Qu

"Cassandra King has written
women helping other wom
romance and surprises along

"This novel about friendship, heartache, self-discovery and love—in all its wounding, wacky, and wonderful forms—had me laughing out loud, and then moved me to tears."

—Sandra Brown,
author of *Ricochet*

"*Queen of Broken Hearts* is an absolutely fabulous story of healing and hope, filled with irresistible characters that are beautifully drawn and have great insights into life. I laughed and cried, and you will too . . . I absolutely adored this book! Congratulations, Cassandra King, on a monumental success!"

—Dorothea Benton Frank,
author of *Full of Grace*

"These are not 'The Same Sweet Girls,' but all those who loved that novel will love this one even more. Cassandra King's characters are fully drawn, richly imagined human beings, whose lives will continue to resonate long after you've turned the last page."

—Mark Childress,
author of *One Mississippi*

Praise for

The Same Sweet Girls

"King brings sympathetic characters to vivid life and explores the bonds of friendship. This winning tale should make her a household name."

—*Booklist*

"The story's gentle Southern humor and warmth shine. The characters are true to life, and readers will sympathize with their struggles."

—*Publishers Weekly*

"[King] has an eagle eye for life as we are living it right this red-hot minute . . . a talent for creating memorable characters who reveal themselves in juicy dialogue and smart-talking commentary."

—*Mobile Register*

"King's previous novels, *The Sunday Wife* and *Making Waves*, have been praised as 'rich,' 'lush,' and 'enticing.' Overall, *The Same Sweet Girls* is no different. Its emotional depth is apparent on almost every page, and it lends itself to the kind of immersion many readers desire in a novel."

—*Denver Post* & *Rocky Mountain News*

"If anybody has written a better book about the power of women's friendships, I haven't read it. Cassandra King has caught the timbre and import of women's voices as they speak to and of each other so perfectly that her jersey should be retired. *The Same Sweet Girls* is tender, funny, heartbreaking, and astoundingly unsentimental. Over all their lives together, these women have felt everything for each other but regret. I really, truly love this book."

—Anne Rivers Siddons

"Cassandra King has the gift of telling stories that sweep you away; settling in with a new book from her is like a weekend in the country. This novel of women's friendship is as original, eccentric, funny, and touching as any in recent memory, and you'll be missing those Same Sweet Girls long after they've taken their vivid lives and loves and left you."

—Beth Gutcheon

"Just try and resist the allure of *The Same Sweet Girls*. First of all, you get to sit in the company of a group of colorful, funny, highly opinionated, and infinitely real Southern women. On top of that enough, they will tell you the whole truth, and nothing but, about their loves, deceptions, and struggles. But above all, these women will capture you with the powerful, indelible bond that lies between them."

—Sue Monk Kidd

Praise for

The Sunday Wife

"A wonderful book. Cassandra King catches these quirky, complex people and their world flawlessly."

—Anne Rivers Siddons

"Kept me up till 3 . . . *The Sunday Wife* is a tasty, irresistible treat."

—*BookPage*

"As slice-of-life stories go, this is an extraordinarily generous one: rich, dense, and satisfying."

—*People*

"*The Sunday Wife* is an intelligent, witty novel, skillfully written."

—*Boston Globe*

"A charming read . . . [King] has a sure winner here."

—*Publishers Weekly*

"King explores the nature of love—the destructive power of addictive love, the healing power of mature, mutual love, and the blind worship of an adoring congregation."

—*Birmingham News*

"*The Sunday Wife* . . . delivers some haunting messages about the nature of love and freedom and forgiveness."

—*Orlando Sentinel*

"*The Sunday Wife* is a complex novel alert to the nuances of the Bible-Belt South."

—*The Daily Courier*

"King's unique characters and artfully constructed story are prizes."

—*The Houston Chronicle*

"*The Sunday Wife* is a dazzling tale of deception, heartbreak, and transcendence. Cassandra King has written a novel that sparkles with vitality and truth. Readers will not soon forget this moving story of one woman's journey toward independence and the amazing people who help ferry her toward freedom."

—Connie Mae Fowler,
author of *When Women Had Wings*

"From the perspective of a minister's spouse, *The Sunday Wife* unflinchingly explores the hypocrisy, vanity, and cruelty of leaders and members of a mainstream religious denomination. It's a wake-up call like that of Elmer Gantry. From page one, the reader will be rooting for the liberation of the courageous and talented wife, Dean, from her repressive husband, as Cassandra King's enticing novel challenges the reader to avoid the crippling effects of denial and obsession."

—Sena Jeter Naslund,
author of *Ahab's Wife*

"*The Sunday Wife* is a stunner, a page-turner of a story that's at the same time smart and funny and alert to the nuances of the complicated South. Dean Lynch in the title role will absolutely steal your heart."

—Josephine Humphreys,
author of *Rich in Love*

Making Waves

ALSO BY Cassandra King

The Sunday Wife

The Same Sweet Girls

Queen of Broken Hearts

Making Waves

Cassandra King

HYPERION

New York

Previously published by Black Belt Press in 1995.

Mass market ISBN: 978-0-7868-9119-1

Hyperion books are available for special promotions, premiums, or corporate training. For details contact Michael Rentas, Proprietary Markets, Hyperion, 77 West 66th Street, 12th floor, New York, New York 10023, or call 212-456-0133.

FIRST MASS MARKET EDITION

10 9 8 7 6 5 4 3 2 1

To James Elton King and Pat Williamson King

with love and gratitude

Making Waves

Donnette

I was right in the middle of washing off the rollers from Melissa Mullenix's permanent, getting ready to close up for the day, when Mr. Cleve Floyd called me. Before I could answer the phone, I had to take the neutralizer-soaked end papers off the rods then turn the sprayer on real hard to get that slick chemical solution off; otherwise they'd stink to high heaven. Plastic rollers absorb ammonia worse than anything.

Melissa's perm sure turned out pretty, though. At first I thought that might be her mama calling to tell me how much she liked it. For some reason Melissa was afraid her mama'd think it was too frizzy, which she says looks cheap. So when I finally answered the phone, I was surprised as all get-out to hear Mr. Cleve Floyd on the other end.

Mr. Cleve was not one to beat around the bush, so he got right to the point. He wanted me to come over to the funeral home and fix Miss Maudie's hair.

Normally I'm real polite, but I didn't beat around the bush either. I told him no-thank-you flat out.

"Mr. Cleve, I appreciate you thinking of me, I really do. And I loved Miss Maudie. But there's *no* way I can do that—no way at all," I said to him.

"The pay's good, Donnette." Mr. Cleve cleared his throat,

coughing. "Hairstyling's included in our total package, so we make it worth your while to leave your shop unattended."

"You couldn't pay me enough, believe me. I can't do it, Mr. Cleve. I'm sorry," I told him, and I meant it.

Daddy always said there wasn't a Floyd in Zion County that wouldn't argue with a signpost. Way Daddy told it, every time he and Mr. Verdo Floyd came back from selling hogs in Tuscaloosa and crossed the Zion County line, Mr. Verdo'd start in, fussing: "Sign says twelve miles to Clarksville. Damn fools—ain't no such thing!" Since Mr. Cleve was a Floyd through and through, I was in for an argument.

"Now see here, young lady," he said. I could picture him with his sad funeral-parlor face, cigarette hanging from his mouth, looking real mournful, like he ought to in his business, I reckon.

"You took over that shop from Essie, you got to do her customers, girl," he continued, coughing gruffly. "Essie'd turn over in her grave you refusing to do poor old Maudie—"

"But, Mr. Cleve," I interrupted. I was raised better than to be rude, but I couldn't help myself. "I *swear* I can't do it! I ain't never touched a dead person before—I can't stand the thought. Miss Maudie was my third-grade teacher, Mr. Cleve." My voice was getting shrill.

Mr. Cleve sighed. "Wait just a minute, honey. Hang on, you hear?" His gravelly voice sank even lower. Deep as a grave, Daddy used to say.

I knew why he wanted me to hang on, knew for sure he was fixing to call his wife to the phone. Whatever he couldn't handle, folks said, he turned over to his wife. Since she was a Clark, people listened.

It was my turn to sigh as I held on to the phone, looking around my empty shop helplessly. Mary Frances Floyd was Aunt Essie's best customer, and with her influence in this town, she could make or break me. I knew I was beat. If Mary Frances Clark Floyd started driving to Columbus to get her hair done, then so would all the other old biddies in town, since the Clarks set the standards in Zion. I was beat, all right. I had to do it, no matter.

"Donnette, honey?" Mary Frances Floyd came on the phone. "How you doing, sweetheart?" She was one of those women with a voice thick and sweet as cane syrup.

"Well, I'm doing fine, but what I'm trying to tell Mr. Cleve is—" My voice cracked like I was fixing to cry.

"Now, sugar pie, you listen to me, you hear?"

Miss Mary Frances got even sweeter, practically purring. Actually, she was a pretty nice lady even if they did have all that money and the only funeral home in Zion County. Plus she had so much hair. She got a permanent every two months because it was so fine and there was so much of it. Her twin sister was the same way. Aunt Essie used to tell me that Mary Frances Floyd and Frances Martha Clark had enough hair between the two of them to keep her in business.

"Listen here, Donnette, I know you're scared to do your first one. I remember plain as yesterday that Essie vomited after her first one, Miss Lottie Abrams."

Well, thanks a lot, Miss Mary Frances, I thought. That's just *real* encouraging!

"But if you'll come on out here right now, I tell you what," she said, lowering her voice, "I'll help you. Cleve's fixing to go home for supper, so it'll be just me and you here. And Miss Maudie, of course."

"But—I never touched a dead person—I can't do it, Miss Mary Frances!"

"Well, Donnette, honey, you got to get over that. In your business, they're *your* customers, live or dead. Essie had a rough time, too, but she got to where she didn't mind. She said they were the only customers she had who didn't complain." She chuckled.

But when I sighed again, Miss Mary Frances got aggravated. Like all Clarks, she was used to having things her way.

"Well. Reckon we'll send to Columbus for somebody, then."

I closed my eyes. "No, ma'am, Miss Mary Frances. Don't do that. I'll come."

"Good girl! Come on now, bring your stuff, and come to the back door, okay?"

She hung up before I could say another word. I hugged the phone to me, my heart fluttering like the wings of a hummingbird. Oh, Lord, what had I got myself into? Why didn't they tell us at the beauty college we'd have things like this when we got out in the real world, got our own shop? If I had someone working for me, I could send them. But no, it was only me, and I had no choice if I was going to keep Aunt Essie's customers. Truth was I couldn't afford to lose even one customer, let alone all the blue-haired ladies in Clarksville.

I went over to the sink and finished washing the rollers, laying them out on a towel to dry. When that was done, I picked up a roller bag and began to stuff things in I'd need for Miss Maudie's hair. Setting lotion, blow-dryer, hairspray, lots of clips.

I couldn't help but smile, though. Miss Maudie, bless her sweet old heart, never had a curling iron or blow-dryer touch her head, not with her old-timey hairdo. I'd never fixed it myself, but many was the time I'd watched Aunt Essie do it. She'd part Miss Maudie's thick white hair in the middle, then take her fingers and mold it into big, deep waves. Each wave had to be painstakingly clipped in place with curved metal clips, which they don't make anymore, the kind with jagged teeth. Fortunately I inherited Aunt Essie's collection.

Then Miss Maudie'd get under the dryer so the waves could set, and Aunt Essie'd polish her tiny little fingernails, always a natural rosy-pink. Shell Pink, I remembered, and added a bottle to the roller bag. I figured they hadn't been doing Miss Maudie's fingernails at that nursing home in Tuscaloosa. She ought to have them done for the laying out, she had such pretty little hands. Usually they're crossed at the waist, with a Bible or something in them. It would be a shame for people to file by Miss Maudie's coffin and notice she needed a manicure.

I decided I'd better find Tim and tell him where I was going. I knew he was home, because when I was finishing Melissa's permanent I heard his pickup pull up in the driveway. Melissa heard it too, and she about broke her neck trying to catch a glimpse of him, till I yanked her back in the chair. It was funny that Tim still had that effect on the girls around here.

I locked the shop door, though no one in Clarksville locked doors. But I had fifty dollars in the money box because I not only did Melissa's perm, I'd also cut and styled Ellis's hair as well as doing two shampoos and sets. Not bad with me just opening up. I was pleased with the way everyone turned out, too, especially Ellis. She was going to a reception at the country club in Mt. Zion and wanted to make a good impression. As if she had to worry about that now that she was a Clark, since they own everything and everyone in Zion County.

Miss Mary Frances was a Clark before she married Mr. Cleve. Her brother Mr. Harris Clark set them up in the funeral home business when Joe Ray Johnson died and left it. One thing you could say for them Clarks, rich as they are, Mr. Harris made them all work at something. Well, all except Sonny. Daddy used to say Sonny Clark wasn't worth the bullet it'd take to shoot him. But I'm not so sure about that myself. I know one thing he's good for.

I left the shop and crossed the big front porch, going to the kitchen in back. Me and Tim sure were lucky to get Aunt Essie's house when we got the shop, even luckier to get out of our little trailer. We'd just bought the shop from Aunt Essie when she up and died and left the house to me. It like to have killed my cousin Joleen, the selfish pig, but I for one didn't care a bit. Everybody in town swore Joleen'd get some big-shot lawyer and contest the will, but she never did. She's too lazy, and ever since she left Dinky and ran off with Clerment Windham, she has got all the money she can spend. At least she and Clerment moved to Huntsville and I don't have to see her again, thank the Lord. Everyone knows Joleen can't stand the house anyway, so why'd she want it, except to keep me from getting it? She couldn't sell it—nobody moves *in* to Clarksville; they move out instead. No, Joleen was just jealous of me and Aunt Essie, always had been. Personally I think Dinky's better off and she and snooty old Clerment Windham deserve each other.

I'd most likely find Tim in the kitchen. Soon as he gets off work, he either wants to eat or screw.

"Tim, honey, where are you?" I called out as I entered the kitchen from the back door.

Sure enough, there sat Tim at the table, eating a piece of the lemon icebox pie I bought at Piggly Wiggly, eating it right out of the box it came in. If Tim wasn't so gorgeous, his lack of manners would be more noticeable. But he can't help it, considering the way he was raised—it was a wonder he even knew how to use a fork. The Sullivan boys had to raise themselves out there in the sticks, with no woman around, mother or grandma or anything. Just Old Man Sullivan, who was so bad to drink he finally drank himself to death. Poor Tim, it was a miracle he turned out so good. All the Sullivan boys have, really.

"You're going to ruin your supper, honey," I said to him, sounding ill as a hornet. I was still tense from my conversation with the Floyds, still dreading going to the funeral home. I especially didn't want to go once I'd seen Tim sitting there in his jeans, shirt off, wolfing down that pie. He has the most gorgeous body, in spite of the scars and the lame arm—lean and tanned and muscular. Sometimes I just can't keep my hands off of him, even after two years of marriage.

Tim looked up in surprise at my ill-sounding voice. "Where you fixing to go?" he asked, raising his eyebrows. I was still standing just inside the door, with the roller bag in one hand and my purse in the other.

"I got to go to the funeral home." I didn't know why, but suddenly I didn't want to tell Tim what I had to do.

"You going right now? It's almost supper time." 'Course he'd be worried about his supper.

"I'll be back in plenty of time. Thought I'd fry that fish you caught Sunday."

Tim stuffed a piece of pie in his mouth and talked with his mouth full. "I'm gonna go to the field in a little while and watch football practice."

"Again?" was all I could say. My stomach sank, though. Oh, Lord, not again!

"Coach asked me to. He's starting Tommy at quarterback against County High."

Tim pushed back the hair that was always falling across his forehead, white-blond hair a girl would kill for. You can't duplicate that color with Clairol. I had to turn my back to keep from going to him, going and putting my hands into that soft sweet hair of his. Lord, Lord—after two years!

"What you going to the funeral home for?" Tim asked, reaching into the box for another piece of pie.

Since I never lie to him, I just said, "Miss Maudie died."

"Oh, yeah—I heard that. She was a sweet old thing, wasn't she? She always liked me a lot for some reason."

I nodded, smiling. "She was especially nice to us after the accident. She called me not too long ago from the nursing home, just to see how you were doing." We both fell silent a minute, remembering, then I reached for the door.

"Well, I got to go on." I called back to him as I went out the door and down the back steps, "Why don't you go ahead and clean the fish, get them all ready before you leave?"

I got quickly into my car and cranked it up. It was hot as hell, suffocating hot, even though I parked under a shade tree. I swear I hate summer worse than anything! I can't wait for fall and cooler weather, though half the time in west Alabama it's

November before it comes. I pulled the car out onto the Columbus Highway and the air-conditioning kicked in, making me feel a little better.

Zion Funeral Home is only three miles out from town, on the four-lane highway to Columbus, Mississippi. It stands alone in a grassy field, nothing else around. Across the highway Robby Burkhalter's turned an old Shell station into a tacky video rental store, but other than that, the funeral home looks kind of funny all by itself with only a few scraggly pine trees nearby.

It's not a pretty building: flat-roofed and red brick, with white columns and a gravel driveway in front, big floodlights on the funeral home sign, even in the daytime. It has never been named anything nice and comforting either, like Heavenly Rest or Beyond the Sunset. Just plain old Zion Funeral Home.

I like the funeral home in Columbus—a big old house that use to be an antebellum mansion. When I was at the technical college in Columbus, taking my beauty course, my instructor's husband died and we all went to the funeral home to pay our respects. Lord, was it something! The house itself looked like Miss Melanie's in *Gone With the Wind*. They had a little bitty brass sign out front, otherwise you'd never have known it was a funeral home at all. Inside you couldn't tell it, either. There were real flowers, not silk, in big oriental-looking vases in the foyer, and everything was decorated in shades of rose and dark green.

Best of all were the rooms they put folks in for the laying out. They were real personal-like, with nice furnishings and antiques. Even the Kleenex boxes were in fancy cross-stitched holders. It made you think you were there for a friendly visit instead of in a set-up room with a coffin in the middle. I sure liked it better than Zion Funeral Home. Made a body not mind being laid out in a setting like that.

I pulled the car into the driveway and started to circle the building, going around back like Miss Mary Frances told me to. Next to the funeral home was a brand-new graveyard, but only about ten people were buried there. It's mainly for drifters or Yankees or people who move into town with no family in Zion County. Everyone else's buried in Clarksville on the hill, in the big shady cemetery in the old section of town. There, everybody has tombstones. Here all the poor things have are little markers with their last names on them. In front of each one's a plastic wreath of red roses or white lilies, not azalea bushes and things like folks plant by the graves in Clarksville Cemetery. Why, when Miss Dorothy Davis died, her daughters dug up her whole flower garden and planted her azaleas, gardenias, and rose bushes all around the plot. Folks claim you can see Miss Dorothy there among them like she always was in life.

I parked right next to the hearse. That thing gave me the creeps every time I saw it, but there was no other place to park. Miss Mary Frances's big black Lincoln Continental was taking up the rest of the space. The only other thing in back was a cotton field, and I couldn't park out there.

I grabbed my purse and the roller bag and jumped out of the car, being careful not to look at the big white hearse as I walked to the back door.

The door opened when I got to it and I jumped, startled. However, it was just Miss Mary Frances, standing there holding the back door open for me.

"Donnette, honey, come in this way," she whispered to me. Now why on earth she was whispering, I couldn't imagine. Daddy always said none of the Clark women had the sense God promised a billy goat.

"I brought my rollers and things with me, Miss Mary Frances," I told her as I went through the door she was holding open for me. And lo and behold, there I was whispering too! I guess something about this place made you want to be real quiet.

Mary Frances Floyd stood and looked at me carefully after

she let me into the little hall, I reckon deciding if I was really going to do this. I just stood there like an idiot and stared back at her, blinking my eyes in the darkness of the hallway. Miss Mary Frances's a tall, big-bosomed woman in her sixties, with the Clarks' sharp blue eyes behind silver-framed glasses, making her look kind of bug-eyed. Her hair's about all gray so Aunt Essie colored it Precious Platinum and pulled it in a stiff French twist, the way she's worn it for years. As befitting a Clark, even for ever-day wear Miss Mary Frances dressed fit to kill, and today was no exception. Her dress was a pretty shade of aqua, and she had on lots of aqua eyeshadow to match, magnified by her glasses. I'd have to find a polite way of telling her that at her age she shouldn't be wearing frosted eyeshadow—it shows up every line. A muted earth tone would be better.

"Come on, sugar," she said to me finally, grabbing my arm. "Miss Maudie's back here. She's the only one here now."

She turned down the hallway and I followed close behind her. It was dark except for little globe lamps on the wall, the hall papered with really dreary, dark wallpaper. I didn't like this place one bit.

Miss Mary Frances stopped before a closed door that had a small brass sign on it: KEEP OUT. She turned to me before opening the door.

"Donnette, the hardest thing is to wash the hair. Usually we use a dry shampoo unless they've been sick a long time and it's too dirty for that. Since it's your first time, I went ahead and washed her hair for you, but next time that will be part of it, you understand."

She opened the door and took my arm again, feeling that I needed to be pulled in, I guess.

The room was bigger than I expected and very cold, cold as a refrigerator. I glanced around quickly and noticed that it looked like a doctor's office, with examination tables, big hanging lights, and lots of strange-looking equipment. I wouldn't look at any of that equipment, turning my eyes away soon as I saw strange hoses and things hanging above one of the tables. Instead I stared at the aqua-silk back of Mary Frances's dress. Oh, God, the room smelled funny! Unless that was Miss Mary Frances's perfume.

Miss Mary Frances stopped right in front of me as she led me toward the back of the room, and I almost ran into her.

"Also, honey," she said to me in her loud whisper, "I did you another favor, too. Since Miss Maudie's hair's so thick and would take so long to dry, I went ahead and set it for you, too. I told you I'd help you since it was your first. I do believe it looks real natural the way I fixed it."

As she said this to me, Miss Mary Frances moved out of my way.

Right in front of me, on a long metal table, was Miss Maudie. I was so completely startled that I just stared down at her. Then I caught my breath and let it out real slow, relieved.

Oh, my God, it wasn't Miss Maudie after all! It was some horrible dummy they'd made to look like her. It didn't even look that much like her, but instead was a small, shriveled old dummy, way too little to be Miss Maudie. Though her eyes were closed, her white lifeless face was slack and her jaw sagged, making her mouth hang partly open. They'd dressed her boney shrunken body in a navy blue dress, with white lace at the collar and cuffs, like something Miss Maudie would wear. And Miss Maudie's cameo, the one she'd never go without, was pinned ever so neatly at the neck. But she looked funny all dressed up, because she had no shoes on. The dummy had no shoes or stockings on—she was barefooted! The neat dark dress was way too long for her, and I started to laugh. Her little wax feet looked so silly, sticking out at the bottom of her dress. I started to laugh real loud, and Miss Mary Frances grabbed my arm, hard.

"Donnette—," she gasped. "What on earth—?"

I dropped the roller bag and my hand flew up to my mouth to try and stop the laughter. I saw then that all around the shrunken wax face was pincurls, held in place with little plastic clips. Miss Mary Frances had fixed up the dummy of Miss Maudie with thick white pincurls.

"*No, no,*" I cried. "That ain't right—*no*, Miss Mary Frances!"

I couldn't help myself, causing Miss Mary Frances to grab both my arms even harder.

"Oh, honey, I know, I know," she crooned. "But the poor thing is better off—"

"No, ma'am—that's *not* Miss Maudie—what have you done with her?"

I was crying for good now, tears rolling down my cheeks. So that was what funeral homes did—replaced people with wax dummies made to look like them, laid out in coffins. Now I knew why dead people always looked so unreal.

Miss Mary Frances was about to panic, I could tell. "Donnette, stop this—you are hysterical—let me get you out of here!" She tried to pull me closer to her, but I pushed away and stared at her.

"If y'all are going to fix her up to look like Miss Maudie, the least you can do is get her right." I sobbed loudly, no longer remembering to whisper.

Miss Mary Frances dropped my arms and stepped back, looking at me as though I'd lost my mind. "What in God's name—" was all she could say.

Still sobbing, I turned back to look at the dummy again. Very slowly and carefully, I stepped over to her.

Bending down, I forced myself to look at the dummy of Miss Maudie, staring at the colorless waxen face. The snow-white hair of big fat curls held in place with pink and blue clips was a glaring contrast to the dummy face. I made myself stop sobbing by taking deep breaths as I stared down at it. Then, reaching out with trembling hands, I touched the pincurled hair gingerly. Still damp.

"Miss Mary Frances?" My voice was trembling so much I could

barely hear it myself. Miss Mary Frances leaned closer to me so she could catch what I said. "Could I have some water, please?"

Miss Mary Frances looked paler than Miss Maudie. "Water, hell! I'm going to get you and me both a shot of whiskey. Cleve always keeps some back here."

I couldn't help it, that really made me laugh. Maybe I *was* hysterical after all. "No, ma'am—I don't want to drink it. I need to wet Miss Maudie's hair again."

Miss Mary Frances stared at me, but she turned quickly and went over to a sink in the back of the room where I heard water running. I took another deep breath and began to pull myself together. Reaching down below the table, I picked the roller bag up off the floor.

With shaking hands, I took a comb and began to comb through the dummy's thick white curls after I yanked the plastic clips out. Miss Mary Frances came up beside me then and quietly handed me the glass of water.

I dipped the comb down in the water glass and combed through the hair to wet it, being real careful to look only at the hair and not at the white wax face. Miss Mary Frances then pushed a stool up for me, and I sank down gratefully. It was only after I sat down that I realized how badly shaken I was. My hand shook so hard that drops of water fell from the comb, splattering on the metal table.

Then, as slowly and as carefully as I ever saw Aunt Essie do it, I set Miss Maudie's hair in big neat waves, clipping each one in place with the curved metal clips. It took me a long time because I couldn't stop my hands from shaking, but finally I'd made perfect waves all around the face of the dummy. I got hairspray and sprayed the waves thoroughly, and for a minute the sharp misty smell of hairspray covered the other smell. Mary Frances Floyd must have held her breath the whole time, because when I finished, I heard her let out a trembling breath.

I then took the bottle of Shell Pink nail polish from the roller bag. Biting my lip, I reached ever so carefully for Miss Maudie's withered hand, which lay beside her on the metal table. Her little hand was white as marble and ice-cold, so I took it into my palm as though it was a fragile baby bird.

Carefully I polished the tiny nails Shell Pink. When I finished that hand, I laid it back down beside her, then I reached across the navy blue dress for the left hand and polished those nails, too.

There. That looked more like Miss Maudie. I felt her hair again, and decided it was dry enough for me to remove the clips. When I did, each wave stood on its own, perfect. I couldn't help but feel like Aunt Essie would be proud of me, and I leaned back with a sigh.

Miss Mary Frances had been watching me carefully. The whole time I'd felt her eyes glued to my face. Now she leaned over and looked down at Miss Maudie instead.

"That looks so good, sugar, that we ought to go ahead and do her makeup. Usually I do it, but sometimes the hairdresser does."

I shook my head and wished for a minute that I had that shot of whiskey she mentioned earlier.

"I think I'd like to do it myself." I didn't really want to, but I could just imagine poor Miss Maudie with frosted aqua eye-shadow on. "Only thing is, I didn't bring any with me."

"You can't use regular makeup, Donnette—it won't last a day. We have a special kind. Stay here a minute and I'll go get it."

It wasn't near as bad as I thought it would be. Miss Mary Frances brought me a palette of makeup and I leaned real close to Miss Maudie again. At first I could hardly stand to touch her ice-cold face, but as I applied the thick waxy makeup I began to feel better, because I was making the dummy look more like Miss Maudie. Once the foundation was in place and powdered, I touched the shrunken cheeks with just a bit of color and was astonished at the difference.

For some crazy reason, as I added the rouge to Miss Maudie's face, I thought of Cat. I reckon because Miss Maudie once made Cat sit in the corner when she came to school with some makeup she'd stolen from her mother and put it on all the girls in the class, making us look like a bunch of ten-year-old tarts.

Then I remembered another time when Cat got into even more trouble. Only a couple of years later Miss Maudie caught Cat and Sonny Clark in the cloakroom, Cat with her skirt up around her waist and her legs around Sonny, young as they both were then. Poor virginal Miss Maudie was so horrified. She was a smart woman, had Sonny's number all along, but she never knew what to make of Cat, the preacher's daughter. Cat could be so loving and affectionate, and Miss Maudie loved her in spite of everything, her wild ways.

So Cat got in big trouble with Miss Maudie, and had to stay after school every day for a week and listen to Miss Maudie lecture her on the dangers of playing "certain ways" with boys, but that was all that happened. Miss Maudie never told the principal, or Cat's daddy. Cat swore to me it was just because Miss Maudie never got any herself that she didn't know what she and Sonny were doing, but I didn't believe that. I don't think Cat did either. I think Miss Maudie was such a kind-hearted person, she didn't want Cat to suffer the consequences if her daddy found out.

I decided then and there that I'd try again to get in touch with Cat, let her know about Miss Maudie dying. Thinking that made me feel somewhat excited—maybe she'd even come home for the funeral. Well, probably not. Cat swore she'd *never* set foot in Clarksville again, and she hadn't.

Gently I touched a little rouge to Miss Maudie's icy lips, then powdered them. When I sat back to look at the results, I felt much better.

I saw, however, that this was not a wax dummy after all, that it was Miss Maudie, the life gone from her forever. Looking down at her, I realized the difference between a live body and a dead one. And it's not that bad, knowing the difference. The difference is life itself, of course—movement and stillness. I realized as I surveyed the results of my hairdo and makeup that Miss Maudie would never move again. She would never twitch or raise an eyebrow or yawn or stretch. She wouldn't reach up and pat her hair in place, or hold a mirror before her, turning this way and that, looking for changes. She'd never again stand at a blackboard, chalk in hand, before a room full of restless children. Not in this life she wouldn't, anyway.

Miss Mary Frances leaned over my shoulder, then she patted me. "Why, Donnette!" she said in a whisper. "You did a *wonderful* job. She looks *so* natural, doesn't she?"

Yes, ma'am, I thought to myself. She looks real natural all right—naturally dead. But I had to admit that she sure looked better than she did.

"Can I tell Cleve that you will be available from now on? The pay is real good and I know y'all need all the help you can get."

I picked up my roller bag and began packing it quickly, throwing in the clips and combs and hairspray. I was real anxious to get out of there.

"Yes, ma'am. Just tell him to call me." Surely none of the others could be this hard. And as everyone in town knew, we could use the money.

I grabbed my purse and jumped up. Suddenly I couldn't wait to get out of that building. Miss Mary Frances came with me to the door.

"Bye now, honey." She smiled at me as she let me out the door. "You did a good job—see you next Wednesday, my regular time."

"Bye, Miss Mary Frances. See you then." I hurried out as fast as my legs would take me.

I went down the dark hall and let myself out the back door.

Once outside of the freezing cold building, the heat swept over me. I hurried to my Toyota, passing the big white hearse without looking at it. The sun was just setting, a big ball of blazing pink over the pine trees behind the cemetery.

"And good-bye, Miss Maudie," I whispered as I cranked up the car and hightailed it out of there, tires screeching as I pulled onto the Columbus Highway. "Rest in peace."

My hands were still shaking as I drove back into town. I turned the air-conditioner up full blast and took big gulps of the icy air.

Turning my car off the highway onto our street, Preacher Street, I headed toward our house. Soon as I did, I realized I'd planned to stop by the football field first. I sure didn't want to; I'd rather have pulled into our driveway and started frying those fish. Make some hushpuppies and coleslaw to go with them. Tim loves my hushpuppies. But I felt a strong urge to go on to the field. Tim didn't let on one bit—matter of fact, he was real casual-acting about the whole thing—but maybe he needed me there.

I turned the car down Preacher Street, so-called because three preachers, the Baptist, the Methodist, and the Holiness, all had parsonages on this street. Aunt Essie's big old house—ours now—was at the end of the street, before the highway, then the little brick Methodist parsonage was next to it.

As I drove down the street, I waved to folks out doing the usual late-evening chores. Miss Bobbie Dyer was in her garden, getting tomatoes for supper. Old Man Estes was watering his front yard, which always looked like it was manicured. Sometimes you'd drive by and see the old fellow on his hands and knees with scissors, cutting sprigs of grass that dared to grow between the cracks in the sidewalk. There were little kids playing ball or riding bikes, waiting for the call to supper. I reckon it was the same in every little town everywhere this time of day. There was something real peaceful about it.

I didn't feel very peaceful when I turned the car down the street and headed toward the football stadium, though. I couldn't decide what to make of Tim going to football practice lately, whether it was a good sign or not. Coach had given us season tickets, and me and Tim had gone to the home games last fall—he wasn't able to go the first year, of course—and we'd sat in the stands just like everyone else. Some people acted funny around Tim, almost embarrassed, and they'd avert their eyes when they saw us. Both of us just sat quietly and watched the game, not standing up cheering and yelling like everybody else, which probably called even more attention to us. Sometimes somebody from the other side would recognize Tim as we walked past the visitors' side, and they'd stare at him like they'd seen a ghost, nudging their friends as we walked by, eyes straight ahead. I know that Tim must've seen them, but he never let on. 'Course after all he'd been through, something like that didn't seem real important, anyway.

Unexpectedly I felt tears sting my eyes. Lord, maybe going to the football practice was going to be too much today, after that business with Miss Maudie. Tim would certainly understand if I decided to turn around and go back home, have supper waiting for him when he got there. But I drove on past the high school and pulled into the big grassy parking lot by the stadium. It wasn't quite dark yet but the stadium lights were already on. I parked the car and got out.

Outside the car I was pleased to notice that it wasn't quite so hot now. Maybe it was my imagination, but there was just a little hint of coolness in the air, touching my bare arms ever so slightly as I walked across to the stadium.

I breathed deeply of the heavy, sweet-smelling summer air and felt better. Honeysuckle covered the chain-link fence surrounding the parking lot, and its perfume was the smell of late summer evenings. I could hear the noises now from the field, the grunts and the hits and the coaches yelling and clapping their hands.

Every time I walked into the stadium, regardless of the season, I saw it the way it looked filled with people in the cool nights of autumn. Football season. It was always filled, every single home game. The Clarksville Blue Devils were the pride of Zion County, state champions in their division three years in a row now, written up in newspapers all over the state.

But Clarksville never had a team quite like the one Tim quarterbacked his senior year, with Joey Housel and Tater Dyer and Matthew Pate all seniors that year too. All of them getting those big scholarships—Joey and Tater at Alabama now, Matt all the way up north, playing for Notre Dame. Almost every boy on that team got a scholarship somewheres, it seemed like.

That spring, reporters were calling every day to see where Tim would choose to go—he had so many offers and visited so many colleges he couldn't make up his mind. Coach Mills got to where he wouldn't even answer his phone, finally got him an answering machine. They'd had some great teams in Clarksville, but never another quarterback like Tim, with that throwing arm he had. Lord, the press coverage we got! Suddenly Clarksville was on the map, with coaches from all over the nation coming to our games. People were turning their cameras as much in toward the stands as they were toward the field during those days, snapping pictures of Bear and Pat Dye and Vince Dooley. First time ever, the dinky little motel outside town did a booming business with coaches and recruiters and reporters here every weekend. It was really some kind of goings-on for a little town on the back side of nowhere, as Daddy used to say. Never be anything like it again.

Unexpectedly, I felt my eyes sting with tears and a lump come up in my throat. I had to get ahold of myself—I sure couldn't stay here if I was going to cry. Tim would never forgive me, not after he'd been so brave and never shed a tear through the whole thing. Well, none that I knew of, anyhow.

Soon as I walked past the concession stands into the big open stadium, I spotted Tim. You could never miss that pale blond hair, the way it shone under the stadium lights. I remember how jealous I used to get of all the attention he got, not just for his quarter-backing but for his all-American good looks, too. When the defense would take over and Tim'd go to the sidelines, he'd drink his Gatorade, then pull his helmet off as he stood and watched the action on the field. Never fail, there'd be a collective gasp from the girls on the other side, the stupid little cheerleaders and majorettes nudging each other and giggling like nitwits. Lots of women, young and old ones, too, from all over the state, came to our games just to see him. Made me want to hang a sign on him—he's *mine*, girls, eat your hearts out!

Tim was standing on the sidelines now, behind the benches where the second-string team sat waiting for a chance to go on the field. Tommy was standing beside him, and Tim was pointing with his good arm to something on the field. The offensive and defensive teams, dressed in their dirty white practice jerseys, were lined up ready to go. Tommy was listening intensely to Tim, but the poor thing would never be half the player Tim was, and he knew it. Everybody did. I felt like starting him in the first game was too much pressure to put on a fifteen-year-old. Tim was his age when he started first string, but Tommy just wasn't built for it. He was built more like Old Man Sullivan, shorter, stockier, closer to the ground, without the tight lean body that the other Sullivan boys, especially Tim, had. Would have been better on defense, probably. But I guess Coach figured the way Tommy idolized Tim that he'd try extra hard, and maybe some of Tim's talent would rub off on him. Oh, Lord, Lord, I thought, in kind of a prayer. Maybe things will work out different for Tommy!

Instead of going up into the bleachers where other folks sat watching the practice, I sat by myself down near the bottom, hoping Tim would eventually see me and realize I was there for him, knowing how it must pain him to be here again. I settled down on the hot concrete, which had soaked in a day's worth of sun, and tried to relax. It was hard to do with the memories that came over me whenever I set foot inside this stadium, though.

It was like just yesterday instead of two long years ago now when me and Tim was in school and out here on this same field, every time there was a game. I could picture so clearly the band standing up before the game began, in their snappy blue-and-white uniforms, and everyone in the stands would slowly get to their feet too, always before the announcer came over the intercom to ask everyone to stand. First one of the local preachers would open with a prayer, usually a long-winded one, and then the band would strike up "The Star-Spangled Banner." I would raise my baton in salute, signaling all the other majorettes to do the same, and we'd stand in a contorted stance pointing toward the flag as a Boy Scout slowly raised it high on the flagpole till the breeze caught it and bannered it out above us. That was when Tim and I always managed to make eye contact somehow. Even though the majorettes and the football team were supposed to have their eyes only on the flag, we'd always manage it.

It gave me such a thrill, too, that Tim chose me even after he got so famous. He could've had anybody he wanted at that time with girls from all over struggling just to catch a glimpse of him. But he stayed faithful to me, his childhood sweetheart. That's what that reporter from Birmingham who did the feature story on Tim called me, and folks began to tease me about it. But that's what I'd always been, since first grade. Oh, there were others for both of us ever now and then—we'd break up occasionally, usually after I'd flung some kind of jealous fit—but we'd always end up back together. Though I had some flirtations, I have never loved anyone in my life but Tim Sullivan. I don't believe that he's ever loved anyone like he loves me, either. *No* one.

I watched practice for a few minutes as Tommy snapped on

Sitting a couple of bleachers up from J. D. and his family was Candi Elmore, who'd been a majorette with me. We used to be pretty good friends, but I hardly ever saw her anymore. She had a real good job working for the probate judge over at the courthouse in Mt. Zion. Though to tell you the truth, you couldn't pay me enough to work there. Everybody knows that the courthouse is haunted, a ghost appearing in the window every time it storms. It's even written up in the Alabama history books.

I looked back to the field. Tim was talking to Coach Mills now. Lord, had Coach put on the weight this summer! He used to be a fairly good-looking man. Or at least Cat thought so, saying she was partial to big rugged rednecks. But he was sure getting a beer gut. If I called Cat tonight, I'd have to tell her. I smiled to myself, wondering if Tim'd ever let himself go like that when he got middle-aged. I swear I'd kill him if he did—it'd be such a shame with that gorgeous body of his. There he stood in his tight faded jeans and an old Bama tee shirt, looking better than ever, considering everything. Just looking at him standing there unnoticed, vulnerable and boyish, was all it took to make me start wanting him again.

Suddenly I could tell that someone was staring at me, and an uneasy feeling came over me. Somebody curious, no doubt, even after all this time, somebody who'd seen Tim out there for the first time and was probably watching me for my reaction. I hated that, hated people's sick fascination with other folks' misery. I looked over my shoulder quickly, up into the stands, at the little groups of folks sitting around watching the practice. Candi and some of the others smiled and waved at me, and I waved back. Must have been my imagination, me being so jumpy today after all I'd been through.

But as I turned back toward the field, where Tim was now talking with Tommy, I felt it again. Someone in the stands, just slightly out of the corner of my eye, over my left shoulder, was staring at me. I wouldn't look, wouldn't give them the satisfaction of seeing my discomfort, of letting them know how much I hated them staring. I folded my arms firmly and looked straight ahead.

No use. I could feel it, feel those eyes boring into the back of my head with an intensity I couldn't stand. Unable to stop myself, I turned around slowly to face whoever it was.

Oh my God in heaven—Taylor Dupree! I swear, it *was* him sitting all the way on the top bleacher, staring at me like that. For a moment our eyes locked, and then he looked away, back to the field. Jesus Christ! What was he doing back here? *Here*, of all places! Why in God's name was he back in Clarksville?

I just couldn't help myself. I was so completely astonished to see Taylor Dupree sitting there that I couldn't think straight. Before I realized what I'd done, I picked up my purse, got to my feet, and started walking out. I got out of that stadium as fast as I could move. I saw Tim turn and I think I heard him call my name, but I didn't wait around to be sure. I hurried out of the stadium, hurried to the car as fast as my legs would carry me.

I opened the car door and got in quickly. It was still hot in the car, stifling, unbearable hot. I rolled my window down but I was trembling so bad that I couldn't possibly drive home.

I forced myself to look back into the stadium and make sure it *was* Taylor that I'd seen, before I freaked out over nothing. I'd parked at an angle where I could see right in the front gate, past the place where I'd been sitting. Slowly I allowed my eyes to travel back up the bleachers, tracing where I'd sat to where I saw him. And sure enough, there he was. No question about it. Taylor Dupree, sitting up there just as big as you please, looking like he had as much business here as anyone. I absolutely could not believe what I was seeing. How could he? How could he *dare* show himself around here again?

Since he was too far away to tell that I was looking at him, I was able to get a real good look at Mr. Taylor Dupree. I swear, he had not changed a bit in two years' time! Still beautiful, just completely, breathtakingly beautiful. Not the same kind of looks that Tim has—all-American, the reporters called him—but exotic, movie-star looks, not like anyone in these parts. Everyone says his mama is a beautiful woman—I've never seen her myself—but Taylor must look like his daddy instead, because he don't look a thing like the rest of the Clarks. He always wore his hair different from the other guys around here, but now it was longer than ever, almost to his shoulders. I'd always admired his hair because of its unusual color—a rich chestnut brown, with glints of red and gold, going so good with his dark Cajun complexion and eyes.

Oh, I knew those eyes so well. How he used them to look down his elegant nose at everybody in Clarksville and in Zion County! And his voice, so snooty and cultured, was not countrified like the rest of us hicks—how he used it to put down everybody, saying the most hateful things, always laughing at us. I swear I hated his guts! Everybody did, everybody but Tim, who's too good a person to hate anybody. And Cat, who could never hate anyone who looked like Taylor. She almost screwed his head off as soon as she discovered boys, becoming so totally wrapped up in him that they were inseparable until she left town for good.

I knew what Taylor and Cat saw in each other, but never will understand why he took up with Tim. Taylor sneered at football and everything else in this hick town, most of all good old country boys like Tim. But for some godforsaken reason no one could understand, Tim and Taylor became best friends their first year of high school. Taylor had no friends at all until then, then he and Tim became thick as thieves, Taylor idolizing Tim, following him around like a lost puppy. I reckon Tim was flattered or something, Taylor being a Clark, even if he was the black sheep of the family. It never made sense to me; Tim could have been buddies with anyone else, but no. He seemed just about as taken with Taylor. Cat told me once it was because they were so opposite, that each found something in the other that they lacked, or some such crap. For whatever reason, I knew all along no good would come of it, even that something terrible would happen, and I was right. But now, why was he back? I never, ever wanted to see him again and I felt sure that Tim didn't either.

Still shaking, I cranked up the car. God, what a day, and now Taylor Dupree back. I hoped to God that Tim didn't see him! I pulled out of the parking lot and hurried home as fast as I could.

Almost an hour later, after I'd fixed supper and left it to warm in the oven, I began to feel somewhat better, not so jittery and unnerved by the events of the day. I even felt hungry now that I saw the fish fried up so brown and crispy. Tim would be home any minute now, and we'd both enjoy sitting together in the kitchen and eating our supper in peace like we did every night, just glad to be alive and together and have a place of our own. I set the table with some of Aunt Essie's good ever-day china, thinking it would be nice after such a hard day. Part of the reason I was more relaxed was that I recalled a conversation I'd had earlier in the day with Ellis, as I cut her hair. I hadn't paid that much attention to her prattle at the time, we'd talked of so many things, but now remembering it put a different light on things.

Ellis told me that Taylor's aunt, Della Clark Dean, was not doing well, which would explain why Taylor was back in Clarksville. She said Mr. Harris Clark wanted to close up Miss Della's house and put her in a nursing home in Tuscaloosa. Miss Della was getting real old, on into her eighties. So, it stood to reason that Taylor would come back from that fancy college in New Orleans and see about his Aunt Della. She was the one to raise him instead of that sorry mother of his, Charlotte Clark. No one had seen her in ages; she hadn't even come to Taylor's graduation.

I'd heard all my life how Charlotte ran off and left her little boy and that Cajun husband of hers, ran off to Europe with some rich old man, leaving Taylor all alone when he was just a baby. Mr. Harris Clark had to drive to New Orleans to get him.

People say that Taylor's daddy was not any better, that he left too, out west somewheres, and never contacted his son again. So you could almost feel sorry for Taylor Dupree if he wasn't such a shit.

When I finished in the kitchen there was nothing to do but wait for Tim, so I went to the front porch to do so, since it was hot as hell inside and still light outside.

I was immediately glad that I did. It was a little cooler outside now, and the night noises were soft and soothing. I sat on the porch swing and began to swing real slow, back and forth, back and forth. All of Aunt Essie's flowers, and the yard was full of them, needed watering, but I was too tired right now. I just wanted to sit and swing and not think, not think about Taylor or Miss Maudie or anything.

Next door, I saw the Methodist preacher drive up to his neat brick parsonage with the white shutters and white picket fence. It was hard to imagine Cat being raised in that prim little house. 'Course I lived out on the farm with Daddy then, not next door, but I visited Aunt Essie a lot and spent a lot of time over there with Cat. I always knew something was wrong, knew that I hated to go there, but didn't know what it was then. Now I'm more able to look back and see what an awfully sick family they were, see the poison that finally destroyed them.

The new preacher's family who moved in afterwards, Brother and Mrs. Junkin, were a dignified older couple, just the two of them. Brother Junkin got along well with all the Methodists in town, going around visiting and praying and generally conducting himself like a preacher should. His wife, Florence, did her own hair, even with my shop right next door. Bless her heart, it looked it, too. I could get out that purple tinge if she'd let me try.

The Junkins are a real nice couple, well-liked by everyone, not a thing like Cat's crazy parents. It's no wonder Cat turned out the way she did, her daddy was such a tight-ass. Her mama was nothing but a nervous wreck, crying all the time, finally ended up unable to function, to even go outside her own house. Really, it was pitiful. Cat's daddy used to beat the holy hell out of both of them. Nobody in town knew it but Aunt Essie and me, though. Some people in town actually liked Brother Jordan, thinking he was a real man of God and feeling sorry for him being burdened with such an unsuitable wife and daughter. Aunt Essie never could figure out how such a holy-roller got into the Methodist church, since they tend to be picky about their preachers and even make them go to preachers' college. Somehow, Brother Jordan slipped through the cracks, because he was more like the Holiness preacher, carrying on all the time about hellfire and damnation and the sins of the flesh. The Methodists tolerated him for a few years but finally decided they were too dignified for such carryings-on. They persuaded their bishop to move him to some country church up in north Alabama. Cat was long gone by then, though. It was there, in that little country church away from everybody, that Cat's mama had her nervous breakdown and set the house on fire. She and Brother Jordan, neither one could get out in time. Poor Cat. Such a life she'd had! I missed her so bad and was going to call her tonight. It had been too long, way too long, since I'd talked to her.

Tim drove up just as I was about to wonder what on earth had happened to him. As soon as he parked his truck and got out, I could tell by the look on his face that everything went well at football practice. He must have been pleased with Tommy's performance.

I watched him carefully as he left the truck and started toward me. When he was contented and not too tired, his limp was not all that noticeable. I was sure of one thing—he couldn't have seen Taylor. Thank God for that!

Just as Tim almost reached the front steps, here came that Wanda Wooten from her tacky house across the street. I swear it's embarrassing to have such rednecks living there—it's just a plain ranch-style brick house, but soon as the Wootens bought it, Wanda actually put all her flower beds in old tires and painted them white. As if that weren't tacky enough, she lined the walkway with Clorox bottles, painted them white, and put pink petunias in them, to match her shutters. Like they say, you can take a girl out of the country but you can't take the country out of her—Wanda was raised so far out in the sticks the sun rose a day late.

She waved briefly at me but headed right toward Tim, stopping him before he could go any farther. I wondered what it was she wanted this time. I couldn't hear her, she was speaking to him so soft, almost like she didn't want me to overhear. Every single time her husband was on the road, she was over here wanting Tim to do something around the house for her, playing like she was so helpless and couldn't do anything by herself, big old farm girl like her. I know of course what she *really* wants with him, but Tim's too damn good for his own good, so of course that would never occur to him. Instead he lets her drag him over there and he spends hours fixing her washing machine or TV or stopped-up sink or something. Her kids are plenty big enough to do stuff like that. But what can you expect? Wanda was an Andrews before she married Billy Mack Wooten. Daddy always said there was three kinds of people in Zion County—whites, blacks, and Andrewses.

Evidently Tim promised to come over and fix something for Wanda later on, because I saw her prissing back to her house. She threw me a little wave over her shoulder, smiling. "Bye, Donnette, honey!" I felt like shooting her a bird but glared at her instead. If she thinks Tim'd ever notice her big fat Andrews butt, then she's got another think coming. Especially when he's got me. I try to keep him so satisfied he won't even look at another woman.

Finally Tim came up on the porch and sat in the swing beside me. Neither one of us said a word; we just sat there swinging, back and forth, back and forth, like an old married couple. It had gotten completely dark now, later than we usually eat supper, but neither of us mentioned eating.

The street lights had come on, and the night air was soft and sweet, perfumed with the flowers in the yard. I could see Brother Junkin sitting in his den—reading the Bible I imagined—the lamp next to him shining on his gray hair. Across the street in the tacky house, I saw Wanda Wooten at the sink washing dishes. She'd need to come over soon for me to re-dye her hair—I could see the dark roots, especially noticeable as she bent her head over, from here.

I looked over at Tim. He was relaxed, peaceful, swinging ever so slowly, also looking into the neighbors' houses. "Honey? You tired?" I asked him.

He smiled without looking at me, then reached over and put his hand on my knee.

"Yeah. And I'm getting hungry, too."

"I figured that. Supper's ready, all we got to do is go inside and help our plates when we're ready."

But neither of us made a move to go in, still swinging slowly. I took his hand and squeezed it.

"Tim? What are you thinking about?"

He turned his head slightly and looked past me at the beauty shop. Originally it'd been a front bedroom in the house, but that was before I was born, because it'd been a beauty shop as long as I could remember. It worked out well as a shop because it was both separate from the rest of the house and connected—you could only enter it from the porch.

It was mighty convenient to have your work at your home. I remember Aunt Essie canning her tomatoes, peas, and corn in between customers, running back into the house to check on the vegetables, then into the shop to check on the customers. It used to tickle Daddy; he said she'd can a head of hair and shampoo an ear of corn if she wasn't careful.

The only thing, the shop hadn't been modernized and had lots of old-fashioned equipment in it, heavy old hair-dryers and ugly black sinks. I hoped to be able to make enough within a year or so to fix it up.

"You thinking about the shop?" I finally had to ask Tim, since he kept on looking at it so long.

"Yeah, I was. I was thinking that you ought to name it," Tim said. "Essie never needed to, everybody knew it was here. But times are different now."

"Tim—what a great idea! Why hadn't I thought of that?" I squeezed his hand hard. Thank God he hadn't seen Taylor Dupree at the stadium and that football practice went well! And that he was able to think of something else for a change.

"What should I name it?"

"Well, what about Donnette's?" He smiled at me with a twinkle in his eye. He knew I'd never liked my name, named after my daddy Donald. I swore I'd never do that to a girl, though Tim teased me that our first daughter would be Timmette.

"*No way!*" I pulled my hand away from his playfully. "I'll come up with something better than that, don't worry."

"Think of a real catchy name. Then, if you put a sign up front, folks from the highway can see it. It might be that you'd have folks passing through from Tuscaloosa to Mississippi who'd notice it, maybe stop by."

I was really surprised. Tim *had* been giving this a lot of thought, and he was coming up with some good ideas. He surprised me even more, with what he said next.

"Tell you what, Donnette. I still got all my painting stuff from rehab, so I'll paint you a great big sign, hang it up for you. How about that?" We stopped swinging and looked at each other.

"Tim, that's wonderful! Would you really do that?"

"Of course I would." He smiled at me. "The least I can do if you're going to support us."

I smiled back but felt uneasy. It was a casual remark, meant teasingly, but I'd been afraid once I got the shop that something like that might come up. Though he never let on a bit, I knew that our situation had to bother him, to begin to eat away at his manhood and his pride. But I didn't think now was the time to discuss it, not tonight after I'd had such a hard day and seen Taylor and everything. I couldn't handle anything else. I decided to change the subject instead.

"Oh—I forgot to ask you. Were you pleased with Tommy at practice today?"

I could tell that was the right move as Tim's face lit up. He was awful crazy about his little brother and determined to help him make something of himself. Since Old Man Sullivan died, Tommy had been living with a great-aunt of theirs way out from Clarksville, but Tim hoped before too much longer we'd be able to have Tommy with us. We had the room, now that we had Aunt Essie's house—we hadn't in our little trailer before.

"I think Tommy's going to make it, Donnette. He's got the potential, and he sure has the drive. He wants to go on to college real bad—you know he's always wanted to be a vet, the way he loves animals. I hope to God he can do well enough to get him a good scholarship somewheres. He sure won't be able to go otherwise."

Tim had his left arm on the back of the swing now, and he began to twirl my hair around his fingers, absentmindedly. Suddenly he stopped and frowned at me.

"Hey, I just remembered. I saw you at practice today—saw you tear out of that stadium like you'd just seen a ghost. I hollered for you but you didn't hear me. What on earth was the matter?"

I looked down at my fingernails, pretending to pick at a cuticle. I hated worse than anything to lie to Tim, because he never lied; he was honest to a fault. I thought for a minute about telling him, telling him about Taylor back in town and how I felt when I saw him. But I couldn't do it. I couldn't bring all that up again, with him so relaxed and peaceful lately, not tormented like he'd been the last two years. God forgive me, I just couldn't do it.

"Oh, nothing. I just remembered I'd left something on the stove so I had to run home before I burnt the house down." It wasn't so hard to lie if I continued to look at my fingernail instead of into his soft blue eyes.

"You sure?" Tim asked me doubtfully. "You looked like you were about to pass out or something. You sure it wasn't anything else?"

"What else could it be?" I'd picked at my fingernail till it went to bleeding so I quit. Instead I looked down at my feet, gently pushing the swing, until Tim reached over and touched my face. I looked up at him then.

"You know as well as I do what it could be—being back at the stadium, seeing me on the field . . ."

I tried to look away but Tim took my chin in his hand, his big calloused hand both rough and gentle.

"Donnette, listen to me, honey. You got to stop worrying about me. I'm okay. Really I am."

"You sure?"

"It's been two years. God knows, there's been plenty of times when I didn't think I'd make it. But I got to put all that behind me now."

"But I don't know that we can do that, Tim. Ever."

"Yes we can, baby. We have to. I'm lucky to be alive and to have you. And now, to own this house, and the shop—things are looking better for us. Nothing bad's going to happen to us now, honey. I promise you."

"Oh, God, Tim—" Before I could stop myself, I was crying. Tim took me into his arms, using his left hand to place his lame right arm across my shoulder. I sobbed and sobbed while he held me close, cradled on his chest. "God, Tim," I kept saying over and over, like a prayer. But as I quieted down and my crying stopped, I knew how much I wanted to believe him, wanted to believe it was all going to be over. Finally, after two long, tortured years. If I hadn't seen Taylor earlier, maybe I could. But I couldn't think of that now, or I'd start crying again. I had to pull myself together, for Tim's sake. So I said the first thing that came to my mind when I raised my head and dried my eyes.

"Tim? I've been thinking about Cat Jordan all day today. You know how you get people on your mind like that, just out of the blue sometimes?"

Tim nodded. "Don't you reckon Miss Maudie up and dying made you think of Cat, that and going back to the stadium? Made you start thinking about the old days?"

"I reckon so. Listen, I thought I'd give Cat a call tonight, tell her about Miss Maudie," I told him.

"Really? Do you even have a number for her?"

"Far as I know, she's still in Atlanta. I believe we'd heard from her otherwise."

Tim was quiet as he stroked my hair. I could tell he was doing some thinking, and finally he turned my face toward his again.

"Donnette? Tell you what—don't call her, okay?"

I was surprised. "Don't call her? But—how come?"

Tim shrugged and frowned. "I don't know. I guess because she's part of our past. Let's try and forget *all* of it, okay?"

I knew I'd never forget Cat, but I also knew I'd do anything on earth to help Tim.

"Sure, honey. If that's what you want—it was just a thought, anyway."

Tim pulled me back into his arms and I snuggled close to him. All the unsettling events of the day seemed far away then. As always, when Tim held me close, I felt like nothing could hurt me, that nothing could ever come between us. I closed my eyes and the day swam before me like some kind of crazy kaleidoscope.

I thought about Miss Maudie and the funeral parlor and how I'd fixed her up to look so good. I raised my head and smiled up at Tim.

"Tim! I've got it—I've got a name for my shop!"

"Okay. From the look on your face, it must be a good one."

"I'm going to name it *Making Waves*."

Tim looked at me, puzzled, his face dark. Then his expression cleared, and he laughed out loud. It'd been a long time since I'd heard him laugh like that.

"Making Waves, huh?—I love it!"

I jumped up from the swing and grabbed both his hands in mine and began to pull him to his feet.

"Me and my shop's going to be making waves in Zion County like nobody's ever seen before! Now, come on, Mr. Tim Sullivan. Let's go eat that fish—I'm about to starve to death."

And I was, too. I felt like I could eat anything now because I knew that Making Waves was going to be a new beginning for us, that we'd be able to put the past behind us. And I knew that Tim was finally, finally going to be okay.

Taylor

I hung up the phone after Aunt Della's call and stood in my bedroom shaking, feeling low-down, like the jerk-off I am. Lately I'd been getting off on feeling like the lowest of life forms. An amoeba. Or Prufrock's pair of claws—not even a whole creature, scuttling across the very bottom of the ocean.

"So what else is new, Dupree—when haven't you felt like a lowlife?" I'd also been talking to myself lately, a sure sign of my advanced stage of insanity. Getting worse instead of better, in spite of what my shrink said. What did he know anyway? Only what I told him. And I was very careful about that, doling out bits and pieces, enough to satisfy him, get him off my back. Or give me some more pills, whatever.

Of course my looniness was always worse after talking with Aunt Della, as the shrink loved to point out, scribbling like hell on his notepad. Sometimes I'd go almost two weeks without hearing from Aunt Della, and during that time I'd be functioning pretty normally, going to classes, working, boozing it up, screwing around, my usual routine. Then I'd get to missing her so much that I'd call her, or she'd call me, and I'd feel shitty all over again.

But this time—it was really bad. She'd fallen again, gotten so she couldn't get around without a walker. She had sounded so frail, so damn *old* suddenly. I couldn't picture that; she'd always been so energetic, so youthful. It never fails to amaze me how incredibly bad life sucks. I swear I never want to get old. I'd much rather be six feet under, any day, than be old in this society where old folks are treated like lepers, stuck away in modern leper colonies called nursing homes. Lots of things are worse than croaking. Lots and lots of things.

I put the phone back by my bed and walked into the kitchen area. Getting a beer out of the fridge, I popped the top and noticed that as usual, the kitchen was a disaster area, dirty dishes and crap piled everywhere. I'd have to clean the place tomorrow since the sublease was almost up and I had to clear out, get back into the dorm.

I hated living in the dorm but sweet Charlotte wouldn't pay for anything else. I guess she fantasizes that if I'm in the dorm, I can't get into as much trouble—though she pretends she only wants me to truly experience college life. Whatever. I gave up trying to figure that woman out a long time ago.

The beer was good, icy, icy cold, a contrast to the hot, hot apartment, and I plopped down in the only chair available. I wanted to get Aunt Della's call off my mind. Guess I'd have to drink the whole six-pack before that happened.

Why did she have to beg me to come home? Looks like after all this time she of all people would finally get the message. Women. I swear, no matter what age they are, they're nothing but a pain in the ass.

Aunt Della knew better than anybody that I had no intention of setting foot in Hicksville again. But she knew me so well, she must have heard something in my voice lately that made her start in on me. She hadn't mentioned my returning for ages; now all of a sudden, here she goes again.

I guess the woman *does* know me better than anyone. She knew exactly how I felt right after the accident, when I first came here, and she never mentioned me coming home then. Not that I could have even if I'd wanted to, of course. Just the thought of returning to Clarksville made me wake up with cold sweats and the pukes. Even the shrink knew better than to try to make me go back then.

But now, two years later, I'd begun to have some strange feelings about the old homeplace. I almost wanted to see it again. And of course I wanted to see Aunt Della—she came to see me a couple of times the first year and it almost killed her, so she'd not been able to come here again.

All this nostalgia shit started when I got fired a few days ago for chasing Cat all over the streets of New Orleans. The memory of it makes me laugh at myself now. Of all the things I've done, few things have made me feel like such a fool—which inevitably makes me long to be back in my hometown, where I was king of fools.

It *was* a weird experience, though. There I was, busing tables at Antoine's Courtyard like I did every afternoon. I'd just cleared off a particularly crappy table, full of beer bottles and soggy cigarette butts—one of those shitty messes I hate. And I swear and be damned, I saw Cat Jordan, plain as day, strolling down St. Ann's Street.

Totally ignoring the fools sitting around nursing happy-hour specials, I yelled loud as a country bumpkin raised in Alabama: "CAT!" And she didn't hear me because right in the middle of the street was a monkey and an organ grinder—an *organ grinder*, of all the damn things, out there noisily grinding his organ, a crowd of gaping tourists around. So I yelled again, "*CAT JORDAN!*"

This time everybody in the place stopped drinking long enough to really look at me, and I saw Jacque and the other waiters nudge each other. They all thought I should be committed anyway. So there was Cat, walking away from me, almost to Bourbon Street, not hearing me because of that damn fool monkey music—all like something out of a Woody Allen movie. I couldn't stand it; I'd longed for her for two years, no contact—all my letters returned unopened, and now she was walking away from me. So what did I do?—I hauled ass after her, actually jumping over a table and knocking down two chairs.

There I went, running like a fool in my cute French-waiter outfit, apron and all. I lost her soon as I got into the crowd of drunken idiots on Bourbon Street, of course. But then I spotted her again, long dark hair flowing out behind her, bare slim legs striding confidently along, crossing Bourbon and heading down Royal.

"CAT! CAT—WAIT!" I yelled like a madman as I ran after her, bumping into tourists and pushing aside tables and chairs from the zillion outdoor cafes I encountered on the way. Of course folks stared at me like the fool I was, a strange sight in a city of strange sights. As I ran across Chartres, I heard a cop yell, "Hey you!" but I continued on, determined, until I finally caught up with her in Jackson Square. I grabbed her from behind and stood huffing and puffing like a pervert as I turned her around to face me.

And of course it wasn't Cat after all. Damn woman was forty if she was a day, good-looking all right, but definitely not Cat. She thought the whole thing was funny as hell, but my boss didn't. I didn't care; the jerk-off paid me less than minimum wage all summer, promising to promote me to waiter. So I was glad to get out of that situation.

But having free time since then, plus seeing Cat, that got me thinking about Clarksville all over again. Okay, truth time. I had not thought of anything else. Obsessive behavior, said my shrink. Get some healthy outside interests. Go to your group meetings, like you're supposed to. Exercise. I popped the top on another beer, the only exercise I got lately. Yeah, buddy. Sure. Like all that crap was going to help me, a certified psycho.

Actually there *was* one other time, before the great street chase, that I got like this, right at the end of the semester last

May. But I bounced back from that, got the apartment and the job, and got my mind on other things. Hey, maybe the shrink had a point after all.

Guess I had spring fever then or something, but I couldn't concentrate on my classes, damn near flunked out. It was *really* weird, gave the shrink a tizzy. Suddenly every classroom I went into became a class back in Clarksville High, and I'd lose touch with reality. Actually, confusing Tulane and old CHS is more than weird; it's ludicrous.

But there I would be, sitting and taking notes in a world history class, old fart professor going on and on about a revolution somewhere in some godforsaken country no one gives a shit about. I would lose contact with the present, the room would fade out, and suddenly I'd find myself back in Clarksville High, dizzy and disoriented. The eminent Dr. Reinhold Dietrich's face would blur and become the blobby face of Old Man Holman in my eleventh-grade American history class. The whole class was a hoot, one of the few I really enjoyed because we gave old Holman pure hell.

Holman would have bored us shitless reading aloud from the textbook every class but he was such an idiot he couldn't pronounce the words right, entertaining us with his attempts. *Laissez-faire* became *lassie fairy*, *Shiloh*, *Shill-oh*, and Cat and I screamed with laughter.

Of course we were the only ones who knew the difference. Tater Dyer slept the whole time, once so sound asleep that he fell out of his desk and busted his fat ass, everybody laughing like hyenas as he bled like a stuck pig. I tormented old Holman relentlessly, putting on a Cajun accent, pretending I couldn't speak English, mocking his every word. Cat sat in front of me and I'd goose her and feel her up, so she'd be cussing and slapping hell out of me until Holman'd have enough and send us to the principal, who'd sigh and roll his eyes when he saw us coming again.

We cheated like politicians, too. During the exam every Friday we'd be passing our papers back and forth right under Holman's big hairy nose, which he would often pick in front of us, then carefully inspect the loot. Once I started a special fund to send him to college, putting posters all over the school, claiming he'd never been. God, poor old fellow must have hated my guts!

The only serious student in there was Tim, and he'd shut us out completely, lost in the unbelievably boring details of the War Between the States and Reconstruction. We threw spitballs at him and tried to distract him, but he ignored us, asking Holman questions the idiot couldn't come close to answering. Holman always put Tim off by changing the subject, inquiring instead about an upcoming game. Which pissed me off, folks treating Tim like a dumb jock, and I'd end up looking up the answers for him and despising Holman even more.

I got over that sicko classroom fixation though, once the semester was over. And I'd been doing pretty good until the famous chase and now the call from Aunt Della. If only she hadn't begged me to come home again. 'Course she had a point—two years is a long time, and she said it was time I put that behind me and got on with my life, what everybody else told me, too. Only problem was, they didn't tell me *how* the hell to do it.

The beer and the heat got to me eventually and I fell asleep in the chair, clutching my empty beer can like a teddy bear. When I woke up, it was dark and the damn phone was ringing like hell. I didn't know how long it'd been ringing; I was so disoriented I didn't know where I was. Finally I stumbled back into the bedroom and fumbled around until I found it.

"Taylor? Taylor, baby, is that you?" Aunt Della again. Except this time she was crying.

"Aunt Della, what's wrong? You okay?"

My voice was sleep-slurred, but hers . . . oh God, her voice killed me. I loved her rich Southern drawl, conjuring up magnolias and mint juleps. But now—now it was so feeble and so old-sounding.

"Taylor, Mary Frances just called me—Maudie died," she cried.

For a minute I couldn't think, couldn't connect a name with a person. Then I saw her, plain as day, my third-grade teacher, Miss Maudie Ferguson. One of Aunt Della's cronies. They'd been raised together in Clarksville and were the best of friends. Poor Aunt Della.

"Oh, man. I'm so sorry, Aunt Della. What happened to her?"

"Well, she hasn't been right since she fell and had her hip replaced. She just never bounced back. Then she had a stroke—" Her voice broke again. "Oh, honey! I hate it so bad, her dying like that, off from home in that awful place. Though I know she is with Jesus now."

Aunt Della was a real Jesus freak, always had been. But I kind of liked her Jesus. The way she talked to him was cool, even to a sinner like me. Sometimes I wished I could have such a simple faith. Or any faith at all.

"Maybe it wasn't so awful, Aunt Della. I'll bet she was well taken care of."

There I went, bullshitting about something I knew nothing about, trying to make her feel better. But she was having none of it.

"*Huh!* That's what breaks my heart. Since I'd gotten to where I couldn't go see her, nobody else did, with Sarah Jean living so far away. Maudie went down in a hurry after I quit coming. It just breaks my heart."

I couldn't resist stupid platitudes, still trying to cheer her up. "At least she had you, Aunt Della."

That turned out to be the wrong thing to say, too, because it hung in the air between us. *Unlike you*, it said, *unlike you who has nobody but a disappointing jerk like me.*

"Taylor, baby. I hate to ask you again. But reckon you could come home, take me to the funeral?"

God, I hated how broken her voice sounded, how it hurt her pride to beg me like that. Still, I hesitated.

"I—I just don't know if I can, Aunt Della." I then added lying to my sins: "My job—you know . . . I'll have to see. . . ." Of course, I hadn't told her I got fired.

"I know Harris won't let me go." Her soft voice was resigned.

I wanted to argue with her but didn't even try. She was probably right. It'd be just like Daddy Clark not to let her go to the funeral. Oh, for her own good, of course. Then the hypocrite could tell everybody how he had to look out for his poor, failing old sister. Damn him. It was almost enough to make me go just to show him that somebody else could see about her. Almost.

"Tell you what, Aunt Della. I'd dozed off, I've been working so hard." *Liar. Creep.* "So I can't think right now. Let me call you back, okay? Let me think a while, then I'll call you back, hear?"

And then her soft voice, breaking my heart. "No, baby. Don't you worry about it. I wish I hadn't asked you—I know how it hurts you to think of returning here. Just forget it."

With anyone else, you'd think that a manipulative move, but Aunt Della is the most honest person I've ever known. I knew she meant it.

"No, really, Aunt Della—I want to. Let me think, okay? When's the funeral?"

"I don't know for sure yet. She just died, just a minute ago. Mary Frances called me soon as Cleve got the call. Ordinarily she'd be in state tomorrow night, but there's a delay. Her niece who's in charge of everything—you remember Sarah Jean? Well, she's overseas, attending some kind of meeting, so it won't be till she gets here. Friday, maybe. I'll have to let you know."

"Okay." Silently I blessed the unknown niece and the delay that bought me some time. "Okay, I'll call you back after a while, hear? I'm real sorry about Miss Maudie."

"Me, too, honey. Except I'm sorry for myself, losing her, not for Maudie. She's with Jesus now, out of her misery."

Well, there was sure something to be said for that. We said our good-byes and I hung up, my hands shaking like hell. I needed another beer. And a cigarette. I'd been quit for a month, but I knew now that a bona fide basket case like me would never make it without all my props.

I ate cold leftover pizza for supper and drank two more beers. Then dessert was the long-awaited cigarette, which I eagerly lit once I had settled into my favorite spot.

Since the place wasn't air-conditioned, and the humidity unbearable in August, I had to raise all the creaky, grimy windows. The apartment was so damn cheap it was the only one in the Quarter without a balcony. So, I'd taken to sitting in the windowsill of the back window and looking down St. Peter's Street, out over the seedy back alleys. Made me feel like Stanley Kowalski, except I usually skipped the tee shirt and sat there in my briefs. One up on old Stanley.

You could see the Mississippi from here, sort of, and there was always something going on, fights and yelling and all sorts of seamy little human dramas. I especially liked to watch the two old drunken sisters in the top apartment across the alley, Blanche and Stella fifty years later, two Southern belles fallen on hard times.

But tonight, instead of seeing the drunken belles, I imagined I was looking out the window of my room in Aunt Della's house, a room that had gone unoccupied, untouched, for two years. The blinking neon sign of the sleaze bar across the alley became the white neon cross of the Clarksville First Baptist Church, and I smiled to myself, remembering. Once Cat dared me to paint "At the Clarksville Savings and Loan" under their "Jesus Saves" sign, and of course, I did.

Cat was the most irreverent person I'd ever known. I went along with her crazy, wild schemes most of the time, except for one in particular. She always begged me to do it on the altar of her daddy's church. Not at night, mind you, but in broad daylight, claiming the risk of discovery would add to the thrill. She got furious at me when I wouldn't cooperate, calling me chicken shit, fag, impotent, among other niceties. Then she tried shaming me into it by threatening to get my cousin Sonny to instead. I knew better than that. Sonny talked a big line and swaggered around like the original macho man, but I had his number: he really *is* chicken shit. No one would ever believe that because he's such a cocksman and good-ole-boy, but I know Sonny through and through. He was, and I'm sure still is, nothing but a spoiled baby. I'd bested him so often it wasn't even fun anymore. As a result, he hates my guts more than anybody I know, and believe me, he's got some competition.

Cat never forgave me my cowardice in refusing to participate in her crazy scheme and pouted on and off as long as we were together. However, her daddy was so deranged I figured he'd come in and shoot my bare ass off. Hers too. I didn't want that wild-eyed fanatic after me any more than he was already. But Cat loved to taunt him; it really turned her on.

We did all sorts of other stuff just to get him riled, Cat constantly dreaming up new ways of tormenting him, with me her willing accomplice. Though after that first time, it was a wonder I ever did again.

When we were ten, we stole some of Aunt Della's fruitcake wine and replaced the communion grape juice with it. The communion stewards prepared round silver trays with tiny one-shot glasses, pouring in the Mogen David innocently. During the solemn communion service later, we were disappointed that nothing happened at first. Until old Estelle Hendricks, an avid teetotaler, knelt her fat ass at the altar and turned up the cup Brother Jordan gave her. She choked, spewing wine all over everybody, and declared loudly that the Welch's had soured. Cat and I managed to contain ourselves through that, but when everybody else who came up began sniffing the cups before partaking, we got to laughing so hard that we both ran out of the church, Cat peeing in her pants in the process. Folks then put two and two together. Daddy Clark came after me, pulling his belt off right out there in the front of the church and belting the crap out of me, ignoring Aunt Della crying and begging him to stop. Cat swore to me that her daddy only prayed for her, that she was all banged up from a bicycle wreck, not a beating. But I never believed her. I always suspected that he jacked off beating her and her mousy mother, too. He was a real sicko.

I lit another cigarette, lost in thought. Thinking about Cat was causing the old longings to stir again and I squirmed uncomfortably in my windowsill seat. Inevitably thoughts of Cat would lead to thoughts of Tim, and I couldn't take that right now. Not now, already being upset about Aunt Della, feeling so rotten and guilty. I just couldn't do it—evidently I hadn't had enough beer yet to numb me and make me sleep. I'd have one more, then I'd hit the sack. Like Miz Scarlett, I'd deal with all this crap tomorrow. I jumped down from my perch and headed toward bed.

Instead of the beer allowing me to sleep soundly, I became catatonic. I stared without blinking at the dark shadowy ceiling of my room, and the old demons returned. Suddenly I couldn't breathe, was smothering in the airless heat. I sat straight up in bed gasping for air like an asthma victim. Oh, God—would it never end! The shakes now, the cold chills next, and then the pukes. Already I could feel the waves of nausea begin to sweep over me. I tried the shrink's deep-breathing exercise but began to hyperventilate instead. *Pull yourself together, you frigging nutcase—don't freak out!* But it was no use, I could feel myself losing it—losing, losing . . . on my bedside table were my tranquilizers.

In reaching for them, all I could see was the phone. I fumbled for it, dropping it twice, then grabbed it and dialed with wet shaking fingers. This was what I needed instead—I had to do it.

I had to go—or I'd be like this all my wasted, shitty, no-good life. I heard it ringing, ringing, then Aunt Della's shaky voice, scared to death. No one ever called this late, I knew, and I felt her fear over the line.

"Aunt Della, it's me. I'll take care of my apartment first thing in the morning. Then I'm coming home. I'll be home by dark." I hung up to her tears, but this time, tears of joy.

And then I slept like a baby. *Home.* I was going home, back to Alabama, at last. Watch out, rednecks—here I come!

I almost didn't make it to Clarksville. Getting out of New Orleans, then out of Louisiana, all the way across Mississippi—I did fine. I stopped for lunch and even began to enjoy myself.

However, when I finally drove into antebellum Columbus, Mississippi, twenty-five miles from Clarksville, I began to get shaky. It was all too familiar, conjuring up teenaged trips to Columbus, cruising the all-girls' college there, wolf-whistling the coeds like rednecks. Then the elegant restaurants, nothing now after two years in cosmopolitan New Orleans, but *the* places to go for special occasions back then. Even snooty world-traveler Charlotte would take me to eat in Columbus, once a decade maybe, when she lowered herself to make an appearance in Clarksville and put on motherly airs.

On the outskirts of Columbus, I pulled into a 7-Eleven that was all too familiar, the last place you could get beer before crossing the state line and entering Zion County—you buy your booze before that dry section of the Bible Belt. The cashier asked for an ID of course, and I produced the fake one I'd used for the past few years. Obviously a fake, but no one blinked whenever I used it.

Back in the car, I suddenly felt like I was getting the pukes again. I got shaky inside and had to lean on the steering wheel, taking deep breaths. However, when I saw the cashier staring at me suspiciously, I pulled myself together and hauled ass, pulling out on the Columbus Highway like a madman.

I was running later than I'd planned—it was what Aunt Della called good and dark now. I'd originally thought I'd be home for supper, so I sped on my way so she wouldn't worry. I met only a few eighteen-wheelers on the lonely dark stretch from Columbus to Clarksville, Alicetown the only place I drove through, a hole in the road named for my great-great-grandmother. It was too late for the locals to be out; they rolled up the sidewalks at dark in this neck of the woods. Well, figuratively speaking—Alicetown has no sidewalks, or anything else.

I almost stopped, still shaky as hell, when I drove over the Black Warrior River, a few miles outside of Clarksville, but forced myself to drive on. I'd have liked to stand on the bridge and look down at the mighty Black Warrior, one of my favorite places in Zion County. All the high school couples used to come down to the riverbanks, picnic baskets loaded down with beer and blankets, get drunk as skunks and make out like mad before either passing out or puking into the river. What we called a fun date in those days.

God, Cat and I had some wild times down there. And me and Tim spent hours sitting our butts on the banks of that river or in the fishing boat, in the misty dawn, fishing like a couple of good ole boys. We'd play the roles, chewing tobacco and spitting into the brown waters, calling ourselves Bubba and Buddy, throwing fishing lines out and then slowly reeling them in while the sun rose over the pines. We all loved the Black Warrior with a passion, but especially me. Of course, whenever I love anything, I tend to do so passionately.

Right outside of Clarksville, I passed the Zion Funeral Home that Aunt Mary Frances and Uncle Cleve run. Except for the big spotlight highlighting the tacky sign, it was all dark. No one there.

Well, Miss Maudie, I suppose. If she died late yesterday, they'd probably have her in state tomorrow. No, wait, Aunt Della'd said they had to hold up till her niece got back in the country. That delay proved helpful to my getting here in time to take Aunt Della to the funeral, which was really going to be rough on her. Aunt Della loved Miss Maudie like a sister. Everybody did, come to think of it. I certainly thought a lot of her, too. I loved the way she looked like a schoolteacher should look, a little bitty woman, dainty and old-world. She had sculptured snow-white hair that I always thought was so cool; it fit her old-maid personality perfectly. Maudie Ferguson was my favorite teacher and she loved me as a student, thinking I was smart as hell. I guess compared to the dumb hicks she taught all those years, I was the Albert Einstein of Zion County. Wonder what old Miss Maudie would think of the way her prize pupil had screwed up his life—what a genius!

I turned off the Columbus Highway by the Phillips 66 station onto Main Street, Clarksville. I'll just be damned! It looked exactly the same. Not a *thing* different about it—not a single thing. From what I could see in the streetlighted darkness, no one had even painted their stores a different color, and no new places at all.

As I crossed the railroad track, I noticed that the old depot still looked like it was going to fall in. The whole place was like a ghost town, especially at night. Not much better in the daytime, either. The town is only two blocks long, the stores lining each side of the street like old soldiers standing silent guard. J. D.'s hardware store, Daddy Clark's bank, the city hall, the library, the barber shop, grocery store—all looking exactly like they did when I drove out two years ago. Main Street dead-ends after three blocks, right past a dilapidated cotton gin that's been out of operation long as I remember.

I turned left on Hiram Street, toward the residential section of town. It has always gotten me that the streets are named like they are. None of them are official, far as I can tell, no street signs or house numbers; folks get their mail at the post office. But everyone in town calls the streets whatever name has caught on over the years, based on something notable about that street.

There's Main Street of course, the only one that makes sense. But the others—Doctor Street, for example, right off of Main Street. Old Dr. Davis's office used to be located there, actually in his house, but that was years and years ago, in Aunt Della's time. Now there's a new clinic outside of town, toward Tuscaloosa, but still, Doctor Street it remains. Preacher Street, running parallel to Main, is the one with the three parsonages on it, and Magnolia Street is lined with huge magnolia trees. Hiram Street, with all the big houses on it, was named after Aunt Della's daddy, Hiram Clark, who built the house where she lives now. He's been dead for decades, but it's still not hers, according to the locals, for it's known as Hiram Clark's house. My favorite one of all is Cemetery Street, so-called because it ends up at the cemetery. Now who'd want to live on Cemetery Street? You spend all eternity at that address. But it doesn't seem to bother the folks who live there one bit. What a bunch of zany characters this town breeds!

As soon as I pulled up into Aunt Della's side yard, I knew I was home—the only home I've ever known. I'd always loved this house passionately, from my first sight of it.

They say you don't remember your infancy, but I swear I do. Sometimes it rolls over me in slow motion, like one of those old home movies, blurred and hazy with weird colors, but also clear in other ways. I remember the first time I saw Aunt Della's house, though I was only a baby. Of course it seemed overwhelming then, huge with endless cool, dark rooms. I especially loved the front porch that wraps all around the house, and the startling shine of the tin roof in the sunlight.

The yard, though, sealed my fate—I fell madly in love with

it immediately. It was fantastic to me, a child's fairyland of azalea bushes and dogwood trees, everything overgrown and voluptuous. Exotic trees there fascinated me as I grew older—granny graybeard with fragrant white beards drooping; purple Japanese tulips; strong-scented sweet shrub with its tightly curled red buds; the inevitable giant magnolias I built tree houses in. Of course as an adolescent I came to appreciate the edibles: apple, pear, peach, and pecan trees, plum thickets, blueberry bushes and grapevines. An unbelievable smorgasbord.

When Daddy Clark took me from his cold, loveless house and brought me here to live, I felt I'd died and gone to heaven, early on confusing my Aunt Della with one of the heavenly host. At that time, I wondered if this bustling gray-haired woman was actually my mother instead of the mysterious Charlotte, whom I couldn't remember. No doubt I blocked out my earliest memories for a reason, for I hid behind Aunt Della when Charlotte finally reappeared in my life. Old Charlotte the harlot, my sainted mom, coming in with too little too late, not realizing she'd been replaced in my affections by an aunt she'd always scorned.

I sat in the car a minute, taking it all in, unable to believe I was home again. It seemed like forever, like I'd been around the world or on a long ocean voyage. But here it was, my home. Suddenly tears stung my eyes and a huge lump came in my throat. Damn. I'd missed the old place more than I realized.

I lugged out my suitcase but didn't bother with the other junk I'd thrown in the backseat in my haste to get away. As I slammed the car door and started up the dark walkway to the porch, I saw the front door open slightly, and Aunt Della peeked out. Unable to contain myself, I shouted, "Aunt Della—it's me!" and practically knocked her down bounding up the steps and grabbing her in my arms.

"Oh, Taylor, oh, my baby!"

She was crying and laughing at the same time, and so was I.

It had been months since I'd seen her and I couldn't get enough of her—I hugged and hugged and laughed and laughed. The prodigal returns.

Aunt Della had killed the fatted calf for me, too. She refused to talk to me, to even answer my questions about how she was doing, until I'd eaten supper, late though it was. I put my suitcase down and she got back into her walker, a new apparatus I hadn't seen before.

"Be patient with me, honey," she said as we began the walk down the long dark hall to the kitchen in the back of the house. "I can't get around like I used to."

That proved to be an understatement. As I walked beside her, both hands out ready to catch her if she fell, she limped along, bent over the walker, moving painfully and slowly.

"God, Aunt Della—I expected to find you really bad off, but you look great!" I lied to her as we walked along together. Again the lump in my throat. God, how could she have gone down so much since I saw her last?

Aunt Della was a big-boned woman, though not fat, who'd always looked robust as hell to me. She had short-cropped gray hair that she had no patience with, never going to the beauty parlor like her cronies. But I saw now it was almost entirely white, and much sparser. Her print summer dress was wrinkled instead of meticulously ironed and spotless. I noticed for the first time that even in this unbelievably hot house, she had a shawl around her rounded shoulders. She'd completely changed, turned ancient now, her gnarled liver-spotted hands clutching the aluminum walker desperately.

"I made all your favorites," she said as we went into the kitchen, and I felt even worse. How could she have managed? Why hadn't I been considerate enough to bring in some hamburgers for supper—damn it to hell. I didn't know if I would be able to stand this.

Aunt Della led me into her big old kitchen to what she called the breakfast table, as opposed to the dining room table in the musty dark dining room in the front of the house. She was of the old school; if you ate in her dining room, you had the antique lace tablecloth and linen napkins and gold-rimmed china. We used to eat like that every Sunday and every time company came. But at the little round breakfast table in the back corner of the kitchen, under the bay window, you could eat out of old plates and not have to worry about such niceties. The breakfast table was for serious hunger, which I sure had a case of now, despite my guilt.

"You sit there at the breakfast table, sugar." Aunt Della directed me with a nod of her head. "You serve your plate while I fix you a glass of tea."

And with that, she hobbled over to the fridge, getting out the pitcher of iced tea she always kept there.

I did as she said, sitting down at the table and removing the soft old tablecloth that covered the supper. It was weird to me how she always had leftovers on the table covered with a cloth, sitting out all day, yet no one ever got sick from them. That covered table was another childhood delight of mine—I used to love to peek under it and marvel at the display of goodies, sticking my fingers here and there, tasting like a bear after honey.

I grabbed a plate and dug into the unbelievable bounty spread out before me, food Aunt Della must have labored over all day. There was a platter of fried ham in clear red gravy and a bowl of red-skinned potatoes beside it. Then the vegetables—field peas and creamed corn from her garden, crispy pods of fried okra, fat slices of red tomatoes. The iron skillet was full of cornbread except for the one wedge she'd taken earlier. I ate half of it, sopping up gravy and pea-juices as I did. I ate like a starved man, not even raising my head from the table while Aunt Della stood over me with a satisfied smile.

The finest French cuisine in New Orleans couldn't satisfy my lust for the food of Zion. It was disgustingly greasy and full of cholesterol and calories, but I craved it and always had. I stuffed until I was about to puke, and then Aunt Della proudly brought me out a huge bowl of her peach cobbler, which she'd kept warming in the oven.

"Oh, God, Aunt Della—not your cobbler, too," I said to her, astonished. I knew what an undertaking that was, having seen her pick, peel, and stew the peaches, then roll the crust out, and carefully weave the whole concoction into a dishpan-sized delicacy that she was known throughout Zion for. How on earth had she managed? Greedy hedonist that I was, I grabbed a spoon and dug in as she stood leaning on her walker and smiling at my gluttony.

I've always been a peach freak, especially craving the small tart peaches from her trees out by the chicken coop. Every summer me and Cat would make ourselves sick on them, sitting cross-legged under the shady trees and stuffing ourselves. We both had ravenous appetites—I guess that figures. Even as teenagers we pigged out, but with a different twist then. Cat was the most sensual eater I'd ever known. I'd get aroused just watching her eat a peach, juices running down her chin and through fingers she'd suck on slowly, laughing salaciously at my misery.

I finished off the bowl of cobbler and looked up at Aunt Della with gratitude, since all her wondrous comfort food had finally appeased both my hunger and my guilt. It quickly came back, for she looked terrible, still standing servile, hanging on to that damned walker. I jumped up and put my arm around her.

"That was unbelievable, Aunt Della. But *you're* going to bed and *I'm* gonna do the dishes. Tomorrow we can catch up on everything."

"Leave the dishes." She protested feebly, but her voice shook, and she willingly let me lead her to her bedroom down the hall. This walk was even slower and more painful for her than the one when I first arrived; she was evidently totally exhausted after all the cooking today.

"You go straight on to bed, you hear? We'll catch up on all

our talking tomorrow." I gave Aunt Della a long hug outside her bedroom door. Her age-spotted hand shook as she wiped tears from her eyes.

"Oh, Taylor. My baby boy. I'm so glad you've come home to me," she said as she squeezed me tight with her last bit of energy. "God is too good to me."

With that, she went on into her bedroom and closed the door after her. I knew she'd go right to bed and to sleep, as soon as she said her prayers. She always prayed for about an hour every night, then she slept like a baby. No booze or sleeping pills for her.

After cleaning the kitchen and unpacking my car, I finally made it to my old room, the front bedroom with the bay window on the side, across from the First Baptist Church. I pushed the door open and stood there for a minute before going in, as though I were a toddler and expected monsters to be lurking in the shadows.

Like the town of Clarksville, my room had stayed the same. It was huge, of course the best room in the house; Aunt Della insisted that I have it as soon as I was old enough. An elegant room with tall ceilings, massive oak furniture and heavy dark drapes. Like a cave or a tomb, it had always been dark and cool, even with no air-conditioning in the house.

I don't think any of the old folks in Clarksville had central air; some of them had window units and closed off different rooms, as Daddy Clark did, but most of the houses were built long before air-conditioning. They were big open houses with breezy, wide porches, dark rooms, and high ceilings with ancient, slow-turning fans. So everybody stayed fairly cool except in the dead of summer when no breeze stirred the searing heat. The dog days of August.

I piled all my stuff on the extra bed—Aunt Della had twin

beds added just for me when I was a kid, evidently expecting lots of stay-over buddies, which I never had. Then I collapsed in the big leather recliner, tired as hell, fishing around in my jeans pocket for a cigarette. However, I was suddenly so exhausted that I decided to do as I'd ordered Aunt Della and go straight to bed instead of delaying as I smoked. Stripping down to my briefs, I turned off the lamp then yanked back the heavy quilt on my bed and did a nosedive into it, sinking into the feathery softness, sighing deeply. I was so exhausted I should be asleep in no time.

Shit. I'd never sleep in here without the overhead fan on to stir the stifling air, and without opening up the windows. Reluctantly I dragged myself out of bed and switched on the wheezy fan. Then, I went around the dark room, lugging on the creaky old windows. When I pulled open the last window, I was overpowered by the scent that was Clarksville to me. The smell of honeysuckle. It grew like a jungle on the side fence, mixed in with Aunt Della's wild red roses like some mad florist's bouquet.

I sank into the bay window seat and breathed deeply of the heavy sweetness of honeysuckle, and I wanted to cry. My throat closed up as I looked out of that dark room into the greater darkness of the night, smelling honeysuckle and listening to the cicadas and crickets in symphony. I knelt by the open window and laid my head down in my arms, feeling an overwhelming loneliness that I hadn't felt in years. *Oh, God. Why had I come back here?*

I stumbled back to bed and climbed in again, knowing that sleep would not come easily. I wished to God that I had a beer, but I'd left them in the car, and I wasn't about to go back out there. If I did, I might just drive off into the night, wearing nothing but my undershorts. I settled for a cigarette, fumbling around where I'd tossed them when I flung my clothes off. Propping myself up on my pillows, I looked out into the dark, starlit night as I inhaled.

God, how I'd missed this crazy old town. No one would have believed that, no one. Not a soul understood how I felt about this place—old Charlotte the harlot snorted when I tried to tell her once. None of the family or friends who lived here understood it either; they just assumed I hated it as bad as Cat did. They mistook my interest for ridicule, my amusement for mockery. Nobody but Aunt Della saw that the town and the people in it had always fascinated the hell out of me.

Not that I wasn't miserable all the years I lived here, though, in the way kids can be. I poked a lot of fun at the locals and mocked them, flaunting my imagined superiority and intellect. I was always embarrassed to tell anyone where I lived; on the rare occasions when I visited Charlotte in Baton Rouge, I'd mutter something about west of Tuscaloosa, and she'd smirk knowingly.

Charlotte may have suspected my true feelings. All mothers, whether they're worth a crap or not, seem to have some kind of ESP when it comes to their offspring. Right now, though, she was so pissed with me I hadn't heard from her all summer. Of course, she was traveling in Europe with a new lover and that gave her an excuse. This past Mother's Day I sent her a Mother of the Year plaque, thinking it'd be a hoot. Evidently the new lover raised eyebrows at that and she practically quit speaking to me. I sent Aunt Della a dozen silk roses of her favorite color, mauve. I'd rather have sent the real thing, but the way she kept things, they would stay in her house forever, dead as hell. Aunt Della never threw anything away. Especially not me, the prodigal. When everyone else was through with me, she hung on for dear life. Probably saved me, I was in such bad shape then. I refused to let them cart her off to some smelly old nursing home, no matter *what* I had to do.

I put out my cigarette and settled back on the pillows, feeling my eyelids get heavy as the night air from the open windows got softer and sweeter. I could feel sleep coming on now, thank God. The last thing I thought of before I slept was Tim, and the thought was a sudden stab of pain, like the piercing earaches I had as a kid. I couldn't help it; until now I'd been successful at putting him out of my mind. But I'd have to face him again, now that I was back in Clarksville. I'd have to do it eventually.

The next day, as promised, Aunt Della and I caught up on two years, yakking on and on way into the morning.

She had risen early and baked biscuits to go with the fig preserves she'd just put up. No matter that she could barely stand without the walker; she and her cousin Carrie, almost ninety, and old black Eula Mae, who'd helped her do these things for years, tended a garden and canned and pickled and preserved its harvest. I figured anyone who could do all that wasn't ready to be put out to pasture.

But in the morning sunlight as we sat at the breakfast table, Aunt Della looked frailer than last night, even. Her age-spotted hands shook as she poured my coffee, and her voice was much weaker than on the phone. Even so, she was more like the Aunt Della I remembered, and I hid a smile as she rattled on and on, like she had as long as I've known her, talking to herself when no one else was around. I just drank coffee and stuffed myself with hot biscuits and preserves, letting her talk to her heart's content.

"It's Harris, hon," she told me. "He's the one insisting I can't stay by myself anymore. Oh, give him credit, he did offer for me to live with him and Frances Martha in that three-ring circus he calls a home. Ha! Papa would turn over in his grave—he knows me and Harris never got along."

Aunt Della always referred to her papa as though he were still alive. It used to tickle the hell out of me, but now it seemed unbearably sad, and I blinked rapidly when tears stung my eyes.

Every time she started to bite her biscuit, she'd think of

something else to tell me and began blabbering again. She hadn't eaten a whole biscuit yet.

"I been here eighty-two years, right here in this house. Papa wouldn't want me to go anywhere else," she said. "And he sure wouldn't want Sonny living here."

That got my attention.

"*Sonny?* What's he got to do with it?"

"Why, I thought I'd told you, sugar." Aunt Della's cloudy blue eyes narrowed as she continued. "Oh, it's not just Harris—it's Sonny and Opal, too. They've decided that they want my house for Sonny and that prissy fool he married."

I laughed and buttered another biscuit.

"That really slays me, Aunt Della. I can't for the life of me picture Sonny married to that mousy little Glenda Rountree. Ever since you told me—"

"Lord, I thought I called you back about that!"

Aunt Della was also getting more forgetful, I'd noticed.

"I had it all mixed up, Taylor. That's what I could have sworn Opal said when she called me—that Sonny married that Glenda Rountree you finished school with."

"You mean they didn't get married after all?"

Old Sonny the hell-raiser had shocked everyone last month by up and marrying suddenly. I figured she was pregnant. But I was astonished to hear that he'd married a former classmate of mine, a girl so plain and unknown I had to look her up in the yearbook to remember her. Then I couldn't believe my eyes. What a hoot.

"Oh, no, he didn't marry Glenda, dear." Aunt Della gave up on her biscuit and stared at me wide-eyed. "He married the older sister, the one with the funny name."

I was flabbergasted at this news. "*What?* Ellis Rountree—you don't mean to tell me that Sonny married Ellis Rountree, the Baptist preacher's secretary?"

"Yes. That's the one. Ellis." Aunt Della sat back in her chair and sipped her coffee.

"But—Aunt Della—that's just not possible!" I was bowled over at this news, stunned. "She's much older than me, so she'd be—what? Four or five years older than Sonny?"

"I was older than Rufus when we married," Aunt Della reminded me, primly.

"Yeah, but—Sonny! Naw—I cannot believe it!"

Old holy-roller Ellis Rountree, marrying Sonny! It was too much for me this early in the morning. Ellis Rountree—memory flooded over me and I felt my face flush hotly. Oh, God. Ellis Rountree, married to my cousin Sonny—what if she told him about . . . no, she wouldn't. I could count on that. She'd never tell anyone that. I glanced sheepishly at Aunt Della and saw her forlorn face.

"Well, it seems that Miss Priss Ellis has long coveted this house, working right across the street from us at the Baptist church and seeing it out her office window every day. I can remember now, her always stopping to talk when I was working in the yard, asking about things. But I never thought nothing of it. Guess she thinks she's found a way to get her hands on it now."

I couldn't think straight, couldn't process this new information. "Where are the newlyweds living?" was all I could think to ask.

The Rountrees were a strange family, raised in a little frame house out from town and keeping mostly to themselves. They were religious as hell, about all that I or other folks in town knew about them. The Rountree girls never wore any makeup nor took part in any of the school activities like everyone else. Old Man Rountree didn't believe in frivolities. They went to some foot-washing primitive Baptist church out in the sticks that the other Baptists in town looked down on. It was hard to imagine Sonny in that family!

"They're living with Opal, of course, at Harris's, with everybody else," Aunt Della said with a sniff. "Miss Priss is really putting on the airs now. She quit her job at the church, went off to Columbus to some business college for a year, and now thinks that she can run all the Clark businesses! Can you imagine? And she's gotten that old fool Harris eating out of her hand. Of course, Opal's so glad Sonny's settled down that she dotes on her, too. Beats all I've ever seen."

That it did. I couldn't help it. In spite of Aunt Della's look of disgust with the Clark clan, in spite of learning that Ellis was the new bride and not her mousy sister Glenda, I started laughing.

"Next thing you know, ole Sonny will be working," I teased her. Sonny played the role of the good-ole-boy so well that he'd never worked a day in his life.

"Oh, he already is. He's with Cleve at the funeral home," Aunt Della told me solemnly.

That really cracked me up, and I strangled on my coffee. Aunt Della went on with her story, oblivious.

"He drives the hearse. You know, I must say that Sonny looks right nice in a dark suit, with his hair cut short. He's never looked a thing like his daddy, though. Always favored Opal's folks to me, especially Hoot Hamilton." She bit into her biscuit again.

Not only did Sonny look like his maternal grandfather, I thought, wheezing and coughing, Sonny was his namesake and took after him in other ways, for old Hoot had been a notorious womanizer, finally shot by a jealous husband, over at Mt. Zion. Caught in the act, so to speak. One of our local scandals.

I never knew Sonny's daddy, my uncle Harris Jr. He was one of Zion's war heroes, killed in Vietnam when Sonny was a baby. Aunt Opal'd lived in the big old house with all the Clarks ever since. She and Aunt Frances Martha stayed on and ran the house for Daddy Clark after Grandma Clark died, years and years ago. It took two women to wait on that old geezer, he was so used to having everything his way. My mother's father, yet I'd never felt one ounce of affection for him. Nor he for me, nor my mother. What a loving family we were.

I turned my attention back to Aunt Della as she began telling me about other family members, cousin Carrie and Aunt Mary Frances and Uncle Cleve and their daughters. I let her go on and on, but I was only half listening. At some point, I planned to stop her and ask about Tim and Donnette. She hadn't even mentioned them in almost a year. She had kept me posted on Tim's progress after the accident, when he got out of the hospital and rehab and began to recover, then when he and Donnette married. After that, she wouldn't mention them again and was evasive when I asked her, claiming she didn't get out or see people like she used to. For all I knew, they could have moved or divorced or something. But somehow, every time I'd open my mouth to ask about them, I'd stop myself. Aunt Della was talking about Miss Maudie now, and the funeral arrangements, so I decided to wait until later and ask about Tim. After I'd been home a day or so would be better. One thing at a time.

The phone rang and interrupted our breakfast, finally. I started doing the dishes while Aunt Della talked and talked on the phone to Aunt Frances Martha. Though I grimaced and waved soapy hands to her, trying to signal her *no*, Aunt Della told her all about my arrival and detailed everything we'd eaten since then.

To make matters worse, Aunt Della then accepted a dinner invitation for me to go to the Clarks' that night. Shit. She'd be so horrified if I didn't go that I had no choice. She was of the old school, and, despite all their differences, to Aunt Della family was family and that was that. If you came back into town after two years' absence, regardless of the reason for your leaving, you visited all your relatives. Period. End of argument. Oh well, I might as well get it over with. I needed to talk with Daddy Clark about Aunt Della anyhow.

Aunt Della and I spent the rest of the day doing my laundry,

Finally I reached the end of Clark Street, where I could see the dark red ancestral manor looming way back from the sidewalk, looking deceptively dignified and grand. The Clark house was the grandest one in Clarksville for sure, but certainly not in Zion County. Other folks in Zion who had money lived in modern houses with swimming pools and central air, not old Victorian monstrosities like this one. Even an antebellum heart-of-Dixie number would have been better than this Dickensian horror. Despite its impressive size, the Clark house was embarrassingly tacky, with gingerbread swirls and gothic turrets and iron reindeer on the sterile manicured lawn. The black iron fence around the whole monstrosity made me think of a cemetery, appropriately enough. I opened the heavy gate and started up the walkway. I hated the way all of the trees and shrubs were so thoroughly pruned here, such a contrast to Aunt Della's lush yard.

In the backyard I could see John Moses Jackson, a black man who had to be in his eighties yet was still considered Daddy Clark's yard boy. Anxious to flaunt my liberal views, not to mention bug hell out of the Clarks, in the past I'd tried to befriend old John Moses. But no; he was such an Uncle Tom he insisted on calling me Mister Taylor, bowing and scraping, so I gave it up as Daddy Clark smirked at my failure. Of course, if John Moses hadn't been so servile, he'd never have lasted with Daddy Clark, even though the old geezer pretended to accept all "Nigras" as brothers in Christ. Putting up with that kind of shit all his life eventually softened John Moses's brain; he was notoriously senile. Last few years he'd taken to pruning hell out of the shrubbery so it was practically denuded, forcing it into unnatural shapes, tottering around talking to himself. Even from here I could hear the crazy old fart as he attacked the bushes in the back with his pruner, muttering away: "Yassir, Mist' Harris—I done tol' you these dogwoods looks bad . . . uh, huh, sho is."

As I walked up the long brick walkway to the front of the house, I noted that in spite of the overall tackiness, there was a really spectacular porch, going all the way across the front and around the right side, heavily latticed like icing on a cake. I'd never really noticed it before because the Clarks would never lower themselves to sit outside like ordinary folks around here do, so I'd never been on the porch. I saw for the first time elegant rattan furnishings and showy giant ferns, looking almost like something you'd see in New Orleans. Wait a minute—the reason I'd not noticed it before had to be that it wasn't there. Well, the porch was, but not the furnishings. Evidently they'd started using it after all.

Which was the case, because as I climbed the curved brick steps leading up to the house, out of the corner of my eye I could see someone waiting for me on the side porch. Suddenly I felt my insides contract and a wave of nausea hit. Welcome home, old boy. As usual, I felt the urge to run instead of facing up to my two years' absence. Swallowing hard, I made myself turn away from the front door and head straight toward the porch on the side of the house.

Damn—it was only Sonny. He was standing there on the porch, hands in pockets, watching me the whole time. We stared warily at each other for a minute, then I stuck out my hand to him.

"Well, well. Cousin Sonny. How are you?" False, hearty smile. Hypocrisy runs in the Clark family.

Sonny shook my hand quickly, as though I were contaminated and he couldn't wait to get his hand back into his pocket, which he did immediately. I looked him over carefully, trying hard to conceal the smirk I felt coming on. He always brought that out in me.

Sonny had put on weight, quite a bit actually, looking a lot like Elvis in the later years. His jowls were becoming prominent, and the famous sleepy eyes rather saggy now; looking, as folks in Zion County say, like he'd been rode hard and put up wet too many nights. I'd never understood why the girls thought Sonny good-looking, suspecting it was because he was the only real Clark heir. Cat said he was sexy, but I never saw it. He looked like a plain old redneck to me.

Still, I had to admit to some improvement now, in spite of the added weight. Sonny's dark hair was neatly cut and sleeked back stylishly. And his dress—he was wearing starched khakis, loafers, and an Izod instead of his usual jeans and Bama tee shirt. Old Sonny was finally settling down. My smirk widened.

"How you, Taylor?" was all he could manage to say. As usual, though, he looked me over with disgust and disapproval.

"Me? The question is, how are *you*, Sonny? I understand that congratulations are in order." I tried hard to keep from grinning like a jackass. Even more so when Sonny actually preened at my comment, intended sarcastically.

"Yep. I finally got roped into matrimony—tied the knot," he said with a grin. Jesus—after all the girls chasing him, here was Sonny acting like he'd pulled in big bass by catching old Ellis! There was something weird going on here. Surely *she* wasn't pregnant.

"I can't wait to see your blushing bride again. Aunt Della first thought you'd married Glenda, but when I found out it was Ellis instead—well! I just can't tell you how astonished I was."

"Ellis is looking forward to seeing you again, too—she just stepped in to get us a drink."

Sonny was trying hard not to, but he couldn't keep his eyes off my hair. Finally I could stand it no longer.

"What the hell you looking at, Sonny?" I was determined to be civil to all of them, for Aunt Della's sake, but it was going to be difficult.

"How come you come over here with that faggy hair, Taylor? And dressed like that? I swear! You know Daddy Clark will have a shit-fit." Sonny wouldn't look at me; instead, with hands jammed deep into his pockets, he turned from me and stared out over the manicured lawn.

"It won't be the first time. Everything I do gives him the squirts."

"My God—he's an *old man* now, Taylor. Why can't you grow up?" Sonny glanced sideways at me, then back at the lawn.

"Like you have? Spare me." Anger burned under my damp tee shirt, causing my face to flush hotly.

"Why'd you come back here anyway?" His voice was low and I barely heard him.

"Excuse me?"

"You heard me—why in the hell are you here?"

"You folks been asking that ever since your dear Aunt Charlotte got knocked up by a Cajun bartender," I said, smiling at him. He didn't smile back but glared at me instead.

"Oh, crap, Taylor. I could feel sorry for myself, too, you know—most anybody could. Take somebody like Ellis—"

Fortunately I was spared the rest of Sonny's philosophical remarks. As if on cue, the front door opened and a woman came through it, carrying a silver tray. It was Ellis Rountree Clark—I'll be damned! I tried not to stare, but my mouth fell open and my eyes bulged. Old Ellis, the Baptist preacher's prissy secretary! It couldn't be.

"Why, Taylor Dupree!" This strange creature smiled broadly, setting the tray down and turning to face me. She stood right in front of me as I gaped at her. "What a surprise—I couldn't believe it when Aunt Frances Martha told me you were back in town and coming for dinner tonight. It's been a long time."

Sonny's change was in his added weight and new preppy appearance; he was still the same redneck-looking Sonny to me, in spite of that. But old Ellis Rountree—I would not have known her. Never.

Ellis was as tall as Sonny, a big-boned country girl with large flat feet and really prominent boobs, undoubtedly her best feature. When I last saw her as the preacher's secretary, she was dowdy and painfully plain, dressed in homemade polyester dresses and clodhopper shoes. Makeup and haircuts were against her religion, so her mousy hair had never been cut, and she wore it sleeked back and pinned in a tight bun. Her face was obscured by big dark-rimmed glasses. You'd have never noticed her except to marvel how anyone could be so out of date and fashion. Only in Zion County.

However, marriage to Sonny had evidently transformed the old Ellis into the society queen of Clarksville. The glasses were gone, replaced with bright purplish-blue contacts, and the once-unadorned face was as heavily made up as a country singer's. No more tight prim bun—her hair was cut short and stylish now, dyed a Dolly Parton silvery-blonde. Diamonds sparkled in her ears and on her fingers, and she was decked out in an expensive white linen sundress. I struggled to remember who she reminded me of, and conjured up my tacky Aunt Opal, whom Sonny's dad had married off the farm and brought to live with him in the big city of Clarksville. Holy shit. Ellis was Aunt Opal thirty years ago—Sonny had married his mother!

Ellis stuck out a diamond-ringed hand to me and I grabbed it blindly, still gaping at her like a fool.

"Ellis—," I finally managed to stammer, "I-I wouldn't have known you."

"I brought you boys drinks," she said as she smiled, motioning to the silver tray she'd placed on a rattan table. "Would you care for some sherry?" I'd forgotten her habit of enunciating her words precisely, as though taking old-fashioned elocution lessons. She held her pert little nose elevated, her head tilted; that, along with the prissy way of speaking, gave her a snooty air.

Sonny guffawed before I could answer. "Good going, Ellis. I'm sure Taylor sits around the French Quarter and sips sherry during happy hour every single day."

Ellis blinked thickly mascaraed eyes at him and frowned, puzzled. I shot Sonny a look of disgust and turned back to her. "Actually, I adore sherry," I said. "Happens to be my favorite."

Ellis poured me a tiny, gold-rimmed glassful and I forced myself to kill it. Sonny laughed like hell.

"Sugar, how about pouring me some burgundy instead?" he said with a snort. "I don't have Cousin Taylor's refined tastes, evidently."

I ignored him and turned back to Ellis. In spite of her friendly greeting, now that we were actually face to face, I saw that she was uncomfortable. Unless she had gone senile, she'd *have* to remember our last encounter, and remember it with shame. She didn't look my way but fiddled with the tray of drinks instead.

"So, Ellis. You are now one of the family," I said. "How did you and Sonny come to marry? I didn't even know you were going together."

At this, Sonny moved in protectively to his new bride and put a big flabby arm around her. "A good friend fixed us up. Luckiest day of my life."

He grinned his lopsided Elvis grin at her and I stared in astonishment. I'll be damned. I believed old Sonny might be in love after all!

However, I couldn't resist goading him. Old habits die hard. "I hear that you are not only blissfully married, Sonny, but also that you're actually working now. With Uncle Cleve, driving the hearse."

Sonny preened at this and ducked his shiny, sleek head, looking at Ellis shyly. "That's right. Gotta provide for the little woman here."

They continued to moon into each other's eyes and I continued to marvel. Sonny didn't like it that I was watching them, for he turned suddenly and jumped my ass.

"Now listen, Taylor. After that last stunt you pulled, things are just beginning to settle down here. I don't know what kind of crap Aunt Della is telling you, but we're all fine. Perfectly fine. We don't need you coming in here and stirring everything up again."

"That's the last thing I want, Sonny."

"Daddy Clark's health ain't so good either, though he never lets on. He sure don't need you messing everybody's life up again."

"Since when did you get so solicitous of Daddy Clark, Sonny?"

"He's getting on in years, and as I said, his health—"

I laughed at that. "Oh, come on. The old fart will outlive both of us and you know it. I just want him to lay off Aunt Della. That's the only thing I'm concerned about. She wants to stay where she is, not have him stick her in some smelly nursing home."

To my surprise, Ellis turned sharply and glared at me, her nostrils actually flaring like a feisty mare. "You don't know what you're talking about, Taylor! I figured Miss Della was telling people that. Nobody's trying to force her to do anything. You just don't know how she's gotten lately."

I was about to tell Ellis to mind her own prissy business when Sonny laughed rudely.

"How could he know? He's not been here to see about her; we have. He's so worried about her, when he's the one who almost put her in an early grave. She was doing fine until two years ago, when he almost killed Tim Sullivan—"

Ellis grabbed Sonny's arm as I took a step toward him. As usual, Sonny took a step back. "Shut up, Sonny," I snarled at him. "You shitass—just shut up about that." Damn. And I was determined not to blow my cool.

Saved by the bell. At that very moment, the front door banged open and my Aunt Frances Martha came out onto the porch. Without hesitation, she squealed my name and held out her arms to me. "Taylor—oh, precious baby Taylor!" She'd always called me "Tay-were," which folks around town thought cute as hell.

I rushed into her fat open arms, safe and sheltered again by a dear old aunt who'd been another mother figure to me. She crooned and patted my back and hugged the breath out of me, as Sonny and Ellis stood there in disgust.

Aunt Frances Martha would be the village idiot if she weren't a Clark and such a sweet old thing. Instead, she was everybody's pet. Evidently some mild brain damage at birth caused her vacancy, for she'd been like this all her life. Sweet, simple, completely uncomplicated, incapable of any malice or guile. She turned to Sonny and Ellis and smiled over my shoulder as she patted it happily, like she used to burp me as a baby.

"Oh, look who's here—mine and Sister's baby boy! Mine and Sister's wittle baby boy, come home."

Sonny rolled his eyes and downed his burgundy.

Aunt Frances Martha had come out to call us in to supper. It was typical that Daddy Clark hadn't come out. I'd have to pay homage to him in his lair; he'd never condescend to greet me. Pulling me by the hand, Aunt Frances Martha dragged me into the house and then to the dining room, where Daddy Clark stood waiting at the head of the table.

"Come on in, Taylor, baby. Here's your Granddaddy Harris waiting to see you," Aunt Frances Martha lisped as she pulled me right up to him. Good thing she did. My knees suddenly went weak on me as I approached him. I hated like hell to let go of her soft protectiveness to face the godfather.

Daddy Clark stood glaring at me, probably madder at me for holding up his supper than for returning to Clarksville. Unlike Sonny and Ellis, he hadn't changed one bit. He was a massive old man, bald as a coot, with a stern bulldog face, always looking to me like an unforgiving Old-Testament God.

Daddy Clark was no Southern Big Daddy, drinking and cussing and womanizing, no sirree. Part of the fear he instilled was from his puritanism. He was straitlaced as a Southern Baptist, disapproving of anything he considered unchristian or un-American. He had been chairman of the board of Clarksville's First Methodist Church as long as anyone could remember, and his word was God there, like it was in most local business dealings. Daddy Clark, the God of his little world, Zion County.

I walked over to him and held out my hand, despising myself for feeling six years old and tongue-tied again.

"Good afternoon, Daddy Clark," was all I could manage to say.

His piercing blue eyes behind the gold-rimmed glasses took in my long hair, my ragged shorts and my college tee shirt with distaste. He shook my hand scornfully without saying one word to me. I could feel Sonny gloating as he and Ellis watched.

"Sit down, boy."

After two years' absence, that was all my granddaddy had to say to me. No solicitations over my health or inquiries about my college life. I knew there wouldn't be any, either.

"Frances, tell Annie Lou that we're ready to be served now," Daddy Clark said as we sat down. This surprised me, because the maid Annie Lou used to stay and serve dinner only on special occasions. Maybe I was wrong—could this possibly be a special occasion for the Clarks after all—the return of the prodigal?

Annie Lou came in and stood respectfully by the sideboard, giving me a little wave of her hand. I noticed then that the good china serving dishes were on the sideboard, steaming hot and smelling wonderful. Turned out I was hungry after all. Daddy Clark prayed for what seemed like an hour in his gruff old voice, blessing the food to the nourishment of our bodies and then begging the Lord to be merciful and forgive us of our sins. Wonder what sins he was referring to? The old fool never forgave me for being born.

Aunt Frances Martha, seated next to me, grabbed my arm as soon as we all raised our heads from the prayer.

"Taylor, baby, your Aunt Opal wanted me to be sure and tell you she's *so* sorry she couldn't be here tonight. Her circle's fixing supper at Miss Maudie's." Aunt Frances Martha shook her head sympathetically. "Poor old thing."

I wondered if she meant Miss Maudie or Aunt Opal, whom I hadn't noticed wasn't here until now. She had never been one of my favorite people, since she was who Sonny inherited his charm from. As Aunt Della was prone to say, the apple never falls far from the tree.

"The United Methodist Women are always there when there's a death in the church, like they should be," Daddy Clark said as he nodded in approval. Sonny nodded as well and I grinned. Yessir, keep them womenfolks in their place. I watched fascinated as Daddy Clark stirred about ten spoonfuls of sugar into his glass of iced tea. It would take more than that to sweeten him up.

As Annie Lou began to bring the fancy serving dishes to the table, I became more and more sure that in spite of his coldness, Daddy Clark might actually be glad to see me. Why else would they put on the dog so? Annie Lou was dressed in a crisp maid's uniform, and she was using the best Clark china and silver. Pleased in spite of myself, I relaxed somewhat for the first time since arriving here.

The food wasn't to my liking, however. I'd seen this sort of spread often in the past, at fancy dinners and banquets and so forth. It was Clarksville's attempt at gourmet sophistication, shit like processed ham, or chicken cooked in Campbell's Cream of Mushroom soup; store-bought rolls with that fabulous taste of styrofoam; canned vegetable casseroles topped with crushed potato chips and full of crap like pimentos, olives, water chestnuts. I picked around at the plate Annie Lou put in front of me, pushing pukey cherries off my ham slice, thinking longingly of Aunt Della's good old country cooking.

Glancing up, I saw Daddy Clark chewing away, Sonny sawing on a piece of ham, and Aunt Frances Martha stuffing her expressionless face with a roll dripping butter. Ellis, sitting right across from me, was the only one not eating. Instead, she was watching everyone closely, peering with her heavily made-up eyes first at one, then the other. She looked down quickly when she met my eyes.

"Mighty good, sugar." Sonny smiled at her as he continued to wolf down the awful stuff.

Daddy Clark nodded agreement, still chewing, his fat jowls stuffed like a guinea pig. Aunt Frances Martha smiled sweetly up at me, then looked over at Ellis. "Winn-Dixie's English peas are better than Piggly Wiggly's," she told her new niece brightly, as though she'd just discovered the theory of relativity.

It hit me then—Aunt Frances Martha was not the only retard in the family. Ellis did all this! The new bride showing out. She must have seen my look of realization, for our eyes met and she looked directly at me, her silver-blonde head tilted, erect and proud. And the old girl wasn't doing it for my benefit either—the maid, the citified food, the good china, none of it. What a fool I was to even consider that. No, Ellis was the Lady of the Manor now, the new First Lady of Clarksville. I choked on the artichoke casserole and reached for my iced tea, coughing like hell. Daddy Clark glared at me as though I'd just farted at the table.

There was little conversation at the Clark table, something I'd forgotten in my absence. An occasional remark, "Um—these rolls are mighty good," or some such inanity; eating was a duty to be done and not enjoyed in Daddy Clark's house. It was a relief when Annie Lou cleared the dishes and brought in the dessert. I almost lost it then and looked out the heavily draped windows at the setting sun to keep from cracking up. Ellis took the cake platter from Annie Lou and held it up for us to see.

"Who wants some of my mama's delectable Black Forest cake? It's an old family recipe," she asked, batting her eyelashes.

I had to bite my lip when she turned to Sonny and said, "Your favorite, Hamilton, dear."

Hamilton! I'd forgotten Sonny's real name. That was funny enough, but I'd bet my last dime Ellis's redneck mama thinks the

Black Forest grows around the Black Warrior River. Old family recipe, my ass.

The famed Black Forest cake turned out to be a chocolate cake mix soggy with Cool Whip and canned cherries, which Ellis must have a thing for. I forced a couple of mouthfuls down and thanked God this dreary meal was over. It was easy to turn down Ellis's offer of instant Maxwell House. I had to get up my nerve to talk to Daddy Clark about Aunt Della. He pushed away from the table, grunting, "Mighty good, Miss Ellis," and started out of the room, but I stopped him.

"Daddy Clark. Could I speak to you a minute, please?" I could tell by his disapproving frown he expected me to hit him up for money, but he nodded curtly and I followed him out of the room into the hall. I saw Sonny and Ellis exchange glances but ignored them. My heart sank when he ushered me into the front parlor, the stuffiest, hottest room in the house. He was determined for me to sweat it out. Literally.

He sat in a large brocade chair and I took the sofa across from him. Before I could open my mouth, he jumped me.

"You in trouble again, boy? Because if you are, you can forget it. I've bailed you out my final time—still paying hospital bills on the last one." Again, the cold piercing eyes nailed me and I squirmed uncomfortably.

"No, sir. It's not that. It's—"

"And I've not heard hide nor hair from your mama. Far as I know, she's still overseas, whoring around Europe. You heard from her?"

I shook my head, feeling shame, as though it was my fault. "N-No, sir," was all I could manage to stammer. Damn! Hand it to the old coot, he could still make me feel like a shit. But I remembered Aunt Della's forlorn face and slumped shoulders, and I cleared my throat.

"Daddy Clark, Aunt Della tells me that you want her to go to a nursing home," I blurted out.

"So? I've not made a secret of it. Della is unable to stay by herself. I've asked around, talked to all the Nigras I know—I cannot find *anyone* to stay with her, Nigras, white trash, anyone. People nowadays rather stay home and collect welfare than do an honest day's work. So I don't see Della has any alternative. 'Course she could come here and live with us, let Frances take care of her. But oh, no, she's too stubborn. Says she don't get along with me and Frances."

Sweat was pouring down my shirt, and I'd have sold my soul for a cigarette. Wished I had a drink, too. I'd even have settled for a snort of old Ellis's sherry. I cleared my throat again.

"Daddy Clark, Aunt Della feels that you are going to force her to go to a nursing home. And she hates the idea. It absolutely kills her! She thinks that's why Miss Maudie died."

Daddy Clark grunted and rolled his eyes. "Some of Della's foolishness, talk like that! Della has always run her mouth too blame much. Maudie had been in poor health for years, and she died of a stroke. If Della don't want to go to a home, then she can live here. It's that simple."

I looked down at my hands. "But she doesn't want to."

"Well, boy, wouldn't life be wonderful if we got what we wanted?"

I shook my head sadly, knowing I couldn't reason with him. He was on a roll now and I'd have to listen to the whole tirade.

"Della has always been mule-headed. Got no use for a stubborn woman, never have. What's going to happen is that she's going to fall and break her hip, then she'll *have* to go to the home. No retirement wing for her then. If she'll go on now, she can go into the retirement section and adjust before ending up in the nursing wing. But I can't do a thing with her. Papa was the only one Della ever listened to, and he spoiled her rotten after Mama died. That's what's wrong with her now."

"But Daddy Clark! Surely you can see where she's coming from. She's lived in the same house all her life, her papa's house.

She wants to live out her life there, not in some strange place. Surely that's a reasonable request."

"As I said, boy. Too bad we can't do what we want in life." He started to get up, slapping his hands on his thighs and sighing deeply. I could tell the subject was closed as far as he was concerned. In my desperation to communicate with him, I overstepped and he got me. He always did. I haven't bested him yet, the sly old bastard.

"You're just afraid of what people will say of you, letting her stay alone there," I told him hotly, my voice shaking. "Doesn't matter that's what she wants—you're afraid people will say you're not taking care of your sister!"

He didn't say anything for a minute, but stared at me with those cold steely eyes instead. Clark eyes, just like Charlotte's. "Well, I'll tell you what, son. She can stay there. That's fine with me. She can stay there until she dies. *You* stay with her. How about that?"

"Daddy Clark, you know I can't do that. I'll be starting my junior year at Tulane next year."

"You could transfer, drive over to Alabama every day like a lot of boys around here do. It's up to you."

"But—Daddy Clark, surely you see—I mean, I'd do anything for Aunt Della, but—I can't *live* here—"

There was a dead silence and Daddy Clark pulled himself up heavily and started out of the room. Just as he got to the door, he turned back to me.

"Don't you talk to me anymore about Della, boy. Not *you*. She's given you everything and you've done nothing but break her heart. She was in good health for her age till all that business with you and the Sullivan boy like to have killed her. But no, you can't give her anything in return, can you?"

He paused one more time to twist the knife before going out the door and leaving me alone. "Reckon you're just like your no-good mama after all."

The door slammed, and I sat for a minute staring at my hands, my heart pounding, unable to move. The hot room started closing in on me and suddenly I jumped to my feet and ran out, out the hallway and the front door, not even bothering to close any doors behind me. I ran down the brick steps and the long driveway leading up to the house. I heard Aunt Frances Martha calling after me, but I didn't stop to look back.

Goddamn him! I hated every last one of them—Sonny, Ellis, Aunt Opal—the whole shitty family was nothing but a bunch of assholes. I wished to God I'd never gone there. I swore I never would again.

I had no intention of ending up at the football field. I don't even know what made me do it. I started out walking blindly away from the Clark house and just walked without noticing where the hell I was going. I got to the end of Clark Street, then turned down Railroad Street, paying no attention to anything around me, I was so distraught. I couldn't go home to Aunt Della yet. It would upset her too much to see me this pissed.

Before I realized it, I'd walked down by the high school. I stood and looked at it a minute without focusing on it. It was as ugly as most high schools, a sprawling one-story brick building with a flagpole in front, surrounded by a mound of flowers in the school colors. Blue and white petunias.

I walked past the front entrance, around the side of the building where the gym and some other smaller buildings, the bandroom, shop, were. Everything was perfectly quiet and deserted. I sat down on the hot concrete steps of the Ag building and fumbled for my cigarettes. I didn't see a living soul as I lit up, hands shaking like a fool. Then a blue pickup drove by, and the rednecks in it stared at me, but I flicked them a finger and they drove on. I chain-smoked two cigarettes, lighting one off the end of the other, then got to my feet. Without thinking where I was going, I walked down the little street behind the gym.

That's when I remembered that this street led to the stadium. And I saw it dead ahead. The lights were on in the early evening dusk. A bunch of cars were in the field next to the stadium, so something must have been going on there. They always called this field a parking lot, but it looked like a cow pasture, which caused us to be the butt of jokes from the visiting teams.

Like a damn fool, I kept right on walking through the cow-pasture parking lot until I got to the entrance of the stadium. A bunch of high school kids sitting on their cars were smoking and giggling as I walked past them. I noticed they were too young to have been in high school when I was, so I didn't know them and evidently they didn't recognize me either. I saw the girls nudge each other and simper, but I walked on, into the stadium like I was in some sort of trance or something.

As soon as I got inside the stadium, I saw what I should have remembered: football practice, every evening in August. As I walked in, pulled as if by a magnet, the sounds from the field and the smell of fresh-cut grass got to me so bad it almost bowled me over. I always hated football and the redneck passion for it, but because of Tim, I went to every damned game played here. It all came back so clearly that I felt like I'd been hit in the stomach. I needed to sit down, fast.

I went into the stadium and hurried over to the concrete bleachers, ignoring the little groups of folks sitting around talking quietly. I heard some of their gasps and whispers as I stumbled past them, but I dared not look at anyone. I even heard someone from one of the groups call my name, but I ignored them and got as far away from everybody as I could. Way up on the top of the bleachers, underneath the press box. This section was concrete, the reserve section for the home team fans. Adjoining these bleachers on each side were the wooden ones for the band

and the students. Down next to them on the left was the locker room for the visiting team, brightly colorful with winning seasons and Blue Devils painted on it. The art of Clarksville.

Soon as I sat down, I reached for my cigarettes and drew deeply on the burning smoke, beginning to feel better. Funny how something like the smell and sounds of a football field could revive so many memories. But not all unpleasant. I sat quietly smoking before I looked out on the field. The team was dressed out in their white practice jerseys, no flashy blue devils now, and the running backs were running patterns.

I never played on any team here, not football or baseball either. In Zion County, sports are such a passion, that didn't help me in the polls. I saw old Coach Mills's fat ass out there on the field, still dressed in the same blue shorts and blue-and-orange Auburn jersey. He looked exactly the same, except he had more of a beer gut than I remembered. I bet he even had the same wad of Red Man chewing tobacco tucked away in his jaw. He used to get by with chewing and spitting into a paper cup even in class because he was head coach. God, what a jerk! He always despised me. It pissed him off that I was well-built and agile but wouldn't play any of his good-ole-boy sports. Actually I liked baseball and might have played except that I hated him too much to give in. It like to have killed him that Tim and I were so close, and he did everything he could to turn Tim against me, tormenting me endlessly in P.E. class. Boy, I bet he gloated over my downfall. Brokenhearted as he must have been over his beloved Tim, I'll bet that a part of him was glad that he'd had my number all along, that I'd cause Tim nothing but trouble, just as he predicted.

The team was lined up to scrimmage. They all looked alike with their helmets on, so I didn't recognize any of them. Doubt that I'd know anyone anyway.

All of a sudden, I saw Tim. I sat stunned, unable to do anything but stare. God, it *was* him! He was standing right there on the sidelines, talking to his little brother. Tommy was shorter than Tim and looked much broader in his shoulder-padded jersey. I remembered him clearly, the way he always followed Tim around so with adoration.

Jesus, Tim looked exactly the same—I'd have known him anywhere! These past two years of worrying constantly about him, and he was the same—just Tim. In spite of all my nightmare images, I saw now that there were no scars, no horrible deformities—instead, he was the same person I last saw two years ago.

I realized I'd been holding my breath, and I let it out, squeezing my eyes shut. Aunt Della had kept assuring me that things would be okay, but I was afraid she was just trying to protect me. I knew that until I actually saw Tim for myself, I'd never believe that, not the way he looked when I saw him last. After all the agony of these past two years, Tim was really okay, not nearly as bad as I had feared. There must be a God after all.

Tim had his arm around his little brother's shoulder and was giving him some pointers on the game, evidently. As I watched them, Tim took his arm from Tommy's shoulder and turned in order to point out something on the field. *Oh Jesus Christ*. For a minute I thought I was going to puke at what I saw. Tim's arm! He used his left hand to remove his arm from Tommy's shoulder, then his right arm fell limply to his side. Even from this distance, I saw that the right arm was lame, and I closed my eyes. Oh, no. God, what a stupid asshole I was! Sitting here, trying to convince myself he was all right, when I knew better. *I* was there—I saw his broken body. Oh, yeah, Taylor. He's fine, just fine—just keep telling yourself that. Of course he can't use his right arm, but other than that—Jesus!

I knew that this telltale moment was what I had been running from for two years. I had to protect my precious ass above all else. I had to spend all my time seeing therapists and popping pills, so afraid I was having a breakdown. But safe—oh, yeah, safe as hell two states away while Tim was the one really suffering.

I *saw* him—the blood, the mangled body; I went for help that night—I knew how bad off he was! But during these past years, after I'd run away, unable to face what I'd done to him, I'd convinced myself that his injuries weren't so bad after all. And I believed it because I had to. I could not face this moment of seeing for myself how bad he really was, what I'd done to him. My therapist told me repeatedly I was heavy into denial. No shit.

I looked around wildly for an exit, a way to get out of here without anyone, especially Tim, seeing me. God, I couldn't believe that I walked up here big as you please, ignoring people's stares and whispers. It was a wonder they hadn't stoned me.

Then I saw Donnette and I froze, rooted to my seat. I turned my head quickly, almost panicking, taking deep breaths. Maybe it wasn't her. Dumb blondes are a dime a dozen around here. Turning slightly, I looked back to where she sat by herself on the bleachers.

It was Donnette, all right. Donnette Kennedy Sullivan. She was still good-looking, even more filled out than in high school. No doubt still an airhead, though. God knows how she ever finished school; Cat helped her every night and she still made Cs and Ds. Donnette always hated me, too stupid to realize that I didn't have anything against her personally. I never thought she was good enough for Tim, true. He could have done so much better with all the girls for miles around after him. If only things had worked out; if he'd been able to get out of Zion, gone off to college, he wouldn't have married Donnette, no question, though he fancied himself in love with her. That was only because he'd never gone with anyone else, had been with her since childhood. She was too possessive of him, too jealous of his relationship with me—they'd never have made it outside of this sheltered environment.

I realized I was staring at her, and suddenly she felt it and looked right at me, her big dark eyes wide and startled. It was too late to turn away. She was so surprised to see me that she jumped to her feet and bolted like a scared colt.

As soon as she got down off the bleachers, Tim turned and called after her. He took a few steps toward her, a puzzled look on his face, and I felt as though I'd been punched in the stomach again. His right leg dragged as he walked the few steps toward the fence. I sat stunned, unable to move for what seemed like an eternity as I stared at Tim. Oh, God, I had to get out of here! Oblivious to all the gaping fools in the stands, I too jumped to my feet and stumbled down the bleachers, not stopping to look at Tim, at the field, or anywhere. I just got my ass out of there as fast as I could. All I wanted to do was go home, back to Aunt Della's big safe house. I wanted to crawl in my bed and pull that heavy dark quilt over me and not come out again. Ever.

That night I had the dream again, although I'd been free of it almost a year. It had haunted my sleep for months after the accident, but with therapy and pills, I thought it was exorcised for good. I should have known that returning here would bring it back.

This time, however, the dream was a little different:

It's darker, a darker night than usual. It's raining, too, not hard but a soft summer rain, enough to keep the windshield wipers going steadily. I'm driving the sports car, not fast at all. Maybe too fast on a wet country road, but not dangerously so. Not then, anyway.

Tim, sitting next to me in the dark car, is talking, gesturing with his hands. He's happy, excited as we talk of our plans, going off to school together next week. We laugh a lot and plan together; I give him a playful punch on the leg. I tell him that even though he has to live in the athletic dorm, he can hang out in my room most of the time.

Then he says we can't do that after all, because he's taking her with him. I don't hear what else he says, but he's upset now. I shouldn't have said what I did, but I can't stop myself. He's begging me to shut up. The light on his face is eerie; it catches the pale gleam of his hair but hides his face from me so that his voice is coming out of the dark. Now he's angry, shouting. No, no, that's me shouting, saying those awful things to him, cruel things, meant to hurt him. My foot is heavier now and the rain is harder. Tim is grabbing for my arm. His eyes are in the light now and they are wild with fright. He is yelling at me to slow down.

I'm laughing at him, but in anger, incredibly angry at him for being such a fool. For not understanding what I'm saying to him . . . I plead again. No, it is Tim pleading instead, Tim grabbing my arm, causing the steering wheel to slip . . . we're airborne now, flying, flying, and how I laugh! Then I'm crying, crying, and I can't see anything. I hear a terrible crashing and my own screams.

Now I'm the one flying, free and flying through the dark silvery rain. How soft the rain is on my face and on my hair. I am on the wet grass somehow, dazed and muddy but unhurt. I see the car, crashed in the mud, but I don't see Tim. Struggling to my feet, I plunge around in the darkness, looking for him.

Always at this point in the dream I wake up, calling Tim and shaking so hard I can't breathe.

But tonight, back in Clarksville, dreaming, I search the dark woods for him instead. I call him and stumble around the wet bushes, crying. Then I see him. Thank God, there he is, propped up against a tree. I crawl to him in relief, whimpering. He's propped himself up against a tree and he looks fine. There's some blood on his face; his jeans are torn and his Blue Devils jersey is muddy and soaking wet, but he's fine. He's looking at me in relief, so I laugh and crawl over to him.

When I reach him, I see that he's not looking at me after all—oh, God! His eyes, glazed, stare unseeing at the falling rain. When I touch him with trembling fingers, his skin has the cold clamminess of a corpse.

Della

Every night before I go to sleep, I talk to Jesus and tell Him how my day went. I take all my troubles to Him, always have. I don't kneel beside the bed or anything like that; I just lie down, tucked in for the night, and start talking.

It tickles Papa to hear me talking to Jesus. Now that he's up there at the Lord's right hand, he enjoys hearing about everything going on down here. Just like when I was a child and he'd stand outside my door every night listening to me, chuckling to himself. "That Della," he'd say, "she talks to the Lord like He was a next-door neighbor."

I reckon there's some truth to that. Except Lonnie Floyd is my next-door neighbor and I sure wouldn't tell her half of what I tell Jesus. Sure as I did, she'd run and tell Velma, then half of Zion County would know about it before sundown.

I start off every single night by counting my blessings, and I've sure been blessed my eighty-two years on this earth. Oh, there has been troubles, too, and plenty of sorrows as well, long as I've lived. Sometimes the sorrows have been so bad I thought I'd die, but the Lord has seen me through. One thing I've learned is not to think too long on the sorrows—I think on the blessings instead, which gets me through a lot of heartache I couldn't stand otherwise.

After counting my blessings, I thank Jesus for my daily bread, just like He taught his disciples. Folks nowadays seem to take that for granted, but not me.

What a bountiful garden we had this year, Lord, I say to Him. I've seen plenty of times when there wasn't enough in the garden to fool with canning. But this year the tomatoes are the prettiest I've seen in Lord knows when. And the peaches this summer! How I wish Papa could taste them. Him and Taylor love peaches better than anybody. Those tree limbs were weighted down by mid-June with fruit sweet as could be. It broke my heart that half of them rotted on the ground. Me and Eula and Carrie just couldn't get them all picked to save our lives. You can't give food away nowadays—people too sorry to even come get it. Eula got her preacher to put a notice in the church bulletin that anyone who'd come get them could have all they picked, but no. Not even the colored would.

After I count the blessings of the day and thank Him for my daily bread, I lift up each and every one of my family members to Jesus, petitioning the Lord on their part. Since I'm kin to almost everyone in Zion County, this takes a spell. I spend more time on some than on others, because some folks need the Lord's help more.

Take that fool Harris. Every night I beg the Lord to touch Harris's hard heart. The very idea of him telling me that I got to go to the nursing home! He knows it would kill me, that I can't even stand the thought of it. But he don't care. Harris has always been that way, as You know, Lord. Everybody thinks he's the biggest Christian in Zion, but You and I know better. Oh, he does what he thinks is right, setting quite a store in whether or not something's the right thing to do. The only thing is, it's got to be right according to *him*, not according to Almighty God. Almighty Harris Clark, I call him, behind his back.

I don't mean to sit in judgment on him, only the Lord can do that. But my religion and Harris's just ain't the same. I remember plain as day when Harris got religion. He didn't get saved or converted like most folks do it, not him. When he turned twelve years old, he announced to Papa that he was joining the church. Just like that. No tears or nothing. Then he joined the youth group and started getting himself elected to things, and he joined everything else in the church from then on. He started running all those groups, the Official Board and the Methodist Men's Club and the Christian Athletes group and everything. It was about the same time he started running everything else in Zion County, because he's got to have things his way, and the church is no exception.

I've never approached religion that way myself. Why, even the way Harris and me pray is different, me talking to Jesus every night and him standing up in church and rambling on and on about sin and forgiveness and salvation. His voice trembles in fear as he prays. I guess if I was as bullheaded as Harris, I'd be afraid, too.

It does take me a spell every night to lift up all my relatives to Jesus, and sometimes I just skim over the ones in Mt. Zion that I haven't seen for a while. Like Fannie Clark's bunch; I haven't heard from any of them since Christmas was a year ago. But they're still kin, so I do it, regardless. All except one, that is. I hope You understand and forgive me, Jesus. I just can't bring myself to pray for the newest relative, that Ellis Rountree.

Every night, I save the dearest or neediest relative until last so I can spend extra time on them. It used to always be you, Papa, as you know. But now that you're with Jesus, you don't need me to do that for you. And Rufus, while I had you with me, it was you. But now it is my dear boy Taylor who's always last.

Oh, how I thank the Lord every single night for sending me that precious boy to bless my old age! Only You, Jesus, know how much that boy means to me. I've grieved so these past two years, night after night, but I've always known that You'd return him to me. I couldn't have gone on otherwise.

Before You sent my sweet baby to me, how I grieved over not being blessed with a child of my own. It's been the worst cross I've had to bear, worse than losing Mama and Papa and Rufus, because one day we'll all be together in paradise. But not to have my own little baby! I begged You to grant me that one thing. But once You called Rufus home, I knew then I'd never have a child of my own, because I'd never lay with another man except Rufus Gardner Dean, and I never did.

Yet You still answered my prayer, sweet Jesus! In my old age, when I'd given up hope, you sent me a boy child, my own flesh and blood kin. How I had to fight for him, though! Harris planned for Opal to raise that boy right along with her own boy Sonny, but it wasn't Your will. Opal never could stand Charlotte, so she refused to take in her child. Mary Frances and Cleve had their girls all half-grown and didn't want no baby around.

I did feel bad about poor Frances Martha; she wanted him worse than anything. But she ain't right, never has been, and she wasn't able to raise him. Just to spite me, Harris was going to let her have him, though, until I convinced him that everybody would talk about him something awful if she didn't half watch that baby and something happened to him. Worse than everybody was already talking about his daughter Charlotte for deserting her own flesh and blood. And that did it; nothing Harris hates worse than being talked about. Like Sarah in the Bible, I laughed with joy and clapped my hands when Harris gave in and brought Taylor to me.

Oh, the blessing that child brought into my lonely life! At first it was a lot of heartache. How that poor little child suffered, no one but me and Jesus knows. Poor little thing was so lost and scared at first, he cried himself to sleep every night. Crying for his mama, cries that would tear your heart out to hear. He was half grown before he saw his mama again, and by then all his tears for her had dried up. And he never saw his daddy again—nobody even knows where he is now. Charlotte met him when

Harris sent her off to Louisiana to some fancy girls' school—I tried to tell him no good would come of it. He wasn't no college boy, either. Nothing but a bartender, dark as a colored and couldn't half speak English. Charlotte up and married him just like someone common, instead of a Clark from Zion County.

Jesus, You alone know about that early heartbreak in Taylor's life, being deserted by his mama and daddy like that. But only me and You know how hard he tried to cling to all of us once he knew we was the only family he had. For the first time since Papa died, I was glad he wasn't here, for it would have killed him to witness Harris's coldheartedness. It broke my heart the way the boy Taylor tried to take up with his granddaddy, toddling around after him, begging him to take him riding in his car, or fishing, or anything. But Harris was so hurt with Charlotte, and so unforgiving, that he couldn't stand the sight of the boy. I can't help it—I hope that You'll forgive me for this, but I've had no use for Harris since then, though he's my only brother. No matter how big of a Christian and a Methodist he is, I've got no use for him at all.

I've done everything I can to make it up to Taylor for his parents being so sorry and his granddaddy so hardhearted. I'd do anything on earth for him. I believe sure as anything that You will forgive me for the lies I've told these past two years. I know me lying means that I'm no longer pure of heart and will not see You face to face. But I did it for my baby, and I'd do it again.

After I count my blessings and lift up my kin, ending up with my sweet boy Taylor, I then tell Jesus about my day. Somehow just going over every little detail with Jesus makes it more bearable. Shared blessings and shared sorrows.

This morning I woke up with a heavy heart, and I had a lot of trouble getting up to face the day. Poor Maudie. I can't believe that this afternoon I'll have to go to her funeral! It don't seem right that she's gone. Why, it hasn't been two weeks since Mary Frances drove me and Frances Martha and cousin Carrie over to Tuscaloosa to see her.

It broke my heart right slap in two to see her in that awful nursing home. We found her in her room, sitting in her wheelchair, just looking out the window. She hardly noticed when we came in. I couldn't believe it was my dear Maudie, sitting and staring like that, like a shell of the person she used to be! That's all she did once she went in that home, just sat and stared out that window. I wanted to run to her and grab her and cry, "Oh, Maudie—what are you looking for?"

I guess there was nothing else to do there in that nursing home, but sit and wait for Jesus. And He finally came and took her home with Him, after all her waiting and watching. So I know in my heart that she's in a better place now. But I'll miss her so much. She'll never sit with me on the front porch again and watch the sunset, or help me pick peas, or set out the azalea plants. Maudie Ferguson was just like a sister to me, since I'm so much older than the twins and never felt close to them. No, Maudie was my soul-sister, although I never told her so. Wish I had now.

I guess I aggravated Maudie a bit these last few years, and I regret it now. She never married and I used to worry about her being alone. In our younger days I was always saying to her, "Maudie, you ought to go on and marry Corbett Pate and quit teaching. Raise a family of your own, instead of all them schoolchildren of yours."

I reckon that might have hurt her feelings, like she didn't have anybody. She didn't much; her mama and daddy both gone for years, her only brother down in Florida.

"I think of my schoolchildren as my own," she'd always say quietly to me. Bless her heart, she sure did. She loved her teaching and her children more than anything. I guess that's what finally broke her spirit and turned her into an old woman, when you think about it. The school board had to call a special meeting and ask her to retire after she turned seventy-five. Bad thing was, there wasn't a thing wrong with her; she was just old. People nowadays act like being old is some kind of a disease instead of a natural part of life. All the young parents, students that she'd taught when they were little, having a fit because she was still in the classroom, wanting someone just out of college with all the new methods of teaching with computers and things. It broke Maudie's heart. She never was the same after her retirement. I reckon the school board had a right to do that, but it never seemed right to me, after all those years she gave them.

But it's wrong of me to grieve too much for Maudie when she's in heaven with Jesus now, walking them streets of gold. I sure hope that Maudie finds heaven to her liking. Funny thing is, one of the last conversations me and Maudie had before she fell and ended up in the nursing home was about heaven. A while back now, but I recall every detail like it was yesterday.

Me and Maudie were sitting on her front porch. It was right after she'd retired and I'd gone over to sit a spell with her, to take her some of my peach preserves and some butterbeans I'd gotten up and picked early that morning. That was back when I was able to get around pretty good.

We sat there on her porch in the late afternoon, shelling them butterbeans, rocking and talking. It was a hot summer afternoon . . . I can see it plain as day.

Thing is, we started out talking about the library. Maudie was fussing, telling me the librarian Ima Holliman told her how they were going to start opening half days since the town council had voted to cut back on their funds. Maudie was more upset about this than I was. She always did a lot of reading, all kinds of books imaginable, while I only read the Bible and the *Guidepost* magazine. She'd said the only good thing about retirement was that she'd planned on doing all the reading she wanted, and now the town council had cut back the funds. I never heard Maudie talk ugly like she did that afternoon.

"Damn bunch of rednecks!" She ranted and raved. "Country bumpkins—only thing they ever read is *The Tuscaloosa News*. The sports section and the funny papers, at that."

"Why, Maudie!" I'd said. Maudie was such a lady I couldn't recall ever hearing her use profanity before.

She went on and on about the library for a while before finally quieting down. Then me and her just sat rocking and shelling them beans, watching the sunset. Maudie's porch faces west, and the sun was setting in a blaze of pink. That hushed us because both of us had always loved to see the sun setting over Clarksville. We have one of the best sunsets in western Alabama, right here in Zion County. Maudie said it sometimes looked like her schoolchildren had colored it with their crayons, all red and purple and pink mixed together.

Then out of the blue, with us sitting there shelling butterbeans and looking at the sunset, Maudie turned to me and said, "Della, are you ready to go?"

Well, at first it like to have shocked me to death because Maudie was so well-mannered I'd never known her to be rude. First profanity and now rudeness. But when I looked up from my butterbeans at her, I saw she wasn't looking at me at all but was staring at that red sunset. Her lovely face and snow-white hair reflected the reddish-pink glow. Then I knew plain as day what it was she was talking about.

"No, Maudie. I ain't quite ready yet. I want to see Taylor finish school, maybe go off to college. 'Course I'd love to stay on and see him settle down eventually, too. How about you?"

She had stopped shelling beans and her hands were perfectly still in her lap. A smile came to her lips and she shook her head, the beautiful white waves stirring ever so slightly.

"I don't believe I'll ever be ready to give it all up. I'd really rather stay right here, in Zion County."

Maudie's like me; she'd lived in the same house all her life, her daddy's house. But then she glanced over at me and continued. "But you know what, Della? It won't be long for either one of us, will it? After all these years together, it won't be long now."

Neither of us said anything for a while; we just rocked and shelled quietly as the sun sank lower. Maudie finally raised her head to me again, and this time she really did surprise me.

"Della, do you think there's a heaven?"

At first I couldn't even answer her, I was so shocked. Why, Maudie was as good a Christian as they come. She had taught Sunday school and the women's missionary society long as I could remember. I just couldn't imagine her asking a question like that.

"Why, Maudie Ferguson! You read the Bible same as me. You know that Jesus tells us that if it weren't true, he wouldn't have told us."

"He says there are many mansions, Della. What do you think that means?"

"Well, I believe it means big, nice palaces. And pearly gates, and streets of gold. Just like the good book says."

"But, Della," Maudie continued, frowning. "Neither you nor I would want to live in a palace, now would we? I don't care how fine it is, if it isn't home."

I couldn't think of a thing to say to that. Then, bless Pete if Maudie didn't turn to me with a funny expression on her face and say, "If there is a heaven, I just don't believe it's going to be like that at all."

"Why, Maudie Ferguson!"

"I don't want a mansion or a palace, Della. I want a schoolroom, filled with little children, with readers and crayons and paints and chalk. Little children, all big-eyed and eager to learn. And I'd want a big library. The biggest library you've ever seen. One that's opened all the time, not just half days. That's what I hope heaven's like."

Oh, I hope so too, Maudie, dear, dear friend. I hope and pray that's where you are right now, in some big heavenly library, reading to your heart's content.

It was hard to get myself going this morning. I've got to get my mind off Maudie and her funeral today and go on with what needs to be done. It's so hard for me to do anything anymore. It takes me so long to drag around in this cumbersome old walker—I pure hate it. But I can't walk without it. That really scares me sometimes. I always think about what Papa said to me not too long before he went to be with Jesus.

"Della," Papa said, "you return to the earth the way you came into it, a helpless little baby again. No teeth, no hair, and somebody else having to take care of everything for you, even your bodily functions. When you get to where you can't walk, your time is coming. You are about ready to go back to where you came from."

I sure hope Taylor is feeling better today, bless his little heart. He was about sick yesterday, moping around, not talking. I told him that I believe it's the heat that's got to him. I know that this is one of the hottest summers that I can remember.

Cousin Carrie, however, declares that the summers have been hotter for the past twenty years. She says ever since we put a man on the moon it's been happening, that the summers and winters both are getting hotter. She thinks the Lord will take men up into the heavens when He's good and ready for them, and not before. Just think about the Tower of Babel, she says. Some things the Lord don't intend for us to mess with. She may be right.

If it's the heat that's got Taylor feeling so bad, I guess I ought to get a window unit put in his room, though I don't really believe in them myself. But I could call old Pleese Davis and get him to come out here and put one of those units in—it ain't the money. It's that every single Sunday since we air-conditioned the church,

I've come home with a headache. It didn't use to be that way. When Papa was still with me, we about died, it was so hot at church, and everybody fanned and sweated the whole time. But everybody was there regardless, never missing a single service. Now the air-conditioning is going full blast and you about freeze to death in the sanctuary. Then you walk out the doors and the heat hits you. Nowadays you have to beg folks to go to church, like the church needed them instead of the other way around. So I know part of the problem with people today—it's air-conditioning.

I can't help but worry about poor little Taylor. I kind of hope it *is* the heat instead of him being upset to be back here. Yesterday morning I got up early and fixed pancake batter. Rufus always declared that my pancakes were so light they could float across the room. But Taylor slept until dinner time, so I had to dump the batter down the sink. It's just not any good when it sits out like that; that's what makes pancakes heavy.

I figured rightly that he hadn't eaten a thing over at Harris's the night before because Frances Martha can't cook worth a hoot. It used to worry Mama to death. Main reason Frances Martha never half learned to cook ain't because she's not right. Everybody knows Maylene Hendricks is slower than Frances Martha, yet she wins prizes at the Fair every year with her cakes. No, Frances Martha just would *not* listen to Mama. Instead, she got it in her head to use a cookbook instead, because she loves to look at the pretty pictures of the food in them.

Frances Martha only finished the eighth grade, but she took Home Ec that year and got her a Betty Crocker cookbook that she's been using ever since. For some reason, her doing that like to have tickled Papa to death, but me and Mama didn't think it was so funny. What does a Yankee like Betty Crocker know about cooking purple-hulls, I asked Frances Martha. But she didn't care; all she liked was the pretty pictures in there, and sending Papa to the A & P all the time for Bisquick.

Guess Frances Martha is happy now that she's got someone else like her at Harris's house. Annie Lou told Eula now that Sonny's new bride Miss Ellis is there, she makes them try all kinds of fancy recipes from them *Southern Living* magazines. Annie Lou's like me, she's got no respect for a woman who has to read a book in order to put a meal on the table. Besides, Annie Lou can't even read! She's about ready to up and quit and I don't blame her, even though she's been with Harris for years. She don't like Miss Priss Ellis one bit, not any better than I do. I know them Rountrees and how good-for-nothing they are and so does Annie Lou. The coloreds know these things. Taylor told me about the supper they fixed him and how it wasn't fit to eat. Must have really made him sick because he wouldn't even talk about his visit. I'll bet you anything that Harris was ugly to him. And Sonny—he's always tormented Taylor, calling him a sissy and making fun of him. Sonny can't understand anybody being as tenderhearted and sensitive as Taylor is.

Sonny's as mean as a snake, just like his mama. That Opal Hamilton made her bed well when she married Harris Jr., that's for sure. Harris Jr. was a good boy, God rest his soul. He was like his mama, too. Seems boys tend to be like their mamas, and girls more like their papas. Harris Jr.'s mama, Mary Nell Pate, was as good a woman as ever drew a breath. I never could see what she saw in my brother Harris. At least Harris Jr. took after her. I believe if he'd not gotten himself killed like he did, Sonny would have turned out better, too. Opal spoiled him rotten after that.

I reckon I'll wait till Taylor gets up this morning before I mix up any more pancake batter. Guess I'll put on some vegetables for dinner since we'll have to go to the funeral right afterwards. Lord, I haven't even seen Maudie yet! Taylor felt so bad last night that I couldn't bring myself to remind him that he'd promised to take me to the funeral home. Mary Frances called me to see why I hadn't gone, and I told her I wasn't able to. Didn't figure anything else was any of her business. She means well, I know, but me and her have never been close. There's just too much difference in our ages, for one thing. Anyhow, she had to tell me about how Essie Kennedy's niece Donnette fixed Maudie up so nice, and how natural Maudie looked all laid out.

Lord have mercy! I clean forgot what else she called about. Mary Frances made the arrangements, and Frances Martha is going to pick me up at nine o'clock this morning. We're going over to Essie's to get our hair done for the funeral. I usually don't set no store in going to the beauty parlor, but I can't go to Maudie's funeral looking like this. Oh, goodness! Well, I'll just have to fry some bacon and eggs for breakfast and forget about the pancake batter. I don't have the time to fool with it now.

Taylor came into the kitchen just about the time I got through fixing breakfast. The smell of bacon frying must have woke him up, like it used to on school mornings. He was rubbing his eyes all sleepy-like, looking the world like a little boy. I see that he looks a little better this morning, too.

"Good morning, Aunt Della." He smiled sleepily at me, giving me a hug and a kiss on the cheek. He's the sweetest thing in the whole world; I can't understand why some folks never have liked him. Lord, he sure does need a haircut, though. Maybe he'll go with us this morning and get it cut. No, guess he couldn't do that, not with Donnette there. She's never got over what happened, blaming and talking awful about Taylor, though everyone else knows he didn't go to hurt Tim. Looks like she'd have sense enough to realize that if it hadn't happened like it did, Tim wouldn't be with her now. Probably wouldn't have married her either, once he got away from here and had lots more choices. Well. All that's in the past now.

"I'm so glad you're up early, honey," I said to Taylor instead of bringing up the subject of the haircut. "We got a busy day today." I put the bacon and eggs on the table and sat down.

"What time's Miss Maudie's funeral?" Taylor yawned and

stretched. I'd have to get him to put something on besides his undershorts before Frances Martha got here. It would embarrass her to death, him being half-naked.

"It's at two." I started in on my eggs since I had to hurry. "Honey, you remember Maudie's great-niece Sarah Jean?"

Taylor thought for a minute as he chewed on a piece of bacon. I always get the thick-sliced kind when he's home.

"Yes, ma'am, I believe I do now. She teaches at Florida State, doesn't she? Good-looking for an old lady—great legs."

"She's about the only family Maudie has left. Anyhow, she called me yesterday afternoon and wants us to come over after the funeral and eat supper with her. Says there's the most food over there you've ever seen, and no one but her. And she really wants to see you, too. She and your mama are good friends."

"I can't say that endears me to her, but the part about all that food sounds good." Taylor finished off his breakfast by wiping the plate with his toast. Papa would be tickled to death—he said you can tell a person's attitude toward life by their attitude toward food.

We finished our breakfast, and I figured I might as well go ahead and tell Taylor that I had to go to the beauty parlor. Maybe I won't even mention Donnette Sullivan. Probably he doesn't know that Essie died, and he'll think Essie's going to do it. I know that's called lying by omission but I believe the Lord will understand. He sure knows all the heartache Taylor's had these last two years without me bringing up any of it again.

"Listen, sugar," I told him, "in a few minutes Frances Martha is coming to pick me up, and we're going to the beauty parlor to get our hair fixed for Maudie's funeral."

Now I didn't see a blame thing funny about that, but Taylor did. That boy could laugh at some of the strangest things!

"Aunt Della, you look fine just the way you are," he said, smiling at me. "I mean it. Don't let Miss Essie fix your hair like Aunt Frances Martha's—it looks like cotton candy." Taylor then jumped up to help me as I pulled myself up on my walker. Before I could drag myself over to the sink, he grabbed the breakfast dishes and started scraping them.

"You leave these dishes alone. I'm going to do them while you get ready, okay?" He made a pan of dishwater before I could protest. "Go on, Aunt Della. I'll take care of this."

"No, sugar, you get out of my way. I've got to fix us some vegetables for dinner."

"Now, Aunt Della, didn't you just tell me that we were going over to Miss Maudie's this afternoon to eat? There's no point in your fixing lunch—let's eat a tomato sandwich. Quit fussing over me and go get dressed for the beauty parlor, okay?" And Taylor practically pushed me out the kitchen door, walker and all. It tickled me because it proves he's feeling better this morning and back to his old self again. I gave in with a smile.

I no sooner got my housecoat off and my teeth washed out when I heard Frances Martha pull up in the driveway and blow the car horn. I hurried and buttoned on my dress, because Frances Martha will sit out there blowing that horn until I come, and Lonnie next door will about break her neck trying to see what's going on.

Frances Martha surprised everyone by learning how to drive the car. I never learned myself and neither did Mary Frances; most girls in our day didn't. So it was even more of a surprise for Frances Martha to learn, since she's not able to do many other things. But one day she just up and went outside and cranked Papa's Oldsmobile, then backed it in and out of the driveway. Mama like to have had a conniption, but Papa decided it was a good idea. He helped her learn until she got her license. When Papa died, I tried to get her to trade his old Oldsmobile in and get herself a nice car. By that time, she'd moved in with Harris and Mary Nell. See, me and Frances Martha just can't quit fussing when we get around each other. I can't help it; she gets on my nerves so bad. Since she's always thought Harris hung the moon, she decided to live with them instead of me. She never really cared for Rufus, either. Since he worked over at the university a lot of people in town, including my own family, thought he was stuck up. But really he was just shy. Frances Martha didn't like him, though, and me and her fussed all the time, so she moved in with Harris. It tickled me because Harris refused to let her drive his car. She carried on so and got everybody in town feeling sorry for her, and talking about Harris, so naturally he gave in. Ever since then, she's been driving Harris's big fancy cars all over the place. I'm about the only person in town who's not scared to ride with her, and she takes me to visit and to the grocery store and the doctor. It don't bother me none. She sure drives better than she cooks.

It took me forever to get out of Harris's car, unfold my walker, and walk up the steps to Essie's old beauty parlor. Frances Martha made it that much harder on me by trying to be helpful. She almost tripped me just as we got to the top of the steps, on Essie's front porch.

"Frances Martha, would you quit trying to help me?" I shouted at her because I was so aggravated. "You like to have made me fall down the steps!"

Frances Martha's big blue eyes filled and she hung her head. That was one way she got on my nerves bad. She was so blame sensitive you couldn't say a thing to her. It use to drive Mama crazy, too. Next thing you know, she'd be squalling.

"Don't you start fussing at me, Sister," she said, her voice tear-filled. She started calling me Sister when she was too little to say Della. She couldn't talk plain until she was half grown.

"Besides," she added, "we're right next door to the preacher's house, so you need to keep your voice down."

She held the door that leads into the beauty shop open for

me. I can remember when it was the front bedroom in Essie's house. But that's been a long time ago, before me and Rufus married. The last time I was here myself was before Taylor left for college, before the accident, of course. That June I believe, when Essie did my hair for Buddy Clark's daughter's wedding. I had to serve punch. As I entered the shop, I noticed that everything looked the same. Reckon Donnette can't afford to fix things up.

Donnette was standing over at the sink, washing some hairbrushes or something. When she saw us, she turned the water off and came over to help us.

Donnette's a pretty girl, I always thought so, tall and blonde with big dark eyes. Essie was sure proud of her and bragged on her all the time. I never felt comfortable around Essie or Donnette after the accident, though it wasn't Taylor's fault what happened. I don't believe anybody but them ever thought so.

"Good morning, Miss Della, Miss Frances Martha." Donnette smiled at us, just as friendly as can be. I felt relieved that she was being friendly and not acting so hurt, like she used to do. Evidently she's gotten over it now, and everything was all right. She hurried to the door, trying to help me, too. I swanny, I do better when people just leave me alone!

"Come on in here, Miss Della," Donnette said to me as she grabbed my right arm. Frances Martha was still hanging on to the left. "Let's get you shampooed first, okay?"

Donnette was pulling on one side of me and Frances Martha on the other, me hanging on to the walker for dear life. They were trying to pull me to the sink, but Frances Martha tripped over my walker again and I stumbled. Donnette gasped and about broke my arm, she held on to me so tight.

"I swear, Frances, if you trip me one more time I'm going to end up flat on my fanny-butt!" I tried not to raise my voice but couldn't help it. This was really getting on my nerves.

"Don't you worry, Miss Della," Donnette chimed in sweetly. "I'm not gonna let you fall."

She continued to pull me to the sink, and I saw her look across me and wink at Frances Martha.

"Let's go ahead and get you shampooed, hear? Is that all right with you, Miss Frances Martha?"

Without waiting for a reply, Donnette pulled the walker away from me, turned me around, and plopped me down in the black plastic chair at the sink. Still moving quickly, she pumped it up with her feet until I was even with the sink. Then she pumped it back down, realizing I was taller than I looked, hunched over that blooming walker.

"Now, then, Miss Della. I'll have you ready in no time," she said as she began running the water, feeling it with her long, red-tipped fingers for the right temperature.

Frances Martha sat down in a pink chair under a dryer, pushed the dryer out of the way, and sighed, loud. She was acting like she was pure worn out from having to help me into the shop. I saw her cut those big childish eyes over at Donnette, and I knew she was looking for sympathy. She loves sympathy about better than anything.

"Essie, Sister is being *so* aggravating this morning. I declare I don't know what's wrong with her," she said, looking wide-eyed at Donnette.

"Frances Martha, you hush your mouth," I said to her, rather sharply. Sometimes you have to be firm with her. "That is *not* Essie, that is her niece Donnette. Essie's been dead for months now and you know it. Don't act crazier than you are."

Donnette looked at us nervously, like we were going to fight or something. Guess she's too young to know that me and Frances can't help fussing every time we get together. Most folks don't pay us any attention. But I didn't want Donnette to get too nervous, so I smiled up at her as she lowered my head into the sink.

"Don't worry, Donnette. Me and Frances always go on at each other. Don't pay us no mind," I said.

Donnette smiled but about yanked my head off as she pushed me farther back into the sink and started to shampoo my hair. Now that's another reason why I don't ever go to beauty parlors. The shampoo smelled like rotten apples, and the water was about to blister my scalp, it was so hot. Just pure torture, that's what it was.

"How have you been getting along, Miss Della?" Donnette asked as she began to scrub my scalp as though it were on a washboard. And me so tender-headed I could hardly stand it. "I hear you've not been doing too well lately."

"No such thing," I told her rather sharply. Harris was probably telling people stuff like that so he could send me away to a nursing home. "I can't walk real good, but I'm just fine."

"Don't you listen to her, Essie," Frances Martha butted in. "She can't get around good enough to take care of herself. I don't know what we're going to do with her."

"That's not true, not a word of it. I'm fit enough to stand this water burning the devil out of me," I said.

"Oh, I'm so sorry, Miss Della! Why didn't you say so?" Donnette cut the water on ice cold now. I should've kept my mouth shut.

Meanwhile, Frances Martha was about to have a conniption fit.

"Sister, you know that we are right next door to the preacher's house, and you talking ugly like that! I don't know what's got into you, unless you've got that old-timer's disease."

"There's not a blooming thing wrong with saying something is hot as the devil, Frances," I reminded her. "Says so in the Bible. And Papa used to say it, so it can't be wrong."

"No such thing, Sister," Frances Martha said loudly. Had to be loud for me to hear her over the sound of the water running. "Papa never said any ugly words in his life and you know it! Harris is just like Papa and Harris says it's a sin to talk ugly. Especially next door to the preacher's house. I'm going to tell Harris what you said."

I couldn't help it, Frances Martha was beginning to make me mad. I had to raise my voice even louder so she could hear me over the water running in my ears.

"Harris is not a thing like Papa and you know it! Papa says that Harris is just like his Uncle Henry, the orneriest Clark who ever lived. You know that's true, Frances—you know it."

By this time Donnette was through washing my hair and had pulled me up in the chair. Cold water dripped all down my back. Raised up, I could see that Frances Martha was looking all hurt and teary-eyed again. Lord have mercy! I wisht I'd stayed at home.

Donnette began combing through my dripping wet hair, slinging water everywhere. She acted like she was trying to stand right in front of me so I couldn't see Frances.

"How you want your hair fixed, Miss Della?" she asked me.

I was about tempted to tell her to forget it and go on home. Already I felt worn out and the worst was yet to come. However, I couldn't go to Maudie's funeral looking like this.

"Well, just roll it around my face a little, I reckon," I told her. "I don't want to look tacky. I'd like to look nice at Maudie's funeral."

"What are you wearing?" Donnette asked me as she continued to sling water every which way, combing my hair.

"My navy blue suit. With a white lace blouse, I guess. And Mama's pearls."

"Oh, your hair would look so pretty with a toner on it, Miss Della! Silver and navy go so nice together."

Donnette turned me around to face the mirror while she rolled my hair. I saw her pretty face reflected in the mirror and she looked so young and hopeful. I hated to tell her that I didn't want any of that mess on my hair. Silver and navy, my foot. But I didn't want to hurt her feelings. I noticed that her hands were shaky like she was nervous. I kept forgetting that she just opened the shop up, that she's only a year younger than Taylor. Just a child, really. I was about to tell her to put a toner on just so as not to hurt her feelings. But I remembered that Taylor wouldn't like it a bit.

"Just plain gray will do for me, honey. I've been plain all my life and there's no sense changing now. So fix it nice, okay? For Maudie. Today's *her* day."

Donnette began to roll pincurls around my face and I relaxed some. I might as well relax and get this over with. I noticed that Frances Martha was nosing around, looking at a sheet of paper lying on the table by the dryer. I too had to be nosy and ask, then wished afterwards that I'd kept my mouth shut.

"What is it that you're looking at, Frances?"

"I don't know. Looks like somebody is drawing something."

Frances Martha started to put it back down, but Donnette stopped her. She quit rolling my hair and went over to look at the piece of paper on the table.

"Oh, Miss Frances Martha—you've got to see this—it's the cutest thing in the world."

She held the piece of paper up and looked at it. I couldn't imagine what on earth she could be talking about.

"This is the drawing that my husband Tim made for a sign he's going to make me for my shop. I want you to see it." She held it and smiled like it was a baby or something. "Isn't it just the cutest thing you've ever seen?"

Frances Martha pushed her glasses up farther on her nose and peered at it real hard. "Well, I'll be. It *is* real pretty. And he's colored it, too. Who did it?"

"Tim, my husband. You know him, Miss Frances Martha. He's going to make me a real nice sign for my shop."

Donnette leaned over Frances Martha like she was hard of hearing and pointed it out to her. "I'm so proud of it. It was his idea to make it for me."

You could tell that Frances Martha really liked it because of the pretty colors. From here, I could see that it was real colorful.

"What does the sign say?" Frances asked. I don't know why— she can read as good as a fifth grader. She can really get on your nerves. I just wisht I hadn't said anything about it. I sure didn't want Donnette to start talking about Tim. And I hoped Frances Martha didn't say anything about Taylor being home. It'd embarrass all of us for that to be brought up now.

Donnette pointed to the sign. "It says 'Making Waves.' That's what I'm naming my shop. And I'm getting him to put my name on it, too, and the hours I'll be open. See—Donnette Sullivan, owner. Ain't that something?"

"How come you naming it Making Waves?" Frances asked. She could be so childlike!

"Well, I don't know. I just liked it. It reminds me of Miss Maudie, in a way. Don't you think it will be nice to have a sign like that hanging out front? Nobody else in town has one anything like it!"

"I sure do think that will be pretty. You say your husband drew it?"

"Yes, ma'am. He's already cut the wood out at the lumberyard where he works. Now he's got to paint it. He's real good at painting. Tim can do anything he sets his mind to do," she added.

Donnette then remembered me sitting there dripping wet. She came back over and started rolling my hair again. Frances was still staring at that piece of paper with Donnette's sign drawn on it. Making Waves. That did sound real cute, and nobody else in town had a sign for their place.

But then I noticed Frances looking first at the sign and then at Donnette. I could tell by the expression on her face that she was about to ask a stupid question—I could just tell.

"You're married to that Sullivan boy, ain't you?" Frances may be slow, but she can be as cunning as a fox sometimes. I've never seen a slow person who couldn't be. She knew good and well who Donnette was married to! Then Frances began to look at me with a look I knew so good, too. She was putting two and two together. I had to get her talking about something else, or she'd be saying something that she shouldn't, embarrassing us all.

"Mary Frances tells me that you fixed Maudie up for the funeral, Donnette," I said loudly, before Donnette got a chance to answer Frances. Donnette finished rolling my hair and was now wrapping a hairnet around it.

"Oh, yes, ma'am. I did. I sure didn't want to at first, I'll admit it. But I went over there and fixed her hair and did her makeup. I thought she looked real good when I finished."

Donnette pulled me up from the chair, and with the help of my walker, got me over to the dryer. After plopping me down in the seat, she stuffed cotton over my ears and turned the dryer on full blast.

"Mary Frances says that she was really pleased with the job you did on Maudie," I managed to say before the dryer came down over my head and I couldn't hear a thing. I just hoped to goodness that'd be enough to get Frances Martha talking about the funeral. Anything but Tim.

Donnette got me all situated, sticking an old *Guidepost* magazine in my hands, and then she went back to Frances and started washing her hair. I could tell they were talking, though I couldn't hear what they were saying, and I got real nervous. I couldn't help myself. I finally just yanked the cotton off my ears and listened.

Sure enough, even with the water running I could hear Donnette talking about Tim making her that sign and what colors he was going to paint it. So I stuck my head out from under the dryer and practically yelled so they could hear me over the noise of that thing and the water running too.

"Donnette, this dryer of yours is hot as hell!"

Well, that worked. Frances Martha like to have had a fit, squawking about the preacher next door and telling Harris on me. Donnette came running over, fussing about me taking the cotton off my ears. She turned the dryer down and fixed me back up. As she tucked me back in, I whispered so that Frances couldn't hear me, "Why don't you tell Frances Martha about how you fixed Miss Maudie up for the funeral? She loves to hear things like that."

Sure enough, a few minutes later I eased the cotton up and listened, and that's what they were talking about. Frances's eyes were as big as saucers, and she was taking in every word. Thank you, Jesus. And I didn't have to lie either. The hair dryer *was* hot as hell.

In spite of the nerve-wracking morning at Donnette's beauty shop, I was pleased with the way my hair turned out, so I felt as good as could be expected when me and Taylor got to the church that afternoon for Maudie's funeral. Donnette fixed some soft curls around my face, which went real well with my navy blue suit and lace blouse. I was glad, when we got ready, to see that Taylor had on a dark suit and looked so nice. I hadn't seen him in a suit since his senior prom. He really is a handsome young man. I was proud to have him escort me into the church.

I wanted to get there early to get a good seat and get my walker folded and out of the way. So we were half an hour early. Also, I knew the casket would be open at that time. I wanted to see Maudie, one last time. Taylor couldn't understand that, I could tell. He looked at me like I'd lost my mind when I told him the reason I wanted to get to the church early. He was too young to understand what it meant to me, to lose the last friend

I had left on this earth. Young people can't understand things like that. Maybe it was just as well, otherwise they might never want to grow old.

Taylor helped me walk down the aisle of the church once we got inside. Thank goodness we were the only ones there. It took forever, poking down the aisle with my walker, Taylor holding my elbow and walking along beside me. I couldn't help but think of the other times I'd walked this same walk, and the people waiting for me at the end of it. Today it was my dear Maudie. And Maudie's casket—it was a pretty one, bronze and shiny, not gaudy at all. Maudie's family, what was left of it, gave the casket arrangement of red roses, Mary Frances had told me yesterday. I had reminded her that I wanted mauve roses on mine, if they could find them. I love that color. My wedding dress was the palest mauve you've ever seen.

When we got to the casket, both of us stood there a minute. I noticed that Taylor looked away, anywhere but at the casket. Lord have mercy, I've never seen so many flowers. Maudie would sure love that, way she loved flowers. Her yard was always as overgrown with plants as mine. Neither one of us could stand to cut anything back. Nearest the casket was a huge arrangement of blue and white mums, and sparkly letters in the center spelled out "ZCS." Zion County Schools. Isn't that sweet! I bet they took up money from the schoolchildren to buy that one. That would mean a lot to Maudie.

Out of the corner of my eye I saw Cleve and Pleese Davis, who helped Cleve out part-time, all donned out in their dark suits. Pleese was always around when there was a funeral. He also worked on appliances, too, just an all-around handy man. Someone told me he dug the graves as well.

I finally made myself get close enough to the casket so I could see Maudie. I wasn't prepared to see her lying there like that; I never was. I almost fainted when I saw dear Rufus in his casket—it was such a shock. People say folks look so natural laid out;

they're just asleep, they say. Well, it's true that they're asleep in Jesus. But, Lord, when you first see them, they look so—*dead*. There's no other way to say it. They just look so dead. I heard the preacher say one time that it's real important when there's a sudden death for the kin to see their loved one in the casket, that makes them know they're really dead. I know for sure if that sight won't make death real, nothing will.

Taylor turned his head quickly away as I took a deep breath and looked down at Maudie. I knew if I stood there for a minute, taking deep breaths, I'd accept seeing her like that.

Oh, dear Maudie! I wisht to goodness you'd sit up and talk to me. Just sit up and talk to me, my dear. But instead she was laying there so very, very still. Her waxy-looking hands were neatly folded at her waist, and her pale face was a lifeless mask, like it never was in life. Even Donnette's makeup couldn't bring life to her face. The rouge looked orangey on her, but her hair did look real good, I had to admit. Just like she always wore it, so neat in those big white waves. Her painted mouth was set primly in a little smile, and I smiled when I looked at it.

"Maudie, they got your smile right," I whispered to her. I saw Taylor look at me startled, but I just couldn't help myself. No one else was around to hear me except Pleese and Cleve, and I didn't care about them.

"Maudie, you look real nice. You'd be proud to have everyone walk by looking at you today, honey. Because you look so peaceful, which lets me know you are with Jesus for sure. And the flowers, they are so pretty. I wish you could see them. Just open your eyes a minute and see them." I couldn't help myself; I started to cry then.

Taylor was shuffling around all embarrassed now, because people were beginning to come into the church, but I didn't care. Finally he took my arm gently and whispered to me, "Come on, Aunt Della. Let's get you seated, okay?"

I let him lead me away, back to the pew behind where the family would sit, across from the one reserved for the pallbearers. I wished I hadn't cried like that and embarrassed Taylor, but I couldn't help it. I couldn't seem to stop myself, either. Soon as I got seated, Taylor fumbled around for his handkerchief and handed it to me. It was none too clean, but I took it anyway. I had one in my purse but I didn't feel like looking for it. I didn't feel too good at all.

Cleve came over to us, looking all mournful and droopy like he always does. He whispered something to Taylor but I couldn't hear what he was saying. Taylor whispered something back to him, and then he put an arm around me. I guess he was assuring Cleve I was okay, not about to have a stroke or something. Maybe Cleve was hoping he'd have another customer. I shouldn't think that; it was nice of him to be concerned about me, even if we've never been close. He's a pretty good man, I guess. He's made Mary Frances a good husband all these years.

With Taylor's arm nice and secure about my shoulders, I began to feel better and was able to stop crying so hard. I never thought it dignified to carry on at funerals. Why, I never cried a bit at Papa's or Rufus's; everybody said I held up so well. What they didn't know was that all my crying was inside me.

Oh, Lord give me strength! I see Harris and all his bunch coming into the church now. The church was beginning to fill up. It would be full because everyone turned out for funerals in Clarksville. Whether you were close to someone or not, you went to their funeral when they died. And everybody knew Maudie. I bet she taught half the people in Zion County. I was sure glad we got here early and got a good seat.

Harris and them came over and sat on the pew with Taylor and me. Wouldn't you know that Harris would do that, wanting everybody to think we're such a close family? That hypocrite. He shook Taylor's hand and nodded at me. I nodded back because

I noticed Estelle Hendricks sitting two pews back, and she'd tell everyone in town if I didn't.

Opal, Frances Martha, and that Ellis Rountree were all with Harris, all dressed fit to kill. I reckon Sonny was driving the hearse today. They all spoke to me and Opal hugged Taylor. Lord have mercy, she was a bigger hypocrite than Harris! Probably just showing off, us being up here in front of the whole church. It beat all; none of them have stuck by him these last two years but me, yet they get in front of the town and act so loving. Bunch of hypocrites!

Opal leaned over like she was fixing to give me a hug, and I nodded to her before she got a chance. Opal has gotten fat as a hog lately. She has always been a big woman, but she has spread out even more. That dress she was wearing really hugged her big fanny-butt.

Then Sonny's wife, Ellis, spoke to me, too, in her prissy way. Opal's dress might have been tight, but at least it was a decent dark color—just you look at how that Ellis was dressed! A red silk suit at a funeral, if that don't beat all. But what can you expect from those Rountrees? Tacky as they come, the whole bunch.

Harris had his old bald head down and his lips were moving, like he was deep in prayer. I knew Harris; the more people came in, the longer he'd pray. He'd stay like that until he got a crick in his neck.

Frances Martha got up and went down the aisle to look at Maudie again. Mary Frances told me she had stayed at the funeral home last night the whole time the body was in state. She just loves funerals. She stood and stared down at Maudie till I saw Opal nudge Ellis. I believe Opal was about to go up there and get her. Ellis wasn't paying attention to her, though. People were beginning to file by the coffin now, so Frances Martha had to come back to her seat, reluctantly. Now Ellis was going to be the one to get a crick, because she kept on looking around to see who all was there. I'll bet she figured this was her first official appearance with the Clark family, except for church every Sunday. At least she's got Sonny going to church regular now. I like to have fainted a few Sundays ago when I walked in and saw him sitting there. It's a wonder the roof didn't cave in.

Cousin Carrie came over and hugged Taylor and spoke to the rest of the family before going up to view Maudie. Me and her are about the only old-timers left now that Maudie's gone. Well, there's old Frank Enfinger, who is blind as a bat and never goes out anywhere. I reckon he will be the next one to go, then either me or Carrie. Unless Harris got his way and stuck me in a nursing home, then I'd go first. I hope Harris would be sorry then. He was finally through praying. Frances told me that he was real insulted not to be asked to be a pallbearer. He was an honorary one, I noticed in the obituary, but so was half of Zion County, including the school board.

It seemed like forever before the line up to the casket dwindled out, and people settled into their pews. Cleve went up then and closed the casket lid and placed the spray of roses over it. This time I looked away so I wouldn't start crying again. Maudie was gone forever. I always had that feeling of finality when the casket was sealed.

Cleve and Pleese went out the church doors and escorted the family into the church. There was nobody but Maudie's cousins from Mt. Zion. Then there was Sarah Jean, all by herself. Cleve sat her down real carefully, like she was fragile. She did kind of look it—I hadn't seen her in ages. She's about the same size as Charlotte, but thin as a rail. That pinstriped suit made her look downright skinny. She used to be such a pretty girl, too. Reckon she's been working too hard at that college where she teaches. I remember Maudie was real upset over her divorce a few years back. Seems like he was a doctor. Sarah Jean's a doctor herself, but one of those that teach at colleges instead of seeing patients.

Brother Junkin did a real nice job on Maudie's eulogy. He

always did; he was such a blessing to our church. I'd already been over every single thing with him that I want in my service. I hope I have as many people as were here today. The church was so packed I felt like I was about to faint, but I wasn't going to let on. Taylor didn't want me to go to the graveside one bit, and if he thought I wasn't feeling well, he'd have a good excuse not to take me. Of course I knew that he didn't want to go because he didn't want to be around people, but surely nobody would say anything to him at a funeral. Folks were always so nice and polite then, especially at the graveside. That was my favorite part.

The choir sung Maudie's favorite hymn, "There Is a Balm in Gilead," and the church service was over. The preacher's wife played the organ real nice as the pallbearers came up and wheeled the casket out. This time Sonny was with Cleve and Pleese as they led the way out, then Cleve came back and escorted Sarah Jean and the rest of the family. Sarah Jean had on her sunglasses now. I bet she was real upset over Maudie; she has always been so good to her. She tried to get Maudie to retire in Florida but Maudie wouldn't do it. Zion County was her home. Oh, Maudie.

Everyone started standing, then moving slowly out of the church. Mrs. Junkin was still playing away on the organ. This time she was doing "The Beautiful Garden of Prayer."

Taylor reached out his hand to help me up, but I shook my head at him.

"Let's wait until the whole church clears out, hon," I whispered. He settled back down, relieved, I'm sure. I noticed he didn't look around at all. Opal reached over me and grabbed his arm.

"I sure hate it that I missed you when you came over for supper the other night, Taylor." She grinned, and I noticed she had red lipstick smeared on her teeth. "I was beginning to think we'd never see you around here again. Thought you'd fallen off the face of the earth! How long you going to be in town?"

"I don't really know, Aunt Opal. I've got a couple of weeks free till school starts back." He didn't look at her, but instead faced the front and watched Pleese and Sonny load the flowers up for the graveside trip.

"I thought Charlotte told her daddy that you were working this summer, waiting tables," Opal said to Taylor.

"Yes, ma'am. I was. It was just a summer job," he replied.

"Well, I didn't know for sure. Thought maybe you'd decided to become a waiter for a living. We haven't heard a thing from Charlotte since June." Opal smirked. "She called Harris on Father's Day, was all. What do you hear from her?"

"Not much." Taylor was polite to his aunt, but refused to look at her as he pretended great interest in them hauling the flowers out—there were so many. Bless his heart, I knew that he hadn't heard from his mama all summer. Opal was looking so sly I bet you anything she knew that too, and just wanted to torment him, for pure meanness. She grinned her greasy-lipstick grin at him and reached for Ellis, who was standing next to her, still looking around at all the people as they filed out of church. Opal pulled Ellis next to her and continued to look slyly at Taylor.

"Well. What did you think of your cousin Sonny up and marrying like he did?" As though Taylor gave a hoot about anything Sonny did.

But Taylor surprised me; he turned around and looked real hard at Ellis, so hard that she blushed and looked away from him.

"I tell you, Aunt Opal, I was really surprised. I thought Sonny would never settle down, become a family man, but evidently he just hadn't found the right woman. Now he has." And he smiled at Ellis sweet as you pleased.

You could tell that really pleased Opal, who stuck out her big fat chest even farther, almost busting her dinner-pies out of the too-tight dress. But evidently Ellis was peeved about something else, because she glared at Taylor instead. I reached up and tugged on his sleeve before they had a chance to say another thing to him.

"Come on, sugar. The church is about cleared out now. Let's go."

It was so hot at the graveside service that I thought for a minute I was going to die myself. Because of the heat, there was not as many people here as in the church, thank goodness. I shouldn't have come, because I really didn't feel good, but I loved it out here so much I couldn't stand not to. The cemetery was all the way out past the houses, at the end of the street called Cemetery Street. Lots of big, shady oaks out here, and the graves were so peaceful. However, it was really hard for me to get around in my walker because of the dry summer grass. Maudie's family plot was down in a little valley, away from the rest of the graves, over in a back corner. I hoped I was able to walk over to the Clark plot before we left because I hadn't been able to come out here all summer long.

Brother Junkin didn't do anything at the graveside service but read some scriptures and say a simple prayer over the grave. I reckon it was just too hot for anything else. I couldn't help but be relieved; Maudie wouldn't care, and I didn't much believe I could stand up another minute. Me and Taylor stood in the shade of the tent, right behind the family, but it was still awful. Soon as the preacher finished the prayer and went over to the family members to shake hands, I motioned to Taylor for us to go. It was a long climb back up that hill and to the car. Plus, I had just spotted Donnette among the crowd around the grave, and Tim was with her. I didn't see them in church; they must have been all the way in the back. So if we left now, we wouldn't have to see them or anyone else. We could go over to Maudie's and wait for Sarah Jean. I'd get Taylor to bring me back to the family plot another day. I know Papa and Rufus will understand why I haven't been able to visit them lately.

I was so glad we came to Maudie's house when we did, way things turned out, and that we stayed on and ate supper with Sarah Jean. The Lord does work in mysterious ways. I know that Jesus led us there, because I almost decided not to go by the time Taylor managed to get me into the car, I felt so bad. But I knew Maudie would be disappointed in me for not keeping Sarah Jean company, so I made myself go. I thank the Lord, for Taylor's sake, that I did.

I almost turned around again and changed my mind about staying when we got to Maudie's house. The house was so still and so quiet. It was a big old house like mine, with a porch all the way around it where me and Maudie used to sit and visit. But it sure looked sad and empty when we got there.

Me and Taylor went into the house like Sarah Jean said for us to do—to wait for her till she got there. So we went to the kitchen. I told Taylor to sit down and I'd fix us some iced tea while we waited for Sarah Jean, but he insisted on doing it himself. He made me sit at the kitchen table while he plundered around in the refrigerator and fixed me and him a glass of tea. Then we decided to take our tea and go into Maudie's sitting room. It was her favorite room, a sunny little room next to the kitchen where she sat and read all the time, day or night.

All Maudie's books were in her sitting room, and so was her rocking chair where she always sat when she read. It made me miss her again so much I almost cried when I walked in there and saw everything. I noticed that her reading glasses were folded and placed on the mantel. She never used them once she got to the nursing home—she quit reading and everything.

Taylor helped me into the rocker and folded my walker away.

I sat down wearily, not having the heart to tell him that I'd rather not sit in Maudie's favorite chair. But I didn't feel like protesting right then.

As soon as he had me settled, Taylor started walking around the room, looking at everything and sniffing.

"This house smells just like an old lady. No offense, Aunt Della," he said, grinning at me. He picked up Maudie's glasses from the mantel, inspected them, and then placed them back where they were. Then he picked up a book of Maudie's and sniffed it, for some reason. Maudie wouldn't care, though. She always loved Taylor to death. I just sat there in her chair and tried to keep from looking around too much. I was afraid I might lose control of myself again, like I did at the funeral. Oh, Maudie. It's not a pleasant feeling to bury your last friend. Not a good feeling at all.

If Sarah Jean hadn't come in at that very moment, I would have started up crying again. I don't know what on earth was wrong with me. But Sarah Jean suddenly came in the room, all friendly-like, and looking so glad to see us that it cheered me up.

Bless her heart, she looked real tired, and her hair was hanging down a bit from the way she had it pinned up so pretty in church, but other than that, she looked exactly the same as she always has.

"Miss Della! It is so good to see you here—and in Aunt Maudie's chair, too. How she'd love that." Sarah Jean smiled at me as she grabbed me into a big hug, though she's no bigger than a minute. She smelled like tea roses as she gave me a soft kiss on the cheek.

Then she turned around to Taylor and got to him right away, telling him something even I didn't know. I could tell it really tickled him.

"So this is Samuel Taylor, all grown up now." Sarah Jean smiled as she hugged Taylor, too. She barely came up to his shoulder. I swear she was the least little thing I'd ever seen.

"How did you know that?" Taylor asked her.

"That you're all grown up? I can see," she teased him, poking him in the ribs, then standing back and looking him over carefully.

"No, ma'am. My name." I knew that was what he meant.

"You didn't know that Charlotte named you after her favorite poet?" she asked him. She reached down and took her heels off, making her appear even tinier.

Taylor at first looked puzzled, then he grinned. "Well, I'll be damned! I swear I never knew that—and I never made the connection. And me an English major! I always figured I was named after one of her boyfriends, since I'm the only Clark without a family name."

Sarah Jean looked up at him. "An English major, huh? Are you a poet, too, like your namesake?" She took off her suit jacket, then pulled her blouse out at the waist.

"Y'all will just have to excuse me, but I thought I'd have a heatstroke at that cemetery. Well, are you?"

Taylor shook his head and smiled at her. "Not really. I'm not any good, but I try my hand every now and then."

Sarah Jean then turned to face me, seated in the chair. "God, it's hot in this house! Miss Della, can I get you a Tom Collins? I've got some already made up in the fridge."

I didn't know what she meant; all I saw in there when I was looking for the tea, before Taylor made me sit down, was some lemonade with lots of mint and cherries in it. Maudie always raised the prettiest mint.

"No, thank you, honey. I got me a glass of tea. Maybe Taylor would like some collins."

That like to have tickled both of them to death, for some reason. I saw Sarah Jean wink at Taylor and he grinned down at her. "Could I please, ma'am, have one—a big, tall, icy one?" he asked.

"Okay, but only if you promise to stop saying 'ma'am' to

me. I may be your mama's age, but I don't want to be reminded. You hear?" She laughed and started walking barefoot into the kitchen, Taylor following close behind.

"Okay—what do you want me to call you then?" I heard Taylor ask her as they went on into the kitchen. I heard the refrigerator door opening and then could hear both of them laughing as they got that fancy lemonade out.

For the first time in two years, I felt a ray of hope. I felt like maybe the Lord was going to let me have my Taylor back. I'd already been trying to accept that my penance for these past two years would probably be having to give him up, but now—oh, Jesus was so good to me! I sat back in Maudie's rocker and sipped my tea. I knew that Sarah Jean was going to be around a few days, until her school started back, she'd already told me. She was going to be busy packing away Maudie's things and closing down her house.

If only she and Taylor could get to be close . . . I almost couldn't allow myself to hope. But maybe, with her training, she could be the friend he needed. Then another thought hit me. I wasn't going to be around forever, and the main reason I've hung on lately is knowing that Taylor has no other family but me. Well, none that counts. But if only . . . Charlotte may be sorry as gully dirt, but she was the boy's real mother. Maybe, oh dear Lord, just maybe, Sarah Jean could be the one to bring Taylor and his mama back together, so he'd have someone after I'm gone.

Oh, dear Jesus. I could still hear them laughing and talking in the kitchen, fixing themselves some more of that lemonade. I believe it might be possible. I hope and pray that Sarah Jean will bring Charlotte back to Clarksville, and back into Taylor's life. Starting tonight, I'm going to add that to my prayer list. I'm putting it at the very top!

Ellis

I never would have gotten involved with all that mess about Tim Sullivan and Taylor Dupree if it hadn't been for Glenda taking a job at the Zippy Mart just so she could be with Dinky Odom.

Now, if it'd been anybody but Glenda, I wouldn't have paid it any mind. I do consider it beneath me to involve myself in other people's affairs. But Glenda—Glenda's never been a bit of trouble to me or Mama or Daddy, not one single time in her life.

Long as I can remember, Glenda's gotten up every morning and gone to school on the bus, then come home, done her schoolwork and her Bible study, and gone straight on to bed. You kind of take someone like that for granted, getting to where you forget she's even around.

When Glenda graduated from high school two years ago, nothing in her life changed much. Mama's cousin Tammie helped get her a job at the daycare center where Tammie has worked for years, so Glenda now goes to work instead of school. And last year, Glenda got a boyfriend for the first time ever. Bless her heart, Glenda's no beauty; I got all the looks in the family.

So she had never gone with anyone before. But when Bobby Ray Hall came to our church as the new youth minister, he started asking Glenda to help him out with the young people's activities, like the Crusade for Jesus. She made posters and rounded folks up to host the youth choir that came all the way from Biloxi, Mississippi. Next thing you know, Bobby Ray was asking Glenda to sit by him at the church suppers, and then prayer meetings. We knew for sure they were an item when he asked her if she'd go with him to the annual tent meeting in Montevallo. Brother Clyde Willis from Birmingham was the guest evangelist, so Glenda was thrilled. 'Course it tickled Mama and Daddy, too. I took Glenda to Kmart's myself to get her a new dress for the occasion.

All the women in the church were having a fit because Glenda was officially going with Bobby Ray, because he's about the cutest thing you've ever seen. He's got jet-black hair, which he combs back so neat, and it's always slick and shiny. And he's a real sharp dresser, too. We all thought Glenda was one lucky girl, especially being as plain as she is. I've tried my best to get her to cut her hair and wear some makeup, but she flat-out refuses. I don't guess Bobby Ray cared, because they've been going steady almost a year.

And now this. Mama sent for me right after Miss Maudie Ferguson's funeral. I swear, I'm going to put in a telephone for Mama and Daddy if it's the last thing I ever do! Looks like Mama would realize how humiliated I feel when she sends Daddy to town for me. Last time she did was when they needed a ride to Tuscaloosa to get Granny's dentures fixed. It's always something.

But this time, we had just got in from the funeral, and there I was in my new silk suit Hamilton bought me at Gayfer's, about to burn up it was so blamed hot, but not wanting to change clothes yet. I'd fixed some iced tea for me and Miss Opal and Miss Frances Martha. I sliced a lemon real thin and put the whole thing in the pitcher of tea—a whole lemon and about two cups of sugar. Then I poured it in those pretty long-stemmed crystal glasses that belonged to Hamilton's grandmother. Oh, my, it looked and tasted good! I couldn't even drink mine for looking at it, whirling that tiny little glass stem around and around.

I convinced Miss Opal and Miss Frances Martha that we ought to sit out on the side porch a spell. I could tell that neither one of them wanted to, but they did anyhow. Hamilton's mother seems like she really likes me and tries to please me, which kind of surprised me. When we first married, I wasn't sure how she'd take to me, me being slightly older than Hamilton.

Miss Opal's difficult for me to understand, tell you the truth. She'd been ill as a hornet since we got home, saying that she like to have died at the funeral, it was so hot, and that the dress she wore had shrunk, that she knew better than to trust Annie Lou to wash it in Woolite. I had to bite my tongue to keep from telling her she'd put on a lot of weight lately. I can't understand a woman in her position having such an attitude, frankly. I mean, the woman has everything in the world, and all she does is complain. She stays on to poor old Miss Frances Martha all the time, telling her she's a crazy old bessie-bug who ought to be committed to Bryce's, and as soon as Mr. Harris dies, that's exactly where she's going. She fusses about Mr. Harris—I mean Daddy Clark—she goes on about Daddy Clark being such a tightwad. Except that's not the way she says it, but I was raised better than to use words like that myself.

And then she goes on all the time about how bored she is, so what does she do—goes over to the country club in Mt. Zion and plays bridge all day.

What a waste of time! I just cannot see it myself. She could go to the mall in Tuscaloosa or Columbus anytime she wants to, buy anything she wants; how can she be bored enough to play card games? Or she could go all the way to Birmingham to shop. They've got the most malls over there that you've ever seen! Hamilton took me to the new Galleria after we got back from our wedding trip to Gulf Shores. Lord, I'd never seen anything like the Galleria in my life! He promised to take me back soon to get my fall wardrobe. But Miss Opal won't go—she says it's too big, got too many stores, and it makes her feet hurt to even think about it. If that don't beat all!

So, true to form, Miss Opal was sitting out on the porch griping about the heat and Daddy Clark being too stingy to air-condition the house, when who drove up in that awful old pickup of his but Daddy. You could hear the truck rattling all the way down the street. I was so humiliated I could die, especially today with all the people in town for the funeral. Then Daddy got out, slamming the door, and started up the walk to the house, and I really was embarrassed. Why did he have to wear his overalls to town today of all days? Usually Daddy will at least put on a nice sports shirt and tie when he comes into town, as befitting a deacon of the church. Something must be up for him to come off looking like that.

Miss Opal was about to break her neck looking, then she sank back into the lounge chair.

"I believe that's your Daddy looking for you, Ellis. Tell him to come on in and get some tea."

I met him on the front steps and made him come on the porch with us, though he didn't want to, I could tell. He hated to come see me at the Clark house. I was bound and determined not to let Hamilton's mama see me be rude to Daddy though, no matter how aggravated I felt. He took off his hat and spoke briefly to Miss Opal and Miss Frances Martha without raising his eyes.

"Daddy, we're just sitting out here having a glass of tea. Let me get you some," I said to him because I wanted him to see those pretty crystal glasses. But he shook his head and twisted the battered old straw hat in his hand, the one he wears in the field.

Then Miss Opal spoke up, trying to be polite, I reckon, but I wisht she'd left it alone, because there's no telling what Daddy will say, and he uses the worst grammar. That's one of the main things I straightened out about myself when I went off to college, because I realized nothing shows up your ignorance like poor grammar.

"Mr. Rountree, would you rather have a Coke or something?" Miss Opal asked, pulling her big rear end out of the lounge chair and almost tipping over.

Daddy swallowed nervously, then looked down at the hat in his hands.

"Well, ma'am, if it ain't too much trouble . . ."

"No trouble at all. I'm fixing to go in myself and let y'all visit, but I'm sure Frances Martha will fix it for you."

Sure enough, Miss Frances Martha jumped up, too. She'd been sitting in the swing looking at a cookbook.

"If y'all got one, I'd be much obliged fer a Grapico," Daddy said.

Now that aggravated the stew out of me. How could Daddy ask for a Grapico when he could have lemon tea in a crystal glass? And he'd drink it right out of the bottle, too, I knew. But I wasn't about to say anything and let them think I was disrespectful to my parents, so I kept my mouth shut. Miss Frances Martha went off into the kitchen nice as you please to get him a Grapico. I knew that we had some in the refrigerator because Annie Lou likes them, too. Naturally.

I was also aggravated with Daddy because he didn't say a blooming thing to Miss Opal and Miss Frances Martha while they were still out there on the porch. When she came back with the Grapico, Miss Frances Martha tried to talk to him about Miss Maudie's funeral; she loves funerals better'n anyone, but no. He wouldn't say a blame thing, just looked down at his shoes and nodded. Him and Mama both are the timidest things I've ever seen in my life, but especially around Hamilton's people.

They're not a thing like me. When I was a little girl, I used to make up stories about being adopted, since I was so different than the rest of my family. Outgoing, that's what I am. I can talk to anybody about anything. I stood there after the funeral today and talked to the preacher's wife like I'd known her all my life. We talked about that article in the Zion County Herald last week, the one about all the chickens in the county dying from heat prostration. That's what I call stimulating conversation. And it paid off, too. Mrs. Junkin invited me to come to the Study Club meeting at her house next Thursday night. Every month they read a different book, and the librarian gives a review on it. I just can't wait. This month the book is *Decorating with Decoupage: The Elegant Touch.*

As it turned out, I was grateful Miss Opal and Miss Frances Martha went back into the house for their afternoon nap and left me and Daddy alone on the porch. I would have died if they heard what he came to tell me about Glenda.

"That's why I come, Ellis," Daddy told me after they left. "Your mama's in bed sick and done took two of her heart pills. She took to bed as soon as Glenda up and quit her job and rode off with that thar Dink Odom."

I was about to get a migraine myself. At first, I didn't understand what Daddy was so upset about. About some things, I'm as slow as Miss Frances Martha!

"But that ain't—isn't nothing to get Mama sick about, Daddy," I said. "I imagine Zippy Mart pays better than Kiddie World. And it's over by the river, so they do lots of business there. I for one can't fault Glenda for trying to better herself."

Then I thought of something. "Just how's she going to get to work?"

Mama and Daddy're so old-timey they don't believe in girls having cars, or wearing makeup, or anything like that. When I finished high school and started working at the First Baptist Church in town, Daddy drove me in and picked me up every single day, in that rattley old pickup. Every day for years, that is, until I decided to change my life.

I'd been saving up my money, since I didn't really have anything to spend it on, so the first thing I did was get me a car. I bought the Baptist preacher's wife's little Ford Escort when she got herself a new LTD. I tell you, getting that little blue Escort changed me. I decided that since I finally had my own car, I could go to business college in Columbus, like I'd always wanted to do. Me, in college! The beginning of a new life for me. I set me some goals and stuck with them, and my whole life has changed. Maybe Glenda had decided to do the same.

"That's jest it," Daddy said, "whut I'm trying to tell you. She's ridin' to work now with Dink Odom. He done picked her up this morning. And you know our place is way outta his way."

"How does Glenda even know Dinky?" I suddenly wondered. People assume everybody in a small town knows everybody else, but there are a lot of folks in Clarksville I don't know, bound to be even more for Glenda, living way out in the country.

"He brangs his young'uns to the daycare center whur she worked. So she knows him real good, I reckon," Daddy said.

I saw then that Daddy was getting real nervous. He's a little bitty man, skinny as can be, and one way you can tell he's upset is when his Adam's apple starts bobbling around in his scrawny neck. The other way is his eyes. Daddy has watery blue eyes that have always been crossed, but especially if he gets upset. I've never thought they were all that bad myself, but Hamilton claims Daddy can stand in the middle of the week and see both Sundays. He's always trying to get me to take him to the eye foundation in Birmingham.

I sighed out loud, since no one was around. My sick headache was intensifying.

"Now, Daddy, I still don't see why y'all should be so upset. Glenda's almost twenty-one years old. And there's nothing wrong with her working for Dinky Odom, really. I mean, he's kind of a redneck, but he ain't—isn't—so bad."

"But, Ellis," he said. Daddy named me after the preacher that saved him, so he speaks my name with lots of reverence. "Glenda didn't even tell anyone 'bout this! Tammie drove up to git her fer work this morning, and she runs out and tells Tammie she done quit. Then that Dink feller comes driving up, and she tells us she's gonna be workin' fer him at the Zippy Mart from now on. 'Cept he can't afford to pay her no full wages, so she done give up a regular job fer part-time work!" Daddy shook his head in disbelief. Daddy has always made his living doing odd carpentry jobs and farming, never having held down a full-time job in his life.

Well, I had to admit, it sure didn't sound like something respectful little Glenda would do. I didn't know what to make of it.

Then Daddy looked all around the porch to make sure no one was listening. One of his eyes looked at me and the other over my shoulder as he whispered to me, "Ellis, it ain't jest that Glenda's acting peculiar sudden-like, no, ma'am. It's worse than that. That thar Dink Odom is *divorced*."

Well, that did it. I got a full-blown headache then. I knew it'd do no good to try and convince Daddy that lots of people were divorced nowadays; it was totally against his religion. And I knew with a swift pain over my eyes that Daddy Clark would feel the same, him being a religious fanatic, too, bad as Daddy in his own way. I'd heard him go on and on many a time about the Decline of the American Way, and how folks getting divorces was the reason. I can remember when I felt that way, too, before I went off to college and broadened my outlook on life. Ever since then, I changed how I felt about a lot of Mama and Daddy's ideas, but it wouldn't do any good to tell them. Here I was, trying to make the best possible impression on Hamilton's people, and now this. I could just choke Glenda.

It ended up with me getting rid of Daddy by promising to ride over to the Zippy Mart and talk to Glenda. I sure dreaded it. It was almost four o'clock in the afternoon, and I'd missed my nap. Now I had a headache instead. I planned a lovely summer dinner tonight of chicken salad on a cantalope half, which I looked forward to all day. Miss Frances Martha made some poppy-seed rolls from her Bisquick this morning, and it was going to be a special supper. Well, it would just have to wait until I got back. Daddy Clark wouldn't like that; he likes to eat right on schedule, and Hamilton wouldn't like it because he wants his wife to be here when he gets home from work. But I couldn't help it. Under the circumstances, I didn't know what else I could do. I declare! Family obligations can be so tiresome.

The Zippy Mart that Dink Odom runs is the one over by the Black Warrior River, off the highway that goes to Mt. Zion. Glenda and me never got to go to the river like other kids, because Mama and Daddy don't believe in it. Our preacher even preached against the sins of the river one Sunday when I was a little girl. The reason is, a lot of high school kids go over there all the time and drink and do all sorts of bad things. Hamilton went down there a lot in his younger days, before he met me and settled down.

I'd never been to the river myself until I got my little Escort, then I drove myself out there big as you please and looked around. At first I was scared to even get out of the car. I reckon something in me believed the devil himself would jump out of that dark swirling water and get me. But in a few minutes I got out, and I stood on the steep bank of the river looking down. The water was a dark autumn green, and you could see rocks and sticks and fish underneath it, around the edge. The trees were changing colors, and in places the golds and reds of the woods around the river were reflected in the deep dark water.

I couldn't stop staring down at the river, almost like I was hypnotized by it. I was baptized in the creek that runs behind our church, a clear, cheerful little creek, not a thing like the

Black Warrior. As I looked into that dark, deep river, I swore I'd come there anytime I wanted to, that never again would anyone forbid me anything so fabulous.

So I took to coming often, bringing my lunch and sitting in the sun, watching the different seasons. Autumn's still my favorite, because that's the way I saw it first, then spring is next, with the soft pretty greens and golds. If I thought for a minute that Glenda had found at the Black Warrior River what I myself discovered, it would be different. I wouldn't be going out there to talk to her. But if all she'd found there was that sorry old Dinky Odom, that was a different matter altogether!

I was glad no one was at the Zippy Mart when I drove up. Dinky's black pickup was parked over to the side, by the restrooms, was all. I didn't care; anything I had to say to Glenda he could listen to.

Glenda was behind the cash register, adding up a pile of figures on a little calculator. She'd always been good with numbers, and I tried to get her to go to business school in Columbus like I did, but no, she's too blame timid to go off anywhere. Except to the Zippy Mart with Dinky, evidently. Glenda didn't look different, though, for someone who'd had a change of personality lately. She was dressed her usual way, in a pink polyester dress Mama made, way too young for her, with a little bow at the waist. Glenda's not pretty but she's neat as a pin. She pulls her long hair back on each side, which looks right nice on her. She's never cut it, it's down to her waist, almost. Lord, I'd love for Donnette to get ahold of it. She did wonders for mine.

Glenda didn't look particularly surprised to see me. "Hey, Ellis," was all she said, then she went right back to the calculator.

"Glenda, I reckon you know why I'm here," I said firmly to her, a little louder than I intended.

"You need some gas or something?" She didn't look at me, still pecking away at that calculator.

"I need to talk to you. You ought to know that Mama would send Daddy to town for me after you up and did what you did this morning!"

I grabbed a package of Anacin and tossed her a dollar. I couldn't take this headache anymore.

Glenda calmly handed me a Coke to wash the Anacin down with.

"Why would Mama send Daddy for you?" she asked. Hand it to her, she did look puzzled. I've tried to get her not to squint her eyes like that; she'll have crow's-feet before she's thirty. Look at Mama. Why, she's more wrinkled than Miss Frances Martha, who's about sixty, and Mama's no older than Miss Opal. But Miss Opal takes care of her skin.

"You know good and well they'd be upset with you quitting your job like that, Glenda. And then going off with Dink Odom! You know how they are, good as I do."

Glenda shrugged. "They never ask me about my job, or anything else, for that matter."

Lord, Glenda could be pure slow sometimes! "Of course not—Mama and Daddy don't know how to make conversation," I reminded her. "You have to be the one to initiate it with them. But that's not the point. Mama's in bed sick, and Daddy's so upset his eyes are wallowing!"

I couldn't believe it; Glenda just shrugged again.

"Mama stays in bed sick half the time. And if I read the Bible as much as Daddy, I'd be cross-eyed too."

Well, my mouth fell open and I stared at her, I was so dumbstruck. Glenda, talking like this! No wonder Mama and Daddy were upset. For once in my life, I couldn't think of a thing to say.

Glenda opened up the cash register and began to fiddle with something in there. "Is that all you need, Ellis? Dink's got RCs on special this week. Or you could get Sonny some Budweiser."

"I don't need an RC and I sure don't need any beer—Hamilton doesn't drink beer anymore. No, I just need to understand what's going on—I need to understand *you*."

"There ain't nothing to understand. I quit my job at the daycare because Dink offered me a job here. Plus, he offered to come by and pick me up every morning, and take me home after we close at night. I love it here, too. It's the first time I've been to the river."

Glenda closed the cash register with a bang and I jumped. Timid little Glenda talking like this! I guess I'd been too preoccupied with getting into the Clark family to notice her lately. But thinking of the Clarks fueled my resolve again. I couldn't let Glenda get by with this.

"Now listen here, Glenda. How do you think it will look to Mr. Harris Clark when he finds out about this?"

She looked at me with disgust. "It's honest work. Why would Mr. Harris give two figs about anything I do?"

I looked around to make sure no one else was in the store. "Use your head, Glenda. Dink is a divorced man. You know what that means to people like Mama and Daddy. Well, Mr. Harris is just as religious as they are, in his own way. He wouldn't approve. You are Hamilton's sister-in-law now, you know. What you do reflects on the whole Clark family."

Glenda began restacking a display of Bic cigarette lighters next to the cash register, purposely avoiding my eye.

"So what if Dink's divorced—he couldn't help it. Joleen ran off and left him. And left him with two little girls he's had to raise all by himself. He's done the best he could. It ain't none of Old Man Harris Clark's business. Or Mama and Daddy's either."

I was so flabbergasted I was again speechless. But I had to ask her what I came here to find out—I wasn't going home without finding out.

"Glenda, are you and Dinky—I mean—what about you and Bobby Ray Hall?"

Glenda stopped her fiddling around and looked right at me. She has nice blue eyes if she'd wear a little Maybelline.

"Ellis, this ain't none of your business either. I never said one thing when you set out to marry Sonny Clark, and everybody knows what he is. But he just happened to be the only Clark available, so you tricked him into marrying you—"

"I *never*—that's a lie, Miss Smarty Pants! Hamilton and I happen to love each other very much." I couldn't ever remember getting mad with Glenda, not once. Now I could've gladly killed her.

Before either of us could say another word, the door swung open and Dinky Odom walked in. He's older than me, a big, hulking man who always wears cowboy shirts and boots with his Levi's. He combs his long hair way over from the back to cover a balding spot on top. What on earth could Glenda see in such an unrefined man?

"What in the hell are you two yelling about?" he said right off the bat, no "How you doing, Mrs. Clark" or nothing. Just plain common. He stopped right in front of the Bic display and glared at me.

"Well, hello to you, too, Dink," I said with all the sarcasm I could muster. I've gotten good at sarcasm since I've been to the business college.

"What do you want, Miss Ellis? Glenda ain't done nothing wrong," Dinky said, squinting as he lit up a cigarette without asking me. I waved the smoke away and coughed.

"Guess I'm here to make sure that she don't, Dinky Odom. How come you had to come along and offer Glenda a job here? She was doing just fine where she was."

Dinky leaned lazily on the counter and looked me over, head to toe, puffing that cigarette disrespectfully.

"Shit. That ain't what she told me. She's been miserable over there for two years, stuck with a roomful of squalling kids eight until five every single day. How'd you like to do that for a living, Miss Ellis?"

"Then how come she didn't just quit?" I asked him with a smile to show him who's got the brains around here.

"She just did," he smiled back.

I swear if Glenda didn't snicker. Now I was really mad. I might have known somebody had been influencing her. A good girl like Glenda doesn't turn into a smart mouth overnight.

Dinky dragged on his cigarette and blew smoke right in my face, causing me to gag and sputter. "Now, why don't you tell me what you really came for, Ellis Clark? As if I didn't know. Lay your cards on the table."

"All right, I will. I want to know this—is Glenda just working for you, or are you *going* with her?"

Before another word could be said, Glenda came from behind the counter to stand by him, and Dinky put his arm around her. I literally felt my chin drop. Dinky grinned at me.

"I guess that answers your question, Miss Ellis."

I was too shocked to say anything—it was as I had feared! Oh, Lord, what would Daddy Clark say? This was all I needed now. Then, for some reason, I pictured Bobby Ray Hall, with his boyish grin and his shining face, and I turned to Glenda.

"B-but, Glenda—what about Bobby Ray?"

"It don't look like the preacher man is much compared to me, now does it?" Dinky smirked. My hand itched to slap his stupid face, and Glenda's too. I had to get out of there fast.

"Y'all are not going to get by with this, you hear me? Glenda Sue Rountree, you'd better listen to me, because I mean it—nothing is going to mess me up with the Clarks, you hear? Certainly not you and this no-good man here!"

I ran out still yelling, too upset to stop myself, my head busting now. I headed straight for the car and slammed the door, not once looking back. Thank the Lord no one was around to see me carrying on in such a way, so unlike my usual dignified demeanor.

. . .

It was much later that I had an inspiration, one which brought me vast relief from this despicable situation. I took two Valiums Hamilton gave me and went to bed when I got home. I didn't let on to any of them that anything was wrong, just that I had one of my bad migraine headaches. I couldn't even eat the lovely supper we'd worked so hard over, and Miss Frances Martha pouted, but I couldn't help it.

Hamilton was so sweet and solicitous of me; he brought me the pills and some cold lemon tea and fussed over me. It almost made me cry. Glenda is wrong about us. I would have married him even if he wasn't a Clark—I just didn't realize it at the time. I admit I set out to catch him, but he hasn't been short-changed one bit. I have made a different person out of him in the short time we've been married. So, maybe it was fate that made me set my cap for him—certainly it was fate or something that made it turn out the way it did. Maybe even God. It was almost like God spoke to me about what to do about Dinky and Glenda.

Dinky Odom is related to Donnette Sullivan. As soon as I remembered that fact, I felt enormous relief. They're not exactly related; he used to be married to her cousin Joleen. I knew that Dink thought the world of Donnette because she helped him with the children after that slut Joleen ran off with Clermon Windham. I recalled hearing folks say that Dink wouldn't have made it through that difficult time without Donnette, that he'd do anything for her. So. Tomorrow I would pay a little visit to Donnette. I needed my roots touched up anyway. Of all people, Donnette knew what all I went through to get where I am today and how I'd do anything to keep from losing what me and her together gained. Donnette would help me out again, I just knew she would! I was so glad I thought of her. Maybe there was a God after all.

. . .

I thought Donnette was not at home when I got to her shop. It was early in the morning—I was just too worried to stay around the house any longer. Hamilton was still asleep, so I left him a note saying I was going to get my hair fixed. He always sleeps late because there's no need for him to go to the funeral home until after lunch anyway. Then, if nobody has died, there's really nothing much for him and his Uncle Cleve to do. They spend a lot of time polishing the hearse. Usually, they go to the cafe in Mt. Zion and sit around with the men who work at the courthouse, drinking coffee and telling jokes all afternoon. There's not a cafe in Clarksville. There's a Coca-Cola and hamburger stand outside of town but that's it. You have to drive twelve miles to Mt. Zion to get a decent cup of coffee.

I opened the door to Donnette's shop and looked in. The lights weren't on, and she was nowhere to be seen. I figured she was probably in the kitchen, so I went to her front door and knocked. But there was no sound coming from the house. I knew she wouldn't care if I went to the kitchen, so I walked around the porch to the back door. If she wasn't in the kitchen, then she must still be asleep, which is not like her. Donnette is determined to make a go of that shop and she works hard at it, putting in long hours. As a matter of fact, she has consulted me on certain matters about keeping her books and running the shop, since I'm a business school graduate. In a way, that's how our friendship started.

The kitchen door in the back has a window in it, where Donnette has hung some cute flowery curtains. Before knocking, I peeked through there to see if she was in. I sure was relieved that I didn't just go barging in, because Donnette *was* in there, all right, but she wasn't alone. Tim was with her, standing with his arms around her. I stepped back, embarrassed.

I didn't really intend to watch them, but Donnette had tied those flowery curtains back on each side of the window, and I could see them plain as day. Tim didn't have on a thing but his underwear! Donnette had on a skimpy little pink robe that didn't cover much.

I couldn't help but take advantage of this opportunity to look and see if Tim had really recovered from that accident as well as Donnette claimed. He like to have died, yet he sure looked fine now. Even though his injured arm was hanging there kind of useless, his shoulders and chest were still muscular and tanned. Both of his legs looked the same, though there was some kind of brace on one. He really did look good. Hamilton has let himself get a little flabby lately. He says it's my good cooking, but I've been trying to get him to exercise some. Maybe I should tell him to take a good look at Tim Sullivan if he wants to see what a man's body ought to look like. I'd never seen anyone's but Sonny's, and now Tim's—except for that one other time. But I couldn't let myself think about that, certainly not now.

I stepped a little closer to the door and saw that the two of them were bending over something on the table that Tim was pointing to. Donnette kept her arm around his waist as they leaned together over the table. Now what on earth could it be that had their attention so completely? I tried to get a little closer, and I'll be—I sort of fell against the door and it banged. Donnette looked up startled and saw me standing there. All I could do now was give a little wave to her. She gave Tim a shove and he hobbled off quickly, down the hall. She then straightened up her robe and motioned for me to come in. I was so embarrassed I could die, but there was nothing I could do now but apologize.

"Oh, Donnette, honey," I began, "I am *so* sorry I interrupted y'all! I was just looking to see if you were in—"

But Donnette, being so sweet and friendly, laughed it off and let me in the door. "No problem—Tim has to go get ready for work anyway. I'm running late; I should have already opened the shop. Come on in."

Donnette pulled a kitchen chair around for me just as casual as could be. I purposely didn't let my eyes wander over to the table, though I was sure curious to know what they were looking at there.

"I hope I didn't scare Tim off," I said to her as she handed me a mug of coffee. I hated coffee but took it anyway because I needed something to do with my hands. For some reason I felt kind of uneasy, like she'd caught me spying on them.

"No, Tim's fixing to go to work," she said as she fixed herself a cup of coffee and leaned against the kitchen counter sipping it.

"Does he like that job at the lumber mill?" I asked politely.

She shrugged. Without any makeup on, she looked about twelve years old, not at all the glamorous girl she usually was.

"It's okay. Just part-time. He does odd jobs there, figures up the bills and invoices and stuff."

"Donnette, you know Mr. Harris would get Tim a job any time, at the bank or any place." We'd been through this before.

"I know. I wish to goodness he'd go to Mr. Harris, but he says that it would make him feel like a charity case. I think it hurt him more than he lets on that, even though they paid the bills, Mr. Harris let it be known it wasn't his responsibility to keep supporting him. That really hurt Tim's pride, because last thing he wants is for anyone to feel responsible for him."

"I know that, but Taylor—" I had to shut up before I could say another word, because suddenly the back bedroom door opened and Tim came into the kitchen, dressed this time. He spoke to me politely and quietly, and asked about Sonny. He's one of the nicest boys I've ever known. It breaks my heart to think about what all he's been through. And to think of where he'd be now, how famous he might be, if it hadn't been for that accident! Life just isn't fair sometimes. I looked away as he kissed Donnette good-bye, then he went out the door. Least he's got her. She's stood by him through it all.

Soon as he was gone, Donnette turned to me, and she looked really awful. So pale and worried.

"I'm glad you came this morning, Ellis," she said. "I've got to talk to somebody or I'll go crazy."

"What is it? Is something wrong with Tim?" Lord, maybe he was having a relapse or something. I could tell by her face that it was something bad.

"No, Tim's doing fine. Just fine, really. The doctors are real pleased with his recovery." Donnette swallowed her coffee nervously. "I want to know what Taylor Dupree is doing back in town!"

Stupid me, I should have known she'd be worried sick over Taylor's return. I would be if it were me. I'd been so wrapped up in my own problems I hadn't thought about how Donnette must be feeling.

"Supposively he came back to talk to Mr. Harris about his Aunt Della, who is not able to stay by herself and is too stubborn to move in with the family, or to go to that nice new nursing home in Tuscaloosa. That's all that any of us know, Donnette. Believe me, we all hate him as much as you do."

Donnette looked down into her cup of coffee, as though the answers were there.

"I've heard that, but I don't believe it. I'm scared, Ellis. I'm scared he'll come around Tim again. I'm afraid that he'll come between us somehow."

"That's *crazy*, Donnette, and you know it. Tim would never have anything to do with Taylor now, after what happened."

She nodded, but her face was still grim. "Oh, I know that. A part of me does. But I keep thinking about how close they were, and how much Tim thought of Taylor. He was always much more of an influence on Tim than me. Taylor even chose Tim's scholarship so that they could be together."

"Yeah, and Taylor almost got him killed, too, Donnette. *You* are his influence now, honey." I could tell that she was listening carefully to me. People respect my logic. We were silent a minute, then I thought of something.

"Has Tim seen Taylor yet?"

Donnette's face went pale. "God, no! I'm doing all I can to make sure that Tim doesn't find out that Taylor is in town. I like to have broke my neck at the funeral yesterday turning Tim all sorts of ways so he wouldn't see Taylor sitting up there with the Clarks. I can't keep this up forever, though. So see what you can find out for me, Ellis. Find out when he's leaving, going back to school."

I felt a lot of pride that Donnette needed me to do something for her, after all she'd done for me.

"Of course I will, Donnette. I'm in the perfect position to find out. As a matter of fact, Taylor came over and had supper with us the other night."

Donnette looked up curiously. "Oh? How did he seem to you?"

"The same as I remembered him, a snob who turns up his nose at all of us. He thinks he's too good for anyone in this town."

"Except Tim. For some reason I can't imagine, he has never been interested in anyone in this town but Tim. And Cat Jordan." Donnette looked like she was about to cry, so I hurried to reassure her.

"Listen, Donnette. Listen to me. You put that out of your mind, you hear? I'll talk to Hamilton about it, see if we can't find out something and let you know. For all I know, he just came to take his Aunt Della to the funeral, and he's going back tomorrow."

I didn't really believe that, though. I believed that Taylor got wind that me and Hamilton wanted Miss Della's house, and he was determined that we weren't going to get it, that's what I believed. He didn't care a hoot about his Aunt Della—he didn't care about anybody but himself!

"Donnette, I need to ask you a favor, too. I hate to even mention it, though, with you so worried about Tim." I forced myself to sip on the coffee some and glanced over at Donnette to get her reaction. To my relief, she smiled and shook her head.

"Tell you the truth, Ellis, I probably need something to worry about besides Tim. He doesn't like me carrying on over him, reminding him of the accident. He wants to put it behind him now," she told me.

"Well. If you're sure. You'll probably think I'm overreacting, Donnette, but after all you and me went through to get me where I am today, I am so afraid of anything that might come along and mess it up."

Donnette pulled up a chair and sat next to me. "Is it Sonny? He hasn't found out. . . ."

"No, it's not that. It's Glenda."

"Glenda? What on earth?"

Donnette looked so puzzled that I almost enjoyed telling her about what was going on with Glenda and Dink. However, she didn't take my concern seriously.

"Ellis! Surely you don't think that the Clarks are so snooty that they'll hold it against *you* that Glenda is going with Dink! And what's so bad about Dink, anyway?" I forgot that she really liked him. I had to be careful not to offend her.

"Donnette, you know as well as I do that Mr. Harris Clark is almost as fanatically religious as my daddy is. He'd be horrified that a relative of his is going with a divorced man."

Donnette just shook her head. "That's crazy, Ellis. This is 1985! Nobody is that old-timey anymore. Are they?"

"Oh yes, they most assuredly are. My daddy is, and Daddy Clark is too. They really are, Donnette. I ought to know—I was raised with it. I believe that's one of the reasons Daddy Clark accepted me into the family like he did, even though we're poor and not in his class. He knows that we'll never embarrass him with a scandal like this could be, Glenda dropping Bobby Ray like she did and going off with an old divorced man like Dink. He's fifteen years older than her, too! People are going to be talking to beat the band—I just know it. What am I going to do?"

Donnette shook her head again and smiled at me. She leaned over and took both my hands in hers.

"Listen to me, Ellis. We've come too far to let anything mess you up now. Tell you what, I'll talk to Dink, okay? I'll explain to him how you feel, how he needs to keep a low profile with Glenda. Trust me, okay?"

I smiled back at her and nodded. Trusting Donnette had gotten me where I was today, so how could I do any different?

Before Donnette and I started into the shop to do my hair, she stopped by the kitchen table and turned to me. "Oh, Ellis—I forgot! You've got to see the sign that Tim is painting me for my shop."

So that was what they were looking at on the table before I came in. Donnette had to uncover it to show me. The paint wasn't quite dry since Tim was still working on it. I went over to the table and stared in amazement as she pulled a large piece of plastic off to reveal a big round sign, almost the size of the kitchen table.

The sign was painted white, with black letters in the center saying MAKING WAVES. But the pretty thing about it was the pictures Tim had drawn on it. Why, it was little pictures of the whole town! The stores downtown, and the library, and the school, the football field, the churches—everything, painted all around the border of the sign. Then in the center, on the bottom, was a replica of Donnette's big old house with the sign hanging in front of it. I'd never seen anything like it.

"Donnette, this is absolutely beautiful! You don't mean to tell me that Tim did this!" I said to her.

Donnette was so proud that her face lit up like a lantern. "Yes, he sure did. I can't wait to hang it outside."

"But—Donnette—this is unbelievable! Has Tim ever done anything like this before? I didn't even know he could draw."

"Oh, yeah, he sure can. You ought to see some of the pictures he drew when he was a little boy. But once he started playing football, that took up all his time and he quit. Coach Mills wouldn't let him draw anymore then—he had a fit. So this is the first thing he's done in years."

"Well, it sure beats all I've ever seen! Is there nothing that boy can't do?"

Donnette's eyes widened, and it was like we both realized suddenly that she was still standing there in her skimpy, sheer nightie. And we both started laughing at the same time.

"I ain't going to answer that, Ellis!" Donnette laughed. "Let me get dressed, then we'll do your hair!"

After I left Donnette's, my hair freshly frosted, I decided I'd go out to see about Mama and Daddy before I went home. I didn't really intend to ride by the Zippy Mart on the way out there, but found myself doing so. I wasn't planning on stopping, just riding by to see if Glenda was carrying on with Dinky. Surely they wouldn't be in broad daylight, but you never know about people. If they were, then I'd stop and give them both a piece of my mind. But if not, then maybe I'd wait until I formulated my latest plan and approach Glenda again, try it out on her and see what she thought.

If Glenda was so dead set on having Dink, and working at the Zippy Mart, then maybe I'd have to change my tactics. A plan began to form in my mind as I drove toward the Zippy Mart.

Maybe I'd better pretend to be on Glenda's side, talk her into doing like I did and taking a room with a widow-lady in town. Then I could keep an eye on her. Maybe Donnette was right; if I could just keep Glenda and Dink from advertising that they were seeing each other, things would be okay. So I decided to ride by casually and check on them. As it turned out, I was sure glad that I did!

When I rode by the Zippy Mart real slow and looked in, all I saw was Glenda waiting on a couple of fishermen, ringing up purchases for their fishing trip probably. Then I saw Dinky out by the Barber's milk truck, and he and the milkman were stocking up dairy products, milk and butter and sour cream. Nothing much there, so I decided I might as well go out and report to Daddy that I had everything under control, was working on a plan.

On impulse, I turned the car down the road that leads to the river. I thought I'd just ride by the river for a minute; I hadn't been since Hamilton and I married. It was almost noon now, so I didn't expect to see anybody much. I sure didn't expect what I saw!

Actually, this time of the year is not one of my favorites at the river. It's not fall yet and summer is dying out. Not real pretty. I rode slowly along the road that runs next to the river, looking for any sign of the leaves turning, some signal that my favorite season might be coming on early this year. I was right, nobody much out this early. There were some fishermen on the river in their boats, and a few women and little children picnicking on the picnic tables under the oak trees along the riverbanks. One little kid was at the river's edge, poking a little plastic boat with a long stick.

I was about to turn the car around and head back when I saw a couple off to themselves, sitting on a big beach towel. They were on the sandy riverbank where it widened before a bend, sort of a private little cove. You couldn't have seen them if you hadn't been looking just right.

At first I glanced at them and didn't pay them no mind. Then I looked back again, startled. Speak of the devil—it was Taylor Dupree and some woman! Who on earth was he with, out here midmorning? Guess I'd better pull over and get a better look, I thought, because from where I was, I couldn't see them all that plain. I stopped the car and stuck my head out the window. They were almost hidden from my view because of the steepness of the riverbank at that particular place.

I must say that I couldn't blame them for wanting to hide from sight. From here I could see that they were sunbathing and that he was rubbing suntan lotion on her, very slowly and suggestively. She had on a skimpy black bikini and he had on swim trunks, like they'd been swimming already. She had her head back and was laughing like he was tickling her. Probably someone as common as Taylor is. No matter if his mama is Hamilton's aunt and a true-blooded Clark, everybody knows his daddy was a Cajun. They got colored people's blood. I was dying to know who he was with, so I fished around in my purse until I found my glasses and then stuck my head back out the window.

Lord have mercy! I had *never* in my life—I could not believe my eyes! That woman was none other than Miss Maudie Ferguson's niece—that college professor! I had met her at the funeral home the other night, actually shook hands with her. And I remembered that Miss Opal introduced her to me as Sarah somebody, saying that she was an old friend of Hamilton's Aunt Charlotte. Good heavens! That'd have to mean that she was probably old enough to be Taylor's mother. If that didn't beat all!

I have never met Hamilton's Aunt Charlotte, but she'd have to be in her forties to have a son Taylor's age. This Sarah woman didn't look that old. She was really a good-looking woman. I recalled Hamilton carrying on about her at the funeral home, whispering lewd remarks to me about what he'd learn with her as his professor and stuff like that. From where I was, she looked skinny as a fashion model in that black bikini, and usually Hamilton prefers women with more meat on their bones. But I'd better be careful. I've heard about women like her, who go for younger men. She might go after Hamilton. He's certainly much better looking than that long-haired, half-colored cousin of his.

Now Taylor turned around and she was rubbing lotion on his back, though he's so dark, looked like he wouldn't need it. He sure acted like he was enjoying it. I could tell from here that his eyes were closed and he was smiling. Looked like he was purring like a kitten. That woman leaned over his shoulder and whispered something in his ear and they both laughed like everything. Well. I could just imagine what she must have said to him!

I'll be—right out of the clear blue Taylor opened up his eyes and looked right at me. I was so surprised that for a minute I just stared back at him. He said something to the woman and she turned to look up at me too, shielding her eyes with her hand. I rolled the car window up quickly and turned the car around fast as I could. I hoped to goodness Taylor didn't recognize me with my glasses on. I sure wouldn't want him to think I cared enough about his carrying-on to be spying on him!

Once I left the main river road I just kind of drove around, sorting all this out. There were plenty of country roads all around the river, and I followed one until I came to a deserted spot. I parked the car and sat a minute to think. Right now the only thing I could think of doing was going back to Donnette's and telling her what I'd seen. I knew that Donnette was more knowledgeable about these things than me. Not that she was fast or anything; she just got around a lot more than I ever did at her age. I bet that she wouldn't be nearly as shocked by this as me. The more I thought about it, the more I thought that's what I should do. I could go tell Daddy Clark or Miss Opal, but something told me not to. Not just yet. I cranked up the car and started back into town to her place. Making Waves, that's what she was going to name her shop. In spite of being so shocked

I giggled. I bet that Taylor and Sarah what's-her-name were making a few waves right about now!

As I drove back into town, I thought about how strange it was that I've gotten to depend on Donnette so much lately. Ever since our friendship started, I have come to rely on her. I really owe her so much. Without her, I could not have changed my life the way I did.

About a year ago, I quit my secretarial job at the First Baptist Church to go off to business college. I don't know exactly what made me up and do it like that. Come to think of it, I'd always been pretty much like Glenda—just a good obedient girl who never gave anyone a minute's trouble.

Mind you, I was not like Glenda except on the surface. I was really bored and unhappy underneath, and I wanted something more out of life than the backwoods and the Freewill Baptist Church. I courted a couple of boys from my church, but never anything serious.

Then I turned thirty years old and realized my life would stay just the same if I didn't do something about it, and do it fast. But even at that, I moped around miserable for a couple of years before I set my mind to exactly what it was that I wanted in life. That's where Donnette came in.

It all started with my hair. Daddy has always said that the Bible says a woman's hair is her crowning glory, and it should never be cut. Mama can sit on hers. Mine has always been fine and stringy and broke off at the ends. But it was never cut; instead I wore braids or a bun as I got older. The kids in school used to make fun of me looking so old-timey, but I couldn't bring myself to go against my raising.

When I went off to business college in Columbus, I realized that I looked like a hick. The next thing I did was to go to

Donnette Sullivan's trailer and get her to cut my hair. I knew her, not real well, but like everyone in town, I knew their situation with Tim's accident. So I wanted to give her my business. At first I couldn't bring myself to get it cut enough for Daddy to notice. I had it cut just to my shoulders, and I still wore it pinned up. Donnette showed me how to make a French twist and Daddy never even noticed. After that, I got my nerve to go to Kmart's and get me some more stylish clothes. A couple of the young men at the business school began to notice me and asked me out occasionally.

To this day, I don't know exactly what it was that made me confide in Donnette. All I know is, I went to get my hair trimmed; there was no one in her shop but me and her, and the time just seemed right. It was late spring, already hot so the window unit was going, which made it cozy with just me and Donnette talking.

Although it was a beautiful sunny day, and things were looking up for me, I was still down in the mouth and unhappy with my life. So for some unknown reason, I just up and told Donnette that.

"Then change it. If you don't like your life, change it," Donnette said to me, not missing a beat as she snipped away on my hair.

"If only I could!" I'd replied, sorry that I said anything. I'd been taught that self-pity was a sin.

"If *you* can't change *your* life, then who can?" Donnette kept right on cutting away without looking at me.

"Oh, Donnette. You just don't know. I'm an old maid. I ain't never had anything exciting happen to me in my whole life, lest you count when the preacher slipped down in the creek at my baptism."

We both giggled. I didn't tell Donnette I'd never had any girlfriends to giggle with before. Daddy wouldn't have put up with such.

"Come on, Ellis," Donnette said to me. "You can do *anything* you want in life if you set yourself some goals."

"That sounds good, Donnette. But I guess I don't really believe it. I'd have to have some kind of evidence."

She laughed at me then. "Okay. I can provide that. You're looking at your evidence."

"What on earth do you mean?" She had my curiosity roused now.

"Well, I'll tell you something, if you promise not to tell. A few years ago, I set myself some goals and decided nothing on earth could keep me from getting what I wanted. And nothing has."

This time she did stop and look right at me.

"What was it that you wanted?" I asked.

"Tim Sullivan." She let that sink in a minute. "Need I say more?"

When I considered all they'd been through, I was sold. Donnette didn't say anything else about that then. Instead she asked me some business-type questions about the shop, since she was fixing to buy her Aunt Essie's place in town when Essie retired. I gave her some good advice, too, and I could tell she was grateful. People admire my good business sense.

It wasn't but a few days later, however, that Donnette asked me a question that really started me thinking. And it was this soul-searching that eventually led me to change my life completely.

She had talked me into getting a manicure that warm spring afternoon, and we were sitting there talking as Donnette worked on my nails. They were in bad shape from all the filing and typing I had to do in business school. I didn't want any colored polish on them, just some clear shine. Daddy would have a bigger fit if I came home with nail polish on than if I got my hair cut any shorter.

"Ellis," Donnette asked me as she filed away on my nails, "who do you admire more than anybody you know?"

I admit, I had again been feeling sorry for myself, talking about how uneventful my life was. I was surprised at Donnette's question at first, but I didn't have to think long about it, not the way I was raised.

"Why, Jesus Christ, of course," I said to her.

Donnette laughed. "You sound like a Miss America contestant. Come on."

I felt sort of insulted. "I'm serious. Jesus Christ."

"A living person, Ellis. Think of it this way—who would you most like to be?"

The answer came suddenly as I looked into Donnette's artfully made-up dark eyes, and her long, sun-streaked hair, curling so perfectly around her pretty face.

"Well. I reckon that would be you, Donnette."

This time Donnette threw back her head and laughed, but I could tell she was flattered.

"There ain't nothing to admire about me! Come on, let's get you shampooed now. Your nails look so nice we might as well do your hair, too."

It was under the dryer that I realized I really hadn't been truthful with Donnette. Oh, sure, I admired her looks all right. And she was married to Tim Sullivan, who in spite of that accident still looked so good any girl would be glad to get him. And I knew from the way she talked about him that she loved him more than anything on this earth. No, it wasn't that. It was that Donnette and Tim, in spite of having such good looks and each other to boot, were just too poor for me. *That* I didn't admire one little bit. We had always been dirt-poor, so poor we couldn't even buy regular groceries; Mama and Daddy had to raise vegetables and chickens and hogs so that we would have enough to eat.

I knew then who I admired more than anybody: I admired the Clarks. Come to think of it, I admired Miss Opal Clark most.

I had seen her many times around town, and of course people talked all the time about the Clarks, so I knew that she had come from a poor family like me. But she had set her cap for Harris Clark Jr., and look where she was now. She had been a widow for over twenty years, but she stayed right there with the Clarks and became one of them. I admired that a lot, too. So. If only I could look like Donnette, have a husband like Tim, and be in Miss Opal Clark's position in town. My goals! I decided as soon as my hair dried I'd hit Donnette with them—see if she thought goals were all you had to have in order to succeed. Ha! She'd faint dead away.

Donnette didn't faint dead away at all—she didn't even laugh. As a matter of fact, she took me very seriously. She listened to me carefully, and nodded when I told her what I'd decided under the dryer. All she said was, "Let me think on that some, okay?" I never dreamed she'd find the perfect answer for me!

Later that same night, I lay in my bed in Mama and Daddy's house and thought about my life. I had made the first step by going away to college, I knew that, but I also knew that it was not enough. I felt almost panicked when I thought about being over thirty years old, and time slipping away from me. The years had started to roll by, one right after the other, and they were all the same. I took deep breaths in order to keep my heart from jumping out of my chest. I had to get away from this. I had to change.

Mama and Daddy were good, good as gold, but they didn't know anything about the world out there. They had always lived by the Bible and what they heard every Sunday in that stifling little church where we'd gone all our lives, that church where no one sings or laughs or wears any makeup on their faces. Then a thought hit me that scared me to death because it was so shocking. Where had all of that stuff my church preached every Sunday ever gotten anyone? Just look at Mama and Daddy and everyone else in our church—poor and ignorant and content to stay that way. Where had their religion gotten them? I mean, look what happened to Jesus. He was good, and He was religious, and look where He ended up! I saw clearly then what Donnette had been saying to me when I thought about Jesus. Goals, that's what He lacked. The man never had any goals.

So I set my goals and Donnette set about seeing that I got them. She called me one day the very next week, all excited, and I hurried out to her trailer. She'd come up with the perfect plan, the answer. My life was about to take a new course.

Oh, at first it was so difficult for me. I couldn't take in the thought of what Donnette proposed to me—that I set my cap for Sonny Clark the same way Miss Opal went after Harris Jr.! I was willing to settle for much less. I tried to get Donnette to just help me get a job working for Mr. Harris, maybe at the bank, and I'd be satisfied. But her plan—there was no way I could go along with Donnette's crazy idea.

I had no experience with men at all, none whatsoever—except that one time, and I'd never tell Donnette or anyone about that. Plus I knew Sonny Clark's reputation with women. I admit, it both scared and thrilled me to death to think about him. I had always thought he was cute as could be, but him being younger than me, I'd never thought anything about going with him.

But Donnette would not hear of me lowering my goals; she'd get real mad at me and tell me to go back to the sticks if I was too scared to do this. At times, I was, then I'd go back to her, and we'd talk some more. The more we talked, the more convinced I became that I had a chance.

Donnette herself was convinced that this could work because she and Sonny Clark had always been real close friends. She claimed that Sonny tried his best to get her to marry him just a couple of years ago, before she married Tim. She swore that he was ready for marriage, that Mr. Harris was putting all sorts of pressure on him to settle down. My timing couldn't be better. Sonny had to marry and settle down soon, or Mr. Harris was going to boot him out of the house. There was no way our plan could fail.

Well, I would have remained totally unconvinced if I hadn't let Donnette make me over into a glamorous, sophisticated woman. She cut my hair real short and frosted it almost white-blonde. Then she pierced my ears, and put makeup on my face. My body was fine; I was strong and healthy from living on a farm all my life. At first Donnette wanted me to diet to trim off a few pounds, but she took a look at Miss Opal and changed her mind.

Donnette's theory is that men marry women who remind them of their mothers. She swears that there is a picture of Tim's mother that looks exactly like her.

Once I saw myself in the mirror at Donnette's trailer, I knew that I had a chance. Then me and her went shopping for clothes. I didn't have much money, so we went to Discount World in Columbus, which has much nicer clothes than Kmart at about the same price. Class, that's what I had to have, Donnette insisted. She picked out colorful sundresses and shorts sets for me, still using Miss Opal as our model.

I then got me some contacts and put away my glasses forever. I tell you, when I walked into my classes that next Monday, people didn't know who I was. It is amazing what a new image can do for a woman. Right away, I enrolled in a self-improvement course at the community college, as well as a remedial English and vocabulary class. If I was going for this, I was going all the way.

As a matter of fact, Donnette's strategy was just the opposite on that particular point. My face blushed a dark red when she first told me how I was going to get Hamilton Clark.

"Fixing you up with Sonny will be no problem," she assured me. "I've fixed him up before, and he'll go with *anybody*. No offense, Ellis. But the rest is up to you. Sonny has never been able to resist anything he can't have. Under no circumstances can you go all the way with him, you hear me? Under *no* circumstances. But you've got to make him want to so bad he can't see straight."

At first I didn't know what she was talking about. "Go all the way? What do you mean?"

"Oh, my God, Ellis. Don't tell me you're a— This may be harder than I thought! Okay. Let me think on this awhile. First you got to take a room in town. Better yet, in Columbus."

Well, I balked and resisted her most of the way, and some of the things she proposed embarrassed me so much that I couldn't face Sonny Clark without blushing when we first started going together. But Donnette was right, about everything. Every single thing worked out according to her plan.

And I don't give the Lord one bit of credit for it like I would have at one time, before I understood who really makes miracles happen. Now that my eyes have been opened to the truth, I finally understand that every person is in charge of his or her own life, and that all the praying and carrying on done every Sunday is not going to help near as much as having a friend like Donnette.

I pulled up in the driveway of Donnette's house, but I didn't get out like I planned. I could see into the shop window, and I saw that someone was in there with her. It looked like Elton Davis's wife from here. I sure couldn't talk to Donnette now about what I'd seen at the river, because Florece Davis is one of the biggest gossips in a town where she has plenty of competition. Not that I cared a bit if everyone in town knew what Taylor was up to, but I wasn't sure yet what to make of what I saw. I decided I'd wait and call Donnette later and ask to see her when no one else was around. I needed to find out from someone in the family when Taylor was going back, too. I could talk to Miss Opal first, before I talked to Donnette. Then I'd have two bits of information to share with her. So I turned the car around and went back home.

On the way I passed Mr. Hiram Clark's house, where crazy old Della Dean lives. Miss Opal was right; it could be turned into a beautiful house for me and Hamilton and our children. I expected to be getting pregnant any time now. I was disappointed that I wasn't already, since that was a major part of me and Donnette's plan. But I would be soon, and we'd need a house of our own. Miss Opal and I had some great plans for the complete remodeling of the old Hiram Clark house. It was going to be so pretty decorated in shades of pale yellow and sky blue. If only Miss Della would hurry up and either kick the bucket or go on to the nursing home, we could get started on it. It was in Mr. Hiram's will that the house go to Mr. Harris if he outlives Miss Della, so Taylor might as well give up and go on back to Louisiana with the other Cajuns. No way he can outsmart me anyway!

I ended up telling Hamilton about Taylor and that Sarah woman at the river. I didn't really intend to, but I couldn't get Donnette on the phone, and I was dying to tell someone.

That night after supper, me and Hamilton sat around with the family for a while like we usually did, then excused ourselves to go upstairs and watch TV in our room. I admit, it was pretty boring sitting around downstairs with the family.

They have a TV down there, but they never watch anything but the Tuscaloosa news because Daddy Clark thinks there's too much cussing and fornicating on TV nowadays. Instead, Daddy Clark studies his Sunday School lesson. He teaches the Men's Bible Class every Sunday, and he puts a lot of work into it, looking up stuff all the time in his complete set of Barclay's Bible Commentary.

Miss Frances Martha either looks through her cookbooks, or

dozes in her rocking chair. Miss Opal usually looks through women's magazines, *Redbook* and *Ladies' Home Journal*, but she always sighs and carries on like she's so bored she could scream. She keeps going back and forth to her bathroom, too. When we first married, I felt sorry for her, thinking she had a kidney problem like Granny Rountree does. But Hamilton says she keeps her booze in there, hidden away from Daddy Clark.

At first this information shocked and disillusioned me, but my outlook on society has broadened lately. I realized that a cocktail could be a very soothing thing. Hamilton doesn't drink hard liquor or beer anymore, but we, too, keep a bottle of wine or sherry in our bedroom. We share a glass of wine or two just about every night.

When we finally went up to our room, Hamilton jumped up in the bed immediately and started flicking the channels around, looking for a wrestling match. But I turned the TV off. I just couldn't wait to tell somebody what I'd seen. I tried to get Donnette on the phone again a few minutes ago, but they'd gone somewhere, I reckon.

"Hamilton, listen to me. You won't believe what I saw today." I hadn't even told him yet about Glenda and Dink. I knew that Hamilton liked Dink a lot and used to hang around with him some, so I wasn't sure if he'd be sympathetic with me being so upset about them.

"Come here first, Mama." He held out his arms to me, and I went and laid down beside him on the bed. He's so loving. He just can't seem to get enough. He says that we have to do it all the time if we want to have a baby. But I wanted to tell him about his cousin Taylor first, so I propped up next to him on the pillows and pushed his hands off me gently.

"Hamilton, listen to me. I rode out by the river this morning. I was just looking around some, you know. I sure didn't expect to see what I saw!"

He lit a cigarette and pulled me close to him again. "No telling what you'll see at the river, hon. You better not go out there again without me."

"Hamilton, I saw your cousin Taylor Dupree out there, all lovey-dovey with a someone on a beach towel."

Hamilton laughed and ruffled my hair affectionately. "Was he queering off with someone now that he has that faggy long hair? I knew his true colors would finally come through."

Hamilton can't stand Taylor, but he's always been able to put him down effectively and not let him get under his skin. And I've given him a few pointers myself lately, sarcasm being my specialty.

"Hamilton, Taylor was with a woman old enough to be his mother!" I told him.

"That doesn't surprise me either. He's bound to have some kind of hang-up, having Charlotte for a mother. Maybe he's looking for a mother figure to screw."

Hamilton really laughed at that. He could be so vulgar sometimes. I just don't know where he gets that; surely not from anyone in the Clark family.

"She sure has screwed him all his life, hand it to her," he added, laughing like everything.

"Stop talking ugly and listen to me. He was with that niece of Miss Maudie Ferguson's!"

This time Hamilton paid attention to me. He sat straight up and looked right at me. "Are you kidding me?"

"No. I saw them plain as day."

"No shit!"

"Hamilton, I've asked you nice as can be not to use words like that around me. I tell you, I saw them carrying on with each other, right there at the river."

Hamilton was as shocked as I was, I could tell. "No shit!" he kept saying, until I poked him in the ribs. Then he took a deep drag of his cigarette and sat back on the pillows. A satisfied smile came over his face.

"Well, well, well. I'll just be damned. Aunt Charlotte's old buddy Miss Sarah, huh?" He continued to smoke and smiled to himself like the cat that swallowed the canary. Then he turned back to me. "Now, Mama, are you sure they were scr—doing it? You mean you actually caught them in the act?"

"Well, of course I didn't actually witness it, but they were sure fixing to!"

"Have you told anybody this?" Hamilton asked me.

"Not yet. I've been trying to get Donnette all day, but I can't."

"Donnette—why on earth would you tell her?" He looked at me as though I'd lost my mind.

I swear, he could be so slow sometimes. "Think about it, honey. Donnette is worried sick about Taylor being back in town. She just got Tim to where he's okay after that accident where Taylor almost killed him. Imagine how upset she is."

"Donnette ought not to worry about that. I guarantee you Tim Sullivan won't have nothing else to do with Taylor. He sure won't get in a car with him!"

"That's what I've told her, too. But she can't help but worry. You know how devious Taylor is. You know better than anyone what he is. What kind of person would go off and leave someone in the shape Tim was in, not caring if he lived or died? And now that he's all better, come looking for him again? I tell you, Taylor is a low-down human being in my estimation, and I intend to help Donnette out all I can."

"I'm proud of you for that, hon, but tell you what. Don't tell anyone about Taylor and that woman yet, okay? Wait and let me think on it awhile. It might be real useful information for us."

"For us? But how?"

"Well, now, just think about it. Reckon Taylor wants his Aunt Della to find out about this? Or Daddy Clark—heh, heh, that would be something!" Hamilton literally rubbed his hands in glee. "So old Taylor is sticking it to Miss Sarah, huh? That may be the best news I've heard in a long time!"

. . .

I tried hard to keep my word to Hamilton not to tell anybody about it, I honestly did. I didn't mean to tell Miss Opal, but she was the one who brought it up. Then I let it slip with Donnette when I was telling her what I found out from Miss Opal.

I kept it to myself for a whole day, because it was some time later before I saw Miss Opal. She stayed out at the country club all that next day playing bridge, and then she had some kind of dinner party out there that night.

The day after that, I finally had to go to her room after lunch and knock on her door, because she hadn't shown up all morning. At first I thought she was still asleep because she took so long coming to the door, and she looked extremely irritated until she saw that it was me.

"Oh, it's you, Ellis. I have a little headache today so I'm resting—I didn't hear you knocking at first."

Her big hazel eyes, which are usually so lively and sparkling, looked bloodshot and tired. Miss Opal has a pretty face but she's let herself get way too fat. I swear I'll never do that, even if I get widowed like her. She just doesn't care anymore, I guess. She was still dressed in her robe, this time of the day!

"I'm so sorry to bother you, Miss Opal. I need to talk to you about something, but I'll come back when you're feeling better," I told her, backing away.

"No, no. Come on in, sugar. I want you to feel free to talk to me any time at all. Just a minute, okay?" She closed her door and I felt stupid standing out there in the hall. Now what could she be doing, I wondered. No point in her straightening up her room for me, I've seen it in a mess before. In a few minutes she opened the door and ushered me in.

I loved Miss Opal's bedroom best of all—to me it was the prettiest room in the house. She had it fixed up in light and dark shades of pink, with lots of hot pink lace, and she had antique-looking furniture of gold and white. Classic, that's what it was.

Right now, it was dark as a cave because she had the shades pulled.

She took me over to a pink satin loveseat and sat down. I'm going to get me one just like it when me and Hamilton get into Mr. Hiram's house.

"What is it, hon?" Miss Opal asked me as she patted the seat beside her, indicating for me to sit down. "You and Sonny haven't had a fight, have you?"

"Oh, no, ma'am. Nothing like that. Actually, I wanted to ask you something for a friend of mine."

Maybe it was my imagination, but it seemed Miss Opal looked real suspiciously at me. "Somebody wanting to borrow money?"

"No, ma'am—I'd never ask you that!" I was a little hurt, but plunged on. "You know Donnette Sullivan, who was my matron of honor?"

"Sure. I've been knowing Donnette and her people for years," Miss Opal said, relaxed now. I noticed up close that her makeup was smeared, like she'd been sleeping when I knocked. And her room smelled funny, too, like liquor or something. Maybe it was just her perfume, though looks like with all her money, she could buy the good-smelling kind.

"What's Donnette's problem?" Miss Opal asked me.

"Well, she's real worried, Miss Opal. You know all that about her husband Tim and Taylor Dupree? She's worried about Taylor being back in town now, after two years. I know he's your nephew, but—"

Miss Opal lit a cigarette and threw back her head as she inhaled deeply. "That little bastard's no nephew of mine. He belongs to the high and mighty Clarks."

I was shocked to hear her talk that way about the Clarks. Maybe it was because she was feeling indisposed. She took a long drag on the cigarette and looked over at me. "Sorry. Go on."

"Well, Donnette wants me to find out when Taylor's going back to college. The kids start back to school here this week, so we figure colleges must be starting up soon."

Miss Opal shrugged. "For all I know, he'll be going back any day now."

She didn't seem concerned about it as she added, "You can't carry on a decent conversation with him, he's so spacey. Probably on dope. And you sure can't get anything out of that old loon Della. Neither one of them got walking-around sense, if you ask me. Hell, Taylor may have flunked out of school, for all any of us know."

"Well, I promised Donnette that I would ask around, see if I could find out anything about his plans," I said.

"Donnette hasn't got shit for sense if she thinks Taylor is going to come around them again! Only reason he ever took up with Tim Sullivan to start with was because no one else would have anything to do with him. Nobody except that nympho preacher's daughter. God knows what ever happened to her."

"I guess you're right," I said, but without much conviction.

"I know I'm right. Tell Donnette to look at the facts—Taylor ain't had the guts to show his face around here for two years. He never even checked up on Tim, offered a penny—nothing. Oh, that fool Della tried to tell us he wasn't able, that he had a nervous breakdown and b.s. like that. Huh! He's just like Charlotte, too sorry to care about anybody but himself."

I guess I still didn't look convinced because Miss Opal looked at me with a crooked smile, then reached over and patted my hand.

"Tell you what I'll do, though. Just to make you feel better. I'll get Frances Martha to talk to Della, one fruitcake to another. Find out what she can from her, and I'll let you know, okay?"

"Oh, I'd sure appreciate that." I smiled at her. "You are the best thing to me in the world." Impulsively I gave her a quick hug, though I must have caught her off guard because she pulled back from me. I stood up to go then.

"I guess I'd better go plan supper with Miss Frances Martha

now, Miss Opal. Anything you can find out about Taylor, just let me know and I'll tell Donnette."

I was halfway to the door, anxious now to be on my way, knowing that I had done what I could to help my best friend out. I'll be—just as I walked off, Miss Opal took another drag of that cigarette and said to me, just as casually as anything, " 'Course I could have asked Taylor myself yesterday. He was actually being right friendly, for him."

"Oh? You saw him yesterday?"

"Sure did. He was at the country club having lunch yesterday. Acting halfway decent, too. But that may have been because he was showing Sarah Williams around."

I came back over to the loveseat slowly, not believing my ears. "Who, Miss Opal?"

"Maudie Ferguson's niece. You remember—I introduced you to her at the funeral home. She's kind of weird, teaches psychology or something like that at the University of Florida, I believe. Or Florida State."

I sat back down on the loveseat beside her. "I remember her all right. Do you think she's attractive, Miss Opal?"

"Yeah, for a skinny woman. Personally I've found that most men like to look at a woman like that, but they like well-rounded women for—other things." She stopped and eyed me shrewdly. "I noticed Sonny giving her the eye, if that's why you're asking."

I pretended not to hear that. "What were she and Taylor doing at the country club, just having lunch?" I asked the question real casually. I can be cunning when I need to be.

"Yeah. And drinking. Country club's the only place in Zion County where you can get a drink. They said they were going swimming there, too, that they hadn't been able to find a good place to swim."

"How do you reckon they got to know each other?" I asked, again pretending to be real casual.

"Oh, Sarah and Charlotte used to be big buddies. When Sarah

was a kid, she came and spent summers here with her Aunt Maudie. So I expect she met Taylor at the funeral."

Miss Opal yawned loudly. I could tell she was really not interested in this conversation. Well, she would be if she knew what I knew, that was for sure!

"Miss Opal," I said, my voice dropping to a whisper. "If I tell you something, will you promise not to tell a living soul?"

I felt it was my duty to tell her what I'd seen at the river. It also made me feel good to have something to confide in her about, since she'd accepted me and been so good to me. At first Miss Opal couldn't believe me, I could tell. She kept asking me the same questions over and over, and asking me to describe seeing them at the river again and again.

"I just *cannot* believe it, Ellis!" she said to me. "The very idea—she's old enough to be that boy's mother! It's beyond me what a woman her age sees in such a young boy. Of course, if it were Sonny, I could understand it. But Taylor—the very idea of those two together is repulsive."

I agreed with her completely. "I tell you, Miss Opal, I've never been so shocked in my life. Of course, Daddy has told me all my life what college professors are like—loose, every one of them."

"Women who go after young boys like that ought to be horsewhipped," Miss Opal declared vehemently to me. "Just hearing about this makes me sick to my stomach. But I want to make sure I heard it right—tell me again *exactly* what they did!"

Miss Opal kept her word and got Frances Martha to call Della Dean that night, but what she found out ended up not being good news for Donnette when I saw her the next day. Della had been praising the Lord over the phone, Miss Frances Martha said. Taylor planned on staying with her a few more days. His college didn't start until mid-September, so he had some time on his hands. I sure hated to be the one to tell Donnette that. I hated it even more when I got to her place and saw that she was already upset.

Tim was outside in the yard when I drove up, fixing the stand the sign was going to hang from. It was an old lamppost Miss Essie had put there which he was painting white. I thought the sign would look *so* nice there, and I told him so as I walked up the driveway to the shop. He blushed and smiled at me. Goodness, I never noticed before what a sexy smile he has. Donnette is sure one lucky girl. I was just about to ask him where Donnette was when she stuck her head out the shop door and motioned to me.

When I walked up to the shop, Donnette pulled me in quickly, then closed the door.

"Oh, Ellis. I just tried to call you to see if you could come over. I need to talk to somebody so bad."

One look at her face and I could tell that she'd been crying. She had her hair in rollers and not a smidge of makeup on. With her reddened eyes, she looked awful.

"You look terrible, Donnette. What on earth are you so upset about?" I was really concerned about her.

Donnette looked out the window to make sure Tim couldn't hear, I guess, then she turned back to me.

"Oh, Ellis. Me and Tim had a big fuss. It was just awful. I wish to goodness I'd learn to keep my mouth shut." Tears welled up in her eyes again.

"Come on, hon. Let's go sit down," I said to her gently. I can be very supportive when I need to be. I even took a course in it at the Methodist Church last year.

"Let's sit over here by the dryers and you tell me all about it." I felt like an old married lady listening to a younger one, for a change. It was a nice feeling.

"It's a lot of things. You see that Tim ain't at work today. Well, that's because—" Again, she started to cry. I reached in my purse for a Kleenex and handed one to her.

Donnette blew her nose and looked at me. "I reckon I'd better start at the beginning. You know Tim works at the lumber mill for Jack Floyd, Mr. Cleve's younger brother. Jack is *so* nice, Ellis. He has always thought the world of Tim, 'cause he was the star quarterback here during his day. This ain't his fault at all. But the lumber business is so bad that he had to cut Tim back to quarter time."

I felt some relief. Not quite as bad as I'd feared. "Well, that's bad, Donnette. But at least he didn't get laid off altogether."

"I know. But Tim thinks Jack needs to cut him completely out but just hates to. It makes Tim feel like a charity case, which you know he hates. It ain't the money so much, Ellis. I think we can manage with me having the shop. It's Tim." She wiped her eyes and looked just like a little girl.

"I can understand Tim feeling like that, Donnette. But if business was so bad that Jack couldn't pay Tim, he'd have to let him go. Tim ought to realize that." I felt proud of my logic.

"I think he knows that. He's just down."

"Well, he ought not to take it out on you."

Donnette looked puzzled, then smiled weakly. "Oh, that's not what we had a fuss about. I wish in a way that he would take it out on me. Anything but suffer in silence like he does."

"If it's not about his work, then what is it?"

"The reason I was telling you about Jack was to tell you that he felt so bad about cutting Tim back that he took us out to the cafe in Mt. Zion to eat supper."

"Me and Hamilton went there the other night. They have the best catfish I've ever put in my mouth," I told her. I love to eat out. Usually we go to Tuscaloosa or Columbus, though, where they have nice restaurants like Shoney's.

"Ellis, you won't believe who we ran into there! You just won't believe it."

"Not Dinky and Glenda!" I had gotten so involved in all this other mess lately that I'd clean forgotten them. Since Daddy

Clark hadn't said anything about it either, I'd been able to put it out of my mind temporarily. And Mama hadn't sent Daddy to town for me lately.

"Oh, no. *Not* Dink and Glenda. I only wish it had been. We were sitting in there, eating our catfish, and who comes in but Taylor Dupree!"

"You don't mean it! I guess there's no way Tim could not see him, that's such a little cafe." No wonder she was so upset.

"Tim saw him all right, and so did Jack. Jack was just as startled as me. Probably more, since I don't think he'd heard that Taylor was back in town. Me and Jack both started talking at once."

"What on earth did Tim do?"

"That's just it, Ellis. Tim never let on one bit. He looked at Taylor, I saw him. Looked right into his eyes. And Taylor stopped right in his tracks and stared at Tim. Can you believe it? The gall of him—right out there in front of everybody, staring like a fool."

Donnette wiped her eyes as they filled with tears again. "I thought I was going to choke to death on my food, I swear I did. Jack was so embarrassed he didn't say a thing after that; he just got us home in a hurry, believe you me."

"What do you suppose Taylor was doing at a cafe like that—slumming? He's not the kind to go to places that serve local people." Suddenly I thought of something. "Reckon he was following you and Tim?"

"I might have thought of that, too, if he'd been alone. But he had his Aunt Della and another woman with him. They got a table over in the corner and had catfish. I tried not to look at them, but I couldn't help it. Have you found out anything about when he's going back to school, Ellis?"

"I found out more about Taylor Dupree lately than either of us want to know, Donnette. I don't suppose that woman with him and Miss Della was Miss Maudie Ferguson's niece, was it?"

"Sure was. Do you know her?"

"Not really, but Taylor knows her real well. If you get my drift. Matter of fact, I saw them together, making out, down at the river the other day. And they've been seen together since."

Donnette's eyes got big as saucers. "Taylor and that woman? Good heavens! That's unbelievable."

"Well, you can believe it, because I saw it with my own eyes. There's nothing he won't do, is there?" Donnette and I just stared at each other at the thought. "So I can see why you don't want someone like him influencing Tim. Did y'all leave the cafe as soon as they got there?"

"Pretty soon after. We had to finish our supper. 'Course I never ate another bite, but Tim ate like a pig. Then he had banana pudding for dessert." Donnette shook her head. "It upset my stomach, I'll tell you. I went back and forth to the bathroom all night."

"When did y'all have a fuss? And was it about Taylor?"

Donnette sighed. "In a way it was. I didn't say a word about it when we got home; I was too scared to. And I kept running to the bathroom. It was this morning. Tim got on to me real bad, Ellis. He said I was a fool to think that he hadn't known all along that Taylor was back in town, to try and protect him like I did. He said he saw Taylor at the funeral and he knew I was breaking my neck to keep them from seeing each other." She smiled through her tears.

"Tim said I had to let it go, Ellis. He said all that with Taylor was over and done with, and that I *had* to stop protecting and mothering him so much. I know he has a point, but I couldn't let it go at that. I had to open my big mouth. I told Tim that I was afraid of Taylor, afraid for them to see each other again. And I swear, I don't understand his reaction! Tim turned white as a sheet, and he just walked out of the room. He walked right away from me!"

This time Donnette was crying in earnest, big tears rolling

down her cheeks, and I didn't know what to do. I patted her on the shoulder while she buried her face in her hands and cried her heart out. I didn't know quite what to make of it, either.

"Tim hates me, Ellis. I know he does. He wants to be independent and forget everything that's happened and I won't let him. I bet he even thinks I *like* having him depend on me. I've never been so worried in my life—I can't live if Tim hates me, Ellis." And on she went, sobbing and carrying on. I didn't know what to say to make her feel better. I was afraid that she might be right. Not that Tim hated her, but that she was overprotective of him and he resented it. Made sense to me.

Suddenly there was a loud knock on the shop door. I like to have jumped out of my skin until I saw it was Tim. I ran and opened the door and stuck my head out.

"Is Donnette all right?" There was so much concern on his face that I knew he really cared for her, and I breathed a little sigh of relief.

"She's a little upset right now, Tim, but she'll be okay. Give her a minute to pull herself together."

Tim looked real uneasy, like he didn't know what to say. Finally he stammered, "I-I got the sign hung and I want her to see it."

I smiled up at him and winked. "That's great, Tim! Just what she needs. Tell you what, let me help her get her hair fixed and some makeup on, and we'll be right out there."

I closed the door quickly. Through the curtains, I could see him standing there for a minute uncertainly. Then he went back to the front yard.

"Come on, Donnette," I said. "Get those curlers out and let's get some makeup on you, honey. Tim has got your sign fixed!"

I was so proud to be able to do something nice for Donnette I decided that since she was already so upset, I wouldn't tell her yet about the conversation between Miss Frances Martha and Miss Della. It would probably be more than she could handle today.

I helped Donnette fix herself up real pretty, but she was still pale and shaky when the two of us went outside to join Tim. She gave me a hug just before we went out the door and told me how grateful she was to me for listening to her problems. I tell you, I sure was proud of that course that I'd taken at the Methodist Church then. Daddy says the Methodists are middle-of-the-roaders and don't have enough religion to suit him, but I think that they have just enough for me!

I will never forget when we walked out to the front yard and saw that sign Tim had painted and hung for Donnette. I always think of myself as a levelheaded, practical person, not emotional at all, but I got tears in my eyes when I saw it.

And Donnette—well, she just started up crying again and ran right into Tim's arms. He held her so tight that I thought he was never going to let her go. I wished she'd hush crying, because her eye makeup that we worked so hard on was running in blue and black rivers down her face. But somehow, I don't think she cared one bit.

I slipped away then and left them standing there, holding on to each other for dear life, looking up at that sign, that big white sign with the town of Clarksville painted so pretty all around the edge, their house right in the center.

Taylor

Aunt Della and I walked heavily down the hall to her room, she scraping along, hanging on to the walker, her head bent over and her back humped, me holding on to her elbow like an idiot, as though that would do either of us any good if she started to fall again.

"Now don't you worry, baby," she said to me, huffing and puffing like the Little Engine That Could, from the story she used to read me every single night as a child. "Don't you worry none, you hear? I'm fine. I just lost my balance, got a little dizzy. I'm absolutely fine."

I couldn't tell if she was trying to convince me or herself. My hands were shaking so that it was a wonder she didn't fall just from me rocking hell out of her. Trying to help and I'd probably end up doing her more harm than good. Story of my life.

I was determined to get her settled into her room and call the doctor or somebody. Maybe Sarah—we'd just let her off, so she couldn't be in bed yet. I might even have to break down and call Daddy Clark or Aunt Mary Frances or Martha. I was that worried.

It was like Aunt Della read my mind.

"Taylor, I want you to help me get into my bed, then I'll be fine. I think I just ate too much catfish tonight. Really, I probably shouldn't have gone, I haven't been out at night in so long. Couldn't see the porch steps and almost fell. Don't you go calling Harris or any of them, you hear?"

At her bedroom door I let go of her long enough to reach inside and turn on the overhead light. Her room was so big and dark that the light from the hanging lamp overhead seemed pallid, lighting only the faded roses printed on the rug underneath it, and leaving the corners of the room in shadows. I faked a cheerfulness that I didn't feel.

"Okay. Here we are. Home sweet home."

I helped her into her room, carefully moving her toward the four-poster bed. Letting go of her elbow, I yanked off the white chenille bedspread and pulled back the sheet. It was hot as holy hell in her room. How could she stand it?

"Okey-dokey, Aunt Della. Into the bed with you." I tried a smile that didn't quite come off.

Aunt Della stood facing me, both hands gripped tightly on the walker. She looked at me, then at the bed, and she shook her head.

"Oh, baby. Bless your heart." Like me, she tried to smile. "Maybe you had better call Frances. I got to go to the bathroom."

For a moment I stood there and just stared at her. She looked at me with those pale watery eyes, so fatigued that they seemed even paler now.

"No, let's don't call her," I said, having absolutely no idea how I'd pull this off with somebody as modest as Aunt Della. "I'll help you go to the bathroom."

I grabbed the elbow again and turned her toward her bathroom before she could protest. But she only said, "Oh, sugar, you don't have to . . ." weakly, and off we went.

"Now," I said when we got her, me, and the walker inside the little bathroom adjoining her room. "I'll go get you a gown while you use the pot. Or do you need any help with that?"

To my relief, Aunt Della chuckled. "Bless you, baby. I don't believe you could help me even if I did."

Somehow I got Aunt Della pottied, nightgowned, medicated, and settled in for the night, ready for her nightly prayers. I even found a bell someone had given her for Christmas and put it on her bedside table with strict orders for her to ring hell out of it during the night if she needed me.

I bent over and kissed her forehead once she was all settled in, with her covers pulled around her like it was wintertime instead of early September. Carefully, I pushed the stray gray hairs off her cool, damp forehead.

"Did you have a good time tonight, in spite of the dizzy spell?" I smiled down at her. She looked so shrunken without her teeth in. Her skin appeared yellowish in the glow of the Victorian lamp on the round table by her bed.

"I sure did. I appreciate you and Sarah Jean taking me with y'all," she said as she smiled up at me. "I do love catfish. Me and Rufus used to get a craving for fish, go to that same restaurant. It's been in Mt. Zion long as I can remember. Used to be a fish camp."

"Sarah's quite a woman, isn't she, Aunt Della?" I knelt beside her and took her hand. "Wonder why she ever fooled with Charlotte? Surely she had her number."

Aunt Della looked thoughtfully up at the lamp then back at me. "I believe Sarah Jean honestly felt sorry for Charlotte. She was the only female friend Charlotte ever had. Maybe she didn't see Charlotte in the same light the rest of us did. Plus, they only saw each other in the summers, when Sarah visited Maudie."

I nodded, getting to my feet then sitting beside her on the bed. "Yeah. That makes sense. And I can vouch that, in Charlotte's case, absence does make the heart grow fonder." I leaned over and gave her another kiss. "We can talk tomorrow—you've got to get some sleep now, okay?"

But Aunt Della surprised me as I turned out the lamp and started out the door, bringing up a subject we'd avoided so carefully since I'd come home. Surprised me and saddened me more than ever.

"Taylor?" Her voice came weakly from the bed just as I reached the door.

"Yes, ma'am?"

"I thought Tim looked good, didn't you?"

I stood poised by the door, frozen, then turned and looked back at her. The light from the hall outlined her eerily in her bed, reminding me of what little I'd seen of Miss Maudie in her casket the other day, and I shivered.

"He looked—okay, I guess."

"Taylor?" If I hadn't been standing perfectly still, I couldn't have heard her voice, it was so soft. "I love that boy. I always loved him, from the first time he started coming around here with you. He was mighty special to me, almost like another son."

"I know, Aunt Della," I said, swallowing hard, painfully.

"I believe he's going to be okay now, don't you? Jesus has promised me he will be."

Yeah, old Jesus really keeps those promises, doesn't He, I thought to myself, but to her I said only, "Yes, ma'am."

"Taylor?" Something in her voice scared me, she sounded so sad. "Honey, I've done that boy wrong. You know that now, don't you?"

I crossed the dark room and knelt again beside her.

"Aunt Della, you couldn't do anyone wrong if you tried." I smiled at her, but she was shaking her head vigorously.

"I've been begging Jesus to forgive me, and now I need to ask you to. Because I see now I not only did Tim wrong, I did you wrong, too." Her pale eyes looked at me pleadingly. Without her teeth, her words were slurred somewhat, like a drunk. I had to lean close to understand her.

"Aunt Della—," I began, but she grabbed my hand hard, surprising me with the force of her grip, her large bony hand covering mine.

"No, baby—you listen to me. When you would ask me about Tim these past two years, I always told you he was okay. But I knew he wasn't—I knew he was lame and that he couldn't use his right arm. But—I was scared, Taylor. I was so scared you'd have another nervous breakdown if you knew . . . so I let you think he wasn't bad hurt. . . ." Her voice broke off in a sob and tears leaked out of the corners of her eyes.

I reached over and touched the teardrops that fell, wiping them away with my fingertips.

"Aunt Della, you did what you thought you had to do. Okay—so it was wrong, in a way. But your heart was right."

Still she shook her head, closing her eyes tightly. "Not for Tim it wasn't. Poor little thing! I let him think you didn't care enough about him to call or—nothing. I don't see how neither one of y'all can forgive me."

I took her chin in my hand, turning her face toward me, and she looked at me with shame glistening in her tear-filled eyes.

"You hush about that, you hear?" I told her firmly. "You and I both made mistakes. But I did mine out of self-centeredness and yours was an attempt to save me. Knowing your honesty, I can only imagine how much that cost you. You've paid for your sins. You can't pay for mine—I gotta do that."

"But—how, honey?" she whispered, looking up at me. "Me and Harris both—give him credit—tried to help Tim afterwards. He was too proud to accept anything from us, even a job at the bank from Harris. He kept insisting the wreck wasn't your fault."

I shook my head. "Damned idiot—he knows better than that."

"I don't know what he'll let you do . . ."

"I don't know either, Aunt Della," I admitted. "But I'll find a way to do something. That I can promise you."

"Baby? You've got to face Tim again before you can do anything else. You've *got* to. Promise me you will." Again her gnarled old hand grabbed mine painfully. "I know one thing for sure—if you give me your word you won't break it."

"I'll see him, Aunt Della. I promise you that."

A faint smile touched her lips, though I could have been imagining it, the light from the hallway was so dim. She let go of my hand and nodded. "I'm putting that on my prayer list. Right now." And she closed her eyes.

I was stretched out in my bed later, smoking a cigarette in the dark. In spite of the scare of the dizzy spell and my fear for Aunt Della, I couldn't help smiling to myself remembering her horror when she realized I was going to have to help her undress. I almost lost it when I looked at her as I pulled her dress over her head and noticed that her eyes were tightly closed. She was like a refugee from another era, somehow caught in a time warp in the eighties. Sarah said that both Aunt Della and her Aunt Maudie were so incredibly naive, it blew her mind. We had a long bullshitty discussion of small-town life and the way it shelters one from the larger world. Actually, we had this conversation the other night on the banks of the Black Warrior, over a beer, passing a cigarette back and forth.

I smashed my cigarette out in the bottle cap I used for an ashtray, dropped the butt down an empty beer bottle by my bed, and turned over, hoping to get a decent night's sleep. Even though Aunt Della scared the hell out of me when we got home, it had been a good night—just being with Sarah made it good. Seeing Tim had thrown me, shaken me up more than I realized until now. And Tim—he'd surprised me by looking as shaken as me. God! I was at an advantage, in a way, having seen him from a distance at the football field my first day back. But me suddenly materializing like that, right before his eyes . . . I bet he almost shit a brick to look up and see me there. At the Catfish Cabin in Mt. Zion, of all the damn places.

. . .

The Catfish Cabin became one of mine and Tim's favorite hangouts after our first trip there, quite a few years ago now. Tim had finished the football season of his sophomore year, the first year he started as a varsity player.

It was sort of a fluke—some good old boy, I can't recall who now, was the first-string quarterback and he got his bell rung third quarter. Desperate, Coach Mills put Tim in and he astonished hell out of everybody with his throwing arm, getting himself written up in all the local papers. By the end of the season, Tim had taken over the starting position and was getting all sorts of attention from state-wide sports writers, heralding him as a young Namath or Montana. The rest, as the saying goes, is history.

So it was after the state playoffs his very first season that we decided to celebrate. I offered to take Tim out on the town for dinner, going into Tuscaloosa to a nice place. I got all dressed up in a dark suit and tie, trying to decide between the Cypress Inn or the University Club, even toying with the idea of going into Birmingham to Southside, when Tim came over. He too was dressed fit to kill, in a god-awful brown polyester suit that he'd borrowed. He had his hair all slicked down and I had to struggle to keep from laughing at him—I couldn't help it, he looked so much like a country boy out for his first night on the town. I held myself together until we got in the car and I told him I hadn't quite decided the best place for us to go to celebrate. His fresh-scrubbed face lit up and he turned to me eagerly.

"The whole time I was getting dressed I kept thinking," he said breathlessly, "reckon Taylor wants to go someplace *really* nice, like the Catfish Cabin in Mt. Zion? I've always wanted to go there."

"Man, you've got to be kidding," I told him, shaking my head in feigned astonishment. "That's *exactly* where I was thinking of taking you!"

After that, going to the Catfish Cabin became our way of celebrating, especially after big victories. The only time we didn't was after Tim's last game, one I'll never forget. It was the first and only time I ever saw Tim drunk.

It was the state championship game, our senior year, Tim's triumph in a career of triumphs. It was his final game, and all the damn reporters, photographers, and TV cameras in the state of Alabama turned out for it. The Blue Devils captured another state championship in divison 3A, mainly because Tim played such an incredible game, completing twenty-four of thirty passes for over four hundred yards and five touchdowns, breaking records like hell. Tim was the one lifted on his teammates' shoulders in the final seconds instead of Coach Mills, though that could have been because no one could lift his fat ass that far.

Donnette, of course, was all over Tim—they were a steady item by then, and pictures of them kissing hit the local papers the next day. She clung so tightly to him that I couldn't get close enough to even congratulate him. I always swore she saw me coming toward him and dragged him to the dressing rooms before I could reach them, unwilling to let me share this triumph with him. Then she stood guard at the door, supposedly to fend off the reporters and all the well-wishers so that Tim could shower and get out of there before being bombarded again.

So I had gone back home then, thinking I'd wait and catch Tim tomorrow, knowing now that the two of us wouldn't be celebrating that night as was our custom. It was a long drive home; the game was played at Legion Field in Birmingham, and I didn't relish driving back alone. Normally I shunned the high school crowd, but for some crazy reason that night, I'd longed to share in the glory of the state championship and resented hell out of Donnette's petty jealousy.

It was much later that same night when Tim and I had our celebration, though at first he almost literally scared the shit out of me. I was sound asleep, sawing logs like an old man, right here in this bed. I never knew what caused me to wake up—my subconscious suddenly knew someone was in my room. I rolled over and Tim was standing there, next to my bed.

"Jesus Christ, man! You scared the shit out of me!" I'd yelled at him. The fool had evidently crawled in my window. It was late November, cold as hell, and even in the dark, I could see a window wide open.

At first he didn't say a thing, just stood there, grinning at me like a possum caught in headlights.

"God, man—I thought you were a ghost or something, appearing in the night—don't ever do anything like that again!" I kept yelling at him. I'd never been so scared; my heart was literally jumping around in my chest like a trout thrown on a riverbank.

Tim laughed like I'd never heard him before. "Hey, Taylor. Were you asleep? Tay-were boy?" Sometimes he mocked Aunt Frances Martha, ribbing me like that.

"Was I—naw, of course not! I'm rarely asleep at three o'clock in the morning; I like to close my eyes and snore like hell and fake it. What in the name of sweet Jesus are you doing here, man?" I couldn't believe my eyes. Straight-as-an-arrow Tim, doing something that weird.

Tim was in dress pants, a button-down shirt, and his blue-and-white letter jacket. The cold moonlight caught the gleam of all the gold footballs decorating the white CHS on his chest. Then I saw a big dark stain on the front of his white shirt. I grabbed my robe off the bedpost and stuck my arms into it, inside out.

"Hey! You okay, Tim?"

I realized then that he didn't look right. His eyes were glazed and he swayed as he stood by my bed in the moonlight, holding on to the bedpost for support. Here I was yelling like a Cajun fishwife at him, and he was hurt or something.

"No, I ain't, Taylor. I'm sick as hell." His voice was slurred, too.

"Oh, goddammit, Tim—why didn't you tell me—me yelling at you like that?"

Stumbling sleepily over my own feet, I reached for the lamp by my bed. Before I could turn it on, though, Tim grabbed my arm, almost falling on me.

"Don't turn the light on, okay? My eyes hurt."

I grabbed both his shoulders and turned him around so I could see him better in the bright moonlight. I was terrified to look at the stain, fearing blood and guts, at the very least. And then I knew.

"Well, I'll be damned! You're *drunk*." The smell of booze was overwhelming—if I hadn't been asleep, I would've noticed it right off. The gory stain was just puke.

Tim started laughing like hell and fell over on my bed. He lay flat on his back and laughed like Br'er Rabbit in the briar patch, a drunken laugh that wouldn't stop, flapping his arms and kicking his feet in delight.

"Oh, shit!" I sank down beside him on the bed. For some reason, the only thing I could think of was that Coach Mills was going to blame me for this, him knowing that me and Tim always celebrated together. He'd love an excuse to beat the crap out of me.

"I can't believe Donnette let you get drunk like this, man," I sighed.

Tim had finally stopped laughing and was now wiping his eyes on my sheets, like a little kid.

"She don't know," he muttered, his eyes closed. "After I took her home, I was coming over here to see you. Why didn't you come to the dressing room after the game, man? I looked all over for you, you damn shitass."

Like a fool, I didn't say anything, not wanting him to think I was trying to turn him against Donnette.

"On the way over here," Tim continued, "I ran into Tater and Matthew and them—Pleese Davis gave us some moonshine to celebrate."

"That sorry son-of-a-bitch white trash! Goddammit, Tim, that rotgut stuff will kill you," I yelled, furious with Pleese, with Tater Dyer's sorry redneck ass, wishing I could beat hell out of all of them, or at least that I could slap Tim sober. He never drank, never broke his precious training, not even for an occasional beer.

"Why did you drink that stuff, you goddam fool—you've got better sense than that!"

Tim just shrugged, giggling helplessly again, and I continued to rant and rave. "And why the hell did you crawl in my window?"

It was the only time I could remember being mad at Tim since we became buddies in the ninth grade. What if I'd seen him at the window, got Aunt Della's old shotgun, and killed his ass? I was thinking I should shoot him anyway, upsetting me like that. His answer was a snore. He'd fallen instantly asleep, lying halfway across my bed.

I didn't even try to shake him awake, having been in his situation enough to know the futility. No, I'd have to let him sleep it off right where he was, lying across my bed, and unload all the schoolbooks and crap from the other bed and try to sleep the rest of the night there. Tim and I had been friends for years, but we'd never slept over at each other's place. What an occasion!

I knew I'd never be able to sleep with the smell of puke so strong in the room, that nostalgic odor of drunken adolescence. So I began to pull Tim's jacket off of him. It wasn't as hard to do as I expected; he hadn't fallen into a total dead drunk state yet. I lifted each of his arms and lugged on the sleeves until I freed the jacket. His arms fell limply down and he snorted loudly again.

I threw the jacket on the floor, then began to unbutton the soiled shirt. God, it stunk like hell! Yanking it off him, I wadded it up and tossed it as far as I could into the darkened room. Turning back, I removed his loafers. Only then did I hear some sort of moaning sound from Tim. He was trying to say something to me.

"I can't understand you, man," I told him. "You're too damn drunk to talk—just go on back to sleep."

Somehow Tim raised himself up on an elbow and glared at me with glazed eyes. "I said, asshole, get as far as taking off the pants and you're a dead man." And he sank back down and closed his eyes.

"Oh, yeah—I'm scared to death." I laughed, in spite of my anger at him. "This is one time I know you can't touch me. Come on, sit up one more time and we'll get you all tucked in for nighty-night. If there's no puke on the pants, they can stay."

But try as I may, I couldn't budge him—this time he did appear to have passed out. So I had to go to my closet and get a blanket for him. I realized the room was freezing because the damn window was still open, and I went over to pull it down. In doing so, I stumbled over the puke-stained shirt, so I tossed it out the window and closed it, still marveling that Mr. Goody-two-shoes Tim, Football Hero perfect Tim, had actually come over here dead drunk and crawled in my window.

I put one of Aunt Della's warm old quilts over Tim, tucking it around his bare shoulders so he wouldn't freeze his half-bare ass off and croak of pneumonia. Assuming of course he survived the alcohol poisoning of Pleese Davis's notorious moonshine. I was going to tell Coach Mills on his sorry ass, soon as I got to school Monday. Just as I got the quilt all tucked in, Tim's eyes flew open and he stared startled at me.

"Taylor! What you doing here?" he muttered, slobbering drunkenly all over my bed.

I sighed and sat beside him on the bed, pulling my inside-out robe closer about me. I was about to freeze my balls off.

Before I could say anything, Tim rolled over on his side. "Oh, God. I'm *so* sick—help me. Please, Taylor . . ." And he retched miserably over the side of my bed, dry-heaving until he fell back exhausted on my pillows.

I shook my head. "There's not a thing I can do. Believe me, I would if I could. Just don't puke on my bed. And try to go to sleep—that'd be the best thing you could do now."

But like most drunks, Tim wanted to talk instead. He closed his eyes a minute, then opened them and looked at me. I was still sitting by him on the bed.

"Taylor?" Tim said. "The reason I came here tonight—I wanted us to celebrate like we usually do, go to Mt. Zion to the Catfish Cabin. Come on, let's go over there and get some catfish, okay?"

Again I sighed. "Tim, you are shit-faced drunk. The Catfish Cabin has been closed for hours. Besides, if you were to eat there now you'd be puking catfish for a month."

Tim looked sorrowful, like he was going to cry.

"Tell you what," I said, to cheer him up, "I'll take you there tomorrow night, okay? If Donnette will let you go, that is."

Tim either missed or ignored my last remark. "You promise?"

"Scout's honor."

There was a minute of silence, then Tim looked up at me solemnly. Again, I had to force myself not to laugh at him. I couldn't help it—it was so strange to see him drunk that it was beginning to strike me as funny as hell. What he said to me next changed that real quick.

"Taylor? You know the real reason I wanted us to go out together tonight?" he said, leaning toward me still slurring his words. "I wanted to talk to you about something. Something serious."

"Talk away. I'm listening." I lit a cigarette, prepared for a drunken sob story.

"Man, listen. I gotta tell you—I'm scared as hell," Tim said.

"The game's over now—you won. No reason to be scared anymore." I smiled at him, drawing deeply and blowing smoke into the pale moonlight. The light coming in the front windows wasn't much, but I could see him plain as day.

"I'm not talking about that, Taylor." Tim's voice began to get a little clearer, not quite so drunken-sounding. "Tonight was my last game here. I'm scared to leave, go off to college. Ain't you?"

"Tim—come on! I've never imagined you being scared of anything," I said, truly astonished.

"Oh, man—you just don't know. I'm scared shitless that I won't make it." He pulled the quilt closer around him and looked up at me. I suddenly realized the two of us were half-lying next to each other on a single bed, so I scooted myself up, propping up on the pillows, giving him a little bit more room. Tim wadded one of the pillows up under his head and looked up at me.

"How can you *not* make it, Tim? You've got everything—you're smart, hard-working, good-looking, a great athlete. You're going to blow them away, wherever you decide to go," I told him sincerely. It was too late, or rather early in the morning, to be bullshitting.

If I thought Tim had surprised me all he was going to that night, I was wrong. What he said next blew me away.

"I wisht I was more like you, Taylor," he said, looking up at me with bloodshot but earnest blue eyes.

Jesus Christ! I stared down at him a minute then started laughing like hell.

"You're drunker than I thought, fool."

Tim reached out from under his quilt and grabbed my arm

with an iron grip. "No, man—listen to me—I'm serious! You don't let things bother you, eat at you like I do. I wisht to God I was more like that. The reason I got so drunk tonight was because I was so damn nervous about the game—I was a wreck. You'd never let anything get to you that much."

"Not a football game, that's for sure. Maybe getting laid, or something really important." I laughed again.

Tim let go of my arm and settled back down on his pillow. "That's another thing—the way you make everything out to be a joke. God, if only I could do that, instead of taking everything so serious!"

"Well, Tim, as you should know, my life is a joke. In the deck of life, I'm the joker."

Tim was quiet for a minute and I looked to see if he'd gone back to sleep. Instead, he was looking at me, frowning. He sure sobered up in a hurry. Thinking about what Tim said to me next gives me a chill to this day. And kind of scares hell out of me.

"You know what, Taylor? I have this bad feeling that I'm *not* going to make it—that I'm never going to get out of this hick town, make something of myself. I just have this feeling."

"That's the booze talking, Tim. You'll be Mr. Football Hero again tomorrow—folks interviewing you left and right. Though I warn you, tomorrow you're going to feel like you've been dipped in shit and rolled in cracker crumbs."

Tim was quiet again, then spoke up, his voice no longer so slurred. "Taylor—level with me, man. You really think I can make it going away to college? Some place like Tulane? I could stay here, play for Alabama. Bear wants me bad."

I looked down at him, dragging on my cigarette before turning my head to put it out. When I turned back to him, he was still looking up at me. "Donnette going with you, Tim?" I asked.

Tim shook his head. "She don't want to go to college. She says she'll wait for me, be here waiting when I get back. I hope so."

I didn't tell him I couldn't imagine her, as possessive as she was, letting him go off anywhere, much less some of the far-away places that had been scouting him. She'd figure out some way to tag along, probably want him to marry her. I hoped he had sense enough not to.

"Donnette thinks I ought to stay here, play for Bama," Tim continued. I lit another cigarette to hide my fury at Donnette's conniving to keep him under her wings. I looked away from him, out the moonlit window, as I puffed angrily. "She says I ain't got the background to pass otherwise," Tim added.

"That's bullshit, Tim! Sure, CHS's not so hot, but they'll have tutors for you jocks. And, if we go to the same college like we've talked about, I'll be there to help you, too."

"I—just don't know if I have enough confidence—" Tim began, but I interrupted him furiously, the only time I allowed myself to say anything against Donnette.

"No damn wonder, hicks like Donnette telling you that you can't make it! Sorry, Tim. But I can't stand to hear you talk like that, man."

"You really think I can make it, Taylor? You really believe in me?"

"Move your ass over; I'm about to fall off the bed," I told him, giving him a push with my shoulder. "Of course I believe in you. Anybody who'd climb in the window of a dark house at three in the morning has the balls to do anything. So shut your damn-fool mouth—I refuse to listen to any more cowardly shit from you."

He was the one not to listen to me, of course, though we talked on and on that night until the sun began to come up over the dead honeysuckle vines in the yard, and it began to gradually lighten in my room. Tim finally just passed out, in mid-sentence.

I sat for a while looking down at him as he slept. I should have realized Tim would be scared to leave here; he'd never been anywhere but west Alabama. I reached down and pushed back the tousled blond hair that had fallen over his forehead, letting my hand rest for a moment on his cheek. Crazy drunk fool. Then I eased over to my bed and fell asleep immediately. When I woke up later that day, he'd dressed in one of my shirts, taken his jacket, and gone. Neither one of us ever said a word to the other about that night.

I knew returning to Hicksville would cause all the old ghosts to come back—stuff the shrink had been trying to pry from my subconscious these past two years. Ever since I'd been back in Clarksville, I'd been haunted by my recurring nightmares of the accident, not half sleeping because of the different scenes tormenting my mind when I woke up gasping for breath and nauseated. The morning after Aunt Della gave me such a scare, I woke up tired and spent, dark circles under my eyes, looking like the haggard Macbeth I was becoming.

And on that morning, who should show up at my door but old Ellis Rountree Clark. Okay, Banquo—let's get all the ghosts out, have a goddamn parade, how about it?

Aunt Della seemed much better when I finally dragged my sorry ass up—I would have laid around until noon if I hadn't been so concerned about her. She was up and dressed, had made the coffee and was even pulling out eggs and crap to make her pancakes. I swear, there's no stopping her—Uncle Cleve and Pleese will be wheeling her out one of these days and she'll sit up, pull the shroud off, and say, "Wait just a minute, boys. I got to make my sweet baby Taylor some pancakes before I go."

I was having none of it today, though. I forcefully put all the stuff back into the pantry and made her sit down, taking her walker away and pushing her into a kitchen chair.

"Aunt Della, you're going to have a rare treat this morning. *You*—lucky you—are going to be the first in Zion County to sample my famous Cajun omelet," I said as I tied one of her aprons around me. Of course I had no idea how to make a Cajun omelet, but I figured I could fake it and she'd never know the difference.

Evidently it worked. Aunt Della fussed like hell, but she picked around and ate the eggs I'd scrambled with onions and bell peppers, with a dash of Tabasco for the Cajun touch. I studied her as she ate; her coloring looked a little better and she didn't appear as shaky. Maybe she was right—the dizzy spell last night was just a result of eating fried catfish and being out so much later than her usual bedtime.

"Now, sugar, I'm feeling so much better I'm going to go bathe and dress," she informed me when she finished.

I jumped up and retrieved her walker. "Let me run your bathwater for you then. You don't need to be bending over the tub."

Aunt Della chuckled as we started the journey out of the kitchen to her room. "Not this morning, baby. I'm going to have what Papa called a spit bath, where I just run some water in the sink and wash only the most important places. I can manage fine."

I kept an ear out for Aunt Della as I cleaned up in the kitchen. It was then that I heard the banging on the front door—Aunt Della had never had a doorbell. And most people knew to come around to the back door. Puzzled, I dried my hands and went quickly down the hall to quiet whoever it was before the banging disturbed Aunt Della. And who should be standing there but old Ellis Rountree Clark!

We both stood looking at each other for a minute. I couldn't help but notice that Ellis almost looked good—anything, of course, would be an improvement. She was all dolled up in some kind of tropical-print jumpsuit which showed off her figure, scooped down in the front revealing some nice cleavage. But she was wearing these ridiculous earrings fashioned like parrots swinging upside down. Well, you can take the girl out of the country but . . .

Maybe old Ellis was changing in lots of ways though, because the first thing she said to me really surprised me, surprised me that she'd ever allude to that other time, if even indirectly.

"Do you always come to the door half dressed, Taylor?" she said in her stilted, prissy way of talking.

I sighed. "Only when I'm expecting you, Ellis. Hang on just a minute."

I left her standing on the doorstep, stepped quickly into my room and buttoned on a denim shirt. I'd be damned if I was going to change from my cutoff jeans, even for prissy old Ellis. Though maybe I did owe her something . . . my eyes fell on my bed, still rumpled from my restless night. It was the spring of the next year, after Tim's nocturnal visit, that I had another visitor to my bed. Only it wasn't night; it was a stormy morning. She had come in to dry off from the rain, and I'd helped her, first loosening her long, wet hair from the tight bun, toweling it dry, then reaching for her rain-soaked blouse, never imagining . . . I shook my head and reluctantly turned to go back to the front of the house.

Ellis had stepped into the hall when I came out of my room. "I didn't come to see you, Taylor. I came to see Miss Della," she said frostily, looking past me down the hall.

"Well, too bad, Ellis. Miss Della regrets she's unable to receive callers this morning. Come on, let's step out here on the porch."

No way, after Aunt Della's spell last night, was I going to let Ellis come around this morning, trying to talk her into coming to stay with them, or going to a nursing home, or whatever the loving Clark Clan had sent her here for.

Our porch was not screened off like the Clark porch—it was

wide open for all of Clarksville to see. I motioned to Ellis, and she sat across from me in a rocker I'd always loved—it looked like it was made from twigs. I sat in the big wicker swing and began to swing lazily, but Ellis sat primly on the edge of her seat, her hands, tipped with long red nails, held together in her lap. We were right across the street from the Baptist Church.

"Your old stomping ground, Ellis." I nodded toward the church, giving the swing a little kick. "I don't guess you miss it, though, now that you are in the rapturous bonds of matrimony with Zion's ex–most eligible bachelor."

She glared at me without saying anything and I couldn't resist aggravating her a little more.

"You know, I've spent many an hour since I've returned trying to figure out exactly how—and why—you captured old Sonny. I'll just bet you that's quite a story! I'm surprised you haven't been interviewed by the *Zion County Herald* on such a momentous feat."

When she didn't reply but turned her head haughtily and looked away from me, I pressed on.

"Yes, indeed—quite a story. Of course I myself have had a little sample of your ample charms and can see how you could put such delights to good use. Though I admit I never dreamed—"

I finally succeeded in getting her attention. She turned to me then, her painted face red and furious.

"You shut your mouth, Taylor. Don't you ever say anything about that again—"

I laughed, causing her to jump up from the rocker and grab her purse. The parrots swung crazily from her ears.

"I was thinking, Ellis—maybe now that you are more experienced you might want to try again. Maybe this time we would have more success—"

I had underestimated old Ellis and pushed her too far. Before I realized what had happened, she had swung her arm back with a deadly looking straw purse in hand. If I hadn't grabbed her arm, she would have knocked hell out of me, right there in front of the Baptists, God, and everybody.

"Whoa! Calm down now, Ellis—I was just playing with you some—" I said, laughing.

For the second time that morning, I found myself forcing a woman into a chair. I grabbed both her shoulders and pushed her back down into the rocker, then stood in front of her so she wouldn't come at me again. Ellis was glaring at me like I was the reincarnation of old Satan himself.

"You sorry, low-down bastard—" she muttered furiously.

I let go of her shoulders and backed away, going back to the swing, but this time I, too, sat on the edge, not swinging.

"People in Clarksville keep saying that, Ellis, but surprisingly, Charlotte did marry my daddy. 'Son of a bitch' might be more appropriate. Try it—I'll even show you how to enunciate—*son-of-a-bitch*."

"You are sick, Taylor. You are really sick," she said, shaking her head. Her jaw was so tightly clenched it must have hurt her. Even the dangling parrots glared at me from their upside-down perch.

I shook my head at her and smiled, relaxing now. "Ellis, you must forgive me for not being a gentleman—it's not in my genes. No pun intended. What you don't know is this: your little visit to me that fortuitous, rainy morning was the stuff fantasy is made of—every male adolescent's dream come true."

"You know perfectly well that what happened—" she said through clenched teeth, "that I was looking for Miss Della that morning—"

"Well, you sure found something else, didn't you? Something that you didn't bargain for, right? How was I to know that you had no experience with men—the vestal Baptist virgin herself, suddenly finding herself awakened to passion by the sight of my half-naked body? Damn, Ellis, that's what I'm telling you—every fantasy I've had since then has stemmed from that experience. Or rather, almost experience."

"So help me God, Taylor—if you ever breathe a word of that to Hamilton—" Ellis was so upset she was no longer talking in complete sentences. Her breath was coming out in little gasps.

"Jesus, Ellis!" I grinned, pushing the swing off again. "I know I'm not even a half-assed Southern gentleman, but I wouldn't do anything like that!"

"I don't trust you as far as I could throw you—" she spat out at me.

"Give me a break, Ellis. I've never told anyone about it—not Tim, not Cat, no one."

"I don't believe you." She folded her bare arms under her boobs, still clutching the murderous purse like a weapon. When she caught me looking at the top of her jumpsuit where her chest heaved like that of a gothic heroine, she hugged herself even tighter.

"Honey, you can believe me, because if I had told anyone, you wouldn't have had to wait so many years to get you a man—they'd have been knocking your door down."

I feared I'd gone too far again because Ellis moved in the chair as though to lunge at me. Then she suddenly sank back and her red-painted mouth drooped at the corners.

"Hamilton must never, ever know anything, *anything* like—that—happened. I swear, if I lost him—" Her voice trailed off and she stopped. I was surprised as hell. Maybe old Ellis really loved Sonny. I certainly knew she had the potential for great passion.

"Okay, Ellis—I'll drop it. My lips are sealed. It never happened, okay?" I began to swing again then, leaning back and looking at her. "What *did* you come here for this morning, if not to catch me half-clad, awaken my sleeping passion again?"

She took a deep breath and looked straight ahead. "I'd prefer to talk with Miss Della."

"I've already told you; it's me or nobody. She's bathing, getting dressed now."

"I don't mind waiting."

"Okay, Ellis—I won't bullshit you. I don't want her talking to you, or Sonny, or Aunt Opal, or Daddy Clark. Not right now, anyhow. She's not feeling well. She had a little dizzy spell last night. So tell me what you want with her."

"All right, I will." Again she looked straight ahead rather than at me. "It's about my sister, Glenda."

"Glenda? What the hell does she have to do with anything?" I remembered Glenda Rountree—or rather I remembered her when I'd looked her up in my old high school annual. If possible, she was plainer and quieter than Ellis had been back then.

"Like me at her age, Glenda needs to get out of her present situation. I have advised her to do as I did then, and take a room somewhere. Mine was in Columbus, but Glenda wants to stay here. She works part-time at—at the Zippy Mart out from town, by the river."

"Oh, yeah. I saw her there recently. And she's going with old Dink Odom now, isn't she? Both the Rountree girls landing them a man in one year!" I grinned. "Fascinating story, Ellis, but why would you want to talk to Aunt Della about it?"

Ellis had relaxed some, and she looked down at her hands. I noticed she was turning her big diamond wedding ring round and round on her finger.

"Well, I thought Miss Della might be interested in renting Glenda a room."

I laughed in spite of myself. "Thanks for asking, Ellis, but it's just as well you didn't waste Aunt Della's time. She wouldn't want anyone else staying here. No offense to Glenda, of course. I know how Aunt Della is."

"Well, Donnette is considering it, because they need the money. But I would prefer that Glenda be with a genteel lady—especially since she's family now."

I studied Ellis a minute and then shook my head. "Ah. I see. Good try, Ellis. Had me going for a minute, there."

She tried to look surprised. "What do you mean?"

"I know what you're up to. The bit about being family gave you away. You want to get your sister settled in this house, then when Aunt Della croaks, or y'all cart her off to a nursing home, you and Sonny can move right on in. Maybe you're planning on moving all the Rountrees in then—bring them out of the sticks into 'genteel' society. Though that ought to be quite a feat."

I could tell by her expression that I'd hit the nail on the head. Ellis stood up, mad again, clutching the hell out of that purse.

"Forget it! Forget I even mentioned it, Taylor! Obviously you still think you are too good for anybody in this town—you and your crazy old aunt, too. Well, I've changed my mind. I wouldn't have Glenda live here for nothing—she might have the misfortune of running into you!"

With that little speech, Ellis started down the steps haughtily. I couldn't resist one more dig before she disappeared down the sidewalk, and I tried to say it loud enough for the Baptists across the street to hear.

"I wouldn't call it a misfortune if Glenda came snooping around here one rainy summer morning and caught me naked and willing—she might like it as much as you did!"

It was a day not only for old ghosts and resurrecting old memories; it was also a day for visits. Since I had no way of knowing at the time what the consequences of Ellis's visit were going to be, I decided I was feeling up to continuing my therapy with Sarah. Naturally she'd been curious as hell about my reaction to Tim's appearance in the catfish restaurant, calling me as soon as Ellis left, checking on Aunt Della and getting the lowdown on my state of mind.

I'd just begun the last few days to talk with Sarah about Tim, and the accident, and my being off my rocker for two years. I never thought I could talk to anyone like I'd talked to Sarah, spilling my guts ad nauseam, going on and on like I'd never done with my shrink in New Orleans.

But Sarah was so different, so easy to talk to. The night before, when I stopped the car to let her out at her Aunt Maudie's house, she'd crawled out of the backseat behind me, then leaned back into the car and kissed my cheek. "Thanks for a great meal," she whispered, her hand in my hair. "And we've got to talk about tonight—call me as soon as you feel up to it."

Of course I'd sat there all moony-eyed watching her walk into the house, delighting in that perky little swing she has when she walks, sighing over the way her hair fell over her shoulders. I had finally found the most unbelievable woman I'd ever known, a woman who could be my salvation, and she was old enough to be my mother and treated me like the son she'd never had! My shrink would have a field day with that one.

Sarah came over and had lunch with me and Aunt Della, since she said she wanted to see for herself if Aunt Della's dizzy spell was anything to be concerned about, or just a passing thing. We pigged out on tomato sandwiches and leftover fish from the Catfish Cabin. After lunch, when Aunt Della lay down for her afternoon nap, Sarah and I sat on the swing and talked until dark. When it finally got too dark to see, Aunt Della came out and turned on the porch light, wanting to know if Sarah would stay for supper. But Sarah insisted she had to go, that she had work to do getting her Aunt Maudie's house ready. She said her goodbyes to Aunt Della, then I walked her home. I didn't even go in—it was right outside her house that it happened.

"Taylor?" Sarah smiled at me, taking both my hands in hers as we stood on the sidewalk outside Miss Maudie's house. "I think

Della's going to be all right—just watch her closely. It could have been a mild stroke or something she had last night. But probably not. Probably the night out was too much for her."

I nodded. "I think so, too. And listen, thanks for hearing me out this afternoon, listening to all my crap. One for the casebooks, huh? Give you lots of material for your classes, at least." Sarah taught psychology in medical school, and she was the only shrink I'd met who wasn't loonier than her patients.

She looked at me earnestly with those marvelous golden eyes. "I think I can help you, Taylor. We've both got some time left here. So let's continue to talk, okay?"

She couldn't have said anything I liked better than that. Any excuse to be with her. Funny thing was, though—she really was helping me. Mainly by urging me to spill my guts and get so much of that shit out. When I talked with her, I could feel the torment begin to ease up ever so slightly, like the way a tranquilizer dulls the searing pain of heartache.

Sarah held out her arms to me and I went into them gratefully. She had no idea how she tormented me, always hugging on me, kissing my cheek, tousling my hair like a pet puppy. If only she knew!

"Oh, honey—you're going to be all right. I promise you, things are going to work out for you. Trust me," she whispered, patting my back.

Of course I couldn't help it—I had to screw everything up. Suddenly I could stand it no longer, the sweet sensual smell of her, the softness of her hair, her lean muscular body. Taking a deep gasping breath, I pulled her tightly to me, pressing her against me, her firm small breasts into my chest. Then I heard her cry out and push me away. At first I was startled, hurt, so I looked down at her. She was staring at the road, at the lights of a car which had slowed down and then sped off quickly.

"Taylor." Sarah raised her head and looked up at me, her

golden eyes wide. "That car stopped right in front of the house, then took off like a bat out of hell when I saw them looking at us."

"Did you see who it was?" I took my arms off her shoulders reluctantly and looked down the street at the receding taillights, glowing like fireflies in the darkness.

"Your cousin Sonny. He got his eyes full."

"Oh, shit. Shit. I'll just bet he did." I sighed.

"And his wife was with him. She was about to break her neck looking at us."

I sighed again and pretended to shrug it off. But knowing Ellis, especially after she'd gotten so furious with me this morning, I could only imagine what the consequences of that little scene might be.

I had only to wait a couple of days to discover those consequences for myself. Aunt Della seemed to be doing okay now, not great, still frail and shaky as hell, but no worse than when I'd reappeared a few weeks ago. Just to be sure, I'd taken her to the doctor in the new clinic outside of town. He'd been a bit more cautious than I'd expected—giving her all sorts of tests and stuff as though he suspected some kind of stroke. But she'd checked out okay, and he'd gotten her to agree to see him more regularly, which was a major feat with her. It irked her to admit she was not as robust as she'd always been.

I was spending lots of time helping Sarah get Miss Maudie's house ready for its new occupant, some old maid cousin of theirs. It was an afternoon, a couple of days later, after I'd been helping Sarah paint the kitchen cabinets, when I returned home to find Aunt Della all agitated.

"Frances Martha is coming over here in a few minutes to pick you and me up, Taylor," she told me as soon as I got in the house. "Harris wants to talk with us. He wanted to come here, but I didn't want him to. Last time he was over here he snooped around—said I wasn't able to take care of the house and all of Papa and Mama's antiques anymore. That's why I don't want him here."

"Crap, Aunt Della—you should've at least made him come to you! His royal majesty can't just command that you come over there and talk with him, especially now, with you not feeling well. What the hell could he possibly want to talk about anyway?"

Aunt Della shook her head and sighed. "I don't know. Last time he came here, earlier on in the summer, was when he tried to talk me into going to a nursing home. I'll bet you anything Lonnie Floyd told him I went to the doctor the other day. Her daughter's the receptionist there."

I rubbed my eyes wearily with yellow paint–stained hands. I was dirty and tired and didn't feel like listening to His Holiness this afternoon.

"Do we have to go?"

"Well, you know Harris, hon. He'll just pester me until he gets his way."

"Okay, okay. I guess it could be worse—they could've invited us to supper."

The whole Clark clan was out in full regalia when me and Aunt Della got there. Evidently Annie Lou or someone had aired out the front parlor, the one Daddy Clark and I'd sat in when I was last over there. The window unit was going full blast but it still was airless, hot as holy hell, and smelled like mothballs, if moths had balls. They were all waiting for us—Daddy Clark, Sonny, Ellis, Aunt Frances Martha—each looking morbidly eager for whatever confrontation was ahead. I looked around dismissively at my dearly beloved family gathered around the Great Bald Wizard of Zion.

"Guess what, Aunt Della," I muttered as we made our entrance. "We ain't in Kansas anymore."

Daddy Clark was standing up, of course, lording over us, leaning against the mantel over the marble fireplace. I walked over to him, shook his hand, then turned back to help Aunt Della fold her walker away. She settled herself in a big satin wing chair, which made her look small and defenseless. I pulled up a needlepoint stool and sat right next to her, taking her hand firmly in mine. No way I was going to let him bully her like he usually did. This time, I was going to be here for her, so help me God. I looked around at each of my lovely family members, nodding curtly to them instead of speaking. I wasn't up to the Clark family scenes today.

Aunt Opal then prissed her fat ass into the parlor, surprisingly. She spent most of her time boozing it up at the country club, playing bridge with all the other bored housewives out there. I thought I was going to puke at the performance she put on, though I couldn't figure out who it was for. She came over when I got Aunt Della settled, ohhed and ahhed over her like so many idiots do around old people, shouting at her as though she was deaf, talking babyish to her, and generally acting like Aunt Della had become a retard in her old age. I swear, when I get old I'm going to keep a cane handy and brain the hell out of whoever pulls that on me.

The true retard of the bunch, Aunt Frances Martha, dear old soul that she is, excused herself right off because she was making a Bisquick pie or some such shit for supper and had to roll out the dough, or so she told us. She'd already enthralled us by describing it step by step on the ride over. Aunt Della ignored her, but I pretended to give a crap and she explained the whole process in detail, getting off on mixing Bisquick with buttermilk and poppy seeds. I guess Daddy Clark allowed her to miss the powwow because he figured she didn't have sense enough to know what was going on anyway. Such Christian compassion.

The happy newlyweds Sonny and Ellis sat side by side on the sofa, holding hands and looking mad enough to shit a brick. Neither one even spoke to Aunt Della or myself, just nodding a greeting instead. I didn't know what on earth their problem was, but I figured I'd find out soon enough. I was sure right about that. I was determined to keep my cool, not blow it, not let any of them know that I was nervous and shaky as usual, just being in this house, especially in my usual subservient position with my grandfather.

I looked up at Daddy Clark standing there, elbow on the mantel, stern and unapproachable, dressed in a starched blue shirt and sharply creased gray trousers held up on his rotund belly with suspenders. Gone was his deadly weapon, the thin belt with the gold buckle engraved with HJC, a belt I'd felt the sting of more often than I could remember.

No matter how hard I tried not to be affected, there was something about this scene that was unnerving the hell out of me, more than his summons or even the memory of the infamous belt could possibly warrant. Suddenly I knew what it was. No wonder I was so nervous—I discovered at an early age that Daddy Clark had a weapon more potent than the belt.

I was five years old, the year before I started school, the year Charlotte reappeared briefly in my life, first time since I was left crying for her in my playpen in a squalid apartment above a lush courtyard in New Orleans. It was years later before I learned she'd paid some old hag to watch me, supposedly planning on coming back for me after a little jaunt to Europe with a new lover, one of her professors, twenty years her senior. The old sot got too plastered to see about me; if the landlord hadn't heard my wails I might have kicked off before my first birthday. Too bad. Saved lots of folks, including myself, plenty of heartache.

Aunt Della, of the old school, use to take me to visit my granddaddy all the time those first five years, damned determined to establish family, especially male, bonding. She gave up only when she realized the old fart really didn't care to have me around, couldn't stand to be reminded of the shame his daughter had brought to the almighty Clark name.

But it was one of those visits; Aunt Della had left me for the afternoon and gone to some church meeting or something. I'd been baking Bisquick cookies with Aunt Frances Martha in the kitchen. She'd then gone down for her nap, and I believed Daddy Clark to be napping too. Like the dumb little bastard I was then, I took advantage of my supposed freedom to snoop around in the forbidden regions of the front parlor, just asking to get in trouble. Something my Aunt Della had told me that very morning prompted my curious snooping. Some of the things about that day are still shadowy and half-forgotten, but others are vivid as hell. Too vivid.

I'd sneaked into the big dark parlor, crawling on the floor like I was a cowboy having to hide out from the Indians who might be chasing me. I can even remember the faggy little cowboy suit I wore, one Aunt Della'd given me for my fifth birthday.

On my hands and knees, I'd scurried behind the sofa, then over to a big old antique sideboard that I'd seen Daddy Clark use, on the few occasions I'd been allowed in the parlor. I'd found what I was looking for, too, in the first drawer I lugged on. It fell open, spilling its contents out onto the polished wooden floor. I cried out, thrilled, when I spotted the photo I'd sneaked in there searching for.

At that very moment, I'd known I was not alone in that room. "What do you think you're doing, boy?" came thundering at me, and I cringed. I'd looked up to see Daddy Clark standing there by the mantel. Evidently he'd been there, fiddling around with something or other, the whole time, and I hadn't seen him in the fantasy of my cowboy games.

To a child, Daddy Clark had seemed the essence of the wrath

of God, scaring the daylights out of me by his sudden appearances, his scornful glare, looking down at me from his massive height. Also like God, he seemed omnipresent, always around, seeing what I was getting into. Not that he really gave a shit, as long as it wasn't anything to shame him. That day, he towered over me and grabbed me by my arm, pulling me to my feet. At that time, though, I was too excited to be scared speechless like I usually was around him. Unfortunately.

"Look, Daddy Clark!" I'd babbled like a fool. I held up the picture I clutched in my chubby little hand, the photo of the beautiful lady I knew immediately was Charlotte Clark Dupree.

"I know this is my mama! Aunt Della told me my mama was coming to see me next week. I know this is her."

"You don't have a mama, son," Daddy Clark said coldly.

That's all he said, but I had to argue, dumb little hick that I was. "Uh, huh, I do, too! Aunt Della told me that my mama—Charlotte, *my* mama, was coming across a big ocean to see me next week."

Daddy Clark looked down at the picture. He took it out of my hand and put it back in the drawer.

"My daughter Charlotte is coming here next week, boy. That much is true. But she's *not* your mama. A mama doesn't desert her child, leaving it to be raised by anybody who'll take it in. She's nobody's mama, not her."

And he closed the drawer with a bang.

Of course the old bastard had a point, but I didn't know it at the time. I'd been too petrified to tell Aunt Della. Because if the mysterious Charlotte wasn't my mother, then who was? Maybe Daddy Clark was right; maybe I didn't belong anywhere, to anyone. I'd been so quiet afterwards that Aunt Della, old-fashioned as she was, had dosed me good with castor oil, thinking I was surely sick. That part I do remember vividly.

I shook aside my happy recollections of childhood days gone

by and forced myself to go back to where I was right then. I wasn't going to let myself be distracted by any more ghosts—I owed it to Aunt Della to be here for her now. Banquo—be gone!

Daddy Clark continued to stand there staring at us, looking disgusted with the whole clan. He peered down at us like Browning's last Duchess, his looks for each of us the same. Aunt Opal, wasting her days playing cards and drinking; Sonny, too sorry to hold down a regular job; Ellis, straight out of the backwoods; and of course me and Aunt Della, his cross to bear, each in our own way. Guess he felt none of us were worthy of the prestigious Clark name. Finally he spoke, turning his attention first to Aunt Della, as I'd expected.

"Della, I promised Papa that I'd look after you when you got to this point in your life. Since you had no offspring, Papa left the house to me, with the stipulation that it was yours long as you lived. However, I've talked with your doctor. He agrees with me that you can no longer stay home by yourself," he said.

Aunt Della opened her mouth to protest, but Daddy Clark held his hand up to silence her.

"Please. Let me finish. I have given this matter much attention in my prayer life. I am not the heartless, coldhearted person you've always made me out to be, Della." He stood more erect and waited for his sister to look ashamed. She only looked frail and forlorn. I squeezed her hand tighter.

"Christ requires that we have compassion one for another," Daddy Clark continued. I sighed. Shit. Now we had to listen to him pontificate as well.

"It has come to me from my prayer life that I honor my papa's dying request by doing what I can to make your final years happy, Della. The Lord has seen fit to answer my prayers. He has sent us someone to stay with you. With her help, you can stay in Papa's home as long as you are able to make it."

Daddy Clark stuck out his chest and waited for the worshippers to fall on their knees in front of him. Something told me he'd already practiced this speech for the town's benefit, probably telling the preacher and his cronies at the church, extolling in how he was going beyond his Christian duty by his poor old sister. But I smelled a rat.

Aunt Della, for once, seemed to not know what to say, since she was expecting he'd already gotten her a room ready in the nursing home.

"Well, Harris," she said finally, faintly. "I do appreciate that."

"Whoa! Wait just a minute," I looked over at Ellis, and sure enough, she was preening and looking at me as if she'd just conceived by the Holy Spirit.

"Daddy Clark? Is this person—this angel of mercy sent by God—is she by any chance Ellis's sister, Glenda?" I asked.

Neither Sonny nor Ellis waited for him to answer; both began protesting at the same time. Even Aunt Opal, who up until now had been thumbing through a magazine, put it down long enough to glare at me.

"She comes as a gift from the Lord's grace, a good Christian girl like her, wanting to live in town, nearer her place of employment," Daddy Clark said.

"Wanting to live nearer Dink Odom," I muttered, but only Ellis heard me. The look she gave me could have chilled the most fainthearted.

"Ellis's sister?" Aunt Della looked confused, and looked around the room at each of them, coming to rest finally on Ellis. And Ellis was smirking at her like she'd pulled off a good one.

"Oh, come on, Daddy Clark!" I sighed. "Aunt Della doesn't want Ellis's sister staying there with her, snooping around for Ellis, waiting for her to kick the bucket so the Rountree clan can move in. Forget it."

Sonny jumped up from the sofa. "You are so ridiculous, Taylor! Such a screwball—now you've added paranoia to your list.

Your shrink will be glad to have some more Clark dough to handle that one, I guarantee you!"

"Sit down, Sonny," Daddy Clark said. Then he turned those steely blue eyes on me. "Don't you tell me to forget this, young man. In the first place, it's none of your business, and in the second, I told you that the Lord arranged this—sent this girl our way right at this time, in answer to my prayers."

As usual, I couldn't keep my temper, hold my tongue and try to reason with him. I ended up blowing it big.

"The Lord, my ass! Ellis is behind this, and you can't tell me she's not. It's her idea, and we won't have anything to do with it," I retorted.

Daddy Clark looked as if he were about to have a stroke at my outburst. His face got as red as Sonny's Crimson Tide shirt.

"Don't you *dare* use that kind of language around me, young man! And there's no 'we' to it—this has nothing at all to do with you."

It was Aunt Della's turn to come to my defense. I jumped when I heard her voice come so clearly from her seat next to me, stronger than I've heard it in ages.

"Harris, you know better than to say anything like that! Taylor is my boy, same as Harris Jr. was yours. I've raised him and he has every right to say what he thinks. Me and him only have each other."

But at that, Aunt Della pulled on my hand and turned me around to look at her. "Taylor, honey. Don't get so upset. I know of Glenda—I've heard that she is a fine Christian girl. I'd do anything to stay home, as you know. Me and you'll talk all about this later."

But I knew, just knew, that Ellis, Sonny, and probably Aunt Opal had hatched up this latest scheme. And I knew the way Aunt Della felt about Ellis, she had to be saying that just to appease me, get me to shut my mouth before I blew it with Daddy Clark.

Even knowing that, I couldn't let it go. I pulled away from Aunt Della and stood up.

"No. No—this won't do," I said. "I haven't asked around yet—I'll find someone to stay with Aunt Della before I go back to school next week."

Sonny laughed out loud. "That ought to be no problem. You're in such good standing in this community—"

Daddy Clark interrupted him. "I have tried my best to find someone. Della knows that. Folks are too sorry to work for a living anymore. Why should they when they can stay home and collect welfare? I admire this young woman for wanting to stand on her own two feet, make something of herself."

It was my turn to laugh. "Yeah, she's real ambitious, all right. Dink Odom is a step up from the footwashers, I guess. All things are relative."

It was at this exact point in all our encounters that Daddy Clark always had enough of me and my smart mouth—I could tell when that moment had come. His eyes bored into mine, and everybody in the room got quiet.

"The matter is settled, young man. Della should thank the Lord that I have everything all taken care of."

I couldn't stand it. From the corner of my eye, I saw Aunt Della rise up in the chair, try to grab my hand again.

"No, sir. It is *not*. Your plan is unacceptable." I turned then to Aunt Della and reached for her hand. "Come on, Aunt Della. Let's go back home."

"I have never been so insulted in all my life," Ellis began to whine from her spot on the sofa. "Hamilton, are you going to sit there and let your wife's people be insulted like this?"

Aunt Opal threw down her magazine and got up to leave. "This whole business is giving me a headache. Y'all are going to have to excuse me."

From previous visits to the house, I knew exactly where Aunt

Opal was headed. "Bring me a snort from your secret stash while you're at it, Aunt Opal," I said to her retreating back. "I'm getting a headache, too."

She threw me a dirty look and slammed the parlor door, making everyone jump.

Sonny, of course, had to defend the honor of his wife and mother, Southern chivalry running like blood through his veins. He jumped up again and took a step toward me.

"Daddy Clark, I'm going to have to speak my mind. I cannot stand this longhaired excuse for a human being another minute. I think the Clarks have put up with more from him than anyone would expect us to tolerate."

"I don't think anyone would argue with that," Daddy Clark said stiffly, as I unfolded Aunt Della's walker and helped her get into it. Aunt Della was shaking like everything. I decided to shut my fool mouth and just get her the hell out of there.

But Sonny wouldn't let it go. "Ellis told me what you did, Taylor. She told me about the morning three years ago when she went looking for Aunt Della and found you there alone, how you tried to get her in bed with you. I intend to settle with you about that, but not in front of Daddy Clark and Aunt Della."

I sighed. "I'm shaking in my boots." I looked at Ellis, and she looked away quickly, her face flushed. So old Ellis had my number, knew I wouldn't tell them the truth, that *she* had been the one to come after me.

"What if I did make a pass at Ellis, Sonny? I was overcome by her charms, her beauty, the passion beneath that plain facade." I grinned at both of them. "Now, let's get the hell out of here, Aunt Della." We began the slow walk to the door.

Daddy Clark sighed loudly. "Stubborn as a mule—you always have been, Della. Well, that's gratitude for you. About what I expected."

I bit my lip to keep from smarting off at him again. All I wanted now was just to get Aunt Della home.

Sonny had gone beyond that point, though. His face furiously red, he turned to Daddy Clark.

"I said Taylor had embarrassed the Clarks all he could, Daddy Clark, but I was wrong. His latest escapade has gotten me where I'm ashamed to show my face in town. Judge Barfield and everybody else at the courthouse was talking about him the other day."

"Gossip." Daddy Clark shook his head. "I've no use for idle gossip. That's all that bunch at the courthouse do all day, anyway—gossip and collect taxpayers' money for doing it."

I grinned at Sonny, unable to resist one last dig. "Guess he told you, old boy."

Sonny turned back to Daddy Clark. "Oh, I can assure you that what they're saying about him is not gossip, Daddy Clark. Just ask Ellis."

I winked at Ellis. "A reliable source there," I said, opening the heavy parlor door.

"Daddy Clark—Taylor has everyone in town talking about him again. He's running around with Maudie Ferguson's niece, Sarah Williams. You know her—Aunt Charlotte's old friend." Sonny's voice was loud and harsh.

Surprising me again, Aunt Della turned in her walker as she was poised to go out the door. She looked right at Sonny, then at Daddy Clark.

"Harris, I hope you can finally see how Sonny has always done all he can to hurt Taylor. Trying to make something out of that! Sarah is a real good friend to Taylor, taking a special interest in him since she knew Charlotte so well. You know better than to listen to such trash."

Daddy Clark shook his head scornfully. "Don't be spreading rumors like that, son," he said to Sonny. "We've had enough—"

But Sonny jumped in rudely. "Ellis saw them! She saw them at the river, fornicating on a blanket. And I admit I wondered myself—then I saw them, too. Right in front of the whole town, in front of poor old Miss Maudie's house. Everybody in Zion County's talking about it, believe you me."

Ellis raised her chin haughtily. "It's the God's truth, Daddy Clark. I swear it."

Aunt Della gasped and turned herself around to face them all. I just sighed and shook my head. Here we go again. Let's crucify Taylor, a favorite game of the Clarks.

"I never heard such filth!" Aunt Della said, taking deep, trembling breaths. "Harris—"

But Daddy Clark had truly had enough now, and he exploded with righteous indignation, his favorite excuse to push everybody around.

"*Enough!*" Par for the course, he turned on me.

"Get out of here, boy. I am sick to death of you and your troublemaking. Will it never end? It doesn't even matter to me whether it's true or not. Frankly, I wouldn't put anything past you, so I don't doubt you fornicating at the river, in broad open daylight, whatever. You're just like your sorry slut of a mother. I want you out of my sight!"

"Harris—" Aunt Della began weakly, trying to take a step forward. Then, right before my eyes, she let out a long breath and slumped. Her head fell forward, her eyes rolled upward, and she lost her grip on the walker. She fell right where she was standing.

"Oh my God! Aunt Della—oh my God!" I grabbed for her. Sonny and Daddy Clark both ran over at the same time, Sonny reaching her first and grabbing for her futilely. I was able to keep her from hitting the floor by falling myself, cushioning her blow with my body, the walker and Aunt Della on top of me.

"Call the paramedics," I heard Sonny say to Ellis, and saw her run from the room. Daddy Clark and Sonny were able to lift Aunt Della off of me. Then they got her over to the sofa, where they stretched her out flat.

Ellis came running back in, Aunt Opal and Aunt Frances Martha in tow. Aunt Frances Martha shrieked, and Aunt Opal ran out again, saying she'd get some smelling salts or something. "The paramedics are on the way," Ellis said to Daddy Clark.

"Go get me a cool washcloth," I yelled. I saw Aunt Della's eyelids flutter. Her breathing was less ragged now.

Aunt Frances Martha ran out and reappeared with a washcloth, which she threw at me. It was sopping wet; I had to wring it out on the floor before I could wipe Aunt Della's face. She was pale as death, but warm and breathing heavily. As I wiped her face, she flickered her eyes open and looked up at me.

"Taylor . . ." she said faintly, then tried feebly to smile at me. "I'm fine. I just got too hot. I'm fine, honey."

I took both of her hands in mine and looked down at her. The Clark clan stood nervously around the sofa, shuffling back and forth. For once Daddy Clark was not in charge, didn't know what to do with himself. Sonny announced he was going out to watch for the paramedics, but I ignored them all, shut them out.

"You're going to be okay, Aunt Della. I know you are," I said. "I'm going to take care of you. I'll ride with you—we'll just take you in to the clinic and check you out, okay? Okay?"

She nodded, closing her eyes. "That'll be fine, sugar. Just so you go with me."

I held both her hands and squeezed them. "I'll not only go in with you, I'll stay with you from now on. I'm going to stay with you, Aunt Della."

I looked up then at the family, gathered around the sofa. I looked at Daddy Clark, standing at the foot of the sofa, arms folded, trying for a look of Christian concern on his stern bulldog face. He probably was pissed at Aunt Della for scaring him like that. Then I looked at Sonny and Ellis, standing next to him, Sonny's arms tightly around his new bride, both looking truly frightened. Aunt Frances Martha was at the door, peeping in, looking both horrified and thrilled at the sudden excitement.

"I'm going to stay with Aunt Della," I said loudly to all of them, and to no one in particular. "I'm not going back to Louisiana. I can transfer over here, be with her. That's what I'm going to do."

And I didn't wait for their reaction, because I really didn't give a shit what any of them thought. I knew with a certainty that's what I had to do, regardless. I couldn't let Aunt Della down now. Maybe this was my chance to redeem myself for all my screwups in the past, who knows? All I knew was, it was the right thing to do, for me. And for her.

The ambulance driver stopped at the end of Preacher Street, before pulling out on the Columbus Highway. They weren't in a rush, having decided from preliminaries that Aunt Della wasn't as bad as it appeared; she'd probably just fainted, gotten upset over the argument and passed out. But as a precaution, we were taking her to the clinic so that her doctor could check her out thoroughly, make sure she hadn't had a stroke.

Stopped as we were by the highway, we were right across from Essie Kennedy's old place, the house where Tim and Donnette now lived. Donnette had taken over her aunt's beauty shop so Aunt Della had told me. She was mostly supporting herself and Tim, though he also worked some at the lumber mill for Jack Floyd, Uncle Cleve's brother.

From the ambulance window in back, I looked at the big old white house. It needed painting, especially around the porch. I could see Donnette's beauty shop, a picture window reflecting the movement of figures inside, though I couldn't make out who they were. Someone pressed against the glass, trying to see who was in the ambulance, I guess.

So this is how Tim had ended up.

An unbearable pain, sharp in my chest, swept over me. Oh Jesus! How would I ever live in this town, seeing his house every day as I passed by, riding to the university? How could I stand it knowing Tim was there, in that shabby house, supported by his wife as he limped through his life, never able to do anything else, working part-time at the lumber mill, helping out at the high school?

Just as the ambulance pulled past the house and toward the highway, I saw the sign. It had been in front of me the whole time, of course. It was right in my line of vision as I looked at the house, but I'd not really noticed it, seeing only that it said "Making Waves" and advertised the beauty shop.

I saw the town of Clarksville, painted all around the edges of the sign—painted by a true artist, an incredible sight in these parts. It was unbelievably good, I realized with a shock, my mind going back to the art appreciation class I'd had as a freshman, the long hours spent in the museums of New Orleans.

Astonished, I suddenly realized the source—I could see it plain as day. Tenth grade, one day in study hall. I borrowed Tim's notebook to copy his notes, and everything spilled out from the back pocket—all the pictures he'd drawn. Incredible pictures. I'd marveled at them, sketches of the football team, the high school, Donnette, me—but Tim had angrily yanked them away from me and refused to let me see them again, or talk about them. No matter how I bugged him, he never let me mention them again.

Tim had drawn the town of Clarksville on that sign. I knew it as sure as I'd ever known anything.

I glanced down at Aunt Della. She had dozed off, worn out from the confrontation and the excitement, no doubt. Wearily, I rubbed my eyes as we pulled onto the Columbus Highway, toward the clinic. I watched out the window as the sign grew smaller in the distance. My eyes began to burn and I blinked back tears, glancing again down at Aunt Della. Oh, Jesus Christ.

Wake up, Aunt Della, and pray to your Jesus for me. Pray that somehow I'm going to be able to stand this—that somehow, some way, I can make it up to Tim for my part in screwing up his life.

Donnette

When I looked out my beauty shop window and saw that Sarah Williams woman standing in my front yard looking at the new sign, I like to have died. I was doing Miss Edna Earl Andrews's hair, and I was so startled that I spilled White Minx toner all down her back. "Oh, Mrs. Andrews! I'm so sorry!" I quickly jumped to get another towel, and when I did, I knocked over the tray of hair rollers that I had by the sink. I was that flustered.

Miss Edna Earl kind of glared at me. She grabbed the towel from my hand and began wiping the toner off herself. I could tell she was really pissed. She's not the friendliest woman in town anyway. Aunt Essie used to shake her head whenever she looked at the appointment book and saw Edna Earl Andrews's name written there. "Here comes Miss Trouble," she'd sigh. Daddy always said wherever an Andrews was, trouble would follow. Of course Miss Edna Earl was only an Andrews by marriage, but that didn't matter; she acted like them anyway. Always bad-mouthing folks and finding fault, eager to look on the bad side of everything—that's an Andrews for you.

Miss Edna Earl was back again this morning because she pitched a damn Andrews fit the other day when I gave her a perm and then the color wouldn't take on it. Never does on a fresh perm, but no, you can't tell her nothing. So I told her to wait a week or two and we'd try the color again. I didn't want to because it was bound to damage her hair, but she wouldn't listen to me. Oh well, at least her hair would match her brain.

I wouldn't have been so thrown off course by seeing Sarah Williams standing in my front yard staring at my sign if anybody but Miss Edna Earl had been in the shop. I tried to hurry and get her rolled up in case Sarah came in here. Well, surely she wouldn't, but in case she did, I didn't want an Andrews sitting there soaking it all in.

Miss Edna Earl was griping as I rolled up her hair. "I swear, Donnette, you are as rough and clumsy as Essie used to be! Not only that, I couldn't do a thing with my hair the way you fixed it last time." And on and on she went.

I kept nodding "Yes, ma'am" polite as all get-out, because I was raised that way, but in my mind I was wishing the old witch would shut up. My hands were shaking like everything so I probably was clumsier than usual this morning. I kept glancing out the window and trying to figure out what on earth Sarah Williams was doing out there. She sure was looking hard at my sign.

I couldn't help but picture her and Taylor together, after what Ellis told me the other day. I knew there were women like her, older women, who go for younger men. But Taylor Dupree! That was beyond my comprehension. Then suddenly it dawned on me, fool that I am. I was so flabbergasted I almost yanked Miss Edna Earl's head off.

"Owww!" she yelled at me, practically coming out of the seat, rollers and all. "Dammit, Donnette, I swear to God if you do that one more time I'm *never* coming back to you again! I've been wanting to try out that new shop at the mall in Columbus, but naturally under the circumstances I wanted to help you and that poor deformed husband of yours—"

I began apologizing hard as I could to Miss Edna Earl, trying my best to get her to shut her face, because now I could see out of the corner of my eye that Sarah Williams *was* coming up the walkway. I knew plain as day she was coming to talk to me about Tim, that Taylor had put her up to it.

"Oh, Miss Edna Earl, I am so sorry—I'm just nervous today. I don't know what is wrong with me—" I blabbered on as I hurried to get her under the dryer.

She was still squawking like a wet hen when I pulled down the dryer top and shut her mouth finally. In disgust she picked up a *Glamour* magazine and flipped it open. But as I started back to the sink, she lifted the dryer to get in one last word.

"You better thank your lucky stars I'm not the kind of person who goes all around town complaining—you'd lose every customer you got. Then where would you be, with an invalid husband to support?"

I'd barely gotten back to the sink when the door opened and Sarah Williams walked in. I stared at her, not believing my eyes that she'd come in here like this. But it did stand to reason that if she'd taken up with Taylor, she'd want to patch things up between him and Tim, to get on his good side.

Sarah was the kind of woman who's sort of pretty and sort of plain. Frankly, I didn't see what all the fuss was about, why all the men in town were slobbering all over themselves because of her. I had called Dink the night before to try and talk to him like I promised Ellis. Sure enough, he wouldn't listen to me; instead all he could talk about was this good-looking woman who'd been coming into the Zippy Mart with Taylor Dupree. Some men will chase anything with a skirt on. Look at Dink, after that plain church-mouse Glenda Rountree.

"Good morning," I said to Sarah Williams as she came into the shop. I pretended I didn't know who she was, as though everybody in town wasn't talking about her and Taylor! But I wasn't going to let on one bit.

"Good morning." She smiled at me, looking kind of curious. She wasn't any bigger than a minute and was dressed in a pair of cutoff blue jeans and an FSU tee shirt. I could tell she didn't have a bra on, and she don't have near as much as I do. Her body's small and trim, like she exercises a lot. Her dark blond hair was pulled back into a ponytail, and she didn't have on a bit of makeup. Lord, there wasn't nothing to her after all! If she'd get that hair frosted and a makeup palette of some peach and gold shades, then she'd be a knockout.

"Are you Donnette Sullivan?" She smiled at me again, coming on over by the dryer. She smelled nice, like some kind of sweet flower. Maybe a gardenia. But I knew what she was here for, and I was on my toes. I wasn't gonna be taken in by no sweet-smelling perfume or friendly smile.

"That's me. What do you need done? Looks to me like you could use a conditioner." I glanced up at her while I cleaned the brushes in the sink, nonchalant-like.

"Donnette. I've heard about you but haven't met you yet. I'm Maudie Ferguson's niece, Sarah Williams." She still was smiling friendly as everything, but I wasn't fooled.

"Oh, yeah. I remember hearing that you were here." No point in having her think I wasn't very bright. Surely she knew everybody was talking about her.

She looked at me kind of knowingly. Her eyes were an odd color, a sort of golden green. With just a little jade eyeliner and a touch of gold shadow—I looked back quickly to the sink.

"I got an opening now if you want to get that conditioner," I told her.

I knew she hadn't come for no appointment, but to my surprise she reached back and pulled the rubber band off her ponytail, shaking her hair out. I was astonished. Her hair was beautiful, thick and heavy as it swirled about her shoulders.

"Sounds great. Maybe you could give me a trim, too, while you're at it."

Well, before I could get her seated at the sink, Miss Edna

Earl threw the dryer top up and stared at us suspiciously. I'd forgotten the old hag was even over there, which was always a mistake with an Andrews.

"Donnette! I need you to check my hair this very minute. And I specifically asked for a time when no one else would be here so you could get my hair right this time."

Her fat face was shaking, she was so mad. She glared at me and Sarah Williams both.

"By all means, Donnette, attend to her first," Sarah told me. She seated herself at the sink and proceeded to brush out her hair.

"She ain't ready; she just got under the dryer," I whispered. But I went over anyway and loosened a curl and checked it. Still wet, just as I knew it'd be. At least the toner took, though.

"You're not quite ready, Miss Edna Earl. Don't you want me to get you a Coke or something from the drink machine?"

Miss Edna Earl never looked at me; she was staring like everything at Sarah Williams.

"Who is that woman?" she said, loud. I was embarrassed to death.

It didn't seem to faze Sarah, but I noticed she acted different with Miss Edna Earl; she seemed more dignified, more like a professor when she turned and looked at her. I could tell Miss Edna Earl wasn't going to rattle her.

"I'm Maudie Ferguson's niece from Florida, Sarah Williams. I believe we met at the funeral home the other night, Mrs. Andrews."

Miss Edna Earl stared at Sarah suspiciously. "I thought Maudie's niece was a doctor. You sure look different than you did at the funeral home."

"I normally don't dress for a funeral every day, Mrs. Andrews," Sarah drawled, turning back to the mirror.

Miss Edna Earl's narrow little pig eyes took in the shorts and tee shirt and sandals. She even went so far as to pick up her glasses and put them on and stare harder. But it still didn't faze Sarah a bit. Hand it to her, she was a cool one.

I hurriedly stuck Miss Edna Earl back under the dryer and went back to the sink, but Miss Edna Earl kept her glasses on and continued to stare. I knew for sure that we'd be hearing from her again.

"I can come back later if you want me to," Sarah said to me.

I quickly shampooed and applied conditioner to her hair so I could get her out. The whole situation was making me more and more nervous, like a long-tailed cat in a room full of rockers. I definitely wanted Sarah out before Tim came home for lunch.

"No, no. Don't pay Miss Edna Earl no mind, she's always like that."

"Occupational hazard, huh?" Sarah smiled, her eyes meeting mine in the mirror. I noticed she had smile lines around her eyes and mouth, but that was all. Her skin, like the rest of her, was firm and tight. And she was very tanned from living in Florida, I reckon. Either that or sunbathing half-naked with Taylor down by the river. I shuddered to think of it.

As I was toweling her hair, Sarah's eyes again locked into mine in the mirror. "Donnette, I didn't really come to get my hair done today. Actually, I came to meet you. I'd really like to talk to you."

I combed through her hair carefully. It was shoulder-length and had so much body. It made me feel all stringy-headed with my permed curls going ever which a way. What I wouldn't do for nice thick hair like this!

"I can't imagine what you would have to talk to me about," I lied. "Do you just want the ends trimmed?"

I wasn't kidding about being surprised at her being here. If she was here on Taylor's behalf, looks like she'd be a little more subtle. Maybe that's the way they do things in Florida.

"Yes, please, just the ends." Sarah relaxed in the chair and I began to snip away. "Donnette, I want to talk to you about your husband, Tim."

Well, it all happened at once—Miss Edna Earl threw back the dryer top, and I dropped the scissors, but not before cutting a big gap in Sarah's hair.

"My God," cried Miss Edna Earl, loud as you please. "You cut a hole in that woman's hair, Donnette! She's gonna sue you for sure!"

I got so flustered I was about to cry. I reached down and picked up the scissors and Sarah grabbed the place I gapped. Miss Edna Earl made matters that much worse by saying over and over, "Oh, my God, look at her hair!"

To my relief, though, Sarah Williams tossed her head lightly. "It's no big deal, Donnette. Just cut it a little shorter. It'll be okay. The ends were split anyway."

"Just a minute," I managed to say, swallowing hard, fighting tears. I had to get Miss Edna Earl out of here if it was the last thing I did. She was going to make me have a nervous breakdown. "Let me comb Miss Edna Earl out."

I finally managed to get Miss Edna Earl combed out, and out the door, but not before she like to have broke her neck staring at Sarah, muttering to herself the whole time. She kept saying things like "disgraceful" and "old enough to be his mama," and "no brassiere on," and I kept talking real loud to her so that Sarah wouldn't hear her. But she did, I know. Miss Edna Earl didn't even try to keep her voice down. Daddy used to say she must have learned to whisper in a sawmill.

I breathed a sigh of relief when Miss Edna Earl finally left, but I still had to face Sarah. I went back over to her and held the scissors firmly this time.

"Now. What do you want with Tim?" I have to hand it to her for being one cool cookie; she didn't flinch a bit as I finished trimming up her hair, just like I hadn't even gapped it. But I fixed it up fine, and I had to admit it looked even better when I finished.

"What do you think I want, Donnette?" she floored me by asking. There was a hint of a smile about her mouth and a twinkle in her strange gold-green eyes.

I turned red as a beet, and stammered, "Well—I mean, I just can't imagine—" I grabbed the blow dryer and began to dry her hair quickly. It didn't take but a minute, then Sarah looked at me, real serious-like.

"Donnette, I understand that your husband, Tim, painted that sign hanging in front of your shop," she said.

"He sure did. But how did you know that?"

She shrugged. "You know Clarksville better than that. *Everybody* is talking about it. I heard it in the post office, then again in the drugstore yesterday."

"What are people saying?" I couldn't help but ask. I hated to think about everybody talking about Tim again, after all the talk was finally dying down about the accident.

"Well, as you know, Mary Sullivan at the post office is Tim's cousin. She told me he used to draw all the time, until he started playing football, then he quit. She was glad to know that he could use his right hand now."

When I didn't say anything in response, Sarah fluffed her hair around with her hands and eyed me curiously. "Donnette, can we sit down somewhere and have a Coke or cup of coffee and talk?"

I was determined I wasn't going to take her into the kitchen because Tim would be coming in for lunch any time now. But we could go in Aunt Essie's front parlor. Tim and me never used it, but Aunt Essie had it fixed up real nice because she used to have the missionary society and the study club meetings there.

"Yeah, let's go into the house a minute. I'm finished in here until two."

Sarah reached deep down in her shorts pocket to pay me, then we left the shop and went into the front parlor. I got us a Coke out of the drink machine, and we sat side by side on a stiff old brocade sofa. It was dusty and smelled moldy in there, but at least it was dark and cool.

"Donnette, the sign that Tim painted is unbelievable. He has some real raw talent," Sarah said to me, turning the Coke bottle up to her mouth and downing about half of it.

He has some talent in ways you ain't going to find out about, I thought to myself. I guess she figured if she buttered me up enough, I'd be willing to talk with her about Taylor, talk Tim into a reconciliation with him.

"I'd really like to see some of his other stuff," Sarah said, bold as you please. I was so floored that my mouth flew open. Oh, I just bet you would!

She was looking at me kind of funny. "Do you think that can be arranged?"

Well, I've never in my life! I'd heard about those kinds of arrangements, but I never imagined I'd know anyone who did things like that. So that's what she came here for, I thought, and me imagining she wanted to get Tim and Taylor back together. Instead, she was after Tim herself, going for younger men like she does.

I couldn't say a thing. I knew I was staring at her as though my eyes were going to pop out, but I couldn't help it. She smiled at me and leaned back on the sofa. "If you'd rather, I could talk to Tim about this myself. I just thought we could have a nice preliminary talk, woman to woman—"

"Oh, no. Please don't say anything to Tim!"

I know Tim. Bless his heart, he's so naive, he was liable to agree with anything she said, not having any idea what she was talking about. Tim hasn't been around like I have.

Sarah was still looking at me real strange-like. Maybe she was realizing that I had her number, I thought. "Donnette—" she began. She reached over and put a slim tanned hand on my arm and I jumped.

Before another word could be said between us, the front door creaked open.

I think we both were startled by the creaking door, but me especially. And who should be standing there but Tim! My heart went into my throat. But old Sarah didn't flinch a bit. She leaned back on the sofa and smiled right up at him.

"Well!" she said. "This must be Tim."

I jumped up from the sofa and grabbed his hand, hard. "Tim, this is Dr. Sarah Williams. You know, Miss Maudie's niece from Florida."

"For heaven's sake, Donnette, please call me Sarah. It's so nice to meet you, Tim. I've heard a lot about you since I've been in Clarksville." She held her hand out to him. Tim greeted her politely and shook her hand, and I watched her looking him over from head to toe. I just bet he'd heard all about her, too.

I began to pull Tim toward the door. "You'll have to excuse us now, Sarah. Tim has to have his lunch and get back to work."

Tim looked at me, astonished. I knew he didn't have to work this afternoon, and he knew I knew it. Before he could open his mouth, I yanked on him again. But not in time to stop Sarah Williams.

"Tim, I was telling your wife how much I like the sign that you painted for her shop," she said.

She was really giving him the once-over. Tim stopped and looked at her too. He had to pull on my hand to get me to turn loose of him.

"Thank you," he said, blushing, but he kept looking right at her. There was something about her that kind of drew you to her, as I'd discovered.

"I had not heard that you were talented in art, Tim." Sarah smiled at him ever so sweetly. "Everything I've heard about you has to do with your athletic abilities."

Tim smiled and looked down at his feet. He scuffed around

a bit, then shrugged. "Tell you the truth, when I was little, all I ever wanted to do was draw. But the football coach saw me playing in P.E. one day, throwing a ball, and he got me interested in training to be his quarterback. Only thing was, I had to give up everything else."

Oh, God, I sure didn't want them talking about football, get Tim all moody again, after he'd been doing so well lately. "Tim, come on, honey. Let's go get your lunch. Sarah will excuse us, I'm sure," I said, smiling, phony as all get-out.

"Donnette!" Tim looked down at me and raised his eyebrows. I knew he was surprised at my rudeness, knowing I was raised better. "Dr. Williams—er, Sarah—is visiting us right now."

"Please, don't let me keep you from your lunch, Tim," Sarah said. "I would like to talk to you sometime, though." Still cool as a cucumber.

"I ain't got to eat right now," Tim said, and I'll be, if he didn't just sit right down there across from her, as big as you please. Oh, I was going to kill him later!

I forgot about Sarah being a college professor and plenty smart, so I let her pull one on me. She sure thought fast and handled things smooth, hand it to her. I was astonished at what she came up with so quickly to cover her motives, pretend she didn't come here to look Tim over, see if he was going to be next on her hit list.

"Tim, you remember my aunt, I know. You were one of her students, weren't you?" Sarah leaned forward and looked right into his eyes. I noticed Tim didn't take his eyes off her the whole time she was talking, like he was hypnotized by her or something.

"Yes, ma'am. Miss Maudie taught me in third grade."

"Oh, God, don't say ma'am to me—you make me feel a hundred years old," she laughed. "So Aunt Maudie did teach you—wonderful." Sarah took another sip of her Coke and looked at both of us. There was nothing for me to do but wait this out.

"I'll bet Aunt Maudie encouraged your art, didn't she, Tim? She always tried to bring out the creativity in her students."

"Yes, ma'am—I mean, yes, she sure did. Actually, she was the one who first saw some of my drawings. She gave me a paint set for Christmas that year, and taught me how to use it."

Sarah beamed at that. At this time, I didn't know what she was concocting—I thought she was just making small talk while she looked Tim over. There was no way I could stop that, but one thing I sure as hell could stop—she wasn't going to get her greedy hands on him. I'd beat out tougher competition than her, plenty of times. Even with him laying half-dead in the hospital, the nurses were always pawing all over him, young ones and old ones both. Tim has that effect on women. But I put a stop to that right off the bat.

"Perfect, Tim." Sarah smiled. Somehow she managed to turn the Coke bottle up to her lips, finish it off, and still not take her eyes off him.

"Let me just go ahead and tell you what I'm getting at, Tim. Last year, about this time, Aunt Maudie called me from the nursing home and asked me to come up and see her, that she had something important she wanted to talk to me about. Her mind was still clear then; that was before she had that last stroke. Anyway, she had some very explicit instructions for me."

She stopped her telling long enough to look carefully at each of us, to make sure we were following her, I guess. Then she continued.

"Aunt Maudie didn't have much money, but she did have a dream. She decided she wanted what little money she left behind to go toward creating a scholarship for someone here, in Zion County. A graduate of this school system. She wanted me to help her set it up. Her main specification was that the recipient be one of her former students and that it have something to do with the humanities, especially the creative arts, since that was what she treasured so all her life."

Well, I had to hand it to her. It was pretty damn clever to use that scholarship thing to worm her way into Tim's good graces, ask him to help her find someone, maybe. Give her a chance to be around him a lot. I'd have bet anything that's what she was up to!

But then Sarah Williams surprised me even more. She leaned over toward Tim and looked him right in the eyes.

"Tim, if you should choose to pursue your talent in art, there is no doubt in my mind that *you* could get that scholarship. No doubt at all."

I looked at Tim, astonished, and I could tell that he was floored, too. He sat there for a minute, staring at her, then he just shook his head.

"I don't know what to say," was all he could manage.

Sarah stood up then to go. She walked over to Tim and stood right in front of his chair so that he had no choice but to look right up at her. Reaching over, she touched his arm gently with her long tanned fingers, like she'd touched me a minute ago. What a touchy-feely woman she was.

"You don't need to say anything right now, Tim. What you need to do instead is think this over. Think about it *very* carefully. On something this important, you shouldn't make a quick decision, but you should weigh all your options. Think about it, and discuss it with Donnette. And we'll talk again, okay? I'm going to be around a few more days, getting everything settled. I hadn't planned on moving this quickly on the scholarship, actually; I'd planned on waiting until next year. But no reason not to have this settled before the university starts in a couple of weeks, now that I've found the ideal candidate. I'll be back in touch with you."

She took her hand off his arm, finally, then she turned to me, smiling sweetly. "Donnette, it was so nice to meet you. I'll be talking with you again soon, okay? Thanks for the haircut."

And without another word she was gone, leaving me and

Tim sitting there in that musty old parlor, staring at each other, astonished.

If me and Tim had gotten a chance to talk about Sarah Williams's suggestion right then and there, things might have turned out different. Guess I'll never know that for sure. But just as Tim looked at me, shook his head and said, "Damn—what do you think?" there was a loud pounding on the back door.

Both of us jumped out of our skins, then got up together to go to the kitchen and see who it was. I got to the door first and opened it. Somehow it seemed like Providence that Coach Mills should be standing there, since he was the man who turned Tim's life in another direction when Tim was so young.

"Donnette—you sweet thing! You're looking mighty fine, hon," he grinned. Coach didn't wait for an invitation, just pushed his way right on into the kitchen. He saw Tim and his face lit up.

"My lucky day—I just ran to the post office and thought I'd stop and see if I might catch you in, son. Reckon we could talk a minute?"

"Sure, Coach," Tim said, flustered. Everybody after him all of a sudden, it seemed. "Want to have a seat?"

"You ate your lunch yet?" Coach Mills asked Tim, but reached over and pulled me to him, sneaking in a feel in the process. "Or did I catch you two up to something else?" He leered, shifting the wad of tobacco in his jaw.

"No, sir. We were about to eat. You want to join us?" Tim said, and I wiggled out of Coach's embrace. His hand lingered a minute on my bottom before he let me go.

"Tell you what," he said, turning his attention back to Tim. "Let me take you out, son, get us a hamburger. I want to talk with you about Tommy. Big game coming up Friday night, as you know, and Tommy's got the shakes, bad. I need you, Tim."

As had happened so often in the past, before Tim and I could talk or anything, Coach Mills took him away. When they went out the door, Coach looked over his shoulder, winked broadly at me and said with his dirty grin, "Honey pie, you keep it hot while we're out talking man-talk, you hear? I may keep Tim out late. If I can talk him into staying for practice, I believe we can get old Tommy-boy straightened out." And he ruffled Tim's hair as they went out the door, slamming it practically in my face.

I hated to see Tim get so tightly back into Coach Mills's clutches again! First Sarah Williams and now Coach. Tim told me the other night that when he told Coach he'd been cut back at the lumberyard, Coach had promised to see if he could get Tim a little extra pay from the school board for helping some with the football team during season, now that Tim was able. Bless his heart, Tim seemed so excited about that prospect. I couldn't help it; I had a thought that made me feel so guilty that I put it right out of my mind. I couldn't help but think that, in spite of the horror of the accident, having Tim all to myself these two years had been good. So very good, in spite of everything.

Much later that night I lay in Tim's arms in our big old four-poster bed in Aunt Essie's front bedroom. It was a beautiful night; the moon was almost full and so bright you could see silvery shadows outside. The night air was not as hot and heavy as it had been; there was a hint of the coolness of autumn. And there was a breeze, too. The sheer curtains lifted softly in the white moonlight shining through them.

Tim was almost asleep; our coming together tonight had been quick as a flash. He seemed surprised at first at my eagerness for him. It was almost like I felt I had to hold on to him so tightly he'd never let go of me. Images of Taylor and Coach and Sarah Williams all played on my mind as I waited for him in that dark, moonlit bedroom. When he finally slipped into bed beside me, coming in late from football practice, I was almost frantic with wanting him. He only laughed soft-like as he held me close to him.

"Tim?" I whispered afterwards into his chest. His good arm he kept around my shoulders, but I knew he was drifting into sleep as I felt his grip begin to relax. "Did everything go well at practice?"

"Um," was all he could manage to murmur. I hated to pester him, but we hadn't had a chance to talk yet.

"Tim. Do you want to talk? About Tommy, or Coach, or—anything else?" I whispered.

"No. I want you to shut up so I can go to sleep," he muttered. His eyes were closed and I noticed how innocent and young he looked all sleepy. I brushed away the lock of hair that always fell over his forehead.

"What about Sarah Williams?" I just couldn't go to sleep without asking.

"Donnette," he said, then sighed and pulled the pillow halfway over his face, "let's *please* just go to sleep now."

"Tim!"

"Okay. Sarah Williams is one good-looking old lady. Now can I go to sleep?" he asked from under the pillow.

"That ain't what I meant and you know it." I was wide awake now, but he wasn't. And he'd turned his back on me.

"And I don't think she's so pretty, myself. She don't wear hardly any makeup, fix herself up. You know what I'm asking you about—that scholarship thing."

"Donnette, I do not want to talk about that now. We will, but not yet. I haven't had time to think about it."

"Okay. But I want to be in on your thinking, you hear? Don't you do anything or talk to her anymore until me and you talk first."

Tim muttered something incomprehensible under the pillow

and went right on to sleep. I swear, just like a man! If I had something like that hanging over me, I couldn't sleep a wink.

It was a few days later that I learned what I did about that scholarship offer by Sarah Williams, something that made me determined to do everything I could to keep Tim from even thinking about taking it. I'd made up my mind to give Tim some time to himself to think. I was able to turn loose since he seemed to be doing so well and was not all tied up in knots like before.

Personally I didn't think Tim had an ounce of desire to be an artist. Why, the idea was near-bout funny to me! Artists are weird people with crazy lives, not ordinary folks like Tim. I've never known any artists, actually, but I've seen TV shows about them. I just didn't think Tim had any business trying to do something like that. But, I'd made up my mind to let that be *his* decision; that is, until old Sarah let the cat out of the bag and I got her number good and proper.

I may have been content to let Tim have some time on his own to mull over the idea of the scholarship, but evidently Sarah Williams was not. If I wanted proof that she was only doing this to try and get her paws on him, I soon had it. Even though she had said she'd leave him alone while he thought about it, she just happened to run into him only a couple of days later. Supposively she went out to the lumberyard to get Jack to cut her some two-by-fours for something she was fixing up in Miss Maudie's house. A cousin of theirs from way out in the sticks had bought the house and was moving in once Sarah got it all fixed up, or so everybody said. Some senile old lady who couldn't do the fixing herself, or some such story. Sounded pretty fishy to me. Made me wonder if Sarah didn't want an excuse to hang around Taylor longer. But anyway, when Tim told me about Sarah's visit to the lumberyard, I was furious. Oh, I never let on to him, but I was mad as hell. The very idea of her going out there looking for Tim!

"Sarah asked me if I'd thought about the scholarship," Tim said to me.

We'd just gotten home from church that Sunday and were changing out of our Sunday clothes. I pretended to be only casually interested, but actually I was steaming.

"So, what did you say?" I asked him as I wadded my slip up and tossed it in a drawer. I should have cut her throat instead of her hair, I was thinking.

Tim didn't say anything. He undressed and hung his Sunday suit up. Then he put on some jeans and a tee shirt. It took him forever to dress now, but at least he didn't need anyone to help him anymore. He hated that.

"Well. I ain't never thought about doing anything in art," was all he said. Just as I thought.

"She did say," he added as he tied on his tennis shoes, "that I could teach art to kids, if I got in the right program. I kinda like that idea. But . . . I just don't know."

Tim finished dressing and started out the bedroom door. He always visited his brothers on Sunday afternoons. Since his daddy died, he was the only father those boys had. He stopped at the door and glanced at me, then looked down kind of sad-like.

"Guess I just never figured on having another chance at a scholarship," he said, and then he went on out the door.

For a moment I felt a lump in my throat and my eyes stung. I then remembered Sarah Williams going out to the lumberyard, trying to talk him into this idea, and anger replaced the sadness. I was sure Taylor had told her all about the accident and the death of all of Tim's dreams. That made it downright cruel for her to be prissing around here, talking to Tim about another scholarship. It would do nothing but bring up all that mess again, the last thing on earth I wanted. I was going to have a little talk with old Dr. Williams myself, tell her a thing or two.

. . .

As it turns out, I had a legitimate excuse to go to Miss Maudie's house that afternoon. Otherwise, I'd probably have lost my nerve.

I'd cornered Ellis after church, trying to find out what she'd heard about Taylor. I was not a bit surprised to hear that he was going to stay a couple of more weeks until his school started back. Supposively he was trying to line someone up to stay with Miss Della or something like that. Ellis was sure he was just trying to keep Miss Della out of the nursing home to prevent her and Sonny from getting her house. Evidently the house is willed to Mr. Harris, but it's Miss Della's as long as she lives or something. I have to admit I wasn't paying that much attention to Ellis. Seems like she's gotten a little greedy. First, all she wanted was Sonny and the Clark name, and now she's got her heart set on that house.

Anyhow, when Ellis was telling me about Taylor, she told me about how much time he was spending with Sarah Williams, supposively helping her fix up Miss Maudie's place. She also told me that he and Sarah had been having an estate sale from there, getting rid of some of Miss Maudie's junk. I decided that would be the perfect excuse for me to go and see Sarah. If I got to the house and Taylor was there, I'd leave. But if I caught Sarah Williams alone, I planned to tell her to stick with Taylor Dupree and leave me and Tim alone.

It turned out I was in luck when I got to Miss Maudie's house—I caught Sarah alone. I thought no one was home at first, she took so long coming to the door. And then she was half-dressed, wearing only a pair of shorts and a halter top. I swear if I was as flat-chested as that woman, I wouldn't go around advertising it. I'd get me a good Maidenform instead.

Sarah was all tousle-headed and sleepy-eyed when she opened the door for me, so I knew she'd been napping, though she denied it. Unless, of course . . . I tried not to let her see me glancing around, but I wondered if she had some man hidden back in the bedrooms. Probably only Taylor. Or maybe even Dink, since he was so interested. At least I knew where Tim was.

"Oh—it's you, Donnette," she said sleepily. "Come on in."

At first I played it real cool. "Sarah, I heard you're selling some of Miss Maudie's things. So I thought I'd look around, if that's all right with you."

I followed her into the parlor, and then she turned to me.

"I wish you'd said something earlier, Donnette. I think it's about all gone." She rubbed her eyes, and her voice was husky. I wanted to ask her if she'd had a rough night.

"Anything in particular you're looking for? I had lots of furniture earlier this week," she said.

I hadn't planned on her asking me that, so I had to think fast. "Uh—mirrors. Mirrors I can use in the shop."

She looked around the dim parlor. The drapes were pulled and it smelled funny. I swear, though, it looked just like Miss Maudie. Everything appeared to be a hundred years old. There wasn't any vases or whatnots left, just furniture, but there was one huge old mirror over the mantel. Sarah pointed to it.

"I don't know if you'd be interested in this one or not. I believe it's the only mirror left." It was a big old ugly thing with a dark wood frame. But I pretended to inspect it. Sarah and I looked wavy and speckled in its reflection.

"Um. Pretty nice mirror," I said as I scraped at a bad place on it with my fingernail. "I like it."

Sarah frowned. "Well—if you're sure. It's pretty ghastly to me. It's so heavy you'd have to send Tim over to see if he can lift it before you got it."

"I don't believe I like it after all." Just her mentioning Tim made me mad again. I folded my arms and looked at her, and she looked curiously back at me.

"You didn't really come to see mirrors, did you, Donnette?" she asked me with a little smile.

"No. I reckon you know why I came." I didn't feel quite so

mad now that I was face to face with her, but I still was determined to tell her to bug off.

Sarah chewed on her lower lip while she studied me. "Tell you what. I planned to walk over to the cemetery this afternoon, check on Aunt Maudie's grave. Why don't you and I walk over there together so we can talk?"

So Sarah and I ended up walking all the way out Cemetery Street to the graveyard. I guessed right when I first saw her that she was a jogger; she changed to nylon running shorts and Reeboks.

We had a good brisk walk out there since it wasn't so hot that afternoon. Matter of fact, it was clouding up like it might rain. We didn't see a single soul as we walked. Everybody in Clarksville reads the Sunday paper and then naps on Sunday afternoons, resting up between morning and evening church services.

Sarah and me both were somewhat winded when we got over to the little corner section of the cemetery where Miss Maudie was buried, and both of us stood taking deep breaths and looking around. Miss Maudie's grave was nothing now but a big mound of red clay. The casket wreath of red roses lay on top of it. Sarah bent over and began pulling dead flowers off the wreaths and straightening up the stands that'd fallen over.

"I'd planned to check on her before now," she told me as she yanked the wilted flowers ruthlessly from the pretty arrangements. "When my ex-husband's father died, kids came out and vandalized the gravesite. I couldn't stand it if anybody did that to Aunt Maudie's."

There was the sound of thunder in the distance, and the smell of rain in the rose-scented air. I stood silent for a minute, then it seemed only natural that I help Sarah pick off some of the dead flowers.

"I was surprised to find out how long it takes for a tombstone to be ready," she remarked as she straightened herself up and stretched like a cat. I pressed the wire frames of the wreaths firmly into the ground so they wouldn't fall over again. I was surprised to turn and see Sarah standing there just looking at me.

"Come on," she said to me. "Let's go find the Clark plot."

She led the way and we found the old graves of the Clarks, but not before stopping and looking at some of the others on the way. It's a big cemetery. Seems like there's a lot more people out there than there are in Clarksville.

I really wasn't that interested in the Clark family graves, and neither was Sarah, as it turned out. Instead, she'd remembered there was a big old magnolia tree on their plot, with a granite bench in the shade under it, and that's why she suggested we go there. We sat side by side on that bench, right across from the grave of Hiram Aldophous and Frances Della Clark, the parents of Miss Della Clark Dean, Taylor's aunt.

"You don't seem particularly bothered by graveyards, Donnette, like a lot of people your age are," Sarah said, looking at the rows of graves spread out as far as we could see from the bench.

I shrugged. "Well, I don't like them all that much, but they don't really bother me. I mean, people get born and then they die."

She smiled at me. "If only it were that simple. It's the stuff in between that causes us so many problems, isn't it?"

"Yeah. But people make their own misery, lots of times." I looked at the graves and realized how very peaceful it was here. I'd never known such a peaceful place.

"Well. Sometimes. But sometimes we have it thrust upon us, as you well know."

We were silent a minute, and then she turned to face me.

"But that's not really what we came to talk about, is it? Why don't you tell me what I'm doing that's bothering you?" she asked.

"I—I appreciate your offer of the scholarship, Sarah, I really do. But I think it'd be better if you didn't talk to Tim anymore about it," I blurted out.

Sarah sat quietly for a minute, looking at me puzzled. I felt uneasy and turned slightly from her, looking at the graves down the hill from us.

"Donnette, I can't understand for the life of me how you can feel that way. Perhaps you can tell me where you're coming from."

I knew she had the right to ask that, but still I resented it. I didn't have to explain anything to her, if I didn't want to. Besides, I wasn't sure I could make her see it from my point of view.

"Well. Let's just say that I think you may have an ulterior motive for telling Tim about that scholarship," I finally said.

Again, she looked puzzled. "What kind of motive?"

But I wouldn't answer her. If she was so smart, she could figure it out herself. Damn if she didn't reach over and put her hand on my arm again. I've never seen anyone who liked to touch people like she does. It took all I could do to not jerk my arm away.

"Donnette, can't you see how gifted Tim is?"

"I know he can draw good—he always could. But he's no artist. Folks around here think drawing and stuff like that's sissy."

Again, she studied me before replying. "I assume that's why Tim never developed his talent, that kind of small-town thinking," she said, rather sharply. "But Donnette, please believe me. I am completely serious about this scholarship for Tim. I'm committed to seeing that he takes it—I certainly hope that you will be, too."

I thought for a minute. In spite of my misgivings, she sounded so sincere I could see that she had a point. "I—I reckon Miss Maudie would have loved to see Tim do this. Sounds like something she'd been tickled about," I admitted.

Sarah nodded and smiled. "Oh, yes. She would have been very pleased to help him develop his talent."

"She always loved Tim. But Tim an artist—I just don't know about that!"

"Donnette, there are any number of things Tim could do with an art degree. Matter of fact, he would probably have to. Most artists can't support themselves strictly with their art. Tim could teach. Don't you think he'd like that?"

I thought of Tim with Tommy, and him working with the other boys on the football team. He'd originally wanted to be a coach, so he'd like teaching. He was sure good working with kids.

"And he could drive over to the university, Donnette. You wouldn't have to uproot, since you're just getting your business established," Sarah continued, so earnestly.

That was true, all right. I wanted to believe that Sarah might be right and that I should give this idea more thought.

"Well?" Sarah said, with a smile. "What do you think?"

"I don't know, Sarah. It—well, it sounds like it might be something good for Tim, maybe."

"Oh, Donnette. If only I could make you see what this would do for Tim. I feel sure that this could be just the thing to help him get over these last two years. I can only imagine how awful it must have been for him, to lose everything like he did in that accident! And how awful it was for you, too." She sounded so sweet and convincing, so concerned.

But wait a minute—something she said made me stop and think: How did she know so much about Tim, and how these last two years had been for him?

I turned and looked at her suspiciously. "How come you know so much about Tim?"

She seemed a little taken back by my question, then it hit me. What a fool I was—what a damn fool! Taylor Dupree put her up to this. Oh, my God, why hadn't I realized that before!

"It's Taylor, ain't it, Sarah?"

"What about Taylor?" She tried to look puzzled.

"Listen, what you and Taylor Dupree do when you get together is none of my business; I don't even want to think about it, much less hear it. But if he is the one—"

"Wait a minute!" Sarah stared at me, grabbing my arm. "What do you mean—what Taylor and I do when we get together?"

"It ain't none of my business."

"Donnette!" Suddenly Sarah put her head down in her hands. "Oh, shit. It's true. Taylor has told me that people here would misinterpret things—guess I've been away from Zion County longer than I realized." She raised her head and looked at me. "What have you heard?"

I felt my face getting hot. "Well—you know—"

Sarah stared at me, astonished. If I didn't know Taylor as well as I did, I could almost believe she was genuinely shocked.

"Donnette, listen to me. I can't help what you choose to believe about this. Taylor is a deeply troubled young man as well as the son of my friend, Charlotte. I've been trying to help him. Can you understand that?"

"Listen yourself. I don't *want* to understand it. I don't want to even hear his name. All I want to know is whether or not Taylor had anything to do with that scholarship offer of yours."

But I knew it. Deep down in me, I knew it. It was Taylor who gave her the idea of making the offer to Tim!

Sarah shook her head. "He has nothing at all to do with the fact that Tim Sullivan is a gifted young man who should be given a chance to do something with his life besides waste away in this hick town!"

We stared at each other. "That's *not* what I asked you, Sarah," I said. "Just tell me that Taylor didn't put you up to this."

"Donnette, don't you love Tim? Don't you want what is best for him here?"

"All I want to know is if Taylor had anything to do with it."

"What possible difference could that make?"

I'd heard enough. I jumped up and started walking like a

madman, getting away from her. I'd gotten almost to the gate when she caught up with me and grabbed my arm.

"Donnette, wait. Don't run away—we need to talk all this out."

"Let go of me! Leave us alone—go back to Florida where you came from, Sarah Williams."

"Come on, Donnette. I'm a therapist; I can help you. You have *got* to talk all of this out—you can't stay in denial the rest of your life." She wouldn't let go of my arm.

"You're Taylor's friend, that's all I need to know," I said. "Well, I'm glad that you can help him, because he sure needs it. He's a crazy son-of-a-bitch who almost ruined Tim's life, that's what he is. And because he's a Clark, he thought he could just walk away and everything would be all right." I was so mad, I was about to cry. "Well, take a good look at Taylor, Sarah. And then take a look at Tim. Tim's crippled, and he will be all of his life. What about Taylor—how does he look to you now?"

"Taylor's crippled, too, Donnette. Emotionally he will always be, because of what happened that night. He didn't run off because he didn't care—he ran off because he couldn't deal with the pain and guilt he experienced. My God—he felt like he'd ruined his best friend's whole life; of course he went crazy. Can't you understand that?"

"*No!* Because I don't care about Taylor—I only care about Tim." I was so upset now I wouldn't even look at her.

"If you care that much about him, you'll see to it that he gets another chance! A chance to make something of his life. Taylor wants that—I'll admit it to you. He's the one who told me about Tim's talent. And then the sign appeared. Don't you see—the sign that he made for you! Donnette, you've *got* to let Tim do this. And you've got to let Taylor do this, too."

"Never. Never."

Again, I started to leave her. I just couldn't listen to any more. But again, Sarah caught up with me, right outside the cemetery gate this time. She stopped me and turned me around to look at her.

"Okay, Donnette. Go on home now. I'm not going to keep chasing you. But there's something here you've got to decide."

She took a deep breath and let go of my arm. We stared at each other, both of us breathing hard after all the running around we were doing.

"This is what you must decide, and only you can do it—do you love Tim enough to forget how much you hate Taylor Dupree? Because if you do, you'll give Tim the chance he deserves to make something of his life. You'll forget about your hatred of Taylor because it's not what's important here anyway."

I jerked away from her, still refusing to hear what she was saying to me. Shaking her head, Sarah turned and walked away, back toward the cemetery, pausing only to throw one more thing at me over her shoulder.

"Think about it, Donnette. You know where to find me if you want to talk."

I stood for a minute watching her, watching her walk back over to her family's plot, and then I turned and began walking home. Lightning flashed suddenly, and it started to rain.

For once, I was glad that Tim was so busy with the football team. They'd lost the game last Friday night against County High, and everybody in town was in mourning, especially Tommy and Coach Mills.

Tim took it real well; he said that Tommy showed some real poise and he thought he could work with him on some ways to improve before the game next Friday night. So I didn't see much of him during the week that followed. I was grateful for the distraction of the game because he didn't mention the scholarship again. He didn't bring it up for a whole week, and neither did I.

But I knew Tim was troubled, and I knew it wasn't about the football game, though I didn't dare say anything to him. I just couldn't. Gone was the relaxed way he'd been since that night we sat on the porch and planned to name the shop; everything had changed since Taylor Dupree came back into town, as I knew it would. It hurt me real bad to see Tim sitting and staring, deep in thought, that tormented expression on his face again. All of a sudden I felt my hopes of things being right vanish right before my eyes, like a puff of wind on a dandelion.

Oh, was I right feeling the way I did the night Tim ran into Taylor at the Catfish Cabin, after thinking he was out of our lives for good! I knew his return would bring nothing but trouble. If only he'd stayed away—oh, God! Things were just getting better when he came back into our lives. Him, and now Sarah Williams, probing around, interfering, telling me what was good for Tim and what wasn't. I wish everybody would just leave us alone!

For the next few days following my talk with Sarah at the cemetery, I went about my business, fixing hair and cooking and cleaning, as though nothing had happened. But it was like I was marking time. I could feel it in the air. It wouldn't be long now before something would happen. I was getting knots in my stomach trying to be all nice and friendly with my customers, and normal with Tim. He was so quiet and moody himself that he didn't even notice me acting this way. I jumped every time the phone rang, or someone came in the shop.

It was Ellis who got me out of the house, finally. Thursday she called me, having a fit for me to go with her to the study club at Mrs. Junkin's house next door.

It was the last thing in the world I wanted to do, and I told her so. Lord, sitting over there with a bunch of blue-haired old ladies, listening to Ima Holliman, the librarian from Mt. Zion, talk about some boring old book! What on earth could Ellis be thinking about? Mrs. Junkin had already invited me, she did every time, and I'd made up some excuse not to go. But this time, Ellis begged me.

"Donnette, please! I don't know all those ladies, but you do—please go with me. And I want to talk to you about Dinky and Glenda, too."

Well, I sure didn't want to get her on that subject again. I thought Glenda Rountree better thank her lucky stars a man like Dink was interested in her. Ellis could be so crazy sometimes. But like a fool, I let her talk me into it. You just can't help but like Ellis, prissy as she can be sometimes. She tries so hard and she wants so bad to make something of herself. So I agreed to meet her that night after supper, at Mrs. Junkin's study club.

I was real surprised that Tim wasn't going to football practice. As a matter of fact, he was acting unusually quiet and strange at supper. He never said a word to me, sopping up rutabagas and pot liquor with the cornbread I'd made just the way he liked it, not carrying on about it like he usually does. Maybe he was more worried about Tommy quarterbacking the team than I'd thought. Of course, it could be that all the publicity Tommy was getting as Tim's brother was bringing the past back to him. I'd had two reporters call me just the week before, wanting to do a story on Tim two years after the accident. What ghouls those people could be! I told them to leave us alone, and I sure didn't tell Tim about them calling me.

You couldn't always tell about Tim. I think I know him so well, but sometimes he can be downright strange.

After supper I got dressed, then went to tell Tim that I was going to the study club. I knew he'd be surprised, because I'd always said I'd never be caught dead going to a prissy ladies' meeting like the garden or study club. Only thing me and Aunt

Essie used to fuss about, when she tried to get me to go to her missionary society.

Tim was in the den. I figured he was watching a ballgame on TV, but no, he was just sitting there in the dark. I turned a lamp on and he almost jumped out of his skin.

Then I saw that he had something in his hand. It was the drawing he'd done for the sign out front. But how could he be looking at it in the dark? I swear, all I needed now was for him to turn weird on me.

"Tim? You okay, honey?"

He shrugged. "I guess."

"You don't sound like it. You want to talk?"

He looked down at the drawing he held in his hand. "No. Not now, hon. I need to think some first, okay? Where you going?"

"Next door. To Mrs. Junkin's study club. Ellis wants me to go with her."

Instead of being surprised, he didn't say anything. He just nodded, and continued to stare down at his hands.

"Okay. What time will you be back?" he asked me, finally.

"I don't know—not late. Why?"

"I may go out."

"To practice?"

"No, they practiced this afternoon. Just walking. I kinda need to think some, by myself."

I didn't like that much, but I didn't let on.

"Okay," I said.

I went over and gave him a light kiss on top of his head, but he still didn't move.

"Well. I'll be home soon. Maybe then you'll feel like talking," I said, smoothing his hair down.

"Maybe."

I was miserable at the study club and I wished to God that I hadn't gone. Walking over to the parsonage, I remembered suddenly that Tim had gotten a phone call that afternoon, and that's when his moodiness really started up, even worse than it had been these last few days. He'd talked so quietly I couldn't tell who he was talking to. I'd asked him if it was Coach, or Tommy but he muttered something and didn't really answer me. Now I wondered. Surely it wasn't Sarah, asking him about that scholarship again. I was worried sick about him, about the whole situation. Something just didn't feel right about it. But I was committed now—I had to go on to this meeting, regardless if something was telling me I should be with Tim instead.

I felt sorry for Ellis; she had dressed fit to kill in a short-skirted silk outfit she'd gotten at Parisian's in Birmingham. Look like she'd know by now that the ladies of Clarksville don't dres up that much, especially for something like the study club. Bles her heart, she really looked ridiculous. And I swear, she wa wearing real diamond drop earrings hanging from her ears! To the study club—she ought to know better.

Soon as I got there, I tried to introduce Ellis to everyone and make her feel comfortable, but the women were all staring at her so hard that it wasn't easy. And of course big-mouth Edna Ear Andrews was there. The first thing we heard her say when we came in was, "Who on earth is that woman with Donnette Sullivan?" I imagine they heard her all the way to Mt. Zion, too.

After speaking to all the old ladies there, and dragging poo Ellis around with me, I watched as they began to select seats in the Junkins' little living room. I realized then that I'd never si through the study club meeting. I kept seeing Tim sitting in th dark, all troubled and torn up. It certainly wasn't like him to go out walking by himself after dark, either. I'd never sit still and listen to a thirty-minute talk on how to decorate your home wit decoupage. I had to get out, right now, before the meeting go under way.

"Ellis!" I grabbed her arm and whispered before she could sea herself in the living room. "Listen, I've got an upset stomach. I've got to go home."

Ellis turned big, over-made-up eyes on me. Now, why didn't she keep her makeup like I'd shown her? Simple blues and greens.

"Wait, Donnette, I've got to tell you something," she whispered back.

"If it's about Dinky and Glenda, then—"

"It's about Taylor."

"What?" Oh, please, God. Let her say that he's gone back to school, I silently prayed.

"I was going to wait and tell you after the meeting, so you wouldn't get upset," she whispered, looking around to see if anyone was listening. My stomach did a flip-flop. "Oh, honey, I hate to have to tell you. But Taylor's going to stay."

Oh, God. "What—what do you mean?"

"Him and Daddy Clark had a big fight yesterday. Hamilton told his granddaddy about Taylor and that floozie Sarah woman, and Daddy Clark like to have had a hissy fit. And it upset Aunt Della so much that she had a spell, scared us all to death. So Taylor told Daddy Clark that he was going to transfer to Alabama, stay here in Clarksville and take care of his Aunt Della." She looked at me sadly. "Oh, Donnette. I hate to have to tell you. Maybe he won't. You know you can't believe anything he says."

I felt tears sting my eyes. I couldn't take this right now. "Listen, Ellis, I'm serious. I'm sick at my stomach. I'm going to leave now, okay? You got to tell Mrs. Junkin for me."

"No! Donnette, please, don't leave me here!"

"I can't help it, Ellis. Please, tell Mrs. Junkin I got a upset stomach, okay? You'll do fine." And I got out of that house before Ellis could say another word in protest.

I slipped out the back door of the Junkin house and started over to our house next door. Just as I got to the back porch steps, something in front caught my eye. I don't even know what made me turn and look, but I did.

A dark figure was walking away from the front of our house and was almost to the Junkins'. From here I could see the lights on in their living room, and through the open windows, I could hear the voices of the women seated in their meeting. The light of a lamp caught the sparkle of Ellis's diamond drop earrings.

At first I thought it was someone going to the meeting, but they hurried past the Junkins' house and down the sidewalk. I realized then that it was Tim. And he wasn't walking slow like he was deep in thought, either. He was going along like he knew exactly where he was headed. When he walked that fast, his limp was much more noticeable.

"Tim!" I called out to him, but an eighteen-wheeler roared by on the Columbus Highway, and he didn't hear me.

"Tim, wait!" I called again, but he was almost to the end of the street by then. Big oak trees hung over the sidewalk and I couldn't half see him for their dark shadows. Without even thinking, I took out after him.

I couldn't catch up with him. I was fixing to call after him again, but something told me not to. Where in the hell could he be going? I wisht to God that I hadn't worn my new heels to that meeting; I could barely walk in them. I hadn't worn any hose, so I reached down to take them off. While I was stopped to do so, I lost Tim.

Barefoot now, my shoes in my hands, I hurried down to the end of Magnolia Street, the next street over from us, and looked around. Nothing ahead of me but the back road to Columbus, the one people use to take before the new highway came through. I knew for sure that Tim wasn't going to be walking the twenty-five miles to Columbus tonight! Besides, there wasn't a thing wrong with his pickup, that I knew of. Tim had been acting strange as all get-out lately, but he had never done nothing thi weird. I got kind of scared then. Maybe he was having some kind of delayed reaction to the car wreck, or a scar on his brain or something. He'd been in a coma for days after the accident.

I looked down Railroad Street to my left—nothing there but rundown houses. I couldn't think of a soul that Tim would be going to see there. At least Sarah and all the other big houses were in the opposite direction, so I knew he wasn't running after her. Then I stepped across to the street on my right, trying to remember what was down there. Not many houses at all. Pleese Davis lived down there, and everybody knows he bootlegs liquor, but Tim hadn't ever touched it. Surely he wasn't turning into an alcoholic now.

Then I remembered where this street eventually led, and I felt like a pure fool. I started walking down it anyway, since I'd come this far. Me and Tim could have a good laugh when I caught up with him, make both of us feel better.

This street wound around the back way to the high school. It came up behind the football stadium! I'd been so worked up that I'd forgotten about football practice tonight.

I stepped carefully around the broken glass on the sidewalk as I made my way down the dark street to the stadium. There were no streetlights here, just the bright moonlight to light the way. I sure felt ridiculous, too. In all my years with Tim, I'd never been so suspicious of him before. Wait until I told him, I thought—it would tickle him good.

The football stadium loomed ahead, unlighted and kind of scary-looking in the white moonlight, and I stopped dead in my tracks. There was no practice here tonight—I remembered plain as day Tim saying they'd practiced this afternoon. The stadium was completely dark and quiet. There was no one here. Oh, but I was wrong again. Dead ahead of me, walking through the back gates, was Tim. Again I started to call out to him and stopped myself. A shiver went over me. What in God's name was he doing here? I was really scared now, thinking that he might be having some kind of nervous breakdown. I even thought of running and getting Sarah Williams—surely she was trained to know what to do. But I didn't; I just stumbled barefoot after Tim as he went into that dark, empty football stadium.

He didn't go far. Just as he got to the bleachers, he stopped. Instinctively I stepped back so that he wouldn't see me. The little concrete locker room for the visiting team was close by, so I stepped over there in its shadow.

Tim couldn't see me, but I could see him plain as day. His hair gleamed in that pale moonlight, and his white tee shirt looked almost silver. He just stood there for a minute, his left hand deep in his jeans pocket, and looked around.

Again I felt kind of foolish. Just because Tim seemed different from the others didn't mean that he didn't like to relive his glory days on the football field. I bet he came out here a lot and thought about the good old days. Nothing really crazy about that. I was sure he would not want me to know, so I began to back out quietly. I wouldn't let on that I'd seen this.

Suddenly someone stood up in the bleachers and walked down to where Tim stood alone. I froze where I was. It was Taylor Dupree.

"Tim," I heard Taylor say softly in that unmistakable voice of his. "Thank you for coming."

Like at their meeting in the Mt. Zion cafe the other night, both of them just stood there and stared at each other. Taylor came down to where Tim was standing in the grass, and he stood in front of him.

Tim was about a head taller than Taylor, and they were both the same lean, muscular build. But other than that, there was no resemblance in them. Tim was pale in the ghostly moonlight with his light hair and tee shirt gleaming. Taylor was as dark as the night. The moon was behind him and his face was in the shadows but Tim's was so clearly outlined that I could see his jaw clench

Then Tim spoke to him. "You ain't changed a bit in two years, Taylor."

Taylor shuffled his feet, but he didn't take his eyes off Tim's face. "I wish I could say the same for you." Taylor then turned and looked out over the empty field. "Thank you for coming, Tim. I really didn't think you would, especially not here."

Tim didn't say anything, and Taylor stuck his hands in the pockets of his faded jeans as he said, "I've gotten to where I come out here a lot at night and just sit. Aunt Della goes to bed early, and I come out here."

"How is your Aunt Della? I heard she wasn't doing well now, that she's been having some kind of spells," Tim said. I could hear Taylor's deep voice plain as day, but Tim's back was to me so I had to lean forward to hear him.

Taylor shook his head. "She's not good. I don't think she'll be around much longer."

"Is that why you came back here, Taylor?" Tim asked him.

It was totally beyond me how that stupid Tim could just stand there talking to Taylor like nothing had happened. And why in God's name did he sneak around like this and meet him? I held my breath as Taylor answered him.

"That was part of it. Tim—could we, I mean, do you want to sit down so we can talk?" His dark hair now caught the gleam of the moonlight, too, but his face was still shadowy.

"No. I'm fine." I could barely hear Tim now.

"Are you, Tim? Really?" Taylor took a step toward him, but then he stopped.

Tim shrugged his shoulders. "I'm alive, ain't I?"

Suddenly Taylor turned from Tim, like he couldn't stand to look at him anymore. His face was clear in the moonlight, and I was surprised at the torment I saw there.

"Oh, God, Tim! Shit, man—I wish it had been me instead of you—I'd give anything if it had been!" Taylor's voice, that I'd always thought to be so snooty, was in pure agony.

I could see Tim shake his head, still standing there with his hand in his pocket.

"Don't say that, Taylor." He seemed embarrassed by Taylor's outburst. I couldn't see his face but could tell by the way he hung his head.

There was the flash of a match as Taylor lit a cigarette. "There's one thing you've got to understand," Taylor said as the smoke from the cigarette floated around them. "I swear to God I didn't realize how bad off you were until I saw you the other day—I swear it!"

This time it was Tim who shuffled around and then looked out over the field. "Would it have made any difference if you had?"

Taylor seemed startled, and he threw his cigarette down. He couldn't have taken more than two drags off it. What I heard from him next was so cruel I almost came out of the shadows after him—Taylor laughed.

"Well, I'll be damned, Tim! You haven't changed after all." He lit another cigarette. I never knew he was such a chain-smoker. "One of the things I always liked about you, Tim, was your honesty. No bullshit, no melodrama like me. Just plain old Tim Sullivan."

I'd forgotten Taylor's crazy way of speaking and the way he used long words. I never was able to figure out what he was talking about half the time, which always made me feel stupid around him.

"Let's sit down," Taylor said again, and this time they walked over to the bleachers. I could see both of them plainer now, and they were closer by. I stayed in the shadows so they couldn't see me.

Taylor took a deep drag of his cigarette and leaned toward Tim. "How well you've always known me! And you're right—it probably wouldn't have made any difference, Tim. I went crazy anyway, just thinking of what I'd done to you, how I had ruined your life."

Tim thought on that a minute. "I did wonder why I never heard from you."

"Hell, man, you know why! I'm not strong like you are—I never have been. If I'd gone through what you did, I'd probably have offed myself. I thought about it, anyway. But I bet you never let that kind of thinking get to you."

Taylor leaned back and smoked his cigarette, but his face was still twisted with pain.

"It's okay now. For a while, they thought I'd lose my leg. Anything would be better than that," Tim said. "And my arm is lame and still bothers me a lot, but I can use my hand."

Taylor turned to Tim suddenly, and his face looked real angry. "I wish to God you'd stop being so damned noble about it—you're going to make me puke!" he yelled. "I left you to die, you lost the scholarship and you'll never play football again. You're a cripple for life, and you say it's *okay*? What's wrong with you, Tim—did you have brain damage, too?"

I could have easily killed Taylor Dupree right then. Tim just sat there like the fool he is. I could've killed him, too. He should beat the crap out of Taylor while he has the chance, I thought. To my surprise, it was almost like Taylor wanted him to.

"I thought you'd beat the shit out of me when you got here tonight," Taylor said furiously.

"That might have made you feel better, Taylor. But it wouldn't change anything, would it?" Tim said.

For a minute, it looked like Tim would have to anyway. To my horror, Taylor reached over and hit Tim on the shoulder.

"Come on, Tim. You say you can still use your arm—let's see you do it."

Tim pulled away from him. "Lay off the crap, Taylor."

Taylor shoved him this time, trying to pick a fight. "Come on, man—show me your stuff, like you use to."

Taylor jumped down from the bleachers and ran out on the

field, holding out his arms to catch an imaginary pass. I swear to God he must be drunk or crazy.

"Come on, quarterback. Throw me a pass," Taylor said. "You got a famous throwing arm, all the scouts in the stands are watching—throw me a pass!"

The fool pretended like he caught a pass and then he ran back to Tim. "Which scholarship offer will you take, Mr. Big Shit? They *all* want you—Notre Dame, Michigan, USC—all of them."

Tim looked disgusted finally. "Shut up, Taylor."

Taylor held out his hand like he held a microphone. He was crazy as hell; I always knew it.

"Oh, please give me an interview, Mr. Big Shit. Tell your fans why you are still in this shitty little town instead of quarterbacking Tulane. Tell us what happened to ruin all your plans—to ruin your whole life!"

Taylor pretended to hold the microphone so that Tim could talk into it, and Tim knocked his hand away.

"Come on, Taylor. Crap."

Suddenly it was like all the fight went out of Taylor. He sank down on the bleachers, right in front of Tim, and put his head in his hands. I couldn't believe my eyes—he was crying. His shoulders shook and his voice came out in hoarse sobs, like those of a little boy.

"I never meant for this to happen, Tim. I wish to God I could make it up to you."

Tim put his head down in his hands, too, but he only rubbed his forehead wearily before turning back to look at Taylor.

"You can't change things once they happen, Taylor. I wish it hadn't happened either, but that don't change it. I really wish you could put it behind you, like I've had to."

Taylor fumbled in his jeans pocket and took out his handkerchief and wiped his eyes. "Shit," he said, his voice soft. "I didn't mean to break down like that, Tim. Not with all you've been through."

Tim shrugged. "Ain't nothing wrong with crying, Taylor. I've done plenty of it myself."

"God, I wish I had a drink. Let's go somewhere and get a beer, Tim." Taylor was wiping his eyes on his sleeves. To my surprise, Tim smiled.

"One good thing—we could if we wanted to," Tim said. "I never could go anywhere and have a drink with you—I was always in training." That was for sure. Tim was such a prized athlete Coach made him train year-round.

"Yeah." Taylor nodded. "And you were the only one who never broke training. I only remember one time. Do you remember that night?"

"Oh, yeah. I won't ever forget that night—I've never been that sick in my life," Tim said.

I knew exactly what they were talking about—one of my worse memories. Tim and I almost broke up because I caught him coming out of Taylor's house the day after the championship game, so hungover he was pathetic. I'd been frantic with worry about him, and he had spent the night with Taylor. I knew for sure Taylor got him drunk, too, though Tim made up some story about Pleese Davis. But I knew Taylor was jealous Tim had been with me instead of him on the most important night of Tim's life. No, I'd never forget that, either.

Tim smiled again and looked over at Taylor. "Hey, you remember that dog me and you and Cat found when we were kids—the one that had been hit by a car or something?"

Taylor looked up at him surprised.

"Yeah, I sure do. Cat killed the damn thing pouring whiskey down his throat, trying to revive him. What on earth made you think about that?"

Tim shrugged. "I don't know. Now that you're back, I got to thinking about Cat. Do you miss her?"

"Oh, God, yes. I miss her—and you. Both of you, so damn bad these past two years." Taylor ran his hand through his long, thick hair. He seemed to have himself under control now. "Tim? Can I ask you something?"

Tim nodded, and Taylor went on. "Are you going to take that scholarship of Miss Maudie's?"

Tim looked at him puzzled. "Who—oh, I guess Sarah Williams told you about that, huh?"

"Yeah. And I saw the sign you drew, too. Man, it is really good! I'd forgotten how much talent you have. But you could always do anything you wanted to."

Tim shrugged. "I always liked to draw, but I quit once football got so important in my life. Funny thing is, they started me back in the hospital, in rehab. When I was learning to use my right hand again. I've been doing some drawing ever since."

"I hope you'll take that scholarship, Tim. You could drive over to the university, not even have to move anywhere. Hey—maybe me and you could ride together. I'm planning on transferring there myself."

"No kidding? That'll be great. It's something to think about," Tim said.

Taylor ran his hand through his hair again, but even from where I stood, I could tell that he was more relaxed. I relaxed, too. I saw now that I may have been wrong to try and keep Tim and Taylor apart like I had. If I wanted Tim to get over the whole thing completely, he needed this chance to see Taylor and talk with him. Bad as I hated to admit it, it probably was the only thing that could help Tim put it all behind him. And in doing so, put Taylor and their friendship behind him, too. They had probably grown away from each other during these last two years. I knew for sure that Tim would never feel the same about Taylor and let him influence him like he had in the past. How mistaken I had been!

Tim even teased Taylor some, now that they were both more relaxed with each other.

"Man, I've been hearing all sorts of things about you and Sarah Williams," Tim said. "She's something else, ain't she? I hope Donnette'll look that good at her age."

Taylor laughed, shaking his head.

"All that stuff is not true—unfortunately for me. Ellis and Sonny spread that crap. Oh, I admit, I've got a tremendous crush on her and would give anything if there was any way . . ." His voice trailed off, and he shook his head again. "She's helped me more than I can ever tell you, Tim. She's one hell of a woman."

Taylor glanced over at Tim and then continued, saying, "How does Donnette feel about you taking that scholarship of Miss Maudie's?" My ears perked up at that question.

Tim shrugged. "I don't really know yet. We ain't talked that much about it. Ever since you called me, I've been thinking so much about these past two years that I haven't thought about the scholarship, tell you the truth." Tim studied Taylor before going on. "Donnette's been through too much with me lately, Taylor. I don't know how I would have made it without her being with me. So I definitely will not take that scholarship unless she wants me to."

"But if she wants you to, will you?"

Tim looked out over the field, then nodded. "Yeah. I just might do it. I never thought I'd have another chance like this. Especially in art. It blows my mind. I'm kind of excited about it."

I was glad they couldn't see me standing there in the dark by that smelly old locker room, because tears were rolling down my cheeks and I was smiling like a damn idiot. For the first time in two years, I felt relief. After all the pain and suffering we'd been through, it really was over now.

I started to step out of the shadows and go over to them, but I decided instead to slip back home and wait for Tim instead. Let him tell me all about this. I could hear him and Taylor's voices as they spoke softly, and I heard Tim chuckle over something Taylor said. I could cut behind them and they wouldn't see me.

I put my shoes back on, then slipped quietly behind the locker room. A huge blue devil was painted on the side, looking silly in the white moonlight. I cut behind the tall bleachers where Tim and Taylor had sat a few minutes ago. They were now standing like they were about to leave, too, so I hurried. I was almost past them when Taylor said something that froze me in my tracks.

"Tim. You never told Donnette the truth about what happened that night, did you?"

At first I thought that I couldn't move, that I was paralyzed. I could see them plain as day through the bleachers, facing each other. Holding my breath, I crept closer to them and knelt down behind a post.

"No. I'd never tell anybody that, Taylor."

I'd never heard Tim's voice sound so strange before.

"Tim—I think we might need to talk about it now. I think I finally understand it," Taylor said.

I didn't know what in the hell was going on, what they were talking about. They must have been drinking that night. Or maybe doing drugs. I always felt like there was something wrong about the whole thing. I heard that strange, choked voice of Tim's again.

"Look, Taylor. I think it's best never to mention it again."

"I had awful nightmares, Tim. I lived it over and over." Taylor could barely be heard now. Whatever it was, it was killing him.

"Me, too. That's why we don't need to talk about it, Taylor. We both know we were—crazy that night."

"Oh, shit, Tim! If only it were that simple. But now I understand more about the confusion I felt then. I've had my brain probed by enough shrinks; I should know more. And Sarah's really helped me, too."

Tim looked at Taylor, shocked. "You didn't tell her!"

"I never told anyone else, Tim, I swear to God. But she's helped me work on my feelings and the ambivalence I experienced then."

Bound for Taylor to start using them big words again and talking his crazy talk. I crept even closer when I saw the tortured expression on his face, though. Suddenly Taylor reached over and took ahold of Tim's arm.

"See? I can relate to you now, touch you, as a friend, without that other hell—"

Tim jerked away from him.

"Taylor, goddamn you—SHUT UP! We were both messed up in the head then—I know that. It didn't mean anything, to either of us."

"It meant something to you. You wrecked the car because of it," Taylor said.

Tim was driving! That couldn't be right. I didn't believe this. Taylor cleared it up with his next statement.

"When you grabbed the steering wheel like you did, that's what caused me to lose control of the car," he said.

"Oh, Jesus Christ," was all Tim could say. "I remember now."

"So don't tell me that it didn't mean anything, Tim. There was too much between us back then, man. I've never been so close to anyone, not even Cat—I've never had such strong feelings before. We didn't know how to handle them, did we? Neither one of us."

Taylor's voice broke and he turned away violently. "Oh, God—I was so confused then—" He was crying again.

The look that came over Tim's face as he looked down at Taylor like to have broke my heart in two. I knew then what I'd always known about Tim, that he was too good for this world. I watched in disbelief as he reached out with that broken, useless arm of his toward Taylor. Lifting with his left hand, he put that arm around his shoulders, just like I'd seen him do so many times with his brother Tommy. With their heads bent together, he spoke so quietly that I couldn't hear what he said, but I could tell that the gentleness of his words was easing Taylor's awful torment by the look that came over his face. Then Taylor, still crying like a baby, reached out for Tim.

Suddenly I couldn't watch anymore. I ran away from that dark stadium and those two figures huddled together in the moonlight as fast as I could.

It was not until the next day that I knew what must be done. I had pretended to be asleep when Tim came in because I had to think it through, plan it all out. I was too upset to even think at first; my feet were swollen and my head was throbbing. I was totally exhausted and spent.

Tim was gone to work by the time I got up the next morning—I was so tired that it was easy for me to pretend to be asleep so I didn't have to face him. Then when he came home for lunch, I fixed us a bologna sandwich and we talked about Tommy and the football game. I hadn't said a thing to him about last night, and he hadn't mentioned it to me, either.

But he was definitely different—as though an awful burden had been lifted from his shoulders. Thank God, he finished his sandwich quickly and left; he'd said that Coach was waiting for him at the school. We were going to the ballgame later.

I watched out the window as he went to his truck and I saw he wasn't limping as bad. I'd do *anything* on earth to keep him that way—anything. When I saw Tim reach out to Taylor, I realized someone like Tim deserves a better life than he could have hanging around a lumber mill or a football field, that it was up to me to make sure he got it. Whatever it took. I watched as Tim drove away in his pickup.

Soon as Tim was gone, I went to the shop and called my afternoon customers, canceling their appointments. I could only hope that they'd reschedule them instead of going elsewhere, for I had at least fifty dollars' worth of work coming in that afternoon. Oh, well. That really didn't matter as much as what I had to do.

I went back into the kitchen after I'd canceled all my customers. Still thinking of my plan, I reached for the phone book and made the calls before I changed my mind. My first call was to Ellis, for I had to be sure that she could promise me things would work out with her sister, Glenda, that I could count on it. Then, with trembling fingers, I made the other call.

Two rings and an answer. It was him.

"It's Donnette—I was hoping that you'd be there," I said, breathlessly. I couldn't chicken out now. "I need to see you right away. Come over to my Aunt Essie's old house. That's where we live now. Come in the back door, to the kitchen."

I went quickly to the front bedroom, combed my hair and put on fresh lipstick. On the dresser was the drawing Tim did for the sign. *Making Waves*. That was what I had to do. I took the drawing back to the kitchen with me and sat down at the kitchen table to wait for him.

I didn't have to wait long. The back door opened and he came into the kitchen suddenly, as though he'd run all the way. His long, dark hair was tousled; he was sweaty and dressed in ripped shorts and an old tee shirt, but he was still beautiful. What wonderful coloring he had with that dark skin and those golden brown eyes! You just had to marvel at him, regardless.

"Donnette—I came as soon as you called," Taylor said.

"Come on in, Taylor. Close the door."

I stayed where I was at the table.

Taylor came in and leaned cautiously against the kitchen door as he closed it. He probably thought I was going to shoot him.

Both of us looked at each other a minute, then Taylor spoke. "Well. Last time I saw you, you were Donnette Kennedy, living out from town with your daddy." And he smiled at me.

"Yeah, that's true." I smiled back. "Last time I saw you, Taylor, it was a rainy night, two years ago, just before school started. You and Tim were about to go for a little ride."

The pain caused by my words was obvious in Taylor's dark eyes, and he looked down at the floor.

"Donnette, I understand how you must feel about me."

"I bet you do. I understand a lot of things now that I didn't then," I said to him.

Taylor looked around the kitchen, puzzled. "Tim's not here, I take it?"

"No," I told him. "And he won't be back until late. So we can talk free. No one's gonna be here but us."

Taylor looked at me for a long moment, then motioned toward the table. "Why don't I sit down, then?"

He didn't wait for me to answer, but walked over and pulled out a chair at the table. He then turned it around and sat in it so that we were facing each other.

"God, it's hot today," he said, looking around the kitchen again. "You got anything to drink in here?"

I knew what he wanted. "Help yourself. Tim has some beer in the refrigerator."

He grinned and jumped up. I don't think he wanted the beer as much as something to do besides sit and face me.

"Sounds great!" He opened the refrigerator door and grabbed a beer, popping the top. "I can't believe this is Tim's. He used to never drink."

"Well. He's hardly in training now, Taylor."

His face flushed red and he quickly turned up the beer can and drank from it.

"I know you have a lot of hostile feelings toward me, Donnette. You wouldn't be human if you didn't. I don't blame you a bit—I really don't."

"It doesn't really matter how I feel, Taylor," I said quietly. I kept on staring at him, thinking of how much I despised him, so that I wouldn't lose my nerve.

Taylor sat back down in front of me, beer in hand, so close our legs brushed. Again, I marveled at his smooth brown skin and deep dark eyes. Such a damned shame. Those eyes were looking into mine now, real curious-like.

"Donnette—of course it matters how you feel! Listen, Tim and I finally talked. We got a lot of things worked out."

"I know."

"I'm glad Tim told you. Tim has forgiven me, Donnette. God—I can't believe he can understand my cowardice in running out on him like I did! But he says that he does, now. I can only hope that you'll be able to as well." Those wonderful eyes looked so earnestly at me.

"Actually, I have forgiven you, Taylor. I see now that you couldn't help what happened, and your reaction to it. You just really couldn't help it."

Hope lit up his dark face, and he leaned over toward me, as though to grab my hand or something.

"Oh, God, Donnette—you forgive me, too? I—" He stopped when he saw the drawing in my hands. "The sign! Is that the original?"

I nodded. Taylor put his beer down and took the drawing gently from my hands. Our hands brushed, and I noticed his were cold and trembling. No matter how much I hated him, there was no way I could help but feel sorry for him, sorry as hell for what I had to do to him.

"God, Donnette! Do you have any idea how good this is? If Tim hadn't done that sign, I would have forgotten all about his art. It's amazing how it appeared right at this time!" He shook his head, smiling.

"You know, Taylor, life is just full of amazing coincidences, isn't it?" I smiled back, never taking my eyes off him. "Isn't it funny—the sign appears, and you tell Sarah Williams that Tim painted it. She just *happens* to remember Miss Maudie's plan to give some poor student of hers a scholarship. I'd sure call that an amazing coincidence, all right."

Taylor raised an eyebrow at me and shook his head. "So Sarah told you the truth, huh? I wish she hadn't felt the need to do that. I thought she understood how important it is that no one knows."

"She only told me part of it, Taylor, that *you* were the one to put the idea in her head. I figured out the rest, all by myself. I finally figured out that there never was any scholarship, that you were behind the whole thing. Oh, it was a good one, all right. Had me going for a while, hand it to you. I know that Miss Maudie would have liked the idea, too, if only she had known about it. Where was the money coming from?"

Taylor hung his head. "Shit. I never dreamed you'd figure it out! I got the money. Charlotte sent my tuition money to me this year instead of paying the school directly. That's what gave me the idea in the first place, having that much money on hand."

"So the money *is* available for it—that's for real?" I asked him.

"Yeah." He nodded. "Plus, once we concocted the idea, Sarah decided she wanted to use some of her inheritance from Miss Maudie to help Tim out, too. Only reason she went along with the scholarship lie is that Miss Maudie really was doing it, in a way. But you know as well as I do Tim would *never* accept it if he knew it was from me and Sarah. Especially from me."

I looked at him and nodded. "You're right—Tim would never accept it coming from you."

Taylor pushed his hair back with his hands, like I'd seen him do so often, and he looked at me sadly.

"So now you'll tell Tim what I did, make him turn against me for trying to fool him, right?"

I shook my head. "You're wrong, Mr. Know-it-all. I never intend to tell Tim that scholarship came from anyone but dear old Miss Maudie."

Taylor's eyes lit up, and this time he managed to grab both my hands.

"Donnette! That's—God!—that's *marvelous*. I cannot tell you how much that means to me. And think how much it will mean to Tim!" He squeezed my hands tightly and released them, then he frowned at me. "Shit—what if Tim won't take it, even thinking it's from Miss Maudie?"

"Oh, I'm sure he will. I can see now that going to school, studying art—that's exactly what Tim needs to do. I'll see that he takes it, don't worry."

I looked down at the drawing that Taylor had in his lap now. The painted town around the border swam through my tears. I couldn't help it—this was going to be hard.

Taylor couldn't hide his pleasure.

"Oh, Donnette—that is just wonderful! I can't wait to tell Sarah. Do you mind if I tell her as soon as I leave here?"

I shook my head and wiped my eyes with the back of my hand. I was starting to feel calmer now, calmer by the minute.

"No, go ahead. You'll need to see her anyway when you leave here, say good-bye to her," I told him.

Taylor turned the beer can up and drank about half of it in a long swallow. He then turned puzzled eyes to me.

"Good-bye? Sarah's not leaving until Sunday."

"Not her, Taylor. You. Do you want another beer?"

He shook his head and smiled at me. "Oh—I don't guess Tim told you this part. I'm staying here, Donnette. Right here in good old Clarksville. I'm going to transfer to Alabama, stay with Aunt Della. I got enough money left for that."

I frowned and shook my head. "We'll have to think up something to tell Tim about that. Anyone who could come up with the scholarship idea shouldn't have any trouble thinking up another good one to explain why you changed your mind about staying here."

Taylor appeared to be completely puzzled now. And I'd always thought he was so smart. "But I haven't, Donnette! And Tim thought it was a good idea that I stay—we even talked about riding together. And—" Suddenly he stopped and frowned at me. "What's going on, Donnette?"

"Well, Taylor, think about it. Tim didn't tell me about you and him meeting last night. I didn't know what was going on, so I followed him. I was hiding, listening to y'all. I now know *everything*."

Understanding began to replace the puzzlement in Taylor's eyes. He pulled back in his chair and stared at me, very carefully. "Oh," was all he could say.

"There's no way for you and Tim to continue to be friends, Taylor. Surely you know that, don't you?"

Taylor didn't say anything for a while, then he said in a very low voice, not looking at me, "So. You mean for me to go away, don't you?"

"That's exactly what I mean. All the way back to Louisiana where you've been hiding these past two years," I said.

I never thought anyone as dark as Taylor could turn so pale. "Oh, Donnette. No. You don't understand."

Before he knew what'd hit him, I jumped up from my chair and got right in his face.

"You're so wrong, Taylor Dupree. You've never given me credit for having any sense at all. I tell you what I understand—I understand this: If you want to make up to Tim for what you did to him, you'll give him a chance to do this on his own—you'll take yourself out of the picture."

"I can't do that, Donnette!" Taylor was so stunned he could barely speak. And he always thought of me as a dumb country hick, not good enough for Tim.

"It's your choice, Taylor. If you don't, I'll tell Tim the truth about the scholarship. What do you think that would do to him and his confidence in his talent?"

Taylor could only stare at me in shock, speechless for once. Neither of us said anything for what seemed like an eternity, then he tried another tactic on me, pulled the card I was afraid of, what had almost made me lose my resolve.

"There is something about this that you don't know, Donnette. It's my Aunt Della—she's counting on me. I promised her that I'd be here during the time that she's got left." His voice broke and tears filled his eyes. "I promised her, Donnette."

I shook my head. I couldn't look at him because I didn't want him to see any weakness in me, so I had to make my voice hard.

"I'm sure sorry about Miss Della, Taylor. And I really mean that. But then, I've always felt sorry for her, having nobody but you to love. She's gotten along without you these last two years—where was your concern then? Don't you know it almost killed her? I'll tell you where your concern was—with yourself!"

Taylor was still so stunned he just sat staring at me as I sank back down into my chair.

"Donnette—I love Tim, you know that," he cried. "I'd do anything to make it up to him—anything. Except sacrifice Aunt Della."

"I thought about that, Taylor. I've thought this whole thing through, I tell you. And I talked with Ellis. Glenda will stay with Miss Della. She'll be well taken care of, believe me. I know Glenda. She's different from Ellis. It's not the same as you being there, but you'll still see her occasionally. But living here, being here all the time—I can't let that happen."

"Come on, Donnette. This is ridiculous! If you want me to beg you to forget this stupid idea, I will."

"No, Taylor. I don't want you to beg. I just want you to leave. I want you to leave Tim alone and never see him again."

"Okay, okay, goddammit! I'll leave him alone—I won't see

him. We won't ride together, go to classes together, nothing. How about that?"

I shook my head. "Believe me, Taylor, I thought of that too. That was my first plan. But then I thought, no. No way I can live in constant fear that you'll get Tim in your clutches again. This is the only way. I hate it for Miss Della's sake. And also for Tim's, because crazy fool that he is, he loves you, too. But this is the only way it can be."

"So you decided that you want me to get the hell out of Dodge, huh? Out of town by sunset?" Taylor sneered at me, his face now flushed in anger.

I smiled at him then. Oh, he thinks he's so smart. "No, Taylor. Far as I'm concerned, you can wait until tomorrow. Or whenever. Doesn't really matter to me, long as you leave."

Give him credit, he tried to shame me like he had always done, with his big words and snooty voice.

"Dammit, Donnette—I was always the melodramatic one, not you! What the hell do you think I'm going to do to Tim, seduce him? I was a confused kid then, and so was he. We both confused a rare friendship with—with something else. Tim and I both understand that now."

"Yeah, well, let me tell you something about Tim," I said to him, a little louder than I intended. "He's not a thing like you and me, Taylor. He's *good*. He's a better person than me, and he's sure as hell a better person than you'll ever be!"

Now Taylor was the one to jump up from his chair. "Holy shit, Donnette—don't you think that I know that? Are you too ignorant to see that's exactly what I've always loved about him?"

"Yeah, Taylor. You are right as usual. I am ignorant, just like you've always said about me. Well, let me tell you one thing: I may be ignorant, but I ain't stupid. There's *no* way I'm going to give you another chance at Tim, not while I have this opportunity to get you out of his life once and for all."

At that little speech, I stood up too and folded my arms. Taylor and I stood facing each other, as close as lovers. I didn't blink a single time. Finally it was Taylor who turned away from me. He shook his head, and I knew then that I had won.

"Goddamn you, Donnette. I swear, I never knew that you hated me so much."

"Well, you know it now."

Taylor smiled a crooked smile. "Yeah. I sure as hell do."

"So? You'll do it—go on back to Louisiana, let Tim think the scholarship came from Miss Maudie?" Even as I asked him, though, I knew what the answer would be.

Taylor nodded and pushed his hair back with his hand wearily. "Guess I don't really have a choice, do I?"

I didn't say anything for a while. It had turned out to be easier than I thought. Finally I watched him push that hair back one more time.

"You know, Taylor, you really do have pretty hair. I'd love to cut it for you, fix it real stylish. Long hair is not in now, you know? It went out in the sixties."

Like you, Taylor Dupree, I thought to myself. Out of step with everybody and everything around here—always have been. But now, out of here. Out the door. I walked past him as he stood slump-shouldered in front of his chair, and I walked to the kitchen door.

"Well. Guess you'd better be going now, Taylor."

For one weak moment, I felt strong pity for him, he looked so sad and dejected standing there in the middle of my kitchen. Like he'd lost everything. But I thought of Tim, who because of Taylor really did lose everything once. Now, he had the chance to get some of it back.

"Donnette?" Taylor turned to me. I saw the same torment in his deep brown eyes that I saw last night, and there was also tears.

"Can I have the drawing?" he asked, his voice real soft.

We both looked down to where it had fallen to the floor, an my eyes filled with tears, too. I nodded because I couldn't speak Taylor reached down and picked up the paper. He rolled it u carefully, tenderly even, and he looked around the kitchen on more time. With the back of his hand, he wiped his eyes like little boy.

"Well. Guess you'll tell Tim good-bye for me. Tell him— whatever you need to, okay? Sarah can handle the scholarshi arrangements."

He didn't wait for me to answer but moved quickly to th door. Just as he started out, I grabbed his arm. He stopped an looked down at me, and I blinked back my tears, swallowing hard

"Taylor. If you were in my place, you'd do the same thing.

He looked at me—startled—then nodded. "Yeah. I probabl would." He tried to smile that old mocking smile of his, but h bit his lip instead.

"Well—don't guess I'll see you again," he said. "Take goo care of Tim, okay?" And he went out the door, slamming behind him.

From the curtained window on the door, I watched him wal down the steps and start around front. I ran into the front parlo and looked out the window as he came around the house. Whe he got to the sign, he stopped a minute and looked up at it, bu he quickly turned away and headed down the sidewalk. I watche his walk down Preacher Street, on down Magnolia Street to hi Aunt Della's house, watching tearfully as he walked out of ou lives for good. I wondered what would happen to his Aunt Dell now, but I couldn't let myself dwell on that. At least she'd b well taken care of.

I left the front window and walked back into the kitchen. sat down heavily at the kitchen table, as though I was old an tired. My eyes fell on the kitchen clock hanging over the stove.

It was only three o'clock—I could have called one of m

customers back and gotten a permanent in before sundown. However, I didn't do it—I just sat there numbly, unable to move.

Three o'clock. The ballgame in a few hours. Tim would come in starving and raring to go to the game. Especially now that he thought Tommy was going to be a winner. Then, after the ballgame, we'd have to talk. Plan the future, talk about the scholarship, move fast, so he could start to the university next week. I'd have to think up something to tell him about Taylor. I'd tell him Taylor stopped by here to tell both of us he'd changed his mind, decided to go back to New Orleans. Tim would be disappointed, but not all that surprised.

I kept staring at the clock as the minute hand moved slowly. I hadn't even thought about supper yet. I had to get moving, get something cooking. We'd have to eat early in order to get to the game on time.

I decided to fry chicken for supper.

Tim loved fried chicken, better than anything. It'd be just what he'd want before the big ballgame. And I smiled to myself, thinking what a joy it would be to see how much Tim liked that chicken I would fry, just for him.

Cassandra King
INTERVIEW

When did you start to write fiction?

When I was growing up, I loved to tell stories to my sisters. I'd make up plays and use my dolls to act out all the parts. Later, in elementary school, I took my stories to the playground and I would offer them in installments to my friends during recess, my very own schoolyard soap opera. I wrote them down for entertainment, but I suppose I wanted to be a playwright more than anything else. It was years before I took my writing seriously.

Tell me how the idea for Making Waves *came to be.*

I actually lived in the little town that the story was based on. When I started to write *Making Waves*, I was probably in my mid-thirties. I started keeping a journal of my observations and then began writing the stories about Zion; it was like going back in time. I put it in the book just as it was—situated in Alabama, twenty-five miles west of Tuscaloosa. It was so isolated, so small a town, it was a ripe setting for a book and I began to think in terms of a collection of stories that grew from the characters.

There was someone similar to Della; there was a young man who went to high school with my son who'd had a football injury; he already had a scholarship and he was going to be the big star, but he was injured in an auto accident.

I had not thought about publishing, but I had a friend who was a writing teacher, and he was married to my best friend. I took creative writing from him. He encouraged me to mail stuff off. While I was putting these stories together, we moved back to Birmingham for my husband's work; I decided to go to graduate school in Birmingham and began working on a master's degree. When it was time to declare my thesis, I thought I'd do one made up of my stories of Zion, Alabama. So *Making Waves* was actually my master's thesis.

Did you intend for the reader to see Tim and Taylor as gay?

I grew up with sisters, and really did not know anything about what it was like to be a boy until I raised three sons. During this time, I had observed that males had problems with friendship and expressing affection for each other. With Tim and Taylor, I wanted to write about the sexual confusion between them; the way society operates, they have to ask themselves, "Am I gay?" because of their feelings. I was interested in how males express love in our society, exploring that as my primary theme. It came directly from observing the wonderful friendships my boys had, the really close bonds they had with male friends, but no socially acceptable way of showing their love for each other. It was so much easier for me as a girl to love my girlfriends, to sleep over with them without anyone thinking twice about it. It bothered me that it was hard for boys to show the affection I knew they deeply felt.

How did you come to use the device of telling the story through different people?

I realized that everything I wrote was always in the first person; I love doing it. I also love the way we all see the same things differently; we each have our own perspective.

Was any particular kind of research involved in creating the novel?

No, it was all there in front of me. My mother thought she wanted to be a beautician; she never really worked, but she did go to beauty school. I suffered because my mother experimented on me (with perms). I had really straight, fine hair, and my mother religiously gave me permanents; the worst thing you can do to fine hair is put chemicals on it. Because of that, I know what goes on in a beauty parlor. Every time my mother took me with her (she had a standing appointment at 10 A.M. every Wednesday), I inevitably saw a woman there who had waves and clips in her hair under the dryer. So I knew how it was when I wrote about it.

Is there any particular significance to setting the novel in and around a beauty parlor?

No question about it. We lived right across from a house like "Donnette's" with a beauty parlor in it. She was a really pretty girl; it was big white house with a beauty shop; all the gossip would go on there. It was like what a barbershop is for men; the beauty parlor was the primary place women would go to socialize and gossip, find out about the funerals and weddings, and so on.

What does your book say about life in the South? Who were your favorite southern novelists and playwrights?

Making Waves is about how many people have lived in a town that is so isolated. It's away from the mainstream, like a self-contained world. This is not by any means a good thing. One thing you run into is a certain narrow-mindedness about a lot of issues. You also run into more apathy about what is going on in the rest of world. This is typical of small towns anywhere; it could be a small town in Connecticut. It's a sociological phenomenon. But there is a strong sense of place, family ties, and tradition. Much of that is important in the South. Also the food, the aromas, the heat, and the scent of flowers. When you think of the South, you can't *not* think about the heat. "Cold" is 50 degrees.

Southern writers I have liked are Truman Capote, Eudora Welty, Flannery O'Connor, Carson McCullers, but above all those, Tennessee Williams.

You are married to a southern writer. Where does your vision of the South and that of your husband meet and/or diverge?

Pat [Conroy] feels rootless in the South because he came from a military family and moved almost every year. But I was raised on a huge peanut farm, and was very rooted there. Pun intended.

was the King Brothers' Farm. Pat missed all that; he often
emarks on how related I am to my background, and craves that
eeling of home. His mother was from a farming family, but
ie totally rejected her roots. They were poor farmers, always
truggling; she never wanted to go back to that life. Pat and I
omplement each other because I romanticize the agrarian rural
outh, and he experienced his mother's rejection of it.

READERS' GUIDE QUESTIONS

. Though Donnette is twenty years old, her thoughts and be-
avior can be very childlike. How is this most strongly demon-
trated? What could account for this quality in her?

. What are some of the sensory clues provided by the author
hat this story takes place in the Deep South?

. *Making Waves* is set in a tiny town in Alabama. Can you imagine
he events and characters taking place or existing anywhere else
the United States?

. At no time in the story does the author indicate what is hap-
ening in the world outside Zion County. What is the significance
f this?

What role does the beauty parlor play in the town's affairs?

The author makes the affection between Tim and Taylor ap-
ar to border on homosexuality—or does she? What does Tim
d Taylor's youthful relationship say about the expression of
iendship between men in this country?

7. What other novels have used the device of having different characters tell the story through their own voices? Is this a peculiar feature of southern writing, and if so, why is it so?

8. Does the transformation of Ellis from a drab mouse to a glamour-puss, and her rejections of religious teachings, seem plausible? Could she have been the backbone of the story? What other characters seem capable of taking over the story, or perhaps spinning off a new novel?

9. Presumably Tim's artistic abilities were suppressed for the same reason that Tim and Taylor's love for each other was—it wasn't "manly." What other southern writers are known for employing themes of repressed desires and frustration?

10. Did *Making Waves* alter your impressions of life in the Deep South in any way? What did you learn?

11. Miss Maudie's funeral was the catalyst that starts the novel and brings Tim and Taylor back together. What other new beginnings came about as a result of the funeral?

If you enjoyed
Making Waves by Cassandra King,
you'll love *Queen of Broken Hearts*,
now available
from Hyperion!

Chapter One

At the exact moment the cash register dings and I open my change purse, the chain of bells on the front door of the coffee shop bangs together with a brassy clatter. I hear the sound of voices raised in greetings, a loud and hearty hello in response, and the bells jangling again as the door closes. Curious to see who's making such an entrance, I glance over my shoulder. When I see that it's Son Rodgers, my face flames and my heart pounds. On top of everything else that's happened today, I go to the coffee shop for lunch, and who do I run into? One thing for sure: I have to get out of here before he sees me. It would be embarrassing for me and him and the dozen or so other folks enjoying their afternoon coffee. Instinctively, I duck my head and pull my arms close as if to make myself invisible.

Barely turning my head, I look over my shoulder again to determine the distance between me and the front door. No way I can get out that way without him seeing me; I'll have to exit through the bookstore. Now I wish I'd driven to town instead of walking, even though it would've been ridiculous to drive so few blocks. But my getaway would have been easier. I could have gone through the adjoining bookstore, gotten nonchalantly into my car, and put the pedal to the metal. Instead, everyone in both stores will see me running out of the coffee shop right after my best friend's husband has

walked in. I can only imagine the talk that will follow, since ou
small town has talked of little else all summer except what's gon
on in the Rodgers household. I can hear it now: "Did you know it'
gotten so bad that Clare sneaked out of the coffee shop to avoi
Son? Poor Dory!"

Making my getaway is turning out to be more difficult than
thought. The lethargic, bespectacled teenager behind the counter i
new—his first day, he told me proudly—and he doesn't know th
ropes yet. He takes his time wrapping the two slices of carrot cak
in parchment paper, placing them in a flat white box, then bringin
the edges of the box together. When I see him searching for tape,
say, "It's fine. Don't bother taping it," and hope that my voic
doesn't sound as flustered as I feel. But he shrugs me off and says n
problem, it's no trouble at all. He rings it up wrong for the secon
time, muttering, "Oops." After canceling out the sale, he punches i
the numbers again, glances at me over the top of his glasses, an
mumbles, "Uh, that'll be eight fifty-three."

It hits me that I used all my change by counting out the exac
amount for the veggie wrap and iced tea I had for lunch, plus a tip
I left the money on the table, anchoring my ticket. On my way ou
I decided on impulse to take a couple pieces of carrot cake with me
and I stopped at the counter to place my order. I have nothing but
twenty to pay with. Another glance over my shoulder, and I toss th
twenty-dollar bill at Pokey. In a low voice, I say, "If you could hurr
I'd really appreciate it. I'm running late for an appointment." C
course, I speak too softly, trying to keep Son from hearing m
voice, and Pokey tilts his head sideways to say, "Ma'am?"

"Hurry with the change, please," I hiss.

From the corner of my eye, I see that Son is working the roo
like a politician running for reelection, slapping backs and grinnin
like the Cheshire cat. His greetings are met with cries of "Hey–
look who's back in town!" and "Son! How was your trip? When di
you get home?" I watch him lean over to kiss the cheek of a plum
white-haired lady who coos and giggles and puts both hands to he

face in something resembling the ecstasy of Saint Teresa. He then joins a couple of businessmen from the bank who get to their feet to shake his hand and pound his back with great vigor, buying me a few seconds. Son throws back his head to laugh at something one of them says, which gives me a chance for a furtive study of him. I haven't seen him all summer, the longest span of time since he and Dory married, and that was twenty-five years ago.

Son is casually dressed in crisp, pressed jeans and a white oxford-cloth shirt, the sleeves carelessly rolled up to reveal brown, well-muscled arms. Usually he's in a shirt and tie, as befitting such a highly regarded and important hotshot. I guess he hasn't yet gone back to work in his real estate business, since he and Dory have been home only a couple of days. Even though he has a hand on the shoulder of one of the businessmen and appears to be listening with great interest, I notice that his eyes occasionally search the room to make sure he's kissed up to everyone there. When his gaze comes my way, I turn my head quickly, almost dropping the bills and change that Pokey is counting into my outstretched hand. When he miscounts and starts over, I'm tempted to tell the poor fellow to keep it, even if it would make me the biggest tipper in town. He'd probably be so surprised that he'd ask me to repeat myself yet again, and I'd end up getting caught by Son after all.

With his scrutiny of the coffee shop, it's unbelievable that Son hasn't recognized me yet, even with my back to him and the counter located at a helpful angle. It occurs to me that he hasn't seen me since I've had my hair cut. From the first day we met, Son has gone on and on about what great hair I have. It's nothing but his usual empty flattery, the only way he knows to relate to women. The truth is, my long, heavy hair has always been unruly and difficult. After struggling with it all my life, I gave up and had it chopped off a few weeks ago. Everybody tells me I look like a different person with my mass of hair gone, which must be true. Even so, I'm not taking any chances, not with the way Son keeps looking everyone over, so I drop the change into my briefcase instead of in my purse. Thankfully, the door of the adjoining bookstore is only few feet away.

I've taken a step away from the counter when the young ma clears his throat and says in a loud voice, "Uh—ma'am?" My cheek burning, I turn to see him holding out the box with the carrot cake i it. I yank it out of his hand so quickly that his eyes widen in surpris and his Adam's apple jerks up and down. I feel bad for him, but not a bad as he would feel if Son saw me and caused a scene in the crowde shop. It would *not* be a good way to end his first day at work.

In the Page and Palette bookstore, a glance assures me that th salesclerk is helping a customer in the back, so I step behind a re volving display of paperbacks in order to peer into the coffee shop making sure I got away without being seen. To my relief, I've es caped: Son is still standing with the two businessmen and runnin his mouth, with a big grin on his face. The three of them bend thei heads together as he relates something, and they all laugh apprecia tively, slapping backs again. Satisfied that I've escaped undetected, sling the strap of my briefcase over my shoulder and tuck the box c carrot cake under my arm, then head toward the front door.

Once I'm outside, I'm surprised to find the sidewalks stil crowded with shoppers and sightseers, which is unusual for earl fall. Anxious to get away from the coffee shop, I mutter my apolo gies as I make my way through, wondering if there's a tour bus i town. Although off the beaten path, Fairhope is becoming more an more of a tourist attraction, and it's not unusual to have sever tour buses in town during the summer, but not this time of year. I an effort to avoid a cluster of people blocking the sidewalk in fron of one of the street's many art galleries, I cut through a group c charming and colorful little shops that make up the area known a the French Quarter. And that's where I run into Rye Ballenge quite literally. If I hadn't been hugging the bakery box so close, car rot cake would have gone flying.

"Clare!" he exclaims at the same time I gasp, "Rye!" Then bot of us say together, "What are you doing here?"

I link an arm into his and continue my walk, pulling Rye along with me down the brick-paved lane. Out of the corner of my mouth, I say to him in a low voice, "I'm trying to get far enough away from the coffee shop so I won't be seen by a certain person who just walked in."

Rye plays along with me, matching my stride. "Who is it?" he whispers dramatically, looking around in mock terror. "An ex-husband of one of your clients?"

"Actually, you're close," I say with a groan. "It's Son."

"Son!" Rye comes to such an abrupt halt that I almost trip over a protruding brick. "Did he say anything to you? Tell me the truth."

"He didn't see me, thank God. I hightailed it out of there as fast as I could. Something tells me I'm not on his list of favorite people right now."

With a frown, Rye studies my face. He disengages my arm in order to take my hand in both of his and squeeze it tight. "Why don't you go back and confront him, sweetheart? I'll go with you, by God. I don't like the idea of him bullying you, and he needs to hear that."

"Your problem is, you're much too gallant," I say with an affectionate smile. "Charging in on your white horse and defending the honor of the poor maiden."

He snorts with indignation, his color high. "I've never been on a horse in my life, and have no intention of ever doing so. But I hate missing the chance to give Son Rodgers a piece of my mind."

"All I want to do is avoid him," I assure him. "I'm not interested in a confrontation at this point. Especially now, with him and Dory back together."

"Still no idea how that miraculous event came about?" Rye asks, watching me curiously.

I shrug. "None whatsoever. But I'll see Dory tomorrow at the group meeting, and she's promised me that we'll talk beforehand. Have you—"

Before I realize what's happening, Rye has grabbed me by the shoulders and pulled me out of the way of a large gray-haired woman who barges past us, then turns back to scowl at us for blocking the sidewalk. As we watch her walk away, I send up a thank-you to whatever gods were responsible for sending Rye strolling through the French Quarter at the very moment I turned the corner. From the first day I arrived in Fairhope, the sardonic and irreverent Rye Ballenger has been one of my dearest friends, and there's no one I'd rather see now, after the near miss with Son. Certainly no one else understands my history with Son better than Rye does.

He and I move to stand under the jasmine-entwined arbor of a café, then Rye leans toward me to whisper in my ear, "Lord God Almighty, would you look at that! How ghastly." He nods toward the retreating woman, who's clad in a hot-pink T-shirt with flowered capri pants stretched way too tight across her very ample rear end. "I can promise you that she hails from north of the Mason-Dixon line."

"What gives her away?" I ask with a grin, pushing my sunglasses on top of my head. "The camera hanging around her neck or the Gulf Shores T-shirt?"

Brow furrowed, Rye shudders and says, "Come on, Clare. No self-respecting Southern belle would be caught dead wearing white socks with sandals, and you know it. It's a disgrace, that's what it is. If they are going to run us off our lovely streets, the least they could do is dress properly."

"You're such a snob," I say fondly. "But you know what? I think you love it. You work hard at being the biggest snob in Baldwin County, don't you?"

Pretending to be offended, he pulls back and drawls in his melodious, honey-toned voice, "I just happen to have my standards is all."

When I first met the courtly Ryman Ballenger, a cousin of my former husband's, I thought he had to be putting me on. He has the most pronounced Southern accent I've ever heard, and on the East ern Shore of Alabama, that's saying a lot. It suits him, though, just another of his many charms. In addition to being the most breathtakingly handsome man I've ever had the pleasure of knowing, Rye is also the most elegant. He's always seemed out of place in this offbeat, artsy little town. He should be strolling the lavish grounds of an English estate instead, trailed by a bevy of manservants and Cavalier King Charles spaniels.

"It's strange that I ran into you just as I was running out of the coffee shop," I say, gazing up at him. Rye is one of those people I enjoy just looking at, in the same way I might stop by an art gallery and admire a painting. "Don't tell me you walked to town." In all the years I've known him, I've never seen him walk anywhere. He'll get into his big old silver Mercedes to drive a block.

He looks at me as though I've lost my mind. "Me walk to town? In this heat? I should hope not." With a nod, he indicates a place across the street. "My car's over there. I almost never found a parking place in this damn mob." He points out a small shop on the corner. "I came down to pick up a print that Lou framed for me. But the mat didn't suit me, so I had her redo it."

"Not up to your standards, huh?" I tease him.

Rye studies me through long dark lashes, and his fine gray eyes go soft. "I can't tell you how happy I am to see you. I called your cell phone not five minutes ago."

With a grimace, I admit that I turned it off when I left the office. "You know how hard it is for me to close shop on Friday afternoons. Etta had to stand in the door to keep me from returning for some unfinished paperwork. If I'd kept my cell turned on and one of my clients called, having a crisis, I would've had to go running back to meet them there."

He clucks his tongue in reproach. "Ah, Clare, what am I going to do with you? You promised me that you'd stop giving your private numbers to your clients!"

"I know . . ." My voice trails off, and I look up at him helplessly.

He places a hand on my shoulder. "When you didn't answer

your cell, I got concerned about you, after what happened thi
morning."

"You concerned about *me*? That's a switch, since I'm officiall
the one who gets to worry about everybody else. It's in my job de
scription."

"You can worry your pretty head off about whomever yo
want, my dear Clare, but I'm in charge of you."

"How very touching," I say, trying to keep my voice light. "I as
sume you're referring to a certain letter in this morning's paper?"

"So you've seen it?" With a worried frown, Rye reaches into hi
pocket and pulls out a clipping. "I have it with me, so if anyone dare
to say anything about it, I can tell them what a bunch of hogwash it is

"I've seen it," I tell him dismally. I arrived at my office early thi
morning, bringing the local paper to read while waiting for my firs
client. Like most weeklies, *The Fairhoper* is the perfect antidote t
the grim headlines of the national news. Unless we've had one c
our infamous hurricanes, the articles are full of small-town drama
that can be heartwarming but are more often unintentionall
comic. Dory and I will call each other to read some of the mor
priceless ones aloud. Her favorite remains the obituary writte
about a certain Mr. McMillan, who is said to have died in his slee
so peacefully that it didn't wake him or Mrs. McMillan, either one
The human interest stories are usually pretty good, but last mont
I was embarrassed to find myself named Fairhope's Citizen of th
Month. To my further embarrassment, one of this morning's letter
to the editor, which I read in dismay, referred to my award:

*This letter is written to protest your choice of August's Citizen of th
Month, a self-proclaimed divorce "coach." The honor was based on the na
tional attention that has come this woman's way, praising her innovati
methods of divorce recovery. I have to wonder if those retreats of hers, he
right here in our own conference center, actually do more to promote divorc
than to help people get over them. Surely if folks were encouraged to work o
their marriages instead, the disgracefully high divorce rates in our count
would go down. I hope next month's choice will better reflect the ideals*

ur community and country. The letter was signed by Oscar T. Allen, a 'concerned" citizen whom I'd not had the pleasure of meeting, fortunately.

Rye stands with his hands on his hips, scowling. "I can't tell you how furious I am. And you've got to be, too, though you won't let on. I know how you operate. In spite of all your degrees, you hide your feelings like the rest of us."

"You know better than that." I can't resist adding with a sly smile, "I'd never hide my feelings from you."

"Ha!" he scoffs. "You could've fooled me."

"You've lived here all your life, and you know everyone in town, so tell me who Oscar T. Allen is."

"He's a damned nitwit, that's who he is. The good thing is, no one will take him seriously, because we all know he's batty."

I let out a sigh of relief. "Well, I have to say I'm glad to hear that he's a crackpot. It could've been a pretty damaging indictment otherwise. The reference to the conference center makes my work sound sleazy, like those fly-by-night operations that breeze into town and rent a seminar room at the Holiday Inn. Calling me a divorce coach, which I've *never* been, implies that I find confused, unhappy women and teach them the secrets of pulling off a successful divorce, feathering my nest in the process."

"It's ridiculous," Rye agrees, his eyes blazing. "But don't even think about it harming you professionally. You're too highly respected for that. The newspaper allowing the letter to be printed is what made me so mad."

"To tell you the truth, I'm surprised that this is the first attack I've had."

"I don't like anyone going after my girl," he says gently. "As soon as I read the paper, I called Clyde Ayers and gave him a piece of my mind. I'm sick of him giving voice to every ignorant Bible thumper who picks up a pen. Clyde proceeded to lecture me on First Amendment rights. Me! Can you imagine? I reminded him that I have a law degree from Ole Miss, then hung up on him."

"Oh, Rye." Frowning, I put a hand on his arm. "You and Clyd Ayers have been buddies forever. I don't want you losing an friends on my account. It's not that big a deal."

"Just as I thought. You're trying to blow it off."

"I'm not!" I tell him, giving his arm a shake. "As soon as I ra into you, so to speak, I knew you'd make me feel better, and you a ready have."

He regards me for a long moment, then says in a soft voic "You know I'd do anything for you."

"You're such a dear friend." It's difficult to meet his gaze witl out blushing like a fool. In addition to everything else that went c this past summer, Rye and I had a rather unsettling evening that ne ther of us has mentioned since. We need to discuss it at some poin but I chicken out every time I see him.

"And then there was the other thing, in Miss Dingbat's co umn," Rye goes on. "I can only imagine what your reaction was t that one."

"After the letter, I didn't read any further," I admit. "What's sh done this time?" The society column, "Fairhope's Fairest," is penne by a woman who uses the moniker Ernestine Hemingway, appa ently with no idea that it makes her sound like a drag queen. Gue she figures it gives her more literary credibility than her real nam Ima June Hicks.

"Oh, her column was worse than usual." He glances around b fore taking my arm and pulling me closer to the shelter of the litt café. "While Dory and Son were in Europe, he sent a postcard Ernestine, and she quoted it in her column. It was all abo Fairhope's favorite couple spending the month of August on a se ond honeymoon in France. Ernestine went on to say that they we taking in the sights but mostly gazing into each other's eyes. It w beyond nauseating."

"Oh, Lord!" I wail. "It's pure propaganda on Son's part. No take that back. 'Propaganda' is much too long a word for his voca ulary."

Rye regards me sternly, his head tilted to the side. "I've told you, Clare, that Son will get the best of you if you keep dismissing him by claiming he's not very bright. It's all a part of his good-old-boy act. He's crazy like a fox. Have you seen Dory since they got back?" When I shake my head, he lowers his voice conspiratorially and says, "I ran into the happy couple last night, having dinner at the Yacht Club, and she seemed fine, in spite of all he put her through last year. She looked more beautiful than ever." His gray eyes are suddenly dreamy. "But Dory always does, doesn't she?"

"I'm sure Prince Charming was working the room, kissing ass all over the place, just like he was doing a few minutes ago at the coffee shop."

"Even worse," Rye says in disgust. "With Dory back by his side, he was beaming like he'd just scored the winning touchdown in an Alabama–Auburn game. He held on to Dory's arm and didn't let her out of his sight all night."

"Hovering over Dory? That's so unlike Son," I say sarcastically.

"When I approached their table to welcome them back, he did something that really surprised me."

"Told you that scientists have discovered someone with a lower IQ than he has?"

Rye sighs in exasperation before telling me, "He jumped to his feet and hugged me like a long-lost brother."

"Oh, please!" I groan. "Thank God I wasn't there. A performance like that would gag a maggot."

He regards me with a troubled expression. "I know how disappointed you were when they got back together. Both of us were."

"After the last stunt Son pulled, I thought for sure that she was through with him. Dory may be perfect in every other way, but her taste in men leaves something to be desired."

"You expect too much of people, my dear. Of all of us. You always have." Rye says it casually, without censure, but it stings anyway.

"Maybe I do," I reply weakly.

We avoid each other's eyes until I say, "Listen, I've *got* to go. Dory's coming to the group tomorrow morning, and I'll let you know how it goes, okay?" Before putting an arm around his shoulder and kissing him goodbye, I add with real regret, "If only she'd had the good sense to marry you, instead of Son, when she had the chance! You wouldn't still be looking for the one who got away, and Dory would've had a good man instead of a pain in the butt like Son."

With a seemingly nonchalant smile, Rye shrugs. "You're right about one thing: I've spent my life searching for the right woman." We fall silent, then he says wistfully, "Why don't you change your mind and come to the party with me tonight? Be good for you."

"I wouldn't do that to you," I say breezily. "Think what it'd do to your social life to be seen with Fairhope's most notorious homewrecker."

"It'd be worth it."

"I'm busy tonight and couldn't go even if I wanted to. Which I don't."

He takes me by the arm as though to lead me to one of the wrought-iron tables of the outdoor café. "Let's sit down," he says. "I need a smoke bad." At my expression, he flinches. "No lectures, sweetheart. Eventually I'll honor my promise to quit, but not now. Smoking calms my nerves."

"You've been saying that for years, Rye! You ought to have the calmest nerves in the state of Alabama. I'll put that on your tombstone: 'He died of calm nerves.' "

"Okay, okay. I won't have a cigarette, then—we'll get a glass of sherry instead."

"I can't. I've *got* to get home." Twisting my wrist sideways, I look down at my watch. "Oh, Jesus, I'm running late as it is."

He eyes me suspiciously, tilting his head. "You're two-timing me, aren't you, Clare? Running off with your new boyfriend, that Yankee sea captain. He's the real reason you won't go with me tonight, isn't he?"

"I told you why I didn't want to go," I say flippantly. "If I had to get all dressed up, then make small talk with that snooty crowd you hang around, I'd jump off the municipal pier."

"You're not only heartless, you have no manners, either." Following my lead, Rye goes back to his playful bantering. "It's rude to say that you don't want to go. You should make up an excuse that won't hurt my feelings."

Leaning over, I brush his cheek with my lips, laying a hand on his shoulder. "Oh, phooey. Nobody in their right mind *likes* going to cocktail parties. Well, except you, maybe."

Returning my kiss, he smells delicious, his shaving lotion like rare spices. Holding me close for a minute, he whispers in my ear before releasing me, "You're not fooling me, you know. On my way into town, I drove by your house. Your sea captain is already there. That god-awful vehicle he drives is parked out front."

"Good. We're going to the Landing, and as you well know, we'll need the Jeep. I'm leaving now, my friend. Have a good time at your snotty party tonight. Oh—and by the way, you don't fool me, either. I'm sure you won't be going to the party alone."

"Anytime I'm not with you, my dear girl, I might as well be alone." He says it with that devastating smile of his, the one that's left a trail of broken hearts all across the South.

"Oh, God," I groan. "With that corny line, I'm definitely leaving. See you later, okay?"

At the corner of the alley leading out of the French Quarter, I turn to wave goodbye. Rye's still standing on the sidewalk, his hands thrust into the pockets of his straw-colored trousers as he watches me leave. When I wave, he mouths, "Two-timer," and I chuckle, rolling my eyes before turning onto Church Street, toward my house.

On my walk home, I avoid the sidewalks and walk the shady little alleyways, thinking I'll be less likely to run into anyone I know. I've had a couple of calls this morning about the letter to the editor, but too many things are vying for my attention for me to worry about it. I wonder if Dory's seen it yet, and if she's been trying to reach me. She knows I'll fret over it a while, then blow it off, if I practice what I'm always preaching about troublesome things like that. I tell my clients that three of the most important and powerful words in the English language are "Let it go." Pick your battles, decide which are worth putting your energy into fighting and which aren't. Seeing Son at the coffee shop, the letter to the editor . . . those are things I have to let go before I get home. My days are always full, but today even more so. The next thing on my agenda is the all-important trip out to the Landing with Lex; if I hurry home, we'll have time for a few leisurely moments, maybe even a glass of wine beforehand.

Walking the alleyways was a good decision: I don't see anyone, and I've escaped the tourists. Although I dutifully join in the complaints against them, in truth I can't blame anyone for coming here. I fell in love with this little town the first time I saw it exactly twenty-five years ago this summer, when I came here with my new fiancé to meet his family. Fairhope has a way of casting its spell on everyone who spends any time here. It's such a quaint and picturesque town, with its historic waterfront and beach, but the beauty is only part of it. Seeing it initially, I was enchanted with the quiet, unpaved streets meandering under overhanging limbs of towering oaks and huge magnolias. Almost all the little cottages and stately old homes are hidden from view, which makes them seem sheltered and safe, as though nothing bad could happen to anyone fortunate enough to live in them. A foolish illusion, of course, as I know better than anyone.

The unique, even mythical history of the town is as much a part of its appeal as its beauty, and I'm still astonished that such a place exists in Alabama. Fairhope was founded around the turn of the twentieth century by a group of idealists who dreamed of creating a utopia. Even the name reflects their ideal: The story goes that one of the founders remarked that their project had a "fair hope" of succeeding. I'm surprised they gave it that much of a chance, actually.

A group of Midwestern idealists establishing a freethinking colony founded on the principles of social and economic justice in the middle of the Deep South is a pretty radical idea even now, but especially for that day and age. The founders left their comfortable lives and homes to venture into the unknown, putting everything they had into building a new and perfect society. When I first started conducting the retreats, the idea hit me to draw an analogy between that adventure and the journey of the participants. It's still one of the most popular parts of the retreats. Handing out material on the history of Fairhope, I compare the way the colony was established to the way each of them will be beginning her new life. Like the first settlers of this community, each newly divorced woman is charting an unfamiliar course, setting out for the unknown.

To reach my home, I have to pass the stuccoed, tile-roofed cottage that houses my practice. Because it is not only the home of a therapy practice but also Spanish in style and decor, the locals have nicknamed it Casa Loco. At first I was unamused, but over time the whimsical epithet has served me well. Everyone in town knows its location, and new clients who are directed to Casa Loco almost always arrive smiling. I stand outside it now and wonder if I should go in and get the casework I didn't complete this morning. Then I scoff at myself. Even if I had it with me, when would I have time to work on it? I take a few steps away, then pause. Maybe I should check my messages. Won't take but a minute, and one of my really distraught clients might have called. But no. No, no, no! I pick up my pace and refuse to look back at Casa Loco. Like Lot's wife, I'm liable to be turned into something horrible if I do, and it won't be a pillar of salt. More likely it will be a stack of paperwork.

Going around the curve and arriving at my house, I see that Rye wasn't joking—Lex's beat-up old Jeep is indeed out front. I'm getting here later than I'd told him to expect me, but he would've made himself at home. Over the past few weeks, he's gotten more comfortable about coming and going in my house. It started even before, in mid-July, when I gave him a key so he could keep an eye on things while I was out of town for a conference. On returning, asked if he'd keep the key in case I needed him again. There ar times when neither Etta nor I can free ourselves from work, and don't mind calling Lex and asking if he'll stop by the house whil he's out and let in the plumber or whatever. Unlike me, trapped i Casa Loco seeing clients all day, Lex is constantly coming into tow from the marina, making regular runs to the hardware store or pos office or bank.

Funny, me having two men in my life now. I'm equally fond o both Rye and Lex and often find myself juggling my time betwee them. Our choice of friends can reveal our needs, I think, and that' proved true with those two. I give Rye credit for introducing me t the joys of dancing, since he takes me out dancing whenever I nee a mental-health break, which is fairly frequent in my business. The Lex was the one who insisted that I get my work obsession unde control. When we first became friends, he was appalled at m hours, not believing that I often stayed at my office for hours afte my last client left. One day this summer he barged in and de manded I get a *life,* for Christ's sake.

Lex and I met on an unforgettable night at the beginning of th summer and hit it off instantly. I enjoy his company in much th same way I've always enjoyed Rye's, though I wouldn't put it tha way to either of them, since each teases me about the other. No tw men could be any more opposite in personality, temperament, an appearance than Lex Yarbrough and Rye Ballenger. Rye is witty glib, and urbane, while Lex is playful, outgoing, and full of mis chief. With his looks, charm, and courtliness, Rye is adored b women and envied by men. Being neither seductive nor flirtatious Lex cares nothing for adoration or envy. What you see is what yo get with him. He's blunt and no-nonsense, yet he has more shee magnetism than any man I've ever met.

I'm aware that everyone in Fairhope assumes Lex and I ar lovers, but I'm used to that; people have made the same assumptio about me and Rye for quite a while now. Pushing open the door o my house, which feels blissfully cool after the long walk from town, I find myself chuckling. Well, if certain people think my job is coaching women on the fine art of leaving their husbands and destroying their families, it's not much of a stretch to see me as a woman who'd sleep with two men at once. How disappointed they'd be to know the truth! Setting my purse and the cake box on the table in the foyer, I see that Lex brought in the mail and stacked it neatly on the table. The only piece separate is *The Fairhoper,* and since it's refolded in a crooked manner, I know he's read it. I wonder what his reaction will be. Although laid-back and easygoing to a fault, Lex is not a man I'd want to cross.

"Hey, where are you, Lex?" I call out, heading toward the back of the house. One thing for sure, he will be in either the kitchen or the backyard, his two favorite hangouts here. Not finding him in the kitchen, I lean over the sink and look out the double windows. Yep, he's in the herb garden, knee-deep in thyme. I wonder why it is that the sight of him tending a garden never fails to surprise me. I can't help myself; seeing a man like Lex Yarbrough in my garden makes me think of a story I loved as a child, one about a bull who would rather smell flowers than fight the matador. What was his name, Ferdinand? Kicking off my low-heeled sandals, I push open the back door. It's been a stressful day thus far, but I've learned one thing in my business: Never, ever assume that things can't get worse.

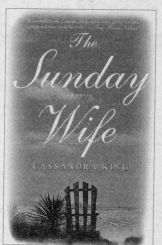

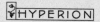